RUBBERMAN'S EXODUS

1st Edition

Joseph Picard

this page has been made intentionally blank.

Why? By whom?

Wouldn't you like to know?

It was me, the writer. So that the legal page is on the right side of the book, and the previous page doesn't have crap on the back of it that kinda shows through the paper version's page in the right light, and isn't tarnished by any...

Aw, frig.

For information, feedback, or other questions, contact the author.

Joseph Picard joe@ozero.ca or joeozero@gmail.com

Cover art by Joseph Picard
Other books by Joseph can be found at www.ozero.ca

/// WARNING! \\\

This book is written using the letter 'u' in a Canadian manner. It's quite a lot like the way the U.K. uses it. It should all still be more or less Queen-approved. I haven't been able to check, since she never returns my calls. I SAID I was sorry about harassing you with chess memes, Liz, they were SUPPOSED to be supportive!

~~~

Re: er

Words spelt with 'er' in the US manner are typically correctly spelt as 're' elsewhere, such as with *center* versus *centre*. In keeping with my Canadian stance, I find 're' to be more coloUrful anyway.

My apologies.

Contents

Dedicated to my mother, who raised me with an interest in creative pursuits of many kinds. She was always a supporter and believer, and showed me the strengths of a twisted wit tempered by an open and compassionate mind.

Dolores Picard
1942-2021

During the late editing phases of writing this book, I was diagnosed with Multiple Sclerosis after a notable initial onset. Among my list of symptoms is damaged concentration and focus. I fear this will likely be my last novel, but I am glad it at least closes the Rubberman series in the way that I had intended.

Thanks to everyone who's backed me in my writing, and everyone who's read them. I hope you enjoyed them.

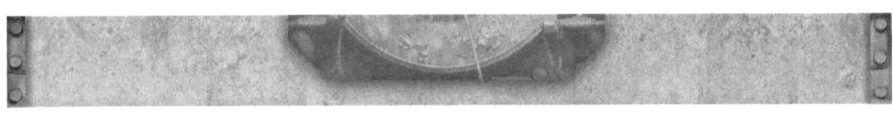

Foreword and Dramatis Personae

The facility, AKA Station Four, has been the backbone of this series, and in a way, a character of its own. It's been explored, fought in, and now, changed. Thousands of residents have to face the world they left above over a century ago.

As usual, I aim to make every book readable as a stand-alone, whether they've read *Rubberman's Cage*, or Rubberman's Citizens – but they do build on each other. I hope that seeing such things come to a conclusion is rewarding for those who have been along for the entire ride. Thanks to the usuals, my parents, and Michelle Browne's keen eye.

Readers who have been with me since before the Rubberman series may find a few surprises as well. What comes after the Rubberman series? Maybe something from before, brought into a new light...

Friends who've lent their names, in order of appearance:

Kevin Leitch Leiver – Engineer Kevin
Gabe Lowe – Provider Gabe
Michelle Patricia Browne – Citizen Patricia
Kara Kettunen – Sergeant Daniel Berryhill
Alison Muir – Corporal Alison Muir
Kay Laird – Corporal Kay Laird
Tavish – Corporal Tavish
Vee Mangual – Colonel Veronika Mangual
Elise Faith – Subject Elise
Caitlin Picard – Councillor Caitlin Aubrey
Becca Moorehead – Councillor Becca Moorehead
Lachlan Picard – PM Lachlan Leon

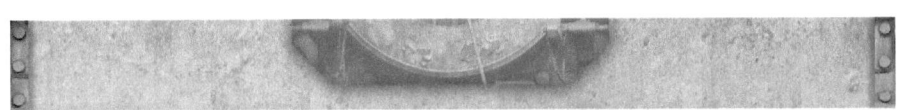

Chapter 1:

Known Issues

Of the thousands that lived here, deep underneath, hiding from the remains of war, only some knew about the Engineering levels. Some called it the heart of the complex, powering everything from its place down below – but a heart is not hungry in the same way that Engineering is.

An atomic generator has a very specific hunger.

Today, it asks to be fed.

Suited up in environmental suits, with her apprentice Sasha by her side, Tara pulled a canister of uranium out of the storage chute, and found it to be unexpectedly light. She held it in the tongs and jerked the canister up and down a little.

"What?!" she said to herself, placing the canister on the ground.

"What, what?" Sasha inquired. She was younger than Tara, and had not been an Engineer during the last refuelling. Sasha was here and suited up to learn about refuelling today, but the lesson was already diverging from expectations.

The next canister had already slipped into the base of the chute, to be taken for a future refuelling, but Tara took it right away. She was even less pleased with it than the last one. She let it fall to the floor and pulled out a third one. And let it drop to the floor as well.

"What's going on?" Sasha nervously asked. Tara didn't reply, dropping to her knees to grab one of the canisters with her shielded suit's gloves. She opened the canister, finding nothing inside, and stared into it for a moment before snapping to Sasha.

"*Geiger!*"

"What?"

"*Geiger reading!*" Tara cried to Sasha.

Sasha fumbled with her belt, and brought a Geiger counter forward. The gloves made using the controls cumbersome, but she managed as quickly as she could.

The counter responded faintly; tick... tick... tick... tick...

"Damn it," Tara hissed, tossing the canister away, and opening another. She brought it closer to the counter for much the same result. "*Damn it!*" Only trace amounts of radiation. They *had* once carried uranium, but obviously, no longer.

"Tara, what does it-"

Tara ignored Sasha, and grabbed the next canister in the chute with her gloved hands. It was too light as well. Also empty. She grabbed the next one. Empty. And the next one. Empty. And the next one.

While Sasha stood back and watched, Tara pulled can after can out of the storage chute. Dozens had piled around them, and Tara's panicked breathing had fallen to sobs as the last empty canister left the chute spent and empty.

Sasha looked at the Geiger counter. The room wasn't *clean*, but it wasn't a threat. She put the counter back on her belt, knelt beside Tara, and took off her headgear. With it off, her timid voice came clearer. "Tara... what does it mean?"

Tara turned to her and took off her own headgear. Tears on her face, she silently held Sasha close.

"Hon?"

Tara sighed, composing herself a little. "Well. I guess I need to make a call." Picking up her headgear, she and Sasha left the shielded storage room. They passed the coolant pool, and exited the dangerous materials section of Engineering through the contamination lock. They didn't have any significant lingering radiation on them, and were spared getting hosed down.

Tara and Sasha passed other Engineers as they headed back to Engineering's main control room. The Engineers could tell by their faces that something was wrong, but Tara's stride alone screamed, "*out of my way, don't ask, not now.*"

She grabbed the handset of the radio built into a panel, checking the settings, then forcefully called out, "*Messy!*" Silence followed, and Tara impatiently squeezed the handpiece, staring at the overhead array of status readouts. "*Messenger! Come in!*"

If Engineering was a heart, or stomach, or whatever, then the Central Elevator was the spine, going up about forty stories , through solid rock, habitat, farming, and various work levels, and up to the surface. And Messenger was the one who ran the Grand Elevator – and was the only one who had regular access to Actual.

"*Messy!*" Tara hollered into the handset. 'Messy', or Messenger, had once been an Engineer like Tara, but had been chosen as the operator of the Grand Elevator, and sole person permitted to speak to Actual. You talked to when you wanted stuff.

"Messy, we have a situation here. A bad one. We need you to get Actual to get us some uranium. At this time, we are running on fumes, soon to be running to backup capacitors. Repeat: *we are out of uranium.*"

This was a situation Tara had never known, nor had been warned about. There had always been more uranium in the dispenser. And now it was issuing blanks.

"Tara," came Messenger's deep voice eventually, "stop calling me Messy, and did I hear you right? No uranium? Is the dispenser stuck?"

"No. It feeds me empties."

Soon enough, fully suited against radiation,the dark-skinned Messenger stood at the dispenser. He went through container after container just as Tara had done, until he felt convinced that all of them were empty. He then found himself standing among nearly a hundred containers.

He turned to Tara, and said through the headgear, "Well, I know where these empties came from."

Tara shrugged, bidding Messenger to continue.

Messenger sighed. "I have taken at least four of these out of here, and up the Grand Elevator to recycling. I *assumed* they cleaned them and pressed them down into usable metal."

"But instead, they ended up back in my dispenser?" Tara asked.

Messenger shifted his weight back and forth a little. "There must have been other steps in between, and I can imagine some paths these containers might have taken, but... it would all rely on someone once making sloppy, stupid decisions, and their successors just following along."

"And *that* would *never* happen."

"Of course. I am going to have to perform an investigation and slap people upside the head whomever needs it. But here we stand, surrounded by empties, and the fact remains right now..."

"We are out of uranium," Tara flatly said.

"Indeed."

"Can you get Actual to get us more?"

"Of course," Messenger said, "but the speed of the delivery is not always predictable. You have back-up power?"

"Yes, Capacitors are nearly as full as they can get. We'll be okay for a while. Two weeks?"

Messenger motioned to stoke his chin, but the headgear and gloves made it impossible. "Is there any way you can... ration the power out? Cut non-critical systems? It might be possible to dim lighting, but that would require some new wiring to facilitate."

Tara looked upwards through the ceiling. "I'd have to access some remote distribution nodes, and there'd be... I could limit disruptions to a section or two, but the end result would be lower light, and..."

Messenger nodded. "I'd have to warn people, which at best, would create ... a certain unease."

From mentally going through the different districts in the facility, and the varying ignorance of the people living in them, even a minor change in lighting could be problematic.

There were Subjects, most of whom had no idea about the world outside their four people and four rooms, and their Manager Rubbermen; then there were the Citizens, quarantined for their violent history, who worshipped Actual like a god; the Providers, who operate most upkeep, repairs and mid-technical minutia; and the Engineers, the most educated of them all who run the generator.

"This could be messy, Messy," Tara said.

Messenger grunted. "Well, I guess my first stop is asking Actual for more uranium, then telling Contact that everyone needs to be warned. You... look into rationing power."

Tara sighed. "I don't envy you, Messy. Then again, I haven't tinkered with the distribution nodes nearly this deeply before. Crap, I don't envy *me*, either."

Chapter 2:

Contact

"Sasha, we're going out."

"I know that Tara. It's been years. Are you slipping in your old age?"

"Shush, child," Tara countered. Their age difference had never been of much importance to anyone but the two of them, worried that others might judge. Such self-conscious paranoia had long faded, and it had matured into a point of gentle jokes and jabs. A sixteen-year-difference in age became less and less conspicuous as the years marched on. Where a twenty-year-old chasing a thirty-six-year-old only raised the most prudish of eyebrows, the current thirty-one-year-old living with a forty-seven-year-old was not even of note – partly because they two had become an established fixture in Engineering.

Sasha stepped closer, to respond to the tease with a hand on Tara's waist, but the hard look in Tara's eyes slowed her down. "Hey, Tara... Bad news from Messenger?"

Tara sighed. "No, no, not really. He's going to talk to Actual to get more uranium, but whether it comes before the backup capacitors run out..."

"Aw, crap."

"But manageable crap. We're going to go to distribution nodes and wire in some rheostats that we can control from Engineering. Cut the light intensity, save some juice, and make some other rationing efforts. Shorter showers, that kind of thing."

"So we're going stink in the dark until we get uranium."

"Not *no* showers, just no basking in them for twenty minutes. So clean, in the somewhat-dim. And of course, hydroponic lighting can't be dimmed without threatening food supplies."

"Good news for Citizenry, then," Tara said. "A lot of those weirdos might react badly to mysterious lighting changes, but since they've recently started farming..."

"Good point. But areas away from their farms will get dimmed. But Messenger is going to make sure they get a warning, and I guess some explanation. Same with the Subjects and Managers."

In past years uncounted, there had been a policy of ignorance. It spanned generations, keeping the bulk of the inhabitants of the facility unaware of each other, or the nature of their home. A Subject's discovery of the surface, and the bloody revolt in Citizenry, had made sizeable cracks in the ignorance. Whether that would be helpful or harmful during power rationing was an obstacle Tara was happy to leave for Messenger.

"Okay, so what do we do?" Sasha asked.

"Well, Messenger is probably talking to Actual by now. I have to configure some rheostats. While I do that, you can gather gear for our trip. Basic tool sets, flashlights, and a generous load-out of cabling."

"And lunches."

"Good idea."

"Is this all hush-hush?"

Tara sighed. "No point in that. Offer explanations if any other Engineers ask. I'm sure it can only calm the rumour mill, but don't let it slow you down. I want to be ready as soon as Messenger comes back to give us a ride to the level with our first node."

At the peak of the facility, at ground floor, the Great and reclusive Actual talked on his communication device to 'Division'. Division was the only person more unknown than Actual. Since the moment Actual took on that mantle, only a handful of people had *seen* Actual. He was old, and only getting older, a pale man with kind eyes, who generally wore the same utilitarian yellow jumpsuits that the Providers and Engineers wore. Sometimes a blue one, like the ones used by Subjects and Citizens.

By contrast, no one had seen Division. Division came along the scorched surface during times when the Enemy bombarded the land with radiation – and yet, it apparently didn't bother Division. Surely Division's version of the Rubberman suit was more formidable and advanced than Actual's. Actual's suit could withstand the regular Enemy barrage outside for a while, but it soon became uncomfortable. He'd never risked more time than that. It was a strange sort of radiation; somehow not registering on a Geiger counter, despite being easily felt by a person, and even threatening one's eyes if the Enemy was looked upon for too long.

Once again, Division's aid was needed to deliver something that the facility could not produce on its own. Typically Division was called on for clothing pieces, light tubes, that sort of thing. But today was a request that was not made lightly, nor often. Actual had never made this call before, but the previous Actual taught him how to ask.

"Division? Come in, Division. This is Station Four Actual. Come in, Division." Actual waited in silence, listening for a response in his headset. Messenger was here, and they exchanged glances. After a few moments, Actual perked up, then replied to the voice on the other end.

"Yes, Division. It is time for a new allotment of uranium rods, x-235u. Our previous supply has been expended. Yes. x-235u."

Actual's expression soured slightly as he listened. This made Messenger's eyes widen slightly.

"We have in the past," Actual said, "Why not now?" That made Messenger's eyes widen much more.

"Fine, fine, if it works the same, we'll take that... plu... anium. What? No one? Well if no one uses it anymore, why'd you even bring it up?" Actual stood from his desk, growing more and more fidgety. "Salt? What? No, I don't care what kind of salt it is, will it work in our generator?!"

Messenger silently gestured with questioning, pleading hands.

Actual held a hand out to calm Messenger a little, while continuing questioning Division. "Well how are we supposed to do that? Do we need a Thor generator? How the heck is that supposed to work? Unless it's really small, that's a lot of work to uninstall our generator – and what, assemble Thor from parts? How is this supposed to work?!"

Actual listened with a grave expression, while Messenger sat frozen, wide-eyed, fist against his lips.

"I can't contact the people who built our generator..." Actual said placidly. "... they died a long time ago... in the war." There was another pause while Division spoke. Then Actual replied. "JeeOhSee? I... I don't know such a thing. If you think it can help. It might be our only hope of resolving this. Yes. Call back when you know. Yes. Thank you, Division. Ov... over and out."

Actual calmly sat again, and put his headset on the desk.

Messenger didn't know what to ask first. Actual didn't make eye contact and just stared at the glow of his computer screen with a sigh.

"Actual?" Messenger prodded cautiously.

"Yes," came Actual's flat acknowledgement.

"No uranium... or ... 'plutanium'?"

"...Correct."

"But why?"

"Division didn't explicitly say," Actual said, "but I can only assume that conditions have deteriorated out there enough that there's no plutarium to spare. They're using some kind of salt."

"Salt? How does that make electricity?" Messenger asked skeptically.

Actual shook his head. "I don't know. Maybe they don't. Maybe they've had to make due without much electricity at all, and salt is being used somehow to compensate on a survival level."

"You said the word 'Thor'."

"Did I?"

"I've read that name before somewhere," Messenger said, searching his memory. "This Thor was linked to the salt somehow?"

"Well, we don't have any Thors, and we don't have any kind of salt that I can imagine helping, so it's moot. Tara should proceed with her rationing plan. I have to work on a longer-term solution. I need to think."

Back in the Grand Elevator, Messenger stood alone by the control panel, headed back all the way to the bottom of the shaft to pick up Tara. As he descended, he racked his mind to remember where he heard the name 'Thor' before. A few pieces came together, here and there. Nothing complete.

When the Grand Elevator came to rest, he pulled aside the large sliding bay doors into the Engineering loading bay. Tara and Sasha stood nearby, laden with gear.

"Ladies," Messenger said, "you don't happen to have an abundant supply of salt, do you? I have a feeling there might be some man with a lot of electricity who might be willing to trade electricity for salt."

"Maybe the farms could extract salt from one of the crops?" Tara said, lugging her share of the hardware into the Grand Elevator's large, round interior.

"What's salt?" Sasha asked as she hauled her share.

Messenger shook his head. "Never mind. Where to, ladies, Provider level?"

Tara pulled out a binder from her stuff, and double-checked a schematic. "Two access panels below Provider, please."

Messenger began closing the heavy door, and Sasha was close enough to help a little. Once the Grand Elevator was in motion, Messenger shared the news. "No uranium's coming."

A moment of silence and staring was filled only with the sound of the lift, until Tara spoke up. "Until?"

"Not 'until'. Sounds like 'ever'."

Tara leaned back against the wall, and slid to a seated position. "Excuse me?"

"Division doesn't have any. He's seemingly been forced into more drastic survival methods. Involving salt, somehow."

"What's. Salt?" Sasha repeated in monotone, staring intently at Messenger.

"Salt," Tara interjected. "It's a part of food, and tears have–"

"No, I know what salt is, but what..."

Messenger huffed. "*You know as much as I do right now.* And I doubt offering our tears up to Thor is going to help us. Actual is working on it. Trying to figure it out. Until he does, your work is critical. Focus on the task you can. Actual and I will focus on *our* task."

Uncomfortable silence was accompanied only by the sounds of the Grand Elevator. Humming from engine sounds sent to them through vibrations in the cables and little sounds of the guide-wheels rolling on the shaft walls.

Sasha made herself busy rechecking the equipment they'd brought from Engineering, but not able to concentrate on it much.

Tara stood. "So, you're warning people of the coming changes in lighting?"

Messenger nodded. "I'm going to be giving that job mostly to the Providers. I'll handle the Citizenry myself; Providers aren't too keen to get close to Citizenry, and Citizenry isn't likely to put much weight on the word of people who live below them."

"Idiots," Sasha said, standing, "but we're all idiots today, aren't we? What, two thousand idiots that ran out of uranium?"

"Speaking of idiots, I'll also be exploring how the emptied containers ended up back in the supply chute," Messenger said, "but I expect it's a matter of me and former Messengers giving the containers to materials management, and them treating the empties just as they would full ones. It raises other questions, like why have empties never popped out of the chute before, mixed in with full containers. At some point, some 'idiot' panicked with a lack of full ones, ignorant of the importance, tossed in the empties, hoped it was good enough, and..."

Messenger pushed a lever on the control panel back, and the Grand Elevator came to a stop. "Here we are. Two access panels below Provider level."

"Ignorance," Tara huffed, picking up her share of the equipment. "Innocent idiots. You know a lot of our problems come from idiots who never meant any harm, but freak out when their ignorance backs them into a corner."

"Don't remind me," Messenger said, "I have to talk to Contact next. I don't relish the notion."

"Good luck. Try not to get his nose stuck too far up your rear end."

Having dropped off Tara and Sasha, Messenger proceeded up two floors to dock the Grand Elevator to the Provider level. Providers knew about most of the operations and other peoples in the facility, but their knowledge of Engineering was rather limited. They were generally well-educated, and some of the brightest among them were approached by Messenger to be recruited as Engineers.

Messenger waited in the Grand Elevator for a few moments. 'Contact', the leader of the Providers, saw Messenger as nearly a holy figure; the one link to Actual, bringer of all blah blah blah. Contact liked someone to greet Messenger in an official capacity when he arrived, and Messenger had learned long ago that it was easier to go along with Contact's dogma than to suffer apologies if Contact felt that Messenger had been disrespected.

It was normal. It was tedious. It was steeped in ignorance.

There were voices coming from the loading bay. Someone had heard the Grand Elevator arrive, and presumably, an 'acceptable' greeter was now in attendance. Bracing himself, Messenger dragged the door open.

Lo, there in all his glory, flanked by a few attending Providers on either side, stood Contact himself.

"Messenger! An honour as always! How may I be of service?" Contact was a large man who evidently lived far more comfortably than the other Providers – although Messenger had never understood quite how or why, but that was a matter for the Providers to worry about. Contact wore yellow, like all Providers.

"I come with a warning of events to come," Messenger said. He saw fear in Contact's eyes already, and continued, "in the near future, most of the lights will have to be notably less bright. I'm not sure for how long, but I don't want anyone to panic when it happens. I call on you to make every Provider aware, and to spread the news among the lower Unit Managers. They might do well to warn their Subjects as well."

Contact needed a moment to absorb this. "Less bright? Why? And Subjects? Managers aren't permitted to speak to th..." Contact paused, brow furrowed. He was aware that the ex-Subject Lenth, (who had somehow become a friend to Messenger,) had been teaching his old Unit Brothers and other Subjects all kinds of things. Things that Subjects were never taught before. Contact didn't like the change, but if Messenger accepted it, it was to be.

"The power that Actual gives us has been stopped," Messenger said. "The one who gives it to Actual can no longer do so. Actual is finding another way."

This caused Contact to stagger back. "*Gives to Actual?!* But Actual is the source of all!"

Messenger sighed. "Just as the Subjects think that their Rubberman Managers provide everything, and as they feel everything is from the

Providers, Providers feel that everything comes from Actual. I know of one more step up. Division."

Contact staggered back further, wide-eyed, jaw agape. Coming from anyone other than Messenger, such ideas would be blasphemous. "Division?! What does his name mean? And where is he?!"

"Knowledge of Division's name has been passed down for generations. At this point, we can only guess the meaning," Messenger said, "– perhaps he divides things from some other source to send us what he does, or maybe he is the division between Actual and whatever world is next."

Contact paced, still wide-eyed, now looking up through the ceiling towards Actual, and beyond to where he imagined Division to be. He pointed up. "Division is even higher... does he have another Grand Elevator? Does he battle the Enemy that you tell us bombards us with radiation?"

"He is not higher than Actual, as I understand it. He comes along the surface at the same height as Actual. As far as we can tell. We see his tracks. The tracks tell us he comes in a large wheeled thing, but walks with feet like ours to deliver what Actual requests. He comes from far away, and during times while the Enemy is about. Division either hides really well, or is just immune to the Enemy's radiation."

"Have you seen him?"

Messenger shook his head. "No, and neither has Actual. This is how it has always been. A request is made, Division comes and delivers in the flood of the Enemy's gaze, and when the Enemy moves on, Actual claims the gifts."

Contact covered his mouth with his hand, and looked at the floor. His eyes moved back and forth as if he were reading the idea. "And he can no longer bring the gifts... does this mean that the Enemy...?"

"No, no, Division is fine. It is just that he can no longer supply what we use for electricity. He no longer seems to have it. For himself, he uses other things. Things we cannot use. Yet. Actual is working on it. If things go well, we'll be able to use the new source."

"Actual be praised," Contact mumbled with awe, "What grand things exist in Actual's world... we would be so lost without him." Contact fell to his knees before Messenger. "And you! Messenger be praised as well!"

It was always uncomfortable when Contact got like this. Messenger could only hope to focus Contact on the immediate, important things. "For the safety of all, spread the warning that lights will be dimming in the near future, and that Actual strives to correct it."

"As you command. If I send thirty Providers to tell ten managers each, plus the other Providers..."

"Sounds reasonable. I'll inform the Citizenry myself."

Contact cringed at the mention of the Citizenry. "O, brave Messenger," Contact lifted his head, looking up diagonally to where he understood Citizenry to be. "This isn't *their* fault, is it?" he sneered.

"No," Contact replied.

Contact looked back to Messenger, then back up to the perceived direction of Citizenry. And back again. "You're sure?"

"Yes."

"*Sure*, sure?"

"The Citizens can no more affect Division than you can," Messenger said.

Contact warmed slowly to the idea. Of course. After all, Citizens were garbage. Savage idiots. But what if? No. As much as Contact tried, he couldn't think of a way that Citizens could affect much outside of Citizenry – let alone the one above the Great Actual.

Chapter 3:

Citizens

"I think that's box p32 ahead," Tara said, pointing her flashlight down the unlit utility access crawlspace.

What the crawlspace lacked in height, just a bit over a metre, it made up for in width. This layer between floors was separated into different-sized sections, spanning over all of the three hundred Units. Some Units were farm space, some did laundry, some performed the more repetitive maintenance on various parts, some sorted garbage, some managed compost, some prepared food disks, and on and on.

All this work performed by separated groups of four 'Subjects', directed by Managers in their rubber containment suits. Typical Subjects were raised in ignorance, unaware of anything outside their Unit. Many Managers weren't that much better educated.

Sasha looked back and forth in the crawlspace area they were heading through. "Hey. which way is Lenth's old Unit?"

"Ehh, might be a few sections over to our right somewhere, why?"

Tara asked. "Did he ever get permission to get other Unit Managers talking to their Subjects?"

"As far as I know, beyond his old Manager, and his girlfriend Karen, I don't think so. Not all of them yet anyway."

They had made it to 'box p32', in a section with only slightly more elbow room than other sections of the crawlspace. It was a metal junction box a metre tall, and two wide. Conduits and wires crammed into it from both sides, and above, with one sneaking in from the side, punched in through one of the ventilated doors on the front. Tara started undoing the screws that held the box's access doors shut.

"Crap," Sasha said, thinking out loud more than anything. "So a couple hundred Units, times four Subjects each, are either going to be freaked out when the lights unexpectedly dim – or freak out when their Rubberman Manager actually *speaks* to them for the first time to warn them. Huh."

"Yeah," Tara said, seeing where Sasha was going, "but, they have the lights dim every day during their sleep cycles." With the last screw out, she lifted the middle door, and started assessing the meticulous mess of wires inside.

"It won't be a huge shock, but it'll never be as bright again unless we get some uranium." As Tara fiddled with one of the rheostat kits she'd prepared before, and compared it to the spot she intended to install it, a heavy silence hung in the air.

"Until." Sasha finally said.

"Huh? Until what?" Tara asked.

"*Until* we get some uranium. We *will* get some. You said unless."

Tara ignored it, only focused on making minor changes to the rheostat.

"You said unless." Sasha repeated quieter.

"Yes," Tara replied just as quietly, getting a soldering gun ready to wire in the rheostat.

"Otherwise what, Tara?"

"Otherwise... we find another way."

"Or die? Freezing in the dark and suffocating on our own breath?"

"Actual will find some way," Tara said flatly.

"Tara, Actual? Really? You're going to put all your faith in the Great and Mighty Actual? We outlived the war, and we're going to die like *this*?"

Tara put down her work and pulled Sasha close. "Hey, now..."

Sasha struggled halfheartedly to free herself from Tara's embrace. "Don't '*hey now*' me! What can we do?! What if this rationing is just putting off the inevitable? We're just making our deaths slower!"

"Sash. Shh. It gives us a lot more of a chance. If there's going to be uranium, it'll be through Actual. If there's some other miracle, it'll be through Actual. And Division. Even if it's something stupid like crying salt for Thor. Some way will be found to get us the electricity we need. We're not going to end up frozen in the dark. Shh, now."

Sasha collapsed into quiet tears as Tara held her tight. "You can't let it get to you like this."

"But it's the end!"

"No, honey. No." But Sasha made a good argument. Maybe it was.

After a good deal of fiddling and adjusting, box p32 was ready for the downshift. "Right then," Tara said. We know what we have in front of us."

"Okay. We call back now? To tell the others what needs to be done?" Sasha asked with a bit of focus anchoring a bit of hope.

Tara held up a slip of paper on which she'd been jotting notes on as she worked. "Patch us in."

Sasha connected a portable wired communication device into a conduit she'd prepared while Tara was working on the electrical systems. "Okay, you're in." She passed the handset to Tara.

"Hello, down there!" Tara called out, "This is yer boss! Pay attention or we die."

A moment passed before a voice returned. "Hey, chief! Kevin here. Aren't we all going to die eventually? Did you discover the secret to immortality?"

"That's right, all hail *me*, Tara, purveyor of perceptual life, for I herald the way. Now listen up. P32 is prepped, and I know what boxes and circuits need attention. Teams ready?"

"Teams ready."

"Take notes."

Messenger took the Grand Elevator to the level of Citizenry. Long considered to be full of savage wastrels, recent events had steered the quarantined region toward productivity – though few in the rest of the facility trusted a Citizen entirely. They remained locked in Citizenry.

He knew that the sound of the Grand Elevator would have alerted them to his coming. He peeked out the slot of the Elevator door into the loading bay. A few lingering Citizens stood nearby, ready to receive the word of the Messenger.

"Citizens," Messenger began with his official Messenger tone, "Call your leader, Leena." He specified who he wanted. Leadership had been a troublesome issue, and although he'd not heard of any revolt brewing, he was always a little nervous that there could be some conflict within Citizenry that could again lead to deaths.

"Yes Messenger!" came the reply, thankfully. One of the Citizens ran off to fetch Leena, while the others lingered nearby, in case Messenger had any random wisdoms to share. Ordinarily, Messenger would have closed the little slot in the door to prevent Citizens from peeking into the Grand Elevator, to enforce the long-held general policy of ignorance. That seemed less important these days. And the Citizens were conditioned so much, and for so long, they dared not try.

– Unlike Leena, who presently marched right up to the slot like Messenger was an old buddy. "Hey, what's up?"

Messenger replied through the Grand Elevator's peeking slot. "Leena, you seem well. How are the crops?"

In recent times, Citizenry had adopted minor farming duties. This was something for which they'd never been counted on for until recently. It was hoped that meaningful responsibilities would give Citizenry something constructive to do.

"Garden three seems pretty good, and its papaya tree is taking root. People decided to name it Mike, after our first tree. It's..." Leena sighed with a soft smile, remembering the human Mike, "I guess it's going to be a regular thing."

Messenger returned the smile. "A worthy tradition."

"Yeh. Kind of a little jab in the heart a little now and then, though." Leena snapped out of her increasingly wistful expression. "So! What brings you around here?"

Trying to not present himself too gravely, Messenger slid somewhat back into his official tone. "There's been an issue with the electrical supply. To conserve power, light brightness will soon decrease in many areas. For the sake of the crops, the special lights for them will go unaffected."

Leena tilted her head. "Crops more important than people?"

"Crops are more dependant on their light. If you're in the dark, you bump into a wall. If they're in the dark they die."

"After which, we starve and die." Leena said.

"Correct."

"So, this darkening... is this just Citizenry?"

"No. Everywhere power is not critical. The main farms below will remain lit, medical situations, and so on. But we have to save as m-" Messenger stopped himself. How much information was too much? Was this a case where some ignorance was for the best? The under-educated Citizens had a history of violence, and if they saw the possibility of running out of electricity as a threat...

"How bad is this?" Leena asked bluntly.

"Actual is looking for a solution."

"So... bad."

"We'll fix it."

Leena leaned in closer, giving a glance to the nearby Citizens, and whispered to Messenger, "A little dim is no big deal. But dark? Full dark, for who knows how long?"

"We'll fix it."

"You're kinda scaring me, Messy."

"Don't be scared, we'll fix it. But maybe talk to trusted people to make them aware of the 'darkening', and the possibility of... more. But we'll fix it."

Leena huffed, and gave her head a couple shakes. "Any chance of

Actual coming to give us a talk like before?"

"Actual's busy trying to fix this, and so am I."

"So Citizenry's *my* problem," Leena said with begrudging acceptance.

"You're strong. You're reasonably wise. You can do this."

Messenger left, and the Grand Elevator rumbled away, upwards to the only section above Citizenry; the Actual. Leena turned away from the Grand Elevator, towards the rest of Citizenry, and grunted. "Reasonably wise. And if it's not wise enough, and this place goes to hell, he can just leave the door locked and ride away."

The Citizens in the loading bay were paying close attention. There was no delaying it.

"All right!" Leena swirled her hand in the air as she marched towards the Citizenry Commons, "Shit is going down! I'm calling a Gathering!"

The majority of the Citizens gathered at Leena's request. Not *all* of them loved her, but all at least respected her. She had brought them through a lot in the past.

"So we're going to get less light because Actual can't keep it on as strong?" A random Citizen asked.

"Is this some kind of Punishment?" asked another.

"No, no," Leena tried to reassure those who had assembled. "Messenger assures me it's temporary. He says the newer lights, the ones for the gardens, will stay strong," Leena reminded them, "so it's not even going to affect us a whole lot. Some of the Lofus in the lower levels are gonna feel it most of all."

"You said we're not supposed to call them Lofus anymore."

"Oops. Providers," Leena corrected herself. "And whatever the other groups below that are called – but most of them work for the Providers anyway, so I'm just gonna call them all that," said Leena.

"But Messenger didn't say when all this would happen?" A Citizen asked, "or how long it would be?"

"Next time he comes by, I'll have to ask."

"If it's not punishment," wondered a Citizen, "why is it even happening, then?"

"*The Enemy!*" another Citizen chirped up. "You told us about seeing a thing that the Actual calls *Enemy!* Could this be the Enemy's fault?"

Leena paused to think. "It... didn't seem to be something that would be too interested in causing darkness," Leena said. "Seemed like if it were attacking, we'd have the opposite problem. It was bright and belching massive radiation from above, darkness was the last thing-"

A Citizen gasped "Maybe Actual is getting darkness together to fight the Enemy!"

"Or he's using it to protect us!" another added.

"Praise the Actual! We need to be strong for him!"

"Folks, settle down," Leena pleaded, "You're starting to sound like that crank Edgar did. All we know is that it will get dimmer for a while in some sections of Citizenry. It's not a call for battle! Your ideas are fun, but it's based on .. not much!"

"But then... why now?"

Chapter 4:

Karen

Contact sat in his office in the core of the Provider levels, confident that the Great Messenger's words had been heeded, and that the Great Actual would be pleased. Yet the impending power reduction was putting him ill at ease. Gabe, the most competent Provider under Contact's command, walked in.

A fine worker, leadership material, perhaps, but Contact felt that Gabe's faith in the Actual wasn't resolute enough, which was a pity. Otherwise, Gabe might make a fine future Contact, or even Messenger. He thought about suggesting to Messenger that Gabe might do well in Engineering, (whatever *that* truly was. Contact had little notion of it) – and moving Gabe out would open room for another, perhaps more faithful Provider to rise. However, at the same time, Gabe was simply too valuable in his current role. The end result was that Gabe irritated Contact, though he couldn't avoid feeling some degree of respect for the man.

"Contact, runners are reporting in. Many are still out there, but given the education levels of many of the Managers, we knew some would take more time to understand."

Contact grunted. "Has anyone happened to run into Messenger lately?"

"Not that I've heard of."

Contact grunted again. This electricity problem could be a sign of displeasure from Actual. In the last few years, there had been disruptions the likes of which the facility had never seen. A killer crawling around in the access conduits. Some little war in Citizenry that had threatened to spill out into the rest of the facility.

Maybe it was that Lenth's fault. Lenth had somehow become chummy with Messenger. What made *him* so special? First Lenth was teaching Managers to talk to Subjects, and suddenly *all* the Managers needed to be educated? Was this electricity issue a problem Lenth caused to accelerate his Manager-education fixation? To what ends?

"Gabe, if the Subjects became violent..."

"You're thinking of that killer, 'Six'? Yes, that's on everyone's mind, but knowing there's a risk, everyone's been mindful."

"There's over a thousand of them. Imagine if they all-"

"Not too likely, Contact. Worst come to worst, they're all already in locked rooms."

"Locked rooms that have broken now and then."

"We'll be fine, Contact."

Contact grunted.

"I'll keep you updated if anything interesting happens, or the last of the runners report in," Gabe said cheerfully, waving as he headed out.

Down the hall, he spotted Karen. She was waiting for Gabe to get closer, out of earshot of Contact. As he got closer, she stepped in line to walk beside him. "I just had a visit from one of your little runners," Karen said.

"Did you tell your Subjects?" Gabe asked. Karen was Lenth's love, and a Manager. This made her Unit to be the second after Lenth's for a Manager to unmask and speak to their Subjects.

"Yeah, they didn't seem worried. I didn't go into detail about what a total power loss would mean, though."

"Your Unit farms papaya, right? So your hydroponic lights will be exempt. If the gloom gets to them, they can just go hang out with the trees."

Karen chuckled. "Yeah, well, ever since I stopped restricting movement between rooms, the farm has been where they hang out the most. They were even sleeping under the trees until I told them it might not be good for the trees."

"Is that true?"

"I doubt it, honestly, but it got to a point where... you're tracking dirt everywhere, you're just plain *filthy,* and you have perfectly good non-dirt beds *right there* in the next room!"

Gabe laughed, picturing Karen above the grate, chasing four dirty Subjects around. "They seem to be doing well after your unmasking."

"Yeah," Karen replied wistfully. "It's been a really good thing. They're my girls, I love being able to talk with them, and just... be a part of their world in a real way."

"You know Lenth hit a milestone last week?" Gabe asked.

"A hundred Rubbermen de-rubbered!" Karen declared, a fist in the air. "Well... this new thing going on... are they rest going to happen like... now-ish?"

"I guess it's going to be up to each Manager," Gabe said.

"Frig..." Karen shook her head a bit. "Lenth's been slow with each one, you know? Helping introduce the concepts gently... If we knew this whole power thing was going to happen, we could have put more people on the job. Not every Subject has a well-lit tree to relax under."

Chapter 5:

Chin & Stripe

Tara and Sasha focused on adjusting the fairly centralized unit so that it would accept a signal from Engineering to set the rheostat they had installed. This would restrict the flow of power to non-essential lighting systems attached to that unit. Meanwhile, they took notes. There were a fair handful of these units to adjust and install rheostats into, and it was no mundane procedure. If she was going to get her crew working on these, they'd need concise instructions.

By now, efficient Provider runners had gotten word of the impending dimming to a significant portion of the Managers. It had already been a time of change for many of the Managers. Some had been given the option to remove their rubber hazmat masks, and actually speak to their Subjects.

As little as four years ago, this was unheard of. In any official measure, at least. Subjects were to be kept sterile and innocent of the rooms beyond their designated little section: four Subjects and one Manager per Unit. The reason was all but lost. Something about tests that could happen at any time – but the facility had waited for generations. To many, the wait was practically a sacred vigil. Much to Contact's chagrin, this vigil was eroding. With the Great Actual's blessing, no less.

Former Subject, Lenth, had been busy learning, and was given permission to teach his old Manager, Phil. Also Phil's Subjects, who Lenth had grown up with as a Brother. All now knew that there were thousands of people in hundreds of rooms outside their own, and that the work they'd always done had a specific purpose which was a great service to all; cleaning air filters.

Similarly, Lenth's lover Karen, a Manager, was helping to teach her Subjects. Her Subjects were a quartet of Sisters, whose job was growing papayas. Slowly and cautiously, more and more Units were taught about the facility to which they'd been essential.

Most Subjects were quite reasonable about the new knowledge, having been raised and inadvertently conditioned to be somewhat meek.

Most. A few settled down reluctantly. Begrudgingly.

Some reacted with anger, that they'd been forced to live such unenlightened lives for no good reason. Eventually, such people had to listen to the reason, as explained by their Managers: they ultimately had no choice.

The few Subjects who chose to remain angry, found that even refusing to work wasn't much use. Managers controlled the supply of food for non-farm Units, and in extreme cases, sleeping gas and behavioural-motivational shocks were also available to the rubber-suited Managers.

It reminded Managers of one of the Subjects who escaped a few years ago. The one named 'Six', who went crawling around in the nooks and crannies of the facility, and killed those he blamed, without even fully understanding what death was. When a few newly-educated Subjects were found to foster negative feelings, it gave Lenth pause about enlightening all of the Subjects.

It gave Messenger pause. It gave Actual pause.

At present, of the three hundred Units, one hundred and twelve were now considered 'enlightened' about their place, and the facility. But not about the war that was. That was thought to be too much to learn just yet, too much all at once.

Lenth went to one of the Units in which at least one of the Subjects festered with resentment. He entered through the Unit's Manager's space, dragging the door open to reveal 'Chin', the Unit's manager.

Chin had once been a Subject. Many Managers were brought up a level, taught the traditions of the Rubberman suit. They were then made the Manager of a different Unit. This sometimes happened when a Subject was much younger than their Sisters or Brothers, and survived them by age.

Chin was taught much about the facility, and became a gentle Manager. Not permitted to show her face or speak to her Subjects until recently, she did her best to be the kind of Manager she would have liked to live under.

"Chin, how are things?" Lenth asked. Chin walked by her Rubberman suit, heaped in a corner on the floor, giving it a small kick as she passed it. Chin got her name from her former Sisters. Subjects tended to name each other based on a unique trait; Usually, something superficial about their appearance. Chin had fairly dark skin, but another of her Sisters was darker. But Chin was shorter than her Sisters when they met, and considerably younger. At the time, she was short enough to fit under all of her Sisters' chins. Now, in her mid-fifties, she was a hand-span taller than Lenth.

"Doing fair enough," Chin said, "still feel the habit to put on the suit when I get ready to go talk to the Subjects. And sterilize myself after."

Lenth gave the neglected suit, with its mask stacked neatly on top, a nostalgic smirk. "Is Stripe still cranky?" Lenth asked.

Chin looked towards the door that led to the Subjects' areas. "Yeah," Chin sighed. "She's not causing trouble, quite, but oh, the glares I get from her. When I first took off my mask, she was as stunned as the others, but the more I explained about other Rubbermen and other Subjects... the snippier she got. Had to... oof, I had to zap her once or twice. That sure as heck didn't endear me to her."

Rubbing his jaw to see if he had any notable stubble, Lenth asked Chin, "Do they know about men?"

Chin scoffed softly. "The basics. Never seen one though. If you want to go talk to them, you could leave your pants here, and save a lot of explaining."

"Ha! I don't want to traumatize them!" Lenth joked back. The momentary merriment melted from Lenth's face gradually as he continued. "Really though, I'm going to try telling them something that very few Subjects have heard. Not a lot of Managers, either."

Influenced by Lenth's change in tone, Chin looked keenly to Lenth's eyes. "What is it? ... Is it something bad?"

"Well, yes. Honestly, horrific, but if it makes you feel better, it was a long time ago, and there's nothing we can do about it now."

Chin tried to rationalize that, and internally guessed at what it could be.

"It's easier if I just tell all of you at once," Lenth said, "let's get in there."

They passed into the Unit's Subject area, and came out onto a metal-grating floor, which stretched out over the four rooms that were these Subjects' entire world. They walked over to the sleeping room, where the four Subject Sisters were just relaxing.

Of course, they heard Chin approaching on the metal grate, and if they were paying close enough attention, they might have noticed Lenth's additional footsteps. One way or the other, they were looking right at Chin and Lenth as they came into view.

"Hay Chinny!" piped up one of the Sisters. Another much quieter Sister sat on her bunk, glowering, with a mildly confused look in her eye, and a scar running down the side of her face, more pronounced on the top end.

"Hello, ladies," Chin said, "we have a visitor."

All eyes were already on Lenth. He gave the silence a moment, and said, "Hi. I'm Lenth."

"You're one of those man-things," one of the Sisters said, almost accusatory, but without malice.

"Yup," Lenth confirmed. "We can talk about that if you want, but it's not the main reason I'm here."

"You got an extra thing between your legs?"

"Wha... oh, well, yeah."

And now all eyes were on Lenth's pelvic region.

Chin snickered quietly. "Told you. Pants."

"Maybe we'll move on to the main reason I'm here," Lenth said with a sigh. He settled to sit on the metal grate cross-legged. "Okay, where do I start... for one thing, I used to be a Subject like you four."

"But then someone attached the thing between your legs and then you weren't a Subject anymore?"

"What? No! Subjects can be men or women."

"I wanna try being a man for a while!" piped up the most energetic Sister.

"It...! It doesn't work like that!"

"You said Subjects can be a man or a woman!"

"No no, let me put it another way. Men *or* women can be Subjects. Does that make more sense?"

"No."

"Well, that's the way it is. The point is, I was a Subject, too. And instead of Sisters, I had Brothers. Men Subjects have Brothers, Women Subjects have Sisters."

"So if you changed from being a Subject, can you change from being a man?"

"No!"

"Have you tried? Maybe rip off the thing between your legs."

Chin was having trouble not bursting out laughing, but Lenth was losing his composure, finally hollering out, "*Do you want to know why we're down here?*"

This ended the increasingly silly chatter, and returned the room to silence. Until Stripe broke the silence.

"I'm down here because Chin makes me work," she said slowly and methodically.

Lenth was fast to counter, replying instantly, speaking much faster, and in one breath. "Yes but guess what? We all work. In different ways, but we all do what we need to for us all to survive as we all hide from the *Enemy*."

It took a moment for people to absorb the little barrage of words, but it was Stripe who was first to ask the obvious.

"Enemy?"

Lenth nodded. "Let's talk about war."

It was another word they Sisters had never heard, but they all simply waited. Lenth continued. "When I say *us* – I mean all of us in the facility that we all help keep alive – Do you know how many people that is?"

"The exercise machines count to a hundred, and Chin said there's that many, three times, of Rubbermen and Units," a Sister said.

"That's right. And with four Subjects in most of those Units, that's twelve hundred of Subjects. Plus the three hundred Manag– Rubbermen, makes fifteen hundred people. Now if we add other groups, we're at about twenty-five hundred people. And we're all hiding from the Enemy."

"If there's so many of us, why are we hiding from one enemy?" one of the Sisters asked.

Lenth sighed. "How do I explain 'billions' to you..." He ran his hand through his hair, paused, then perked up. He grabbed at his hair. "Hey, how many hairs do you think I have in my hand?"

"A hundred?" offered one Sister.

Another grabbed at her own hair. "More. Double, at least."

"A heck of a big number, right?" Lenth said, "Maybe if I counted every hair on my head, it might be hundreds of hundreds. Not exact by any means, I never actually counted, but it's a reasonable thought, yeah?"

The Sisters seemed agreeable.

"But I have more hair than that." Lenth tugged at his arm hair, and reached in the neck of his jumpsuit to tug a chest hair, then to his shins."

"Pants..." Chin quietly commented.

Ignoring Chin, Lenth stood and spread out. "All of my hairs, hundreds of hundreds of hundreds... we might be around a million? That's a big number, a million. Imagine if there was a person for each of my hairs..." He them pointed to Chin, and each Sister. "Two, Three, four, five, six million hairs, six million people."

"What the heck were we talking about again?"

"Six million people used to make an okay-sized city," Lenth said, "Some places had many times that."

"City?"

"Like the facility," Lenth said, "but higher up, and way bigger. There were hundreds of cities up there, each with millions of people."

"*Were?*"

Lenth sighed. "You ladies ever fight?"

The Sisters became instantly uncomfortable. Stripe finally spoke up. "Not usually seriously, but once..." She traced a finger down the scar on her face. Another Sister looked especially ashamed.

"Okay. Have you heard of death?"

Chin bit her lip, and looked away, but the Sisters only stared blankly.

"If you fight too hard, it might cause death," Lenth said. "One person will have killed the other, and that hurt one would be dead. They would sleep, and not breathe or move ever again."

Lenth knew that Chin's older Sisters had died of age, and Lenth had known people who'd died as well. The Sisters were well aware of the mood that Lenth and Chin had fallen into.

"At some point, those people in those cities began to fight. Some were very good at it, and some had tools that could kill a lot of people at once." Lenth tugged his hair. "Poof. A city. Dead. Gone. Then revenge. Another, and another. Tell me, imagine a really bad fight starts between you

Sisters, and one of you kills another!"

"No...! I'd never!" said one Sister, perhaps the one who gave Stripe her scar. Stripe went over to give a hug to reassure forgiveness.

"Well good," Lenth said, "but let's imagine *you* are a million people. A million million. And some of you don't trust *that* million people. And you both have the tools that can kill millions at once."

"But I *wouldn't!*"

"Millions of you wouldn't," said Lenth, "but millions *might*. Or maybe *you* might," he said, pointing to another Sister.

"I don't want to kill, too! Then everyone can trust me."

"Some people won't believe you." Lenth said.

"But I-"

"Boom," Lenth said, pointing at another Sister. "That millions of people just killed those millions," pointing at a different Sister. "Now you have a killer of millions. They might do it again some time."

"Are we supposed to take revenge?" Stripe asked flatly.

Lenth shook his head. "I don't know. With millions and millions and millions of people, someone's bound to think that's the right th-"

"*What? Are we all doomed?!*" a Sister hollered.

Lenth stomped on the grating, followed by a break of silence. Lenth got down on the grating, and spoke softly to the Sister who yelled. He spoke softly, and delicately. "Oh... but what if instead, you stepped out of the fighting, and you hid?"

"But where could...?" she stopped herself, and looked around herself, at the ceiling, and the walls.

"It would be difficult!" Lenth proclaimed. "There would have to be rules, if you were to keep as many people as possible alive in your hiding place. Everyone would have to work."

Everyone was quiet. One of the Sisters was silently crying. Stripe was scowling. Lenth made eye contact with her, and tried to diffuse the scowl with empathy. A kindly stare wasn't doing it. "And the rules have problems," Lenth admitted, "the things I just told you shouldn't be a secret to half the facility. At one time, I'm sure all the rules, and the rubber suits, maybe they were necessary. But it became habit. People just kept using them ... just because."

"What, will I be allowed to go?" Stripe asked.

"Where?" Lenth responded. "Where would you plan to go?"

Stripe shrugged. "Up there?"

Lenth tapped the grating. He looked over to Chin. "Might be something we can do."

"Really?!" Chin said.

"I mean, I can't authorize a ton without Actual's clearance," Lenth said, "but a small visit up onto this floor?"

"Ha, what, just 'cause I asked?" Stripe scoffed.

"Eh, basically," Lenth said, "Rules are changing. Bit by bit."

"Can I just not *work*?" Stripe asked.

"We all still need clean clothes, just as we all need food, clean wa-"

"Yeah, yeah."

"That said, I'd like to eventually make it possible to pick what jobs you do. Like maybe you'd like being a beet gardener better or something."

"Just like that?"

Lenth shrugged. "Not quite that simple, a lot of things have to happen before job-changing is an easy option. But hey, I changed, and no one's choking on stale air. Someone else took my spot in my Unit, and scrubs the filters I used to."

"Your new job is changing rules?"

"No," Lenth said, "my new job has to do with electricity, but I'm only still learning that. Trying to change rules is just something I wanted to do, since I used to be a lot like you–"

"Except with the th–"

"Between my legs, yes." Lenth sighed in exasperation.

"You may as well show them," Chin mumbled, earning only a sullen little glare from Lenth.

Not comfortable with all four Sisters coming up above the grate, Chin opened doors for only Stripe to exit the lower Unit, meeting Lenth just outside, then climbing a ladder to the inter-Unit halls. The minimal lighting was similar to the lighting in the Unit when it was time to sleep. Stripe was wide-eyed, taking in everything she could, even though the hall wasn't that interesting.

The door to Chin's room was nearby, and as they entered, Chin spread her arms out. "My bed, the control panel, the door, ehh, that's about it."

"It... it's smaller than our sleeping area," Stripe said.

"There's just one of me," Chin chuckled. "And I use your exercise machines and stuff when you're in other rooms, or asleep."

Stripe knew that, they'd heard Chin in the other rooms from time to time. "But I thought your area would be..."

"Bigger? Shinier? Have a nicer bed?"

"I... I guess so."

"I'm not up here having a good time," Chin said, "I'm a Manager. I manage things. I make sure your food is in stock, all the machines are in order, the laundry you guys clean gets to the right places, all that kind of thing."

"We all work," Stripe whispered.

Chin nodded. "And people called Providers are my bosses, and they answer to someone called Messenger, and he works for Actual. And I didn't know a lot of that until not too long ago."

"Do you have to stay here? Can you go?" Stripe asked.

"I can go to the Provider areas," Chin said, "but I don't have a lot of reason to."

Glancing at Chin to make sure it was all right, Stripe went over to Chin's bed and sat down. She rested her hand on the blanket. "... Just like mine."

Chin glanced over to her Rubberman suit. "I hated not being able to talk to you girls, you know."

"... Because of old rules," Stripe said.

"Yeah. But since I'm not in the suit ... want to surprise your Sisters?"

"Wh... what do you mean?"

Chin smiled wide. "Wanna see if that suit fits you?"

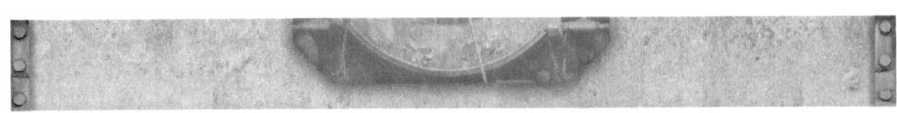

Chapter 6:

The Void

After communicating the basics of what needed to be done down to Engineering, Tara's subordinate crews were well on track. 'Conservation rationing' functions would hopefully be enabled within six hours or so.

"Kay, Sasha hon, since our box is done, let's head back to Engineering where I can keep an eye on the readings from all over, and we can be easy to find if anyone has issues."

"Yeek, it's a long crawl, too bad we can't just hang out on Provider levels until Messenger comes by with the Elevator."

Tara nodded. "Silly, really. Providers should know more than they currently do about Engineering." But this had never been the way, despite many Engineers being former Providers. They headed to the Grand Elevator shaft.

There was a ladder that went all the way from the top of the shaft, down to Engineering. There were easier paths for some of the climb, winding back and forth in the viscera of the facility. This would be safer than directly down the shaft, though slower. There was a great span of solid cement before Engineering, where the Grand Elevator's shaft was the only way.

Tara had a slight hope, and it came to fruition. As they popped out of the access hatch into the shaft, a mere one floor up, the big circular Grand Elevator loomed above, docked to the Provider loading bay.

"Are we hitching a ride?" Sasha asked, pointing at the Grand Elevator. Looking up was preferable to looking down. Down went a long, long way, including that long boring stretch right before Engineering. The length of the dim elevator shaft seemed to reach out to them, a seemingly endless maw. The large span down the shaft without access panels was the distance that the generator required in case something drastic happened to it. A distance that would keep everyone *outside* of Engineering safe.

"Yeah. Let's not dawdle, in case Messenger starts it up." Still laden with abundant gear, Tara and Sasha scampered up the ladder, around the side of the elevator cab, and onto its roof.

"All this crap!" Sasha complained, dumping her gear down beside the anchoring assembly that accommodated the Grand Elevator's cabling. "If I had to carry that all the way down the ladder, I'd be wrecked!"

"Ah, shut up, you've have dropped it all down the shaft after five minutes," Tara joked.

"Two minutes, tops. So now we wait to hear Messenger?"

"Yeah, after he closes the door to the Providers section." Tara knew that if they were spotted by Providers, it would likely lead to Messenger having to have a long, irritating talk with Contact. Tara sat down among their shared pile of equipment and gear, and welcomed Sasha to cuddle in while they waited. Sleep was getting temptingly close, when the sounds of Messenger boarding demanded her attention.

They heard Messenger rattle off official well-wishes and platitudes, in his official authority voice, then drag the door shut. This was Tara's cue to lift up the access hatch, and peer down at Messenger.

"Hey Messy!"

Messenger turned from the Grand Elevator's controls and looked up at Tara with a sigh. "Well, I was just about to come looking for you."

"Found us," Sasha responded as she shoved equipment down the hatch in a controlled pace. Even helping it down gently, being as high as she was over the floor, it would require a bit of a drop. Messenger took it upon himself to help the equipment get to the floor safely. Sasha herself was brave and nimble enough to drop herself down without assistance. She then reached up towards the hatch and Tara. "Come on, old lady, I'll help ya down."

Tara got herself dangling from the hatch, holding on with both hands. Her feet were still dangling a bit more than half a metre over the floor. She gave Sasha a sour glance, and replied in monotone. "Oh, Sasha, my lithe and vigorous, young underling. Be a dear and get under me."

"It's a trap," Sasha said to Messenger.

"Do you two need to be alone?" Messenger replied, already bored with the banter.

"Yeah," Tara said, dropping to the floor with efficiency. "Actually, I wanted a lift to get back down to Engineering, so I could monitor the teams I have running around now. I'll take the cheeky one here with me. What we do behind non-closed doors in Engineering ops control is between me, her, the generator, and all the other consenting Engineers."

"Unless there's any urgency to it, Actual wants you to visit," Messenger said.

Tara, stepped backward slowly, almost tripping over her own gear. "Ac... he wants to see us?"

Messenger looked down with a dour expression. "It's important."

"*It's bloody Actual, I assume it's important!*" Tara said, wide eyed. "Uh... up we go?"

In their roles as Engineers, Tara and Sasha had been in the Grand Elevator many times, but going right to the top to meet with the Great Actual? They'd heard about Lenth going up, and a few others, but to call it a rare occurrence would be an understatement.

Messenger set the controls, and the Grand Elevator lurched upwards. Soon they passed the dock for Citizenry, and kept going up, before finally settling at the top stop.

"Here we are."

Tara took initiative and was dragging the door open before Messenger got over to it. The door opened up to a standard loading bay room – albeit the tidiest one Tara had ever seen, and in the best shape. It underwent the least traffic, after all.

Messenger took the lead and was soon at the loading bay's opposite door, opening it. It opened to a room a few times larger than the loading bay. The walls were white, curving into the ceiling. A stripe of blue material seemed to mark the border between wall and ceiling, as no sharp corner served that role. In the ceiling was an assortment of decorative metal plates that guarded the light fixtures, and scattered the light. The floor was a smooth surface that seemed clear on the top centimetre or so, with glittery flecks of metal suspended in it.

In this large room, three paths and the Grand Elevator bay were visible, making it a hub of sorts. To the left, was a large rolling door that looked like it could be pushed up into the ceiling. There were a few like it in Engineering, but not this large.

To the right of that was just a wide open passage. Down it, another room could be partly seen, with some kind of large counter and other furniture.

Further to the right, comparatively smaller and less decorative than the other rooms, a normal doorway sat with its plain door open. In this doorway stood a man in a normal jumpsuit. His hair and ungroomed beard were grey from age. He saw Messenger, and leaned against the door frame to rest a little.

"Actual!" Messenger hastened to a brisk pace, placing a hand on Actual's arm. "Are you all right?"

As Tara got closer, the aged Actual's eyes told of a lack of sleep, or crying, or both. Actual looked to Messenger with a weak smile, then over to Tara and Sasha.

"Ah, I'm... I'm fine. But you brought... it was Tara? Chief Engineer?"

Tara stood in a straight, formal manner. "Sir! Yes, I'm Tara. I hope you don't mind that I brought my assistant along. I hope it's not breaking any rules."

Sasha waved meekly.

Actual smiled a bit wider, but he only looked more tired for it. He looked down. "Oh, it's fine, it's fine. Rules. We have so many, don't we? But they're all built on the assumption that things keep going well."

"Actual," Messenger cautiously began, "Division... what news?"

Actual ignored the question, and turned to Tara. "You were going to set up a system to ration electricity?"

"Yes, sir. By now, my teams are spreading out all over the facility to make the necessary adjustments."

With a sigh, Actual seemed moderately satisfied. "And once it's all set up, how long do you think our power will last?"

"I...I won't know for sure until it's running and I can see the readouts..."

"A week?" Actual guessed.

"M... more than that, I think, maybe... maybe two?"

"And if we need to use the elevator a lot?"

"What, like maybe twice what Messenger usually uses it?" Tara asked.

"Maybe."Actual nodded as he thought. "But heavy loads."

Messenger stood a little higher, and hints of a smile dared to press at the edges of his lips a little. "Parts for a new generator? One that uses the Thor salt or something?"

Actual's breath shuddered a little, and his gaze kept to the floor. "Tara, I think I need a heavy-duty power conduit installed as soon as possible."

Tara tilted her head slightly. "Uh... I guess so? From where, to where, and for what?"

Actual looked over to the large rolling door to the left. "Well, let's go for a little walk."

Actual led Tara and Sasha to the large rolling door near the Grand Elevator door, as Messenger followed. Tara's eyes darted around every edge of the door, and its latch.

"Your first time, unless I'm mistaken," Messenger said. Tara only replied with an extra rise of her eyebrows. Messenger grabbed the handle of the latch, and heaved it upwards.

Behind the door was a space roughly the same size as the Grand Elevator's loading bays, but this one was cluttered with.... stuff. Boxes of things. Light tubes, plates, clothes, two computer monitors of different types, slabs of wall. Things the facility needed, but didn't have the means to create.

Things from Division.

In the corner sat a few Rubberman suits. The lead-lined type, like the Engineers used around the reactor or the fuel rods.

"Only have three suits here," Actual said as he picked one up for himself.

"I'll sit this one out," Messenger said, "I've seen it."

Sasha's eyes widened, her colour drained. "The... the war land?"

"Yes," Actual said, handing her one of the suits, "I've called it war-ground, but war-land, or battle-field, or whatever... fit as well."

"Where the war was?" Sasha's stare was locked on the opposite door.

"Yes, well, a small part of the war," Actual replied. "The entirety of the war was much larger than what we're about to see." He went over to the door, with little regard to Tara and Sasha not yet having the headgear on. They scrambled to get them on – Sasha with a bit more panic.

Actual unlatched the lock, then pushed the door up, revealing an empty room that was about half the length of the first, before another, identical door. Light brown powder was on the floor, mostly around the far door. The powder showed faint tracks in it. Some from feet, some from wheels.

Now fully suited up, Tara stepped into the newly opened space, and spread out her arms. "Observe!" she declared through the muffling of the mask, "the horrors or war!"

"Very funny, Tara," Sasha said, sounding relieved, "this is just a-"

Actual heaved up the other door, revealing the wastes. Unimaginable width and breadth, a floor that seemed broken, and barely able to hold itself together, a ceiling that stretched savage smears of colours from the edge of oblivion, right across to the precipice of nowhere. Tucked in the edge of that nowhere was a light beyond reason, that bled into the scant figment of reality that sprawled before them.

Tara knelt to touch the fractured floor. It was hard, and at the same time, edges of the pieces wiped off, becoming the same powder she had seen just inside the door. The floor seemed to go on forever, with the walls too far to be seen. Or maybe the impossibly high ceiling, with all these colours, tapered down at some point to meet the floor. Could a person walk to the edge of-

Sasha screamed, fell to her knees, and vomited in her mask. Taking a moment to realize what had just happened, Tara looked away from this unthinkable endless room, and rushed to Sasha's side. By that time, Sasha was crawling back inside blindly. Vomit dripped from her mask unto the floor, as she sobbed and gagged. Once Actual had drawn the outermost door shut, Tara got Sasha's headgear off. Sasha grabbed onto Tara, still shuddering.

"Sasha, Sasha, it's okay. That room is closed off now, you're safe." Tara pulled off her own headgear, and held Sasha tight.

Actual look his off. "That... that's a new one," Actual said. "You're okay? You were never in danger in the suit. And the Enemy was pretty far."

Sasha was slowly settling down, but had no interest in anything beyond hanging onto Tara.

"I didn't see any enemy," Tara said, partly to comfort Sasha, partly to ask Actual about it.

"That bright light, far to the right," Actual answered. "At that distance, the radiation it dumps at us isn't that strong."

Tara looked at the door, and back to Sasha. "*What did it do to her?!*"

"I don't think the Enemy did that. I've seen people react in very different ways to seeing that room the first time. Once was kind of like that, but... without throwing up."

Sasha spat out one of the last bits of vomit, and mumbled "I'm going to dig a hole to get further away from that than Engineering. No wonder the facility exists..."

Tara wanted to tell Sasha that it wasn't that bad, but in all honesty, Tara hadn't gotten a good enough look at it all to form an opinion. It was also difficult to argue with the severity of Sasha's reaction.

Actual knelt down by Sasha and Tara. "Are you going to be all right?"

"Kinda... k-kinda wanna go home," Sasha said, starting to take off the Rubberman suit. Upon realizing the mess she'd made of it by throwing up, she stopped. Then she noticed that she got some of it on Tara. "Oh... oh my, I need to wear this in the shower and just... just hose off everything. Oh, I'm sorry, Tara."

"Shut up with the sorry, Sasha, you're still trembling."

Sasha's eyes went wide again, and she shot a hand out towards the door. "Did you *see that?*"

By now, Messenger had rejoined them. "It didn't go well?"

With a sigh, Actual stood and faced Messenger. "No. Can you take her to the shower? The head Engineer and I still have to address the conduit we need."

Sasha darted her stare between Actual and Tara. "You're going *back out there?*"

"Actual and I have been out there several times," Messenger offered, "even when the Enemy was much closer. With proper protection, we've withstood its attack for nearly an hour before we felt the need to withdraw."

"What kind of attack?" Tara asked.

"Radiation, of course," Actual answered. "It hovers up by that ceiling, far out of reach, and spews radiation in every direction. An odd radiation that doesn't pick up on Geiger counters. Eventually, even with the suit on, if it's close enough, you feel it a bit. It can get quite uncomfortable, but after retreating, the effects usually fade quickly. Once, I was in it for far too long, and...." Actual gestured towards Sasha.

"But you said it was unlikely that the Enemy did that to her!" Tara cried.

"For as distant as it was? And for it to happen so quickly?" Actual frowned at Sasha. More specifically at her condition. "If this is a more severe case like what I've seen before..."

"Six?" Messenger asked, referring to a dangerous Subject who'd been offered exile in the past, and had a similar reaction.

"Well, there's a lot we don't know. But the immediate fact remains, we need to install that conduit." He looked to Sasha with compassion in his eyes. "Go with Messenger. Take a long shower, calm yer nerves."

Sasha picked herself up. She looked to Tara, then she looked to the door. "You're seriously going into that room?" Her voice trembled slightly, her eyes began to well up again.

"I'll be fine," Tara replied softly, "I'll have the friggin' Actual with me."

Actual chuckled to himself. His advanced years did not present the most intimidating visage, but it was known among the Engineers that Actual was the one who'd taken care of that murderer running around a few years ago. Tara gave Sasha a big hug, ignoring any threat of more vomit getting on her Rubberman suit, and headed to the door with Actual while re-fitting her headgear.

At a healthy distance, Sasha lingered long enough to see Tara and Actual open the far door again. Those alien colours were sill out there. That all-devouring emptiness. She stared at it, feeling her trembling gradually increasing. Staring at that beautiful void, she felt a scream building in her chest.

It came only as a startled gasp as Messenger's hand rested on her shoulder, and snapped her out of her trance. "Sasha."

"Shower. Yeah. I... they're safe?"

"Safe, shielded, and getting safer by the minute, as the Enemy gets farther and farther."

"What if it comes back?"

"It won't. It's never come back faster than eight or so hours." Messenger gently and carefully (as to not get messier than need be) pulled Sasha in the direction of the right-most hall.

"Where does it go?" Sasha asked as she finally got moving.

"We've theorized," Messenger said. "It goes more or less in the direction that Division comes from. So maybe it goes to harass Division at his home. But the Enemy shows up coming from the other direction. Maybe it has to go to its own home to refuel. If it works like our reactor does, it has to refuel at *some* point."

"If it's been hassling Division, does it have anything to do with why we're not getting any uranium?"

"Actual hasn't mentioned anything like that, but that's as likely as anything." Messenger showed Sasha to a large washroom with a shower stall, the laundry cart, the towel supply, and her choice of two ill-fitting changes of jumpsuit. Messenger's size, or Actual's size.

Messenger left her to it, and made himself available for anyone who might call for him. Sasha got into the shower fully clothed, Rubberman suit and all. As the water warmed up, she did what she could to clean out the interior of the headgear, turning it inside out, and scrubbing it with soap. When the water had warmed up, she dropped the mask, and gave the soiled section of the suit a quick scrub. She stepped out of it, turned it inside out, and did what she could before moving to the outside of her clothes, then stripping down to finish it off.

She tossed everything she'd been wearing into the nearby laundry cart, then stood under the spray, opening her mouth to let the spray rinse out her mouth. She gargled the water, and spit it out a few times. One gargle was particularly loud, as she let some of that 'scream energy' out.

That room. That maddening room. She stared into the spray, and let her tears join it. Her Tara was in that psychotic room right now! *But it's safe. They all say it's safe.*

Actual's spacious shower was a little too spacious to be comfortable. It could stand to be half this size. And add Tara into it. That would help a lot. Sasha turned up the heat a little, and curled up into a ball, staying in the spray.

It could stand to be a little warmer. She stood, turned it up, and got back down.

Could she just wait here for Tara? Would that be crazy? How long was it going to be before she came back from that room? That settled it, she had to get out of the shower and find out what was going on. Where Tara was.

If Tara got too far in that room with no visible walls, would she be able to see how to get back? They said it was safe, they said it was safe.

But still.

The uncertainty drove Sasha to step out and grab a towel. Sasha put on a jumpsuit from Actual's supply. It was a little too tight and in her haste, she hadn't dried off quite enough, making it even harder to get on. Putting it back in Actual's pile would be awkward and embarrassing.

It clung to her in an embarrassing way as well. It squeezed her in ways that... hmm. Ways Tara might like. But she couldn't walk around looking all plumped up. So she put one of Messenger's suits on top. It was a noticeably baggy on her. She looked like a mess, but a mess without vomit, so that was a definite step up. Onward!

Sasha made her way towards the big door that led to that big room. The closer door was open, and Sasha could see the bay filled with parts and things from Division. Somewhere out in the big room, Division lived. Presumably... hopefully... they had somewhere to be safe. To hide from that Enemy. They must have a place, After all, the things Division brings must be from somewhere. Maybe? Is that an assumption based on ignorance? Even if the things came from somewhere, the things had to have ... had to have been made at some point, somehow.

With her eyes affixed on the closed door to the big room, thirty or forty metres away. Sasha tried to imagine. Division brought things that couldn't be made in the facility. Like light bulbs, zippers, and electronics. Division must have their own facility. That made sense. A place to hide from the Enemy, and make things ... like light bulbs.

The farthest door began to open. Sasha's pulse spiked, her breathing hastened. She stepped back slowly as if that *big empty* out there would somehow come at her. Only seeing Tara and Actual coming in kept her from running. They closed the door, and Sasha's breathing stumbled back into a more normal rhythm, sounding for a moment like a laugh.

"*Eh?*" Tara hollered to Sasha as she walked closer. "What's so funny,

Sash?"

Sasha clasped her hands in front of her chest, and released a nervous chuckle. She wore a giddy, trembling smile, "No, no, absolutely nothing. But... but you're safe, that's good."

Tara came as far as the close edge of the bay, and continued taking off the Rubberman suit, as Actual did the same. "Yup. Totally fine. No issues at all."

"It was going to be getting dark, soon," Actual said, "but that's even safer."

"Dark?" Sasha searched the memory of that room. While the experience of seeing it was seared into the mind, the details were a fuzzy. "I... I don't remember seeing any light fixtures... are they just too high to see?"

Actual huffed. "The Enemy *is* the main light source in there, as insulting as that may be. When it leaves, it takes most of the light with it."

"Then you'd be out there with no walls, and not be able to see where.. no ... w... how could you even know ... anything?"

"How would that be different than being in our bedroom with the lights out?" Tara asked.

"I'd have walls! I'd have control over being in the dark or not!" She glanced towards the door to the big room. "I.. I guess that's it... there's no way to control a room that big. There's no safe place in it."

"I suppose," Tara said, "but if there was anyone dangerous in that room, you'd see them from a long way away."

"And they'd see *you* from a long way away! And if you ran, there's nowhere to hide, you just keep going, and going, until one of you gets tired."

"Sasha, that's a scary imagination you have there!" Tara said, pulling Sasha in for a squeeze.

"If it makes you feel better," Actual commented, "of all the times I've been out there, I've only seen tracks or signs of Division. Admittedly, most of the times I've been out there was shortly after a visit from Division, but there's been no hint of a presence *other* than Division."

"Except the Enemy." Sasha corrected.

"Well, yes. It doesn't touch the ground, but-"

Sasha interrupted with a near-frenzied pace. "If it doesn't touch the ground, then there could be other things that don't touch the ground, and don't leave a trace. Frig, if the Enemy is really bright, who's to say a darker Enemy isn't out there?"

Actual sighed. "There are things we can see above when the Enemy isn't around."

"*Things?*" Sasha's eyes widened, "What kind of *things?*"

Actual cast a glance towards the door. "The biggest is like the Enemy in many ways. It has light, but barely. And it looks damaged. The light it has changes from time to time, as if it's trying to function, but cannot. It looks like small bits of it float around in the dark. Hundreds. I think it once lost a fight with the Enemy."

Sasha clutched Tara tightly, and hid her face against Tara's neck.

She whimpered softly.

Tara held Sasha and patted her back. "Shh, shh, honey, it's okay. It's okay, we're safe."

"Oh, certainly!" Actual added, "Aside from the radiation we need to guard against from the Enemy, it's safe to go out there for a while."

"I can't go there," Sasha whispered in a rasp only loud enough for Tara to understand. "I can't, I can't..."

"Honey, Actual needs a conduit installed that runs to that big r-"

"I *caaaaannnn't* I'm so sorry Tara, I can't!"

"Shhhh shh, honey, it's okay. Can you help me make and config things in *this* room?"

Sasha lifted her head enough to peer over Tara's shoulder towards the door to the big room. Her breathing was still heavy with stress, but the hints of sobbing receded. "I.. yes. Yes I can. Is it enough?"

"I can run what we make through the bay to the big room. If we do it right, that part will be fast. Yes, it will be enough." Tara took Sasha by the shoulders, held her out at half of arm's length, and looked into her eyes. "My brave girl."

"Shut up." Sasha softly punched Tara's shoulder. "Don't tease."

Tara pulled Sasha in again, and whispered in her ear, "Never. Sash." She kissed her ear just because it was handy, then after a moment said, "Okay, let's get crackin'. Where's the measuring tape?"

Actual coughed. "I should try to communicate with Division. I'll be in the back rooms. If you need anything, let me or Messenger know. He's around here somewhere." And with that, and a shared nod to Tara, he headed down the rightmost hall.

Tara held Sasha silently for a while. Sasha was still holding on pretty tight, and wasn't exactly dashing off to find that measuring tape. Tara found that the motion of their breathing had influenced the smallest sway For a while, they stood there silently, holding each other, swaying just a minuscule bit. Sasha eventually released a weary sigh.

"You don't have to be up here and help me make the adaptions," Tara quietly offered. "You could go home and chill out, I can always call out another Engineer."

Sasha's response was prefaced by another sigh, and a pause. "I... I'm not willing to be *that* much of a failure. I can't... I can't do *that* room, but I'm going to help here. Home is wherever *you* are."

With another squeeze, Tara purred. "Ohh, Sash, if I'm not careful, I'm going to just melt us into a cuddle pile, and nothing will get done."

"*Measuring tape!*" Sasha pushed away with enthusiasm. "Cuddle pile later! That's a promise!"

With measurements taken, and cabling cut, the harder tasks involved creating holes in walls and door-frames. The first tool to start a hole was essentially a pickaxe, then they used a heavy electrical saw to refine the holes. Once the cabling was through each hole, they sealed and insulated each hole as they went.

The cable needed connect a main line in the Grand Elevator shaft, though the loading bay doors' frames, (allowing the doors to still close) through the central hub room, then through the door-fames that led the way to the storage bay – and the big room that Sasha dreaded.

As they progressed closer to the void, Sasha's expression slid from focused, working neutrality, to pensive, with a scrunched lower lip, and a sour little glance towards the outer doors.

They punched out the second last hole, having to attack the wall from both sides due to its thickness.

"You plan to punch the last one on your own?" Sasha asked.

"...I can get Messenger if I need extra muscle, so you don't have–"

"*I can do it.*" Sasha growled in the direction of the outer doors. On the floor, below the bottom edge of the outer door, sat some of that light brown powder. It served as a reminder of the vast strangeness laying beyond.

Tara reared back a little. "I... I didn't say you couldn't, but you don't have to."

Sasha placed her hand on Tara's and sighed. "*I can do it.* ... Did I snap? Sorry."

Tara picked up the pickaxe and stood ready to strike. Sasha stood clear of the swing, but didn't leave. She stared at the spot in the wall that would be struck, and nodded.

Tara lifted the pickaxe high. Sasha held her breath and watched the axe come down. It didn't go as deep as expected. "Last one's even thicker," Tara commented as she pried the pickaxe loose again. "Makes sense."

She bent over, and looked into the hole. The metal had a hole, but not wide enough yet. The edges pressed into cement inside. "Brute force it is." Tara struck again. The hole got wider, bit by bit. Soon, small chunks of cement would fly out when Tara stuck, over and over. Progress which had been slow, was getting slower.

Tara looked in the hole, and over to Sasha. "I... I'm probably a bit over half way..."

"You want go into the big room to attack it from the other side like the last one?"

"Yeah. Probably have to, Sash."

"The Enemy might be back."

Tara looked at the door and nodded. "Actual seems to have an understanding of when it's likely to come back."

"Break time," Sasha declared in a weary voice, slumping against the wall, and sliding down to the floor.

"You're stalling," Tara said with a slight chuckle as she slid down beside Sasha.

"Eh, that's just part of my plan." Sasha flopped an arm around Tara, and Tara held Sasha's hand which had become comfortable on Tara's shoulder.

"You're cold," Tara said, giving Sasha's hand a squeeze.

"You're just hot. You've been doing more heavy work than me."

"Sash, you sure you don't want to head home before that door opens again?"

Sasha leaned over a little, and rested her lips on Tara's neck. Without taking her lips off Tara's skin, she said, "No. Me brave. Me just sit over back there when it opens."

Tara tuned her head to plant a small kiss. "Brave girl. Kay, let's get Actual."

As expected, Actual said that the Enemy was still gone for quite a while yet. He came along with the ladies back to the door, and carried a bucket with him.

"Why the bucket?" Tara asked.

Actual handed the bucket to Sasha.

"Oh."

Tara picked up one of the Rubberman suits, remembering that Sasha's was... unavailable at the moment. It didn't matter. Actual walked past Tara. "Leave it. No enemy, no need for the suit."

"In that room? Without even a ..." Sasha's eyes went wide, and as the three of them walked through the storage bay, Sasha seated herself on the floor in the middle of it, next to a crate of plates... holding her bucket near. "I'm good right here."

Tara gave Sasha a soft smile, and continued forward with Actual. Sasha braced herself as Actual reached down, released the latch, and heaved the door upwards with Tara's help. Tara looked so powerful, reaching up as the noisy rolling door receded into the ceiling – which was made all the more striking when the newly revealed view framed her.

A vast, endless darkness spread out beyond Tara. As Sasha quietly gasped, her eyes were able to make out flecks of light above. Countless, shimmering. Were these the broken fragments Actual had mentioned? He somehow made them sound horrifying, but like this, around her love, they shone with a power that Sasha would forever associate with Tara's bravery.

That vast emptiness out there was still intimidating, but with a healthy distance between Sasha and the door, it wasn't... wasn't *so* bad. As long as it stayed out there. She wanted to call out to Tara, *come over here, kiss me, bring those little lights...* but leave that big empty out there.

Only Actual's presence caused her to resist. It would be embarrassing.

A slow gust of cool air reached Sasha, as if a kiss were sent to her. But it did explain why the light brown powder from outside was seen on the floor closest to the door. This all implied some kind of air circulation system functioning in the big room. The fans must be really powerful, but also fairly distant, as the fans could not be heard.

Tara chattered with Actual a little. Sasha couldn't make out what they were staying, but soon Tara was carrying the pickaxe to the spot on the other side that she needed to attack. *Wham.* A delay, Tara looked at the point of impact, standing again. *Wham. Wham.*

As Tara continued, Sasha gathered her own courage, and bringing her bucket, headed closer to Tara and the door. That huge empty was right there, but those flecks of light seemed somehow friendly. And of course, Tara was right there to anchor her focus onto.

Sasha's breathing was getting rougher as she got closer to that unfathomable void, but she kept her eyes on Tara. Brave, invincible Tara. *I'm brave too, Tara. I can be brave for you. I'm trying.*

That dark void stared back at Sasha as she forced herself to edge towards Tara. The sound of Tara striking with the pickaxe seemed distant. That void just seemed to go on forever. The light specks shimmered; some brighter, some darker, seemly swallowed into the nothing. Glittering as they tried to escape, but getting nowhere.

Dozens of them. Hundreds? Thousands?

How hungry was the void?

Sasha felt light-headed. The closer she got to the threshold, the bigger the void seemed. If she went much further, it would surround her. It would consume her, just like the glittering flecks up there.

How long were those flecks up there? Would they ever fall? Or be sucked away?

Would the void bring *her* up there, and people would look up and see a fleck that once was Sasha?

Were all those flecks of light actually victims of the void? Killed in the great war, to be eaten by the void? It all began to melt in her mind. The oppressive crushing emptiness had her. Sasha was unrestrained, but helpless.

She could feel cold on her cheeks where her tears had been falling.

"*Sash!*"

And suddenly, she was safe, she was held.

She surrendered to it, and gasped, only now realizing that she hadn't been breathing. The breathing came back riding trembling sobs.

"Sasha, let's get you out of here." Being guided by Tara's arm around her, Sasha turned to face away from the void, looking back across the storage bay. That much already helped immensely, but she knew that the void was right behind her.

"I didn't throw up." Sasha muttered. When did she drop that bucket, anyway? If she didn't notice that, maybe she threw up and didn't notice. She looked down on herself. Clean. She found her hands clasped together, with Tara's hand over them. "I didn't throw up. So brave," Sasha said meekly, disdain in her voice meant for herself.

"Sasha, Shush. Let's go find you a place to sit down."

"Did you finish the hole?"

"Pretty much."

"I was useless."

"Liar," Tara said.

Sasha was quick to respond, "Less than useless, I'm a burden."

"Shut up."

"I am."

"Stupid bitch," Tara said affectionately as she pulled Sasha closer for a squeeze, "Never a burden."

"Liar," Sasha echoed to Tara softly. She squeezed back hard, but over Tara's shoulder, that endless empty stared back at her. She forced herself not to sob harder, but her sharp inhalation gave Tara a clue to keep them moving. Away from the void of the big room.

"Break time," Tara declared. "Let's go lie down."

In a fairly large room Sasha hadn't been in yet, between the hallways toward Actual's rooms, and the big room, they found a sort of sofa for Sasha to lie down on. There wasn't room for Tara, but she sat on the floor next to Sasha and leaned her head against Sasha's shoulder. "Should I get that bucket?"

"No, tummy's fine." Sasha reached out to find Tara's hand. "Well, that big void doesn't seem to bother *you* much," Sasha said.

It was only now that Sasha noticed that this room had a big rolling door that looked suspiciously a lot like the one to the big room. The big room was so big, that this door might lead to it as well.

"The 'big room' certainly is disconcerting," Tara said.

Sasha scoffed. "Disconcerting." She wanted to ask Tara how that endlessness didn't feel like it was trying to crush her. How the strange things in the ceiling that wasn't there didn't terrify her. How the looming return of that Enemy didn't make her want to take the Grand Elevator back to the bottom and hide under the bed. But she said none of it, and just squeezed Tara's hand.

Tara rested her lips on the back of Sasha's hand while she held it. "Hon, hon, hon. Been a long day."

"Fuck yes," Sasha said in little more than a sigh.

Tara just kept her lips on Sasha's hand. They sat in silence and Sasha found herself melting into Tara's warm breath. It wasn't long before sleep found Sasha.

Tara gently placed Sasha's hand up onto her, and stood. As she went into the central hub room again, Actual was nearby with a concerned expression. "She... is she all right?"

"Sleeping," Tara replied quietly.

"Twice now, she had this reaction to the big room."

"She didn't throw up this time." Tara pointed out.

Actual looked at the improvised conduit that Tara had installed – at least the stretch that was visible from where they stood. "A few years back. that fellow, Six, had a similar reaction. No throwing up, but plenty of panic. I guess it can't be considered all that uncommon."

Messenger walked in from the Grand Elevator loading bay. "Tara! I was just in communication with Engineering. They report being ready."

"Does that mean all the rheostats are installed and responding?"

Tara asked.

"He didn't say as much, but it seems so."

"I should head down there," Tara said. She glanced down the hall to where Sasha was napping. "Can I leave Sasha here?"

Actual looked the direction Sasha was as well. "I suppose. Leave her a note. I'll probably be back in the offices when she wakes up, and who knows where Messenger will be. I can quickly grab a pen and paper for you."

"Oh, good idea. And thank you." Once she had what she needed, she sat near the solidly-sleeping Sasha and wrote,

Good morning Sash!

Went to Engineering to check the responses from all the rheostats, and if everything's good, I'll be activating the rationing. By now, Providers will have gotten to all the Managers and Subjects to warn them, and Citizenry's been covered, so we're all good.

When you wake up, we'll see where Messy is with the Elevator, and either you can come down to me, or I'll come pick you up. Whatever. See ya soon!

Love ya!

Tara put the note where Sasha was likely to step on it when she got up, and leaned in to give her forehead a kiss.

Soon she found Messenger, and was on board the Grand Elevator on the way down. "I should have woken her up," Tara thought out loud.

"Naps are good, and she's had a rough day," Messenger commented.

"She has a bed at home. Who takes naps on the freakin' Actual level?"

"I do," Messenger chuckled.

"You're a *little* different, you *live there*!" Tara thought for a moment, how odd it must have been becoming Messenger, and moving into the top floor. To be suddenly so cut off from Engineering in most respects. No stranger than moving from Provider to Engineer, perhaps... but being the Messenger was a solitary role. "Do you ever miss just being Neil?" she asked.

"Becoming the Messenger is a great honour," Messenger replied.

"That's not what I asked."

"Why, are you looking to take over for me some day?" Messenger chuckled, "You'd be good at it."

"N... no... I couldn't leave Sasha in Engineering."

"Why not bring her? We seem to be all about breaking the rules lately."

Tara looked to Messenger with a serene smile. "Then I'd be taking her out of Engineering, and that wouldn't feel right. I'm pretty content where I am."

Messenger shrugged. "Well, someone will have to take my place eventually when I have to become Actual. Any suggestions for next Messenger? Lenth maybe?"

Tara choked on a sudden laugh. "You're funny. I dunno, I hear Gabe has been getting a lot of good stuff done in the Provider levels."

Messenger nodded sagely in consideration. "I was thinking he'd make a good Contact when the current one keels over."

"Well, there's time," Tara said with a sigh. "I'll try to keep candidates in mind."

Messenger shifted his weight. "I... I don't know how much time."

"What do you mean? is Actual... not doing well?"

"He's old," Messenger sighed, "I'm not saying he's dying, but... you're right, there's time."

"He means a lot to you... besides just being the Great Actual..."

"Yeah..."

Chapter 7:

Click

The Grand Elevator settled at the bottom, and docked to the Engineering loading bay. Messenger had dragged the door halfway open before Tara noticed it, having been lost in her own thoughts. As the door was opening, Engineer Kevin was already there, ready to report.

"Tara, we made it pretty. It's all wired into a new little console we converted from a spare unit. It's installed in the control room," he said.

"Good stuff."

"I've repurposed the extra heat display on the right for this," Kevin said, "it was kinda redundant anyway."

"The right-side one? I alw... eh, yeah, redundant."

When she got to the control room, she saw the 'new' twenty-centimetre unit bolted to the side of a wide control desk. "You have a funny idea of what *'pretty'* is. Someone's gonna bash their hip on this thing, sticking out like this." Tara said.

"It's way over to the right side of the room," Kevin said, "No one goes around that way."

"I do," Tara snapped, "on my way over to check the right-side heat monitor display." She shook her head. "Nah, I'm kidding. And for the time you had to it slap together, it *is* pretty," She admitted.

The control panel had controls fairly typical to the others in the room. Writing in marker labelled everything. Each of the new rheostats were represented, and each rheostat controlled various areas. Despite not wanting to affect them, there were even controls for hospital lights, and the various lights needed by the crops. Each rheostat had a test button, and a three-position switch; normal, half, and off. There was also a "Master Non-Essentials" switch.

"The test buttons send a tiny spike that will show up on the display," Kevin explained.

"I designed it to dip instead of spike," Tara said. "You wanna blow light-bulbs?"

"It's super-minimal, we tested; you can't even see the bulb react." He pressed the button to test Engineering's lights. Sure enough, the correct box on the display showed a little spike in its graph, and the lights around them showed no change. "–and a dip didn't show up on the monitor nearly as well."

Messenger spoke up, "I could be pedantic, and point out that it's still undue added stress, and will shorten the life of the lights before needing changing, but it's honestly a minimal stress. It works."

"Testing next," Tara said,"Grand Elevator shaft... Grand Elevator... Actual... Citizenry... Citizenry crops..." Test after test, they all responded as expected. Tara stepped back a little. "That *master non-essentials* switch controls all the ones we want to ration?"

"Yup," Kevin confirmed.

"Well... okay, here we go!" Tara flipped the switch.

Click.

And the lights went out. Total darkness.

"Haha, very funny." Tara flicked the switch back up, and nothing happened. "I. *said*. very. funny." Surely they rigged that master switch to turn out the Engineering lights as a joke.

But no one was laughing. Scuffing of a few people carefully walking around could be heard.

"Did you flip the switch back up?" came Kevin's nervous voice.

"Yes. I flipped the switch back up." Tara replied in monotone.

"Try toggling the individual switch for the Engineering rheostat," Messenger suggested.

"It's dark, I can't read the control panel, to-" before Tara could finish, the light of a flashlight was bouncing her way.

"Where, where?" said the light wielder, already headed for the right spot. Once she could see the panel, she flipped the Engineering switch off, and on. "Piss all."

Steps came in from the direction of the Grand Elevator. "Shaft is dark, too."

Messenger was heard to huff. "Oh tell me it's just the lights," he said before walking off to the Grand Elevator.

"How wide is this?" Tara muttered to herself. "Damn it, we have a huge surplus discharge ground conduit, you'd think it would have taken the hit of a surge. Whatever." Where was the flaw? Was it every rheostat?

Shrieks flooded the air in Citizenry. They expected the lights to dim, except those for the gardens. But now, gardens and all, darkness reigned.

"Cody?" Leena called out to her favourite, who she knew was still in the room.

"Leena, you okay?"

"Yeah, Cody. Must be everywhere, I hear a fuss out in Commons."

"I bet some of those idiots are thinking this is the wrath of the Great Actual," Cody said, remembering the past rashes of zealotry that plagued Citizenry.

Leena huffed. "Oh, no doubt he's involved in some way, but we don't need people freaking out over it."

"Yeah, well, a bit of freaking out is maybe called for," Cody said with a hint of a tremble in his voice. "It wasn't supposed to be like this!"

Indeed, the Citizens had never known such complete darkness. Yelling could be heard, though it sounded to be mostly confused yelling. People calling out to each other. So far nothing too horrible-sounding.

Leena had found her way over to Cody, and gave him a hug. "I'm gonna go be leaderly or something. If you hear me hit a wall, try not to laugh too loudly."

"You're go...? Leena, the walkway is a heck of a drop to the Commons floor!"

"There's a railing at the balcony. I'm only going that far."

Already, a couple of people could be heard walking up the walkway ramp to come see Leena, but she made it to her destination before they got to her. She faced out into the vast darkness, facing out across Commons, and called out, "*Hey Citizens! It's Leena! How's it going?*"

"How's it going?!" Cody critiqued quietly.

"*Can't see!*" came a reply from a voice further down the ramp.

"*It's dark!*" came a voice from below.

"*Ev... everyone keep calm!*" Leena called out. Hearing the voices from unknown people that she couldn't keep track of made her realize how vulnerable she was in the dark. If darkness like this had happened in more dangerous times in Citizenry, it would have been very, very bad. If any Citizens were inclined to behave very badly... this was the time to do it. "*Citizens together!*" she screamed out an old rallying cry.

"*Citizens together!*" came a reply from the dark, then another.

Leena screamed out again, as she began carefully walking down the ramp. Replies of "*Citizens together*" came back in greater and greater numbers. On her way down the ramp, she bumped into a few people, and gently nudged them to come with her.

Before long, Leena was at the bottom of the ramp, with Cody by her side, and an unseen mass of rallied Citizens around her. The chant had fallen apart as the people drew closer together, and talked in more normal volumes.

"*People?*" Leena called out. They knew her, and gradually hushed to hear her better. "Okay, first of all, I love you people. Everyone safe?"

Agreeable mumbles came from every direction, punctuated by a "*What's going on?*" from someone.

"Don't know!" Leena said, "I guess the dimming thing went a bit extreme. I gotta talk to Messenger, which means I gotta get to the communication device, which is in the the Grand Elevator loading bay."

A flurry of questions without answers came to Leena, to which she answered only, "I don't know yet," and variations thereof, which pretty much continued all the way to the Grand Elevator.

Actually navigating there was an exercise of bumping into people, people's shacks, and a big garden box or two. After a few surprised yelps from smacking into things, Leena began to sense when she was close to something big. Things just sounded a little different. If the ambient sounds of Commons and its people were blocked, or reflected in other ways... she could navigate... if she took things slowly.

When she got to the loading bay, she found the communication box easily enough. She was careful not to change any of the knobs that she wouldn't be able to see to re-tune. A careful hand found the power switch and *click!* The unit's little lights came to life. Static began monitoring for Messenger.

She got the handset, hit the button, and called, "Messenger, this is Citizenry. It's Leena. We're all kind of... a little freaked out right now. Everything went dark. You said dim. This is totally dark other than the communication box's lights." She let the button go to allow the static to resume, and give Messenger a chance to reply.

None came.

"Messenger?" She tried again. Murmurs of worried Citizens around her surged a little. "Shh," Leena requested of them.

"Messenger. Talk to me."

Silence.

"Lenth? You out there?" she tried, wondering if he might be listening somewhere.

Silence.

"Actual?"

Karen pushed her way into the upper section of the Unit that was managed by Chin.

"Who's there?!" Chin called into the darkness.

"It's just me, it's Karen. I came to see how you and your Subjects were."

"It's too dark! We were warned, but this?"

"Well, as long as no one's panicking or anything."

Chin made a trembling whimper. "Oh no panic at all! At least the water works still."

"So far."

"*What do you mean so far?*" Chin rasped.

Before becoming a Unit manager and donning the rubber suit, Karen had been a Provider, and was privy to many of the facility's functions – unlike Chin, who had previously only been a Subject.

Karen explained, "Well, water pressure is maintained by the water tanks keeping filled. I don't know if we've lost more than lights yet, but if there's no power to the water pumps, those tanks are going to empty fast, and at the same time the water processing sections... crap, I never worked in them, but I could imagine the possibility of flooding of dirty water and... stuff."

"Stuff?"

"Stuff."

"So what do we do?" Chin asked.

"Right now, I suppose trying to keep our Subjects calm is the most important," Karen said. "Later, I might try to get up to Provider levels. Maybe help, maybe *get* help, maybe get some info."

Chapter 8:

Gone

Sasha opened her eyes. At least... she thought she did. When you open your eyes, you're supposed to see things.

She felt around her head to make sure there wasn't a blanket or something on it. She touched her eyes, and felt her eyelashes where she'd expect them to be if her eyes were open, blinking a couple of times, just to make sure. She realized this wasn't her bed, and events came back to her, in a muddy, groggy way.

She remembered she was somewhere in the Actual-level. Either Actual turned off the lights, or someone screwed up in the wiring. There was no way the power would have run out already.

She carefully swung her legs around to the side of the sofa, and placed her feet on the floor. As she stood, the heard something sliding against the floor. She bent down and found a piece of paper. It felt like an ordinary piece of stationary, but if It said anything of import, the darkness made it futile. She held onto it, and carefully began to walk.

"Hello?" She called out, "*Actual?*" Which direction was the hub hall? *Bump. Ack, what was that? A chair? It's bulky. definitely a chair though. Okay, another direction.* "Actual? Messenger?" *Bump.* Some kind of desk? She didn't remember a desk, but then, she didn't remember a lot from when she was brought in here.

The last thing she remembered was Tara staying with her until she fell asleep. *Ah-ha.* The piece of paper in her hand was probably from Tara. Or not. She hoped it was. Smelling it revealed nothing. *Bump.* Another chair. *Bump rattle rattle.* What was *this* now? It was a tall mess of smooth little metal rods? The whole thing could spin, sort of, but it seemed to do nothing. Onward. *Bump.* Another bloody chair. *Bump.*

Oh. A wall? A metal wall, which felt like it had horizontal grooves here and there, and... a hinge! Another a bit above, and below. She knew what this was; it was one of those rolling doors. *Oh crap.* Wait, she wasn't by the bay to the Grand Elevator, was she? No, that would be the other way, but getting back that way felt like a challenge at least. This door might lead...

Sasha took a deep breath, and felt along the bottom edge for the latch. She found it, released it, and pulled up gently. Which got nothing. She tried more force. Not so much force that it could whip the thing wide open; just a bit. She felt it come up a few centimetres. No light from the other side. The void could also be dark. Trembling already, Sasha got down to peek underneath.

Just darkness. And no sparkly bits above. Certainly no Enemy. She was fairly sure this was not the void. The air didn't feel like the void's air. It was more stale than the storage rooms of Engineering. She pushed the rolling door up enough to crawl under, and found a ledge. Not high, but it went across the floor in front of her. She found a connected vertical part. They shared a small groove that contained jagged yet worn bits of... of glass. This used to be some kind of window? It was broken, at any rate. The bits of glass were worn down enough that she could crawl over it without much worry. This might be where broken things ended up when Messenger took them away... maybe. She stood, and reached out.

Oh. Another rolling door, right there in front of her. It was only about two metres from the other rolling door. Well, it stood to reason that the rolling doors might need spare parts or replacements as well. This might be spare parts for it. It might mess up her theory of this being a place for broken things. But this one could be broken as well.

Given what a short distance it was from the other door, it could just be blocking her from the rest of this storage space. There might be a flashlight in here somewhere.

She decided to test it, and after finding the handle and unlatching it, gave it a mighty heave up, anticipating the resistance of a damaged device.

Up the door went.

And the void was there.

Blisteringly bright, a white and orange flood blended into a pale blue above. the Enemy was to the left side, and pummelled Sasha as she screamed. Holding out her hands to shield herself from the radiation deluge it must be sending out, she stumbled back, bumping on the metal frame she'd come through, and crashed into the half-open first door.

She collapsed, and crawled backwards. Once over the edge again, she kept her face shielded with one hand, with eyes closed tight, while grasping blindly with the other hand to yank the door back down.

Once hidden from the Enemy, safe in the dark again, she felt her face and hands for burns, but found only dust and tears. There was no pain, but she knew that radiation could be sneakier than that.

Gasping sobs, she managed to whisper to herself, "*It saw me, it saw me. The Enemy in the void saw me.*" She wanted to curl up and whimper, but the Enemy was so close. Just through that door. It might be coming for her. She had to get away.

Much less cautious now, she nearly fell over a chair, then sent the tall metal thing sliding sideways across the floor. If made a horrible racket. Could the Enemy hear that? No sounds from the direction of the void, but if the Enemy flew, it might not make a sound until it burst through. The Enemy didn't look so big when she saw it, but it would be bigger when closer, obviously, and its radiation would–

Sasha's trembling sent her to the floor when she bumped the next chair in her way, and she decided to stay low. Crawling might be safer. Maybe? No chance of tripping and bashing one's head open. Keep moving, keep moving, keep– *Wall*.

A wall, a normal wall. She was confident enough it was far from the void, so still crawling, she followed the edge. She felt around a corner, and was pretty sure she was in the central hub room. This would mean the Grand Elevator was right ahead somewhere. The door with the storage bay and the void was to the right of the Elevator loading bay, and the hall to Actual's rooms was to her left.

"*Actual?*" she yelled in that direction, less worried about the Enemy at the moment, since nothing had followed her so far. No sounds replied, not a voice, nor any sounds of anything approaching from the void.

She turned towards the Grand Elevator's estimated direction, and called out in the dark, "*Messenger?*"

Nothing.

Sasha melted from crawling to lying down, and quietly called, "*Taaaaarrraaa...*" She realized she'd lost track of the piece of paper she had hoped was a note from Tara. It was probably by the door when she was attacked by the Enemy. Ironic that the light the Enemy gave off would have allowed her to read the note, but either way, going back for the note now felt pointless and dangerous.

Weighing her options, going towards the Grand Elevator made a certain sense, but she wasn't certain of the direction. Even if she got to it, then what? Find it locked? Maybe get into it, and fiddle blindly with controls she had no experience with? Or worse yet, find the elevator wasn't there, and go plummeting down the shaft to her death.

No, this wall was much safer. She'd keep following it down into Actual's rooms, and... maybe find a flashlight? Had she and Tara brought a flashlight with them? If so, her best bet to find it would be to grope around for their equipment pile, but there was a very good chance Tara had taken their gear with her, and it would still mean crossing the wide empty middle room. ... And not having her wall to guide her. Then who knew where she'd end up?

No. She'd follow the wall. Into Actual's rooms. She stood, feeling a little safer in her bearings, but kept close against the wall. She found a door that led into a washroom. Not expecting to find any flashlights or anything useful here, she continued down the hall to find another washroom. This was the one she had her shower in. It was equally unlikely to hold anything useful.

The next door was an unknown, so she entered, looking for anything. She found a light switch, with no effect of course. She blindly kicked a bucket, and heard a mop handle hit the floor. Careful not to trip over it, she explored the rest of the room, finding only cleaning supplies, and a large wash basin. It felt like the kind of place someone might store a flashlight, so she made the effort to feel every reasonable surface, but to no avail.

Back in the hall, she was soon at another door. It had been left open, and she soon found out why. Her foot bumped something. It wasn't especially hard, it wasn't bolted to anything, and didn't make a sound. She bent down to feel–

Hair. A head. She felt for a shoulder, and patted it. "Hello? Hello, are you okay?" From the feel of the thinning hair, it was almost certainly Actual. Hesitating, but in growing panic, she felt down to his neck.

No pulse.

No, calm down, relax. A pulse is hard to find. Calm down.

Breathe. Calm.

No wait, breathing. That's easier to feel. She rested a hand on their back. She chided herself for not noticing how cold his neck was.

"*Wake up!*" she yelled at him out of reflex. "Idiot. Wake up," she said in hopeless frustration. She had just called the Great Actual an idiot.

The Great Actual was dead.

Chapter 9:

Bearings

"So?!" Tara said to a couple of her subordinate Engineers, "If you have nothing to inspect, look into at least routing power back to *ourselves* so we can have some bloody light in Engineering, at least! Control monitors and communications would be friggin peachy too, come to think of it."

Messenger stepped up when Tara had a moment. "I'm heading back up. I'll peek into levels mainly to confirm they have no power either, and ... tell anyone I meet that *we're on it*."

"Going to consult with Actual?" Tara asked. "Don't be surprised if you run into Sasha on the way up. I assume she's woken up by now and has seen my..." Tara closed her eyes and sighed. "My note. In the dark. No worries, she's no idiot, she..."

Messenger read Tara's concern, and said with measured confidence, "I'm certain she's on her way."

"Don't give me the *Messenger voice*, Neil," Tara said quietly, "She's on her way. I... I know it."

"Do you want to trade tasks?" Messenger asked, "I used to be an Engineer before I was Messenger, after all. I could tidy up whatever crap you've done to our generator."

"...You're sure?"

"Go. You're no good fixing this if you're going to be stuck worrying."

"I'm supposed to have priorities as first Engineer," Tara growled at herself, "not going off to check on my sweetie when things get hectic."

"Fine then," Messenger said, "As the Messenger of the Great Actual, I command you to find the second Engineer. We'll need her."

"*Fine.*" Tara said, turning away briskly. "Thanks, Neil."

With a boost from Kevin, Tara clambered through the ceiling hatch of the Grand Elevator. She looked around with her flashlight, and straight up into the inky heights. Usually, a series of dim lights lined the shaft, but with them off, this endless tunnel up felt even less welcoming than normal.

She went to the ladder, hooking the flashlight to her waist with the clip on the front end so that the light pointed up for her as she climbed. The motion of her body as she climbed made the flashlight wave around frantically. She decided it was distracting, idiotic, and a waste of electricity, so she turned it off, and continued up in the total blackness.

This was going to be the longest stretch. Engineering was separated from the rest of the facility by a considerable depth designed to protect the rest of the facility if anything went... drastically wrong in Engineering.

It was said that the weapons used in the war were a lot like the generator. Imagining the generator being an object that could be shot around or thrown was a big leap of faith. If there was any truth to the notion, then everyone was sitting on top of a power like that which helped ravage the surface, killing unimaginable numbers of people. And carving out that big room that the Enemy passed through.

Throwing the generator had been a topic for discussion now and then. Hypothetically, how would it be done? The most reasonable answer anyone had come up with was that there could have been machines much like the Grand Elevator, but faster and bigger, to toss a generator at a target. The numbers, based on wildly uninformed estimates, were huge. Impractically so.

Mulling over idle theory was a fine distraction while climbing. The first available rest stop would be an access hatch a bit below Subject level. Messenger crawled up and down in the shaft on a regular basis. If he was the one making this trip, his arms would likely not be feeling this fatigued already.

She paused on the ladder, and turned the flashlight on for a moment to get her bearings.

Well... pointing up, the light was quickly absorbed by the vast darkness.

Down, the light was *also* quickly absorbed by the vast darkness.

Lacking any other evidence, she chose that to believe it meant she was half way to her first rest point. Lights out, up, up...

"Contact?" Gabe called into Contact's dark office, "Are you here?"

"Gabe, is that you?" Sounds of Contact fumbling to stand accompanied the sound of a cup falling to the ground, then rolling away. "*Get these lights on!*"

"I... I'm sure Messenger is working on it, Contact."

"Have we asked him? Properly?"

"I'm not sure where he is. What... what do you mean by asking him properly?"

Contact scoffed. "In recent years, I've seen people addressing the Messenger with less reverence than is *proper* for the servant of the Great Actual. This is all a *warning!* A *punishment!* We must throw ourselves before Messenger and beg for forgiveness!"

"I'm not sure–"

"I blame that Lenth! A mere Subject, and–"

"Contact, the Messenger seems to favour Lenth well enough. If Lenth was to blame–"

"*Whatever!* It's not right! He's a problematic sort!"

Gabe sighed. "Contact, the reason I'm here is just to make you aware that several Subjects are out of their Units. It seems that in light of this unexpected blackout, some Managers have decided–"

"*They're loose!? Subjects running around loose!?*" Staggered footsteps could be heard in Contact's direction, going nowhere, very quickly.

Gabe knew he'd regret telling Contact at all, but Contact would have heard eventually. At least now Gabe could try to manage Contact's reaction. "None of them are above Manager level right now, and they're peaceful. It's only a dozen or two. It's not as if Citizenry's spilled out."

Contact let out a horrified gasp, and then a moment of silence.

"Contact? Are you al–"

"*Has anyone checked that Citizenry is secure?!*"

"From the Grand Elevator shaft, things seem quiet," Gabe said.

"*This is all unacceptable! Find Messenger! Politely! Now!*"

Gabe sighed. Again. "All right. Stay safe here, okay, Contact? I'll... make sure I post a Provider near your door to keep... *problematic sorts* away from you."

"Post two!"

"Sure."

"Four?"

"Sure."

"And do we know where those shock-sticks are?"

"Four guards with shock-sticks. I'll see what I can do."

"Good, good. You're a good man, Gabe."
"Sure."

In the darkness of Citizenry, Leena sat in the loading bay for the Grand Elevator. On one side of her sat her favourite one, Cody. On her other side sat the communication device. In front of her sat, or stood, an uncounted number of Citizens.

From the sound of them, it seemed like around twenty or thirty. They talked amongst themselves sporadically, quietly, as if the darkness pressed their voices down. An occasional minor disruption from the group occurred when someone accidentally stepped on someone else, or bumped into them.

The communication device was on, with its little lights only strong enough to serve its own purpose. It was listening, but so far, found only static.

"Try again?" Cody suggested.

Leena patted Cody's leg, then reached for the communication device's handset, and held the button. "Hello. Anyone out there? Messenger?"

Only static came back.

"Messenger? Providers? Sorry we used to call you Lofus, if I never mentioned before."

Static.

"Actual, maybe?"

Static.

Leena sighed, and put the handset back. A voice called out from the group, "If things are stuck off, does that mean the Grand Elevator, too? We'll run out of food!"

This was a thought that had been in the heads of many, and having it spoken out loud triggered a cascade of similar complaints and worries.

"Calm down, everyone calm down," Leena pleaded in exasperation, "What is *actually* wrong *right now?* We have food, we have water, we're just in the dark. Honestly, big friggin' deal."

"Yeah? How long?"came a reply.

"Have some faith in Messenger and Actual," Leena said, "not because they're Great and Powerful, but because they give a crap, and will fix this."

The overall murmurs seemed dissatisfied. "Seems like we're being punished," came one of the voices.

"Punished for *what?*" Cody called back. "Citizenry is doing the best it has in anyone's memory. We got rid of the cruel ones, and we've started growing our own food, under direct guidance of Messenger. We're doing fine.

This is all just some accident."

The group seemed to mumble in a slightly more positive tone, and the complaints ended for now. This left them all sitting in the loading bay, waiting for ... anything. Leena pulled her Cody closer for reward snuggles. It was still waiting, but it made for slightly more enjoyable waiting.

Eventually, Leena decided to give the communications another try, but to the same result. She attempted to temper her voice to sound more casual, and less ... desperate sounding, as to not fuel unconstructive worry among the Citizens around her.

In the quiet darkness, her mind went to the modest farms set up not far away. The Citizens themselves could live without light but the crops could not. How long would they last in the dark? It had never been something worth discussing previously. She'd grown especially fond of the papaya trees, especially. The first one Citizenry had, they'd named after her previous favourite, who'd been killed.

It would have been easy to drift into the morose melancholy, but being snuggled up against her current favourite curbed that significantly. She gave Cody an appreciative squeeze. He'd fallen asleep. Not a horrible idea.

Leena wasn't even quite sure if she'd actually fallen asleep, when she heard pounding.

A knock against the door!

"Messenger?!" she called to the door. This woke Cody, and the other Citizens sparked to life. "Is he here?" "I didn't hear the Grand Elevator!" "Finally!" "Should we clear the loading bay?"

"*Hush, hush, everyone!*" Leena directed the Citizens, "Messenger?"

"Nope!" came a voice from the other side of the door. It was hard to hear. "I work with Messenger though. You're in the dark in there, right?"

"Y-yes! What's going on?" Leena asked.

"You were told there would be dimming of the lights?"

"Yeah, but–"

"Yes, well, something screwed up. Obviously. I'm Tara, I'm in charge of electricity, and my crew is working on this mess. We have a couple potential solutions we're working on. But it'll be a little while yet. Are you guys doing more or less okay in there?"

"Hey, we have a Tara in here, too," Leena said.

"Hi Tara, I'm Tara!" came a soft voice from the group of Citizens.

"Uh, neat?" Tara, head Engineer Tara, replied. "Anyway, as you might have guessed, the Elevator's not moving. Right now it's at the bottom of the shaft. Messenger's down there too, with my crew, trying to repair things. I've been climbing, and I was passing by, and thought I'd check up on you all."

"We're... we're okay!" Leena reported. "So, can you tell the Citizens... is this an accident?"

"Yeah," Tara moaned, "I gotta take some responsibility on this. The dimming was my idea, to save power, but for some reason, the hardware didn't like my plan, and now it's... it's pouting. But we'll slap it back into shape."

"So, not some punishment from the Actual or anything?" Leena said for the benefit of the Citizens.

"Puni– no, no, nothing like that. Actual's actually a really nice guy, it's not his style, I don't think."

"You can *hear* the Actual?!" a random Citizen called out. The vast majority of the Citizens were under the impression that the Actual's voice couldn't be heard by anyone but the Messenger. This was a myth Tara had never heard about.

"Well, yeah." Tara said.

"Oh!" Leena interrupted, having been one of the creators of that little white lie. "Tara, if you work with Messenger, I guess that means you can hear Actual like he can? I guess all Providers can hear him?"

What the fuck, Tara thought, "Uh, sure. But I'm not a Provider, I work lower. I'm an Engineer. So was Messenger before he was Messenger."

The gathered Citizens listened carefully. These revelations raised many questions about the nature of the people outside Citizenry, and about the Messenger.

"Tara," Leena cautiously ventured, "why do we need to save power all of a sudden?"

Tara sighed. Through the door, this sigh was unheard, but a pause carried as much weight. "Long story short? We're running out, and the source can't give Actual any more. Not the way it has been."

"*Source?!*" Leena asked, voicing the thoughts of all the Citizens. "Actual *is* the source!"

"That's pretty much what I thought," Tara admitted. "It seems Actual is just able to call out to someone named Division. Division comes from far away and brings us things that none of us can make, and one of those things is the stuff we use to make electricity. And *that* stuff apparently can't be found anymore."

This caused a wave of concerned mummers from the Citizens.

"...Div..." Leena stammered, "so... what does this all mean? How long is this going to go on?"

"I'm not sure," Tara admitted. "If my crew fixes what's going on below, it could be any second, theoretically, but I doubt they can pull their job off all that fast. If we rely on Actual's plan, it'll depend on Division's speed, and I personally haven't dealt with Division, so I dunno. You guys are pretty well supplied for the time being?"

"At least a week of food." Leena said.

"Good, good. Even if the Elevator's not running before then, I can find a way to get some supplies in there," Tara said. "That's not all that sustainable if the farms aren't getting light though. Pumps are an issue too. Be stingy with water. Pressure's bound to be dropping already."

"If the Grand Elevator's not working... did you climb?" Leena asked.

Tara chuckled, and glanced down the Elevator shaft. "Leena, you're the one who came down a smaller maintenance elevator shaft to get to Provider levels a while back, aren't ya?"

"Y.. yeah, but Cody got that other little elevator *working*. I've been inside the Grand Elevator, it's... bigger! And you're climbing it?"

"From a lot lower than Provider levels," Tara said, "and I'm sure Messenger's done the climb more than once. But I'm almost to the top. We'll sort this out, Leena. Sounds like you're doing a good job in there. I should get moving."

"... Right. Uh... say hi to Actual for me?" Leena said with a couple of taps on the door.

"Will do. He'll be glad to know you're all doing okay," Tara said. "Bye, Leena. Heh, and bye, other-Tara."

"Bye, other-other-Tara," came a voice from the group of Citizens. With that, Engineer Tara was heard no more, leaving the Citizens in the dark again, but with a slightly better idea of what was going on.

"See? Not a punishment from Actual," Leena said to the others.

"Is it a punishment from this Division guy?!" came a voice from the group.

"Oh, for crying out loud, people."

Elise had been a Subject all her life, though she'd never heard the term. She knew her Sisters, she knew the Rubberwoman in the ceiling, she knew the wheat. Then one day her Rubberwoman pulled her own head off. Her rubber head. It was a chunk of clothing, and a normal-looking person was underneath.

The actually-a-normal-person-Rubberwoman warned them that the lights would become dimmer, and that things would be okay. But things weren't so okay. The lights had gone out completely. Her Sisters screamed, and the Rubberwoman yelled, trying to calm things down, and for a short while, things were a little calmer.

While they were all thinking about how they could farm wheat in the dark, other voices came from above the metal grate where the Rubberwoman lived. Deeper voices. The Rubberwoman could be heard arguing with the deeper voices. Elise's Sisters were worried.

"Get in the far corner of the field," Elise whispered to her Sisters. She had to tell them a few times, trying to be quiet enough that the deep-voiced people wouldn't hear them.

The deep-voiced people and the Rubberwoman kept talking. Still in the ceiling, above the grating, but getting closer.

"Hey Brothers!" one of the deep voices called out, "Are you in here? We're Brothers, too!"

This was followed by the voice talking indistinguishably for a moment before an enormous metal bang, that echoed around the rooms.

"*What are you doing?*" came the Rubberwoman's voice.

"No, it's fine!" replied one of the deep voices before another metallic impact. "We're all looking around, your Brothers can come too!"

"*Nobody needs to be wandering around!*" the Rubberwoman cried "*Someone's going to end up getting hurt!*"

But Elise wasn't so sure.

Chapter 10:

Joined

After a rest at the Citizenry Elevator dock, and having a chat through the door, Tara had only a few stories to get to the Actual's top level. Compared to the span from Engineering, it wasn't much at all. Her rest was appreciated by her muscles, but it was also tough to get moving again. She was extremely ready for her next rest.

When she got to the top, she sat against the door. Pulling her flashlight out, she looked around the door to confirm where the latch was to release it. She turned her flashlight off to save power, and stood to grope the latch open, then began sliding the big elevator bay door open.

A quick flash around with the light let her know the opposite door was open, and the conduit she and Sasha had installed was still in place. In darkness,Tara walked into the hub room area. "*Sasha! You still around here somewhere?*"

"Tara! Tara!" Sasha's trembling voice came from the distant left, so Tara turned the flashlight that way. In the edge of the flashlight's glow,

Sasha's cowering visage offered a smile with weary eyes. "Tara, Tara, you're here!"

Tara began to run towards Sasha, but Sasha held out her hands. "Stop! Tara, stop, I couldn't find the Geiger counter. Is it in our gear here somewhere?"

"Geiger...?" Tara halted. "Why...?"

Sasha clutched herself tight. "The... the Enemy got me. I feel fine, but it got me pretty hard." As they both knew, radiation sickness could take time to manifest symptoms.

"*What?!*" Tara began frantically scanning the flashlight's beam around the nearby gear they had sitting around from the installation. "We didn't have one during installation, Sasha. Did you go into the big room? Did the Enemy do something in here? Where's Actual? I think he has a counter in his office or somewhere over there!"

Sasha let loose a whimpering wail, and Tara turned the flashlight on her in time to see Sasha collapse to her knees. Tara instinctively reacted to run towards Sasha, but only for two steps before Sasha shrieked at her, "Stop! You *can't* get get close to me if I'm a hazard! You have to check me with a Geiger counter first!"

"I... hon, okay, no problem. I have a light, I can go find one quickly, I'll head down and find Actual, and ask him wh–"

"Tara, *no*... no...!"

"Is there something danger–"

"*He's dead!*" Sasha cried out, on the edge of sobbing.

"What?"

"Actual! I... after I stumbled into an attack from the Enemy, I was trying to get as far away as I could, but then I found him."

"How did you find him in the ... oh Sasha!"

Sasha clutched herself tightly again, and her breathing was nearly hyperventilating. She was distracted enough that she didn't have time to protest against Tara running in and holding her.

"No!" Sasha pleaded, trying to push Tara away. "You could be soaking in radiation like crazy right now! Get away from me!"

Tara released Sasha, backing off slowly. "Actual... how did he die?"

Sasha shook her head. "I don't know. I... I'd suspect the Enemy got him, too. If that's the case, he must have had a bigger dose. If he's dead already, and I'm not... but I didn't check for burns on him, I didn't want to search by touch, and it was dark, and there he was, and I called out for Messenger, and you, and there was no one there, and I didn't know where to go, and where I should go, and I–"

"Honey, I'm so sorry! I should never have left you here! I left a note, but I should have woken you up and brought you with me."

Sasha exploded into sobs, smiling, "*I knew it! I knew* that was a note from you! I found it, but I couldn't read it in the dark, but I just knew it was from you!"

"Oh, hon. The power down-shift turned into power-off. The crew and Messenger are in Engineering trying to sort things out. Stay right here, okay?

I'll find a counter and get right back, okay?"

"You... climbed up to find me?"

"Yeah, I should have brought an extra flashlight, but the crew only had so many."

"It's okay. I'm fine in a little more dark. Go." Sasha sounded a little better than before, so Tara gave her a nod, and dashed towards Actual's office.

Sure enough, there was Actual, not far into his office, face down, body laying with his head towards the hall. Across the room on a desk, sat Actual's Geiger counter. It looked neatly arranged, implying it hadn't been used with any great urgency lately. She jumped quickly past Actual in case he was a radiation hazard, and got the counter. She turned it on and checked Actual. Only normal background radiation. Taking a moment to look, there were no visible burns. The side of his face against the floor might have some, but it seemed unlikely.

His expression was pretty neutral. His eyes, open just a little. Tara hadn't seen all that many dead people.

"*He's clean!*" Tara yelled down the hall. She patted him softly on the head, then headed back to Sasha. Sasha was sitting on her knees, waiting silently. She tried to look at Tara approach, while avoiding looking directly into the flashlight.

Tara ran the counter across Sasha, found nothing, and in one motion, turned the counter off and slid down to hold Sasha. Sasha burst into joyous sobs, and squeezed Tara with all her strength.

"*Guagh!*" Tara was being crushed, buy laughed, squeezing back at a more reasonable pressure.

"Don't laugh! I thought I was dying!"

"No, honey, no, you gave me a real scare! I'm just relieved!"

"Been a bad day," Sasha said, just holding her Tara, and feeling her breathe.

"I'm sorry, hon, I'm sorry, it's all my fault. This whole blackout. I screwed up *something* bad in the wiring."

"I saw every step," Sasha said, "It was all good. Had to be hardware. A lot of this gear ain't exactly fresh from Actu..." she sighed, and buried her face further into Tara's neck. Tara just sighed, running a hand up and down Sasha's back. They just held each other in the silent dark for a while, as the inevitable nagging need to get things done crept up on them.

"Hey, his main communication equipment will be down, but doesn't he keep a spare portable one for Citizenry in storage?" Tara asked quietly, trying to not immediately shatter the cuddle. To compensate for the approaching need to stand up and get moving, Tara held Sasha's face, and began a slow, ponderous, gentle kiss, which Sasha deepened.

Tara grabbed Sasha's hips, and pulled them in tight.

"I wish we were just home. I wish all this wasn't going on," Sasha whispered.

Tara huffed. "I know. I know, hon."

"Then let's get going and get things over with. Fix it all, then go home."

One flashlight between two people roaming the cargo bay was inefficient, but they did eventually find the spare communication device. The new batteries inside needed to have their little insulating shields yanked out, but then the unit was ready to go. It was set to the channel designated for Citizenry, so Tara reset it to call Engineering.

"Okay," Tara broadcasted, "This is Chief Engineer Tara on Actual level. Engineering, do you hear me?"

It took a moment, but Messenger's voice came through. "Hello, Tara. How are things up there?"

Tara took a deep breath. "Neil..."

"Neil?" Messenger asked, "Why are you calling me that? Over the air, no less. This is the second time you've called me by my original name today. Am I demoted or something?"

Tara didn't know what to say, and stalled too long.

"Tara?" Messenger probed, "Are you... are things all right?"

"I'm... I'm so sorry..." Tara responded, voice trembling a little.

For a moment that lingered painfully long, no reply came back. Sasha squeezed Tara's free hand.

"*How.*" finally came Messenger's response.

"S... Sasha found him. No obvious cause."

No response, no response.

"Hang on a bit," came the voice of a random Engineer.

"Neil! Neil, I'm so sorry!"

After another long delay, Messenger spoke. "It's not entirely surprising, his heart's been acting irregularly, blood pressure's been up for a long time." His voice carried spite for the truth, and the conditions. "I guess this blackout was... just too much."

"It's... it's my fault the blackout happened," Tara meekly offered.

"No, no," responded Messenger instantly. "You should see the conduits coming out of the backups. They're a melted mass, the capacitors are toast, there's battery acid everywhere. Old gear, rotting in on itself. The sudden feedback from downshifting all that power was all the excuse it needed. There wasn't much avoiding this blackout."

"But the small tests worked," Tara remembered. "If we'd brought each section down one by one, maybe smoothly, it could have been done better."

"Slim chance." Messenger said."By the time we got to the last one, it would have popped."

"Well, I guess we'll never know now. But if Actual had been prepared for the possibility ... if I'd predicted that this could happen ... I should have. How long to repair?"

"Stop second guessing. He was old, it was going to be soon one way or an..." His voice faltered for a split second, but picked up quickly to maintain communication protocol. "The backups are slag. We have no power. Nothing from here's going to power anything in this facility ever again. We rigged the communications with flashlight batteries."

There was a moment of silence before Tara spoke up. "I... I guess you're the Actual now. I.. what do I do now?"

"Don't call me that," Messenger said. "I suppose I am, but I don't want to be called that. Not right now, anyway. We still have his plan. We have his plan, but it won't be easy. Stay there, I'm coming up."

"All right, Messenger," Tara said softly before putting down the handset.

Chapter 11:

Coping

"Please, please return to your Units!" Gabe called out into the darkness. He could hear far too many people wandering in the halls between Manager-level rooms. It was turning exponential. A few Managers decided to give a little freedom to their scared Subjects, curious Subjects got lost in the dark, then other Managers and other Units full of Subjects started to think it might be okay for them to explore a little as well.

The more got loose,the more noise it made, the more normal it became. Old normal was gone as soon as the lights went out.

As far as Gabe could tell, no one was being overly violent. Chatter was quiet, as if a hundred or so (and quickly increasing) people would remain undetected or something. Some manager out there called out, "Okay, let's get back, we don't know where we're going in this darkness."

Voices of reason were often negated with a reply like "Which way?" "Why?" or repercussions of the ignorance that most of the Subjects had been raised in. "Rubberman, are these all my Brothers now?" "There are more people than just my Sisters?!"

A few had been educated thanks to Lenth's efforts in recent years. Others had only had a crash course recently due to the impending power throttling. Some seemed entirely caught off guard – those whose Managers decided not to open up to them.

"Gabe?" came a familiar voice from the other side of a wandering group, "Subjects, can I just get around you over here..."

"Lenth! Is that you?"

"Yeah." His voice was closer now, easier to hear through the mummers of the scattered, confused Subjects wandering around in the dark. "How many do you think are loose right now?"

Gabe laughed a single mirthless 'ha'. "Your guess is as good as mine. Did you just come from Contact?"

"Hooboy..." Lenth responded.

"I'll take that as a yes. How's he doing?"

"He's unhinged. When I found him, he was waiting to be saved by the all-mighty Actual, and begging forgiveness for whatever. He wasn't happy to see me," Lenth said. "He told me he suspected I was the... how did he put it... I'm a suspect or heretical omen, or whatever in his eyes."

"Good to know he's... still Contact. Does he realize how many Subjects are loose right now?" Gabe asked.

"He knows it's some; more than he'd like," Lenth said, "but I doubt he has any appreciation for the number we've got running around down here. He's already talking about sending Providers down here with the stun-sticks and knocking out every Subject."

"*Shit!*" Gabe blurted out, "Is anyone listening to him?!"

"No, anyone with half a brain can do the math. There's four stun-sticks and twelve hundred-ish Subjects. A lot of Providers are scared, though, and Contact's ranting isn't helping."

At that moment, a random Subject bumped into Lenth. "Ah! My sweet thing!" the Subject said, "I dropped my sweet thing! I'm never going to find how to get back to find another!"

Lenth bent down to help find this thing, suspecting the truth. Sure enough, Lenth's hand found two thirds of the 'sweet thing'. It was partly eaten, and Lenth felt the juicy innards. He passed it to the Subject. "It's a papaya."

"Ah! Thank you so much! These are amazing!" the Subject said before wandering off with his prize.

"Yuck. Papaya juice all over my hand." Lenth mumbled.

"Something's gotta be done about Contact," Gabe said, "He's going to end up getting someone hurt."

Lenth sighed. "Seems like it's past time for a new Contact."

Gabe was quiet. "I don't think Messenger would mind."

"Gotta be you, Gabe."

Gabe grunted. "Should have known that's where you were going with this. How do you picture this happening? If he's gonna be officially ... made *not* Contact, it'll get ugly."

"Uglier than how he's degraded already?" Lenth asked.

"Well, I say we ignore that he even exists right now, and just worry about these Subjects," Gabe said. "It should be quietly made known to Providers that Contact's rants aren't worth acting on. I know there's a few zealots that really buy into his 'all mighty Actual' shtick."

"Yeah... some," Lenth said. "Hard to say how many, and how many draw the line between *'Actual is good'* and *'take stun-sticks and go pick a fight with twelve hundred people in the dark.'*"

"Well, when you put it like that. Ha. Okay, let's make sure the exits out of the Manager/Subject levels are secure. I don't have any huge hopes of getting everyone back into their Units at this point, but we don't need them spilling into Provider levels, or finding the access hatch to the Grand Elevator shaft. No one needs clumsy Subjects plummeting to their deaths willy-nilly."

"We're okay there," Lenth said, "before I found you, I found two Providers guarding the panel to the Elevator shaft."

"And I have a few posted to watch Provider-level access," Gabe said. "Okay. We're ahead of the game now. Well... we're not behind. Much. So now what?"

"We just leave this door open, now, do we?" Messenger called out as he passed through the bay from the Grand Elevator shaft into Actual's hall hub.

"Oh, sorry," came Tara's voice, "With all the... everything going on..."

"Understandable," Messenger called back with a sigh. He began dragging the door shut again. He walked across the hub room slowly, surveying the area with his flashlight.

"I... put him on his bed, back in his room down the hall." Tara said as she approached Messenger.

"And Sasha?"

"I'm here," came Sasha's voice from his left.

Messenger swung his light around to see her sitting on the floor, leaning against the wall. She raised her hand to shield her face. He adjusted his aim to make it less harsh. "Sasha, are you all right?"

Sasha lowered her head, raising her hands. "I don't know." She meekly cracked out a weak laugh. "I'm not radioactive, if that's what you mean."

"Wh– why would you be?!" Messenger stammered.

"She was in the big room for a bit," Tara began to explain. "No suit, and the Enemy was out there in full strength, it sounds like."

"Then I found Actual, in the dark," Sasha sighed. By now, Tara had sat beside Sasha, and had an arm around her.

"I'm sorry," Messenger said. "That must have been terrible."

Tara wanted to tell Messenger she was sorry, but they'd pretty much addressed Tara's blame or lack of blame in the matter. Instead, she just squeezed Sasha. "Okay, Messy, now what?"

"First I should give Engineering a call, and let them know I made it up safely, then..." Messenger's voice became notably paler. "... then I check up with... with Division. I suppose that's... *my* job now." He finished with a harsh inhale.

"Neil..." Tara said, "I... you should relax. I know how to use the communication device pretty good, I just need to know the channel. What do I tell Division?"

Messenger masked a sniff with a hard inhalation. "No. I've been listening to Actual's conversations for the past two decades nearly. I know *how* to talk to Division. And I know Actual's plan better."

The three of them went over to the communication device and sat around it, sitting one of the flashlights on the floor facing up to supply at least some workable ambient light. After a quick call down to Engineering, Messenger tuned the frequency. "I hope this portable unit has the gain to reach Division. The built-in one in Actual's office had more oomph."

"We could rig something with the batteries in the flashlights and Geiger counter," Tara offered.

"If it comes to that, yes," Messenger said, "but I don't think these units are entirely feeble. We'll try without an extra boost first." He held the handpiece to his chest, and looked down into the darkness in the direction where he knew Actual's body was, and sighed. "Your timing is terrible, old man," he whispered.

Messenger took a few deep breaths to reinforce his 'Messenger voice.' He held the button. "Division? This is Station Four... Actual. Come in, Division."

Sasha turned her head to the big door where she first saw the big room through... the void... and the Enemy. "He's coming in? What's Station Four?" she whispered.

"No," Messenger said, "It's just part of the way you have to speak to him. He gets confused if you don't talk the way he does." Lacking any immediate response from Division, Messenger repeated himself. "Division, come in. This is Station Four Actual."

As soon as Messenger released the button, a voice was already speaking. The static was noticeable beyond the usual machine to make Division calls, but not horrible. "-sion here, Station Four, what can I do for you, over?" His voice was friendly. And much more casual than Tara or Sasha expected.

"Division, I wanted to check on the status on delivery of my latest request," Messenger replied, "Our main power has irrevocably shut down, and things are pretty tense here."

A few more moments passed, and Division spoke again. "I have a memo about that from the Colonel's desk. Yeah, yeah, it's on its way right now. By ground, but fast ground. About ten hours now, looks like. The Colonel sounds curious as heck about it, but you're getting what ya asked for, over."

Messenger looked about, and saw in what little light they had, that Tara and Sasha were about as confused as he was. Who is the Colonel? But he had to reply to Division in an efficient time-frame, and felt that questioning the existence of the Colonel person might create undesirable results.

"Uh.. thank you, Division. We're ready for it."

"All right then, Station Four," said Division. "Y'all have a good one. Over and out."

Messenger let the handpiece drop to his side, and he flopped back. "Well. It's coming. *'Y'all'*. It is en route. *Which raises a lot of questions.*"

"If you were talking to Division," Tara said, "and Division is in the middle of making the delivery right now, I guess his communication device is a portable one."

"I guess?" Messenger said, flailing a hand upward in resignation. "Not how I envisioned how he operated, but *who the hell is Colonel?*"

"Division might need to keep moving out there," Sasha offered, "to avoid the Enemy."

Messenger remained mostly still, but turned his eyes toward Sasha. Thoughts were turning. "That... makes sense. His deliveries have always been while the Enemy was nearby."

"Is the Enemy chasing him?" Tara asked.

Messenger shook his head. "No, it doesn't add up. The Enemy's patrol times are very predictable. And he... he *always* delivers when the Enemy is near."

"It would be ridiculous to think Division is working with the Enemy somehow, maybe he's reliant on the light from the Enemy? Does Division not have his own light? He has electricity, at least enough to run a communication device, and he has access to light bulbs. And whatever 'fast ground' is."

Messenger put his hand over his mouth, with his other arm wrapped around himself. "Division has always helped us," he said – to himself, more than anything. "We never really understood him that well, but it was always thought that asking too many questions could jeopardize our relationship. With his odd way of speaking, it was feared we might accidentally use a word that meant something else to him, so we always kept things brief and to the point. Simple requests, thank you, goodbye. *But what is Colonel?*"

"And why did he call you Station Four?" Tara asked.

"Division often calls the Actual that," Messenger said, "and the Actual must identify themselves as *Station Four Actual*. We've wondered what it means. 'Station Four' refers to us. Or this room, or the whole facility maybe, from here down to Engineering. It's never been entirely clear, but when an Actual asks for something, he does so on behalf of Station Four, and he asks for the things to be brought to Station Four."

Sasha tucked in tighter beside Tara, holding her arm. "Ten hours," Sasha said. "Will ... the Enemy still be around?"

"Likely," Messenger said, "I don't have any way to tell time right now, but I have never known Division to come when the Enemy was not visible at least a little. After, we can get to work, hooking it up."

"I never actually heard," Sasha asked, "What is Division bringing? I'm guessing it's a power source to hook up to that conduit Actual had us install? A generator that uses that Thor salt or something?"

Messenger shook his head slowly. "Actual was never able to get a clear explanation, but I doubt that an indefinitely sustainable generator is something that gets moved around. It's a guess, but such a thing would likely be a considerable operation to install, assuming we could do such a thing at all. My best guess is some manner of pre-charged capacitor."

"*A battery?*" Tara blurted out, "We're supposed to run everything off of batteries?"

"I assume it would be a type we are not familiar with if Actual accepted the idea."

Tara scoffed with a smirk and a raised eyebrow. "Under normal operating conditions, we eat well over three hundred megawatts in a month, so ... well, we'll just see what he brings. In ten hours. Yeesh."

Messenger stood and stretched out his arms. "Well, we have time. First, I wish to go see Actual. Beyond that, unless we have good reason, I have no particular urge to go climbing down the elevator shaft again. Do what you will, I suppose, Tara, Sasha, – but we should always have someone mind the communications." He took the other flashlight, and began towards the hallway to Actual's bedroom.

Sasha stared at the floor. "Do you... need company?"

Messenger paused to glance back to Sasha. "No, thank you. I would appreciate some time alone with him."

Sasha merely gave a nod as Messenger continued on. The familiar spaces of Actual's level, which Messenger knew so well, now felt so unnatural in the light of the flashlight. Distant, strange. Not like home. Not that this level was ever a hotbed of activity, but now that quiet peace was gone, replaced by a stagnation found only in the quiet of loss.

Actual's door was ahead, closed. Messenger's pace slowed, respect and the procrastination of dread dragged at him. The hesitation of his hand on the doorknob was his last safety. The last step before undeniable verification.

He sighed, and opened the door. Pointing the flashlight towards the bed, Messenger saw Actual laying there peacefully, hands overlapped on his chest. Just the slightest glimpse before Messenger dropped to his knees with a gasp, the flashlight landing on its face, blocking most of its light.

"*Neil!*" Tara called out from the hub room.

"I'm okay!" Messenger called back with a crack in his voice. "I'm... fine." He grabbed the flashlight, and heard Tara and Sasha's footsteps running his way, and the flickering of the other flashlight pointed in his general direction.

"No, no, stop," Messenger called to them with his hand held out to signal them to halt. "I'm fine. I just... I'm fine. I'll come back in a little while. I'm fine. Just wait by the communication device, please."

A pause, then Tara relented. "If you're sure," she said before she and Sasha headed back.

"Thank you," Messenger said softly. He went into the room, closed the door, and put his flashlight on the nightstand facing up to be a weak lamp.

"Teacher, mentor, guide," Messenger said quietly to Actual. "You picked a heck of a time."

Actual's health had been slipping. They both knew the time wasn't all that far away, but now? It was unexpected.

Messenger inhaled sharply, and his eyes burned. "I haven't picked a new Messenger yet," Messenger said. "Honestly, a bit rude, you know. To leave before I was ready."

Messenger took the flashlight, and sat on the floor across from the bed. He turned out the flashlight. In the dark, he could imagine this was all just a dream turned sour. That he could turn the light back on, open his eyes, and find everything would be all right.

He thought of the daily things that had become the boring usual routine. Taking most meals in Actual's company, chatting about dull minutia of maintenance, bringing news of people who lived below. For the longest time, Messenger had been Actual's only real interaction with a person.

Things had changed. A Subject became a friend, and taught other Subjects things that they'd never been taught before. Citizenry had changed. Not gently, but it had changed for the better. Instead of struggling to maintain the rules as every Actual before him, he listened. Often accepted, sometimes even helped directly.

Messenger wondered how much help he himself had been in it all. Bringing people things like lightbulbs and moving food around was the sort of thing he knew to expect from the position. To move things, to bring Actual's will as his Messenger to where it needed to be heard. Where the Actual's guidance was wanted.

And now that had to be him. Little Neil grew up to be an Engineer, confident and bright, and somehow a Messenger thought he was wise, and so little Neil became a Messenger.

And now?

"I'll take the job, Sir," Messenger whispered, "I'll use the name when I talk to Division. To everyone else, *you'll* always be Actual."

Chapter 12:

Proper Order

"*Gabe! Gabe is that you?!*" Contact hollered across his office when he heard footsteps approaching.

"Yes, Contact. It seems the guards have kept you safe?"

"Yes, Yes, but what about this bloody darkness, and what about the Subjects?"

"I haven't heard any new information about the lights, but we can assume Messenger's work continues. The Subject situation... is complicated." Gabe said.

"Complicated? *More* complicated?" Contact growled. "What does *that* mean?"

Gabe paused, thinking of how Contact would like to hear the developments. "Well, Lenth has been extremely helpful, as has Karen, and a number of other Managers. Helping to keep things civil."

"Lenth again," Contact mumbled, "but yes, yes, civil, good. So the Subjects are all back in their Units?"

"...Many."

"*What?* Well how many are still running around unlocked?!"

"Well, Contact, essentially no one has needed to be locked into Units at this pr-"

"*So you mean they're all still loose!*" Contact wailed.

"Now, now, it's not like that, they-"

"*They're going to get up here and go all 'Six' on all of us! We're outnumbered, unless you forget!*"

"Contact, their way to the Grand Elevator shaft, and up to Provider-level are secure. Many are willingly back in their own Units. Some... are visiting other Units. Some are doing their usual jobs, even, what jobs can be done safely without electricity."

Contact scoffed loudly. "Are you telling me, that with sudden freedom, twelve hundred Subjects just... behaving?!"

"There have been... *tensions,*" Gabe admitted, "but most can be reasoned with. The vast majority of them are just finding out how many of them there are, and that-"

"*That they can amass an enormous force to-*"

"To *what*, Contact," Gabe interrupted, "to take over and turn off the lights? The worst we've had is curious, wandering Subjects accidentally doing damage to a few crops."

"*You say that like it doesn't matter! At that rate, we'll all starve!*"

"It... it's a concern, for sure, but it's not as bad as you're probably thinking! Damage has been minimal! The Subjects in farm Units have been graciously protecting their crops, and guiding misguided Subjects out of those Units. The Subjects aren't well informed to say the least, but they see importance to their roles, for the most part. For the most part. Crops and such are easy to understand, though some Subjects needed to have the importance of their work explained to them. Like the air and water filter restoration Units."

"Are you saying... they're just... voluntarily continuing the work they've been doing involuntarily all this time?" Contact scoffed.

"Well, many. They're all finding out a lot," Gabe said. "It's exciting. They're finding out about the jobs of their neighbours – neighbours they didn't know they had."

"Oh that's just darling," Contact moaned, "and when the lights come back, how do we get it all back the way it was?"

Gabe let the question hang in the air for a bit. "Contact, let me handle it. I came to inform you that the change is here. There is no going back. We will have to figure out what it will mean, and how we manage the changes that will be happening; because they will happen. We need to react ... properly."

"Can we construct more shock-sticks?" Contact asked.

Gabe sighed. "That's probably not 'properly'."

Chapter 13:

Outsiders

Tara awoke as Messenger nudged her shoulder. Sasha was fast asleep across her lap. "Messen–"

"I think Division is here," Messenger said, looking into the cargo bay, and the closed rolling door on the other side, which led to the last door to the big, endless room beyond.

Tara gave Sasha's hand a squeeze. "Hon, we have company. Let's get moving."

"Hrm?" Sasha sat up, allowing Tara to get loose and stand. Sasha wasn't awake enough to care yet. Tara followed behind Messenger towards the door to the big room. The sound of large machinery of some kind could be heard out there.

"I've heard Division before," Messenger said, "but this is bigger."

Tara's eyes widened. Her first thought was of the Enemy, but she'd seen the Enemy, and it was silent. At least it was silent at a distance. "We ordered something unusual," Tara reasoned, "so... so Division sounds unusual because of it? It's been a very, very long time since we've ordered uranium as well... did it have a noisier delivery?"

Messenger nodded. "Likely. But now he'll put the delivery against this door, in between the two doors. The Enemy is still out there, probably. After Division goes, we'll have a look." He began putting on the rubber radiation suit, and Tara followed his example. Sasha was still on the far, inner end of the cargo bay, watching carefully. Tara gave her a smile and a thumbs-up before putting on the headgear.

"Messenger, did you get any sleep at all?" Tara asked, her voice partly muffled by the headgear.

Messenger said nothing, and his facial expression couldn't be seen through the suit, but he leaned his head to the side, and wiggled his gloved hand in a 'so-so' gesture.

Footsteps could be heard outside. Tara was anticipating some kind of 'whump' as the ordered item was placed against the door, but instead, there was three smaller bangs, and a voice.

"Sergeant Berryhill with an engineering squad from Yute, here. We have some hardware for you."

Tara and Messenger stood stunned into silence. The voice spoke up again. "I tried to comm in to tell you I was almost here, but I didn't get an answer. Is there anyone here?"

Messenger lifted his headgear a bit so his voice would be clearer. "You... are you working with Division?"

"Yeah, we picked up the gear from requisition on orders from Yute central division, and here we are." Sergeant Berryhill replied.

"We?" Messenger responded, "Just leave the delivery as usual."

"We're told it can't just be left out here," Sergeant Berryhill said, "this is a high-end piece of hardware, it has to be transferred directly to Station Four personnel."

'Station Four'. This Sergeant Berryhill person talked like Division did. And it wasn't just a crate of lightbulbs. Messenger had not been on-hand for the last uranium delivery either. There was every likelihood that it had been a similar situation.

"All right." Messenger turned to Sasha, who was still all the way back across the cargo bay, and called to her, "You're not suited up, get into the loading bay for to the Grand Elevator, and close the door."

Her eyes widened, and she quickly dashed off to obey. Messenger secured his headgear in place, and nodded to Tara. The two of them reached to the bottom lip of the door, and heaved it up.

Before them stood a surprised-looking man in tan clothing with a splotchy pattern, a puzzling assortment of bits of gear attached here and there. His hair was tied back, but obviously long, and a wide variety of colours. His facial hair was trimmed to a goatee, something neither Tara or Messenger had seen before.

Behind the surprised (and surprising) Sergeant Berryhill was a huge metal box on big black wheels. It had small lights on the edges, some of which were on, some of which were not. In the middle looked like a big door, roughly three metres square.

As expected, the Enemy was far above, somewhat to the right.

Sergeant Berryhill raised a hand to chest level, and stepped back, eyes wide. "Is there some kind of active hazard here?!"

"Only the Enemy," Messenger said, "Why are you not protected by something? Are you not worried about the radiation?"

"Tavish!" Sergeant Berryhill called back to the big wheeled box. "Geiger count!"

From the far end of the huge box, a door opened, and a man, kind of short, and kind of wide, hopped out. He was dressed much like Sergeant Berryhill, though bald and with a considerable beard.

Behind Tavish came a... a thing that was not a person, nor was it a tool. It was short, just above knee-height, but long. It was covered in hair, dark in most places, light in patches. It had identifiable eyes, but the nose was sticking forward by about ten centimetres, and its mouth just below was just as long, with big sharp teeth, and a tongue to go with it. It ran on four limbs that ended in spikes or nails of some kind. It had some kind of hairy appendage sprouting from it's rump, flailing pointlessly.

"Clean soo fer, Sarge," Tavish called out, looking at the device, running towards Sergeant Berryhill. "Clean, clean..." He came to Tara and Messenger, aged eyes wide, and held the device out at them. "Clean." He relaxed, dropped his hunched shoulders, and turned to Sergeant Berryhill. The thing that was following Tavish came to a stop beside him.

"Seems clean, Sarge. Wu's th' prollum?" Tavish said, keeping an eye on Tara and Messenger.

Sergeant Berryhill raised an eyebrow, and turned to Messenger. "What... what were you saying about an enemy?"

Messenger pointed at the Enemy. "That one. Are you immune to the radiation it dumps on us?"

Sergeant Berryhill furrowed his brow. "SPF 100. And I have sunglasses in the truck."

"*No!* To heck with the Enemy," Tara cried, "*what is that?!*" pointing at the four-limbed, hairy, toothy mass.

Sergeant Berryhill looked down at the thing. "Casper? She's a German Shepherd. We had need for a bomb sniffer a year and a half ago, didn't have access to one of those fancy sniffer boxes, so Casper was assigned to us. We just never gave her back."

The thing called Casper looked up at Sergeant Berryhill, opened 'her' mouth, and started breathing so heavily that its tongue seemed to be trying to escape.

"Is that thing *smiling?!*" Tara asked, stepping back a little.

"Aye!" Tavish said, "She's a good garl, frandlee an' well trained." He rubbed the top of the thing's head, and it seemed to like it.

"Sir," Sergeant Berryhill said, turning to Messenger, "are you in charge here?"

Messenger paused for a second. "I am ... Actual of Station Four," he said with a slower, deeper tone, in reverence to the title and its former holder.

"Ah. I know Station Four is privately owned," Sergeant Berryhill said, "but what's your title? Or rank? How should I address you?"

Messenger paused a bit too long, so Tara picked up the slack. "We call him Messenger."

"Your name is Messenger?" Sergeant Berryhill asked. "Is that a title?"

"Yes, I guess that's correct," Messenger said, "but I recently gained the title of Actual. There *is* no new Messenger yet. I should be using the title 'Actual'." Tara reached put to give a supportive touch, but through the suit and the glove, it didn't translate that well.

Sergeant Berryhill sighed. "Huh. Well. Okay, Actual, why the whole suit? Do you *really* need all that just for sunlight?"

"What light?" Messenger asked.

"Sunlight. Yeah, you can get a sunburn or even sunstroke if you're not careful, but that suit's gotta be hot!"

To illustrate, Tavish took a small tube from one of his many pockets, squirted out a little blob of white goop into his hand, and smeared it on the top of his bald head. "Du ye want sum?"

"The Enemy's on its way leaving..." Tara said. She reluctantly pulled her headgear off. "Hi, I'm Tara, Chief Engineer. I think you have a toy for me?"

Messenger pulled his headgear off, glancing towards the Enemy, then eyeing the thing called Casper all the while.

"Humans under thar afta all," Tavish chuckled. He turned around to the huge wheeled box, and called out "Aight, boys! Git a muuv on! Whar onloodin'!"

From the same door that Tavish and Casper popped out of, two young women emerged, both wearing the same blotchy tan/yellow outfits as Sergeant Berryhill and Tavish. One had black hair tied back into a ponytail, and wearing glasses with black lenses. The other had a shaved head and wore large, circular-lensed glasses.

"*Oy*, ya old fart," the one with the rounded glasses hollered, "*not quite boys*, here! Casper! *Girl power!* Bite Tav!"

The thing named Casper turned to Tavish, curled up its lips to further reveal its horrifying teeth. A deep growl began to come from Casper, and it quickly came out as a sudden, sharp yell of sorts, as she opened her terrifying mouth wide.

"Ooh, shush, Caspa," Tavish said, wiping Casper's spittle off of his hand. "Doon't speak ta me so moistly." Casper didn't seem to care anymore, and with the teeth quickly put away, she looked suddenly less nightmare-inducing.

Tavish turned towards the ladies and blushed, raising his eyebrows. "Oh! Muir! Ah, what ah mean, ah mean, when ah say 'boys', ah joost mean, uhm, well, ye know whut ah mean?"

Muir walked past Tavish, and broke her scowl for a smirk as she elbowed him. "It's a good thing yer cute, Tav." The other lady snorted with a suppressed smile.

While Sergeant Berryhill and Casper watched, the other three opened up the big door on the big wheeled box, and dragged out a metal ramp. They walked up and in, and surrounded an object about a metre high, and half a metre wide. They made themselves busy detaching half a dozen heavy straps keeping it in place before pushing it on its little wheels towards the ramp. At the edge of the ramp, Tavish and Muir stepped around onto the ramp, while the other lady stayed behind the object.

It could now be seen better. It was a mostly solid piece, with an outer frame on the edges with bevelled handles, similar colour to the outsiders' clothing. The middle was a dull metal with lettering on it, a couple of ports, and a little control panel.

"Oolrght, Laird," Tavish said to the lady still behind the object, "Nayse an' smooth."

Laird leaned into the object, and pushed it onto the ramp, where Tavish and Muir pushed back, to prevent it from rolling down the ramp uncontrolled. It didn't look easy. Once it was on its way, and completely on the ramp, Laird hopped down, and walked over to pet Casper and watch. Once it was off the ramp safely, Tavish patted the big heavy object a couple of times. "One Ryden Octo-Carbun capacitor. Zeera paynt six geega wuts."

Giving Casper a wide berth, Tara slowly walked over to the capacitor. It was labelled as Tavish had said, but now she could see *0.6 Gigawatts* – which had been a little difficult to understand given the odd way Tavish talked.

"This thing? 0.6? In *this*?" Tara asked.

"Honestly, it's old tech, and it's a deliberately clunky unit, built to withstand a grenade or two. Ugly and bloated, but it's reliable. That's what the Colonel authorized," Sergeant Berryhill replied, "if it's not enough, you're going to have to ask *her.*"

This word 'Colonel' again. "Who exactly is Colonel? What is her relationship to Division?" Messenger ventured.

"Colonel Mangual is in charge of most of the functions of the division," Sergeant Berryhill replied, "but if you expected a general, yes, General Westmore is technically in charge of the division, and the entirety of Yute Central as a whole. In short, the General decides what we're doing, and the Colonel directs how it gets done. That's a gross oversimplification, but in general, you'd deal with the Colonel for most things.

"In general, we don't deal with the General, but generally with the Colonel, who is not a General," Messenger mulled over, "and Division... is not a person."

Tavish stepped up. "Are ye feelin' awlright, laddie? Maybe we shood git oota th' sun."

"Son?" Messenger asked.

Tavish pointed a thumb over his shoulder at the Enemy. "Aye, in those heavy suits, tha heat moost be gitttin te ye. Layt's git sum shade." Tavish turned to Laird and Muir. "Boy– er, Ladies, kin ye push the capacitor inside while ah take our host's temp? Mister Messenger, are ye dizzy at ool? Headache?" Tavish reached into one of the packets strapped to his arm, pulling out a little digital thermometer.

"No, no," Messenger said, graciously waving the approaching thermometer away (having no idea what it was, anyway). "I'm fine." He glanced back to the Enemy. "I'm ... I'm fine, but yes, a bit warm."

As they all walked into the cargo bay, out of direct light from the Enemy, Messenger and Tara took off their Rubberman suits, setting them near the doorway.

"You spend most of your time indoors, I guess?" Laird asked, "Sorry, Messenger, your dark complexion doesn't tell many tales, but you..." she turned to Tara, "you look like you haven't seen the sun in a *while*. Don't you get time off, or at least take a lunch break outside or something?"

Tara frowned slightly at Laird, confused.

"Oh shit, that was rude," Laird said. "Sorry. My mouth sometimes, right? Sorry."

"Again, this *son*," Messenger said, "Whose son is this you're talking about?"

"Eh?" Tavish kept his thermometer handy, still not sure about Messenger feeling okay. "Nae anyone's *lad* type o son. The *sun*, the one in th' sky."

"Is that what you people call the Enemy?" Tara guessed.

"What's going on here," Sergeant Berryhill asked, glancing at the Rubberman suits, "I know this facility is all top secret need-to-know type of things, but are my people at risk right now? Is there some contagion loose, bio or nano?"

Messenger slumped against a wall, staring into the floor, so Tara spoke up. "N-no, you're safe in here. Safer than over in that big room with the Enemy right there. That.. 'son'."

Sergeant Berryhill looked hard at Messenger's haunted expression, and called out calmly, "Muir, do us a favour and grab the nano-sniffer from the truck, just in case. Would that be a problem, Messenger?"

Messenger was lost in deep thought, and didn't respond.

"Messenger?" Sergeant Berryhill said louder.

Messenger snapped out of it, and turned to focus on the Sergeant. "Hm? What was that?"

"I asked if it would be all right with you if we brought out a nano-sniffer and did a quick little check around here."

Messenger's brow tightened. "Given I have no idea what a nano-sniffer is, I have a problem answering the question."

"It detects the presence of nanites," Sergeant Berryhill explained, slowly. "They're unlikely, but if they're here, it's an issue. I want to check for airborne nanites, or on any provided samples."

Tara looked around at Berryhill and his people. The talk of these 'nanites' seemed to be making them nervous. "Okay, dumb question maybe, but... *nanites* are...?"

"You really have no idea," Laird said in awe, looking between Tara and Messenger. "Autar? Meston? Densfarn? The whole Erebus thing?"

"Was this the war?" Messenger asked.

"Well..." Sergeant Berryhill began, "it sure felt like it at times, but no, it wasn't an actual war. Those cities were attacked by domestic terrorism. A ton of deaths, but technically not a war."

"How many Cities?" Messenger asked.

"Autar and Meston had to be destroyed to stop the nanite infections," Sergeant Berryhill said with reverence. "Densfarn was saved, mostly."

"And other cities?" Messenger asked with hesitation, "Other cities still stand?"

"A... around the world? Thousands?" Berryhill guessed, "Here in Aguola, a couple hundred?"

"Did they rebuild?" Tara asked, matching Messenger's blank stare, "after the bombs? There were enough survivors to rebuild?"

By now, Laird was roaming around with the nano-sniffer, finding nothing of interest.

"Which bombs?" Sergeant Berryhill asked.

"The... war... world nuclear... war..." Messenger said, "where all the countries..."

Sasha leaned out from around the corner. Muir spotted her, and looked back at Tara. "Both so pale..." Muir said. "Seriously, how often do you two get out?"

"An how many oof ye are thar?" Tavish added. "Sarge, ah'm gittin' the sinkin' feelin' this ain't any black-ops weapons research compound or anythin'."

Sergeant Berryhill looked to Messenger, to Sasha, and to Tara. "How long have you all been here?"

"Our whole lives," Tara answered. "And our parents, and their parents, and so on, back before anyone can remember. The records only go back so far."

"Who was ... I can't believe I have to ask this," Sergeant Berryhill asked, "who was the Prime Minister when your... ancestors came in here? What year was it?"

Messenger broke down, and hollered to the ceiling, "*I've never heard of a Minister, Prime or otherwise, or a General, or a Colonel, or any of this! We're surviving down here, two thousand of us, hiding from the Enemy in that big wall-less room out there as it patrols around belching radiation on us to keep us in here, but where else would we go? It's a wasteland out there, and now you're telling me there's thousands of cities out there? How?!*" He collapsed to his knees, and Tara drew the trembling Sasha close.

"What? Oh shit, what?" Laird said softly.

"It's not April first," Muir added, "two thou..."

"Messenger," Sergeant Berryhill began slowly, "In the history of combat, there have been two atomic detonations. Hiroshima and Nagasaki. After 1945, no one's done that again. There have been threats, scares, but everyone pretty much decided it was too horrible."

Tara covered her mouth. "There... there was no war?"

"There have *been* wars," Sergeant Berryhill said, "but nothing atomic. Nothing nuclear. Land battles mostly, resource conflicts, especially before oil was phased out."

Messenger was silent, staring wide-eyed at the floor. "It... but out there... the world is gone..."

"Out there is the salt flats," Laird explained. "A month and a half ago I was a two-hour flight west from here, sucking margaritas by the beach. My folks live a few hours drive from the north coast, my brother lives in the UK, and was bitching at me this morning about a week's worth of rain."

"Are you people alright?" Sergeant Berryhill asked.

"We were... fine until we ran out of uranium," Tara said. "Oh, the capacitor. There's a lot of people having a bad time right now, we should hook them up with some juice." She looked to Sasha, who, nuzzled up against Tara and was staring out to the big room... to the world.

Sasha's eyes were on the verge of crying. "No... no war?"

Tara pulled Sasha tighter. "I... I don't know right now," Tara whispered to Sasha. She held her while she watched Tavish, Laird, and Muir poking around some of their gear.

Tavish looked amazed at the portable communication device. "Ah knew these still got made, but ah didn't know anyone who *used* them besides retro hobbyists!"

"I saw the cabling you have running through the walls to an open connection outside," Sergeant Berryhill said calmly. "Were you planning on leaving the capacitor outside while it ran?"

"We didn't exactly know what the former Actual had ordered. He might not have really understood himself," Tara said. "Communication with Division was always... mysterious. We usually just ordered stuff like lightbulbs, and some electronics. Stuff we can't make ourselves."

"Does the Colonel know how many of you there..." Sergeant Berryhill stopped himself, "I guess not, if you didn't know the Colonel existed. You've been under the radar all this time, just ordering light bulbs for... decades? Since the 1940s? And now you ordered something high-profile – this capacitor, and it sounds like the Colonel is interested in what's going on here. I guess she's going to be in contact with you soon. Or asking *me* a ton of questions. I honestly don't know where to start."

Messenger slid partly out of his shocked state, and quietly answered. "We start with getting the facility systems powered up. That capacitor isn't a permanent solution, but we need to get people some light. Get air and water pushing through the filters and into tanks. Priorities."

"Yes, Messenger," Tara replied, looking to see how Sasha was doing. Sasha seemed a little better than before.

"Fine, but we're keeping the capacitor indoors," Sergeant Berryhill said. "Folks, drag the cabling back inside and check if it's compatible. Tara, you're chief engineer here? Let's talk about your systems."

Tara huffed. "Right. We can... we can talk about your stories about cities later. There's a lot of scared people down there. First thing's first."

Chapter 14:

Gasp

A cascade of lights popped to life, flowing down the Grand Elevator shaft.

Light returned to Citizenry,
it returned to the Providers,
it returned to the Managers, and all Subjects too.
It returned to the Engineers, who guided it true.

With the capacitor hooked up from Actual level, feeding into the facility's systems through the conduits that Actual had told Tara to set up, and with a little bit of adjustment and checking with the help of Sergeant Berryhill and his team, power flowed almost perfectly.

"Tell me good things, folks," Tara said into the communication device built into Actual's workstation, "Everything where we want it?"

A reply came back quickly from Engineer Kevin. "Non-essential lights at half, farms and clinic at full. Just like we originally wanted."

"Damn, who's the master electrician after all?" Tara chuckled.

"Is the right answer 'you'?"

"Damned right!" Tara laughed.

Kevin laughed back. "We still have this giant melted conduit box that disagrees."

"Bah," Tara said, "Can't let some ancient hunk of junk that can't take the heat get ya down. Bring me the Grand Elevator, would ya?"

"On it. Where'd you get the power?" Kevin asked.

"A little help from a ... a friend of Actual's friend. It's complicated. There's a few other people involved, and something called Colonel. I don't friggin know, but I'm going to have to figure it out. Talk to ya later."

Tara heard Sergeant Berryhill enter the room, and with the crisis averted, it was time for explanations. "Well, seems like the capacitor is doing its job," Tara said. "We'll go easy on it, but it's not gonna last forever. Are you going to be delivering these regularly, or what?"

"I don't have any information about that," Sergeant Berryhill said, "but I wouldn't be surprised if the Colonel will be in contact with you about it."

Tara huffed. "Well, I hope they want to talk about a generator of some kind. I heard something about salt... I have some... some catching up to do. We've been generating our own juice from our uranium supply for a long, long time. The idea of being reliant on fresh batteries from dispatch every few months? gotta say... not a comforting prospect."

Sergeant Berryhill shook his head slightly. "I... don't think you're really getting the situation. You have.. how many did he say? Two thousand people down here? And they think the rest of the world is destroyed?"

Tara paced to the other end of the room, and briskly turned back towards Sergeant Berryhill. "I...! I don't think *you* understand! *How can there be all those cities?* And you're telling me they're all *thriving*? No war? Why are you feedin' me this story?"

Sergeant Berryhill leaned his back against the wall, and crossed his arms. "No story." he looked at Tara's increasingly unsettled eyes, trying to understand. "All the cities, town, villages, whatever," Sergeant Berryhill said, "I'm not saying they're all paradise or anything, but they sure haven't been nuked."

Tara stared long and hard at Sergeant Berryhill, but his relaxed confidence damaged hers. "You're.. telling me things you heard," Tara said with something between a smirk and a sneer. "I mean... it's great that you have people, and have resources and with Division, or however it all works..."

"I've been to a lot of those cities," Sergeant Berryhill responded, "and seen video of so many more. Talked to people in them, have family in many of them."

Tara shook her head and grimaced. She stepped back slowly as if Sergeant Berryhill's opinions on the world might reach out and attack her. But he wasn't smiling, smirking, or anything. He looked sad for her.

The possibility that it was true felt like a pressure on her chest. She hadn't bothered to breathe for a bit, and sucked in air sharply to be able to speak.

"I've been here my whole life! We *all* have! Working together to survive! We all had each other, more or less, and we were doing it! *How can it all be for nothing?!* We see the wastes, the Enemy, the world... you seem nice and all, but how can it be true?"

Sergeant Berryhill said, "Let me show you some pictures?" He pulled at a tube on his wrist, and pulled on its edge. Like a smooth little version of the rolling doors, he pulled a surface out across the length of his forearm, and as wide as the distance between his thumb's tip and middle finger. It stayed rigid across his forearm, and a series of bright little pictures formed along one edge. He touched one, and the whole surface began to show a barrage of little pictures. Before Tara could absorb the functionality of this device, Sergeant Berryhill touched one of the pictures, and it enlarged, filling the entire surface of the device.

Central to this picture was a woman with unnaturally red hair, like one of the colours in Sergeant Berryhill's hair. "My wife," Sergeant Berryhill said before sliding a few gestures across the surface. As he did so, the picture changed, moving through a strange hall, through a square hole in the wall, and moving up, but facing down at an angle.

The view was now of a big room, like the big room the Enemy patrolled. It showed a big structure with strange walls, with unusual openings. Around it, the floor was mostly green. Some kind of short plant life?

"My house." Sergeant Berryhill made another gesture, and the view raced upwards, still looking down. As the 'house' became smaller, others could be seen all around. "Hmm, which way's West from here..." With another gesture, the view flew even higher, and sideways at such a speed that structures became a mere blur before slowing above a dense array of incredibly huge buildings sticking up. Some dark, some light, some reflective. Sergeant Berryhill made a subtler gesture, and the view slid to the side more, now with about half the image being a vast pattern of blue with chaotic white stripes.

"This is the coast." Sergeant Berryhill said, "where the edge of Densfarn City meets the ocean. This is a recorded image." He squeezed a particular spot on the edge the device, and spoke in a near Messenger-like tone, "Live feed?"

The image flickered blank for a moment while a geometric little icon moved around for a moment. When the image returned, it was dark, and the previously blue and white area slowly moved about. What was blue was now black, and the rough white scratchy white stripes were now slim white ripples that travelled generally to the right, vanishing as they reached the edge of the city, which now was bristling with little lights.

"It's like midnight there right now," Sergeant Berryhill said, before squeezing the device again. "Display recording of that spot, twelve hours ago." As the display loaded the requested feed, Sergeant Berryhill glanced over to Tara.

Tara was not well. Eyes glazed over, with a blank expression other than the tears welling up in her eyes, she was barely breathing.

"Tara? You... you okay?"

Her face melted with anguish, and tears flowed. Her breathing resumed with quiet sobs.

"Are you okay? Sergeant Berryhill repeated.

What else could be done?

She screamed.

She screamed at the war that never was.
She screamed at the world that went on without them.
She screamed at the green she'd been robbed of.
At the oceans, at the cities, at the billions of people living a freedom that she couldn't understand.

She screamed.

Messenger ran in, Sasha quickly behind. Messenger took a stance suggesting combat, and Sasha rushed to Tara's side. "*Tara! Tara, what ...?*"

"*I think it might be true!*" Tara cried, pulling Sasha close, "they said the war never happened, but it's true, it's true!"

Sasha held her love close. "I was talking with Muir. It's all... it's all pretty convincing."

"Did she *show* you?" Tara said, trying to refrain from sobbing. She pointed at Sergeant Berryhill's arm, and the device mounted on it. "Did you see?"

"We learned about the Enemy," Messenger said ruefully, "It's apparently called the sun. Muir said it gives life. It gives the right light to crops, and has been doing so for ages. It is far older than us, and it *is* dangerous, but not nearly as dangerous as we always thought."

"The other things up by the far ceiling?" Tara asked, "The ones that come when the Enemy is gone?"

"There is no ceiling," Messenger replied. "They call it the sky. The other large object is called the moon. The sparking fragments are called stars."

Tara whipped out a hand in frustration. "*Moon?! Sun?! Stars?! What is all this?!*"

"You people need a field trip to a farm," Sergeant Berryhill uttered quietly.

"We *have* farms!" Tara screeched, tears running down her cheeks. "We have farms, things work fine, we were safe from the Enemy, *we survived! We triumphed!*" She held onto Sasha, and looked into her eyes. Sasha's eyes were red. She'd been crying, and was still close to it. There was no convenient escape from the things she saw in the Sergeant's device.

"What now?" Messenger asked to no one in particular.

Sergeant Berryhill took a moment to register the question, being stunned by the way reality affected everyone. "W... well," he stammered, "if things are running properly," Sergeant Berryhill said with hesitation and a worried sigh, "I guess my people and I are done here... and the Colonel is supposed to be contacting you soon."

"Very well," Messenger said, turning his attention towards Actual's room. "Now that the immediate crisis is over, I still have a body to deal with."

Tara looked up from Sasha's shoulder, and with tired eyes, looked between Messenger and the way to Actual. "Neil, no. I'll take him."

Sergeant Berryhill looked to the direction everyone else had been looking. "Body?! What body?"

Messenger sighed. "Actual. I'm the Actual now, but our former Actual died during the blackout. Apparent heart failure of some kind. We haven't have time to take the body to ... to composting yet."

"Comp... Oh." Sergeant Berryhill figured it out, and lowered his head. "Sorry for your loss, Messenger."

Messenger nodded. "Thank you, Sergeant Berryhill."

Sergeant Berryhill nodded back. "Hey, you don't need my full rank and name all the time. Just call me Sergeant, or Berryhill. Or Dan. That's my first name. Daniel."

"I don't know most of those words," Messenger admitted, "except for Daniel, and I already know a Dan. Choose Berryhill or Sergeant."

Sergeant Berryhill snorted. "Heh! May as well go with Berryhill, to avoid confusion if you meet another Sergeant. Then... you? Messenger? Or you're Actual now? Or Neil?"

Messenger looked at his own hands. He looked at Tara and Sasha, and down the hall towards the room holding Actual's body. "I... I'm not Messenger anymore, but I can't carry the name Actual. It's too soon." He scoffed at himself. "though I guess every Actual before me has had to pick up the name. Right now, just call me Messenger. It's how I'm known, and this is no time to cause additional confusion."

"All right, Messenger."

It was then that Corporal Tavish walked in, with that short, four-legged hairy thing named Casper walking beside him. Tavish saw Tara and Sasha who were still just holding each other and looking miserable. He nodded to them with a concerned look. He could guess their problem, and having no easy fix, looked to Berryhill. "Sarge. These people awl roight?"

Berryhill looked across Messenger, Tara, and Sasha. "Well, not really. They're... as all right as they can be right now."

"I hope to see you again soon, Berryhill," Messenger said. "We have a lot to figure out."

Berryhill turned to Tavish. "Tav, you have your personal junk on a little civie unit, don't you? Do you have anything personal on your issued comm?"

Tavish pulled a little black box out of a pocket on his chest. It had a little dark pane of glass, and a few buttons. "Nae sir, mah army comm's practic'ly fact'ry settin'." He walked over to Messenger. "Yer old c'muncation gear's antique." He took Messenger's hand, and put the comm device in it. "Whalcome ta th' twenty-secund senchury," he said solemnly. He took a moment to teach some basic functions. "Dun be 'fraid t' call."

Berryhill nodded, and tapped his own comm. "This feels like the kind of situation where I offer rations or something, but you're okay for food and supplies, right?"

"Our farms and production are doing well enough," Messenger said, smirking through an otherwise forlorn expression, "and I doubt your large rolling box thing has enough for two thousand people anyway."

Berryhill nodded. "True. Be safe, all right? Keep in touch. Tav, are we ready?"

"Aye."

With Berryhill and his crew on their way, and an expected call from someone called Colonel on Messenger's new little toy, the task of transporting Actual's body was now at hand. Tara made sure to find her way to Actual first.

She picked him up under his knees and behind the back. His head tiled back in an undignified way. Tara grimaced, and adjusted her arm. His head moved, and now leaned against her jaw. A sorrowful whimper escaped her, and Sasha's hand was quickly on her shoulder.

Messenger entered the room and saw Tara standing there, tears in her eyes, and Actual across her arms.

"Tara... that... that's my job," he said softly.

"It can't be!" Tara cried. "This is horrible for me, but it'd be worse for you. He's been your mentor for... for *how* long?! You've been his only link to the rest of us for so long...!"

"That's why it has to be me," Messenger said.

"No." Tara softened her tone. "At least... to the elevator. I can hold him until we get to the Provider levels." As she said it, she realized that Messenger handing him over to the composting crew would be the hardest step. "Let me at least take one part of this task off your hands." She looked to Actual's face. It was peaceful. She'd never seen him agitated, but this was decidedly different.

She never expected to be so physically close to the Great Actual. Certainly not like this.

Messenger nodded. "Let's go."

Tara let Messenger go ahead a little, and she followed behind, with Sasha at her side. They entered the Grand Elevator in silence, and in silence, Messenger operated the controls.

A few moments after the elevator got moving, Sasha spoke up meekly. "Do you think he knew? About he outside? About... the war?"

"No," Messenger replied with gentle confidence. "He was very concerned with maintaining the status quo. He felt that our agreement with

Division was fragile, and that if we fell out of favour, it would be disastrous." He paused, and had a short, mirthless chuckle. "Instead, disaster found us another way, and it led Division to our door."

"And Actual's gone, and everything's..." Sasha glanced upwards. Up there somewhere was that big room. So enormous, and with far fewer walls and ceilings than Sasha felt it should have. That funny Tavish fellow showed her all kinds of pictures. The big room was a ball, floating in a dark area with no walls, flinging uncontrolled around the Enemy... the... the sun. And no one had ever tied it down!

"I still don't get how gravity keeps us close to ... the sun," Sasha said, "Tavish explained a lot of things, but his explanations needed explanations. *Some people like the big room! And go into it on purpose and enjoy the Ene...!* Sun. They..." Sasha felt dizzy, and leaned against the wall. "I can't... this all..."

Tara and Messenger said nothing. Tara wanted to go hold Sasha, but that wasn't about to happen while holding Actual's body.

The Elevator passed by Citizenry. "I should communicate with them soon," Messenger said. "Hopefully, that Leena lady kept them all sane." Messenger grimaced. "I should have called earlier, given their history."

"I think you had a good excuse to be distracted," Tara said, looking between Messenger and Actual's lifeless face.

Messenger stopped the Elevator. They'd arrived at Provider level. "All right," Messenger said, "give me Actual. After I deal with him, and... whatever I have to deal with Contact while I'm on this level... and the Managers and Subjects... what... what do I tell them all about... the world?"

"One thing at a time, Neil," Tara said. "I've been trying to decide what to tell the other Engineers."

Messenger gave a mirthless chuckle. "Pound for pound, the Engineers have a lot more brains. You won't have to deal with Contact! He's going to melt, if he hasn't already! All right. Give me Actual, you take the Elevator. I can climb up to Citizenry later depending on how smooth things go with the Providers." He walked over to Tara, and took Actual into his arms. "Here we go, old man," he said softly.

"I'll bring the Elevator back up once I've..." Tara shook her head. "I don't know what needs doing down there. Nothing? Everything?" She and Sasha opened up the Grand Elevator's door into the Provider loading bay. Gabe and a few other Providers were there.

Upon seeing Messenger holding Actual's body... the Great and Mighty Actual, the Providers' faces shifted to silent awe. None of them had ever seen Actual. Those who followed Contact's way of thinking were unsure if Actual was even a tangible human being, but here was this body. It didn't need to be said who this was.

Messenger had brought bodies to go to composting before. In bags, on carts, or on a gurney. Never *held*. The light had gone, and the Great and Mighty Actual, provider of all, had fallen. They all stood silent for a moment.

In the past, when Contact greeted Messenger at the Grand Elevator, he would often bow, or kneel, or otherwise make some patronizing gesture of submission.

Today, Gabe was here, and he knelt with respect, with the weight of not having fitting words to speak. The other Providers followed suit.

"It was his time," Messenger said. "The stress of the blackout, it seems. It was enough to..."

Tara clenched her jaw and looked at the floor. If she'd been a better electrician, if she'd see how frail the old systems were, if she'd been more careful...

Gabe looked up. "Does this mean you're Actual now?"

"In function," Messenger said, "but the name does not rest so easily on me. I will be doing his work, and I suppose I will have to be called that by Division over communications, but to everyone else, I am still Messenger."

"Division?" Gabe asked.

"I have so much to tell," Messenger said. "I suppose Contact should be there when I explain."

"One thing at a time," Tara said.

Messenger nodded to her with a very fleeting and very subtle smile.

Tara and Sasha boarded the Grand Elevator while Messenger carried Actual deeper into the Provider level. With the door closed, Sasha and Tara silently collapsed into one another, and melted to the floor.

"That was exhausting," Tara said wearily.

"I'm a dummy, I should have offered to take a turn carrying him," Sasha responded, snuggling in tighter.

Tara squeezed back, and kissed the top of her head. "No, no, hon. It was an honour, really, but even just... just being in the room with his body. You had it worse finding him. In the dark, even! That must have been terrifying. I should have woken you and brought you with me."

"I was only passed out in the first place because I'm weak," Sasha grumbled.

"Well, I killed Actual with my gross incompetence, so I suck more," Tara said with a sigh.

"Not the answer I was expecting," Sasha said, "I figured you'd tell me I wasn't so weak, and not to be hard on myself."

Tara smirked with a little huff. "But I didn't bother saying it, because you know you're stronger than you think, and I'd tell you that even if you were a total weakling, which you're not."

"And I didn't say you're not grossly incompetent, because we both know every Engineer missed how bad this hardware has gotten, and just figured the big core conduits would keep going forever."

Tara squeezed Sasha tighter for a moment. "I guess we're lucky it was a section closest to the generator. I mean, the bulk of those conduits are running the power from that capacitor right now. If it busted somewhere in between, it would have been messier to set up."

"How long until another old section fries?" Sasha asked.

Tara scoffed. "In two seconds? Two decades? We need to look seriously at overhauling every centimetre of the core lines."

"Do we have the parts for that?"

"Nope. Not even close. Gonna have to be real nice to Division, or Corporal, or whatever." Tara kissed Sasha on the forehead and stood, walking over to the Elevator's controls. They were soon underway to Engineering on the bottom floor.

It was logical enough for them to have the Elevator to traverse the longer span between Engineering and everything else, and leave Messenger to maybe have to do some climbing to Citizenry. It was logical enough that it hadn't even been discussed. Nor was Messenger even thanked for lending the Elevator out.

"So, are *you* the new Messenger, if Messenger is the new Actual?" Sasha asked.

Tara looked down to Sasha, who was still seated. "Well. Hadn't thought about it. I would say that I'm quite content as head Engineer, but if we're just going to be hooking up to delivered capacitors instead of running that big ole' generator..."

"Changes coming. Engineering's gonna need you, Tara." Sasha turned her head away, and stared into the floor.

"Yeah, I suppose. At least until we have some kind of stable routine running."

There was some innocuous silence, aside from the sounds the Elevator made while running. Then Sasha spoke. "Do you think Messenger has been lonely being the Messenger? He's been busy all over, but .. but usually alone."

Tara cast an inquisitive glance at Sasha. "Well, he's had Actual all this time, they were pretty close, obviously. Makes ya think how hard his death has been on ol' Messy."

Sasha's breathing had become a little faster, and she avoided direct eye contact. "That's not what I... never mind."

Then it clicked. "Sash... hon... if I got the task of being the Messenger, I'm not going to do it like Neil has. He chose to be the reclusive type. If I have to spend all my time on this Elevator, I have no plan of doing it alone."

"No?" Sasha asked timidly.

"No."

"Isn't there a rule?"

"Rules?" Tara scoffed, "The generator's dead, Managers are talking to Subjects, someone gave the bloody Citizens a farm, what the hell rules are we going to follow? One where I'm not with you every available second? I don't think so! The nerve to think I'd ever abandon you to ride the Elevator!"

Without getting up, Sasha reached out and latched onto Tara's leg. "Stuck with me. Oh, hon, it's been a heck of a day... days? Frig, I actually slept, and I'm still so tired."

The Elevator came to a stop. Engineering.

"Come on, let's go see how they're all doing in there." Tara helped Sasha to her feet, and together they dragged open the door to the loading bay.

Kevin and several other Engineers were there, having gathered when they heard the Grand Elevator approaching. "Welcome back! No Messenger?"

"He's … with Actual, headed to composting," Tara replied.

"Got it," Kevin said with a short sombre nod. "Anyway, congrats for getting us some power!" A number of other Engineers voiced approval and congratulations.

"Yeah," Tara said, "I'm not sure about the details of how it's going to go when we run out of what we have now, but Messy's gonna... gonna work it out with his new..." There was just so much to tell. About the world, the billions of other survivors, the cities, no war. It was so much.

"You okay?" Kevin said, looking back and forth between Sasha and Tara.

"Tired." Tara said. Her gaunt, lost expression said as much, and more.

Sasha, head heavy with knowledge of the truth, just kept her eyes on Tara. Taking her lead, trying not to look at the people who'd have to be told eventually.

"You two look exhausted," said one Engineer.

Tara explained further about the capacitor. That it wasn't a long term solution. That Division and Messenger would be working something out long term. That much, she said flatly with no vigour. No elation or pride. Just facts.

The other facts – they could wait. She couldn't bring herself to tell them. She didn't know how. Not yet. But it would fall to her to tell the Engineers. She pitied Messenger his duties to tell the Providers, and the Citizens.

Messenger carried Actual through the doors to the composting facility. The few Providers on duty nearby stood in recognition of Messenger and his authority, but it was the oldest among them who was first to realize who was being carried.

The eldest Provider here looked to be about the same age as Actual. He looked at Actual's face and grimaced. He quietly said, "Henry. Been a while." He looked up to Messenger's face. "All right. I'll make a note of it. So, you're the new one?"

Messenger sighed. "It seems so. This blackout has brought a great deal of change, above and below."

"I'll say," the elder Provider said, guiding Messenger to a gurney to put Actual on. It was less pristine than the ones in the clinic. This one was only used to move the dead. "I heard the Subjects are runnin' all over their levels," the elder Provider said, "Probably going to cause a lot of issues if the work doesn't get done."

"Some, I'm sure," Messenger agreed, "but Gabe and Lenth are on it, right?"

The man snorted. "And you don't have any faith in the abilities of Contact?"

Messenger smirked with a sigh. "Officially, I owe it to him to tell him some large news first. If you hear him telling his version of it–"

"Everyone knows how he thinks," the elder Provider said "Unofficially, Gabe may as well be the functioning Contact."

"Noted. But I can play the official game a little longer."

After taking a moment to look upon Actual's face one last time, Messenger rested a hand on Actual's forehead. "Thank you. Henry."

Making his way through the Provider level, with arms now empty, his steps felt lighter and heavier at the same time. Most of the Providers who saw him now unburdened, averted their eyes as he made his way to Contact's office.

A Provider stood at the door to the office, holding one of the shock-sticks.

"Messenger."

"Guard duty?" Messenger asked, eyeing the stun-stick.

"You bet, keeping the Subjects from rushing Contact!" The Provider then lowered his voice, "and if he asks you, there's four of us guarding out here."

Messenger raised an eyebrow. "Fought off many Subjects?"

The Provider smirked, shaking his head.

Messenger nodded, and quietly said, "Keep up the good work." Messenger patted the Provider's shoulder as he went inside.

It stank. There was a dark pile of rags in one corner that was probably to blame.

"Contact, how long have you been here?"

Slumped over his desk, Contact popped up his head. "Messenger! The light has returned! The Great Actual has driven it away, but now the Subjects are rioting! Are you here to save us?!"

"I haven't seen any rioting Subjects around here," Messenger said.

"Oh, but they try! Gabe says they're contained, and more or less behaving, but he lies to save my feelings, the sweet boy! I've noticed my guards have dwindled. The other three are surely in bloody combat with a horde of Subjects! May they be victorious in the name of the Great Actual!"

"Contact," Messenger sighed, "Actual... was defeated by the darkness."

"*What?!*"

"One of Actual's last actions was to call for the power that I and others installed."

Contact stood, eyes wide, hands in front of himself. "The Great Actual... is..." Contact's eyes widened even more somehow as he gasped at Messenger. "Then... then *you* are now...!" Contact collapsed to his knees, and bowed low to Messenger. "Actual! Do not sully yourself be being down here among us lessers!"

Messenger put his hands on his hips and sighed. Then... an idea. He cleared his throat and prepared the grandest voice he ever cast upon the ears of 'lessers'. More Messenger-ey than a mere Messenger (and his Messenger-voice was already pretty grand) and worthy of an Actual.

"*Contact!*" he bellowed.

And Contact lifted his face in fear.

"*Rise, Contact!*" Messenger commanded.

And Contact stood, gasping as he remembered to breathe.

"Contact, you have served the Actual faithfully and true," Messenger declared, "and as the former Actual is no longer with us, it is time for The Faithful Contact to take honourable retirement and enjoy the rewards of a life of service!"

"...I... retire?"

"Oh, you seem unsure," Messenger said. "I see, you can't think of who would be able to take your place. Commendable, but you must put faith in a successor to be able to *grow* into the role. Were you as effective as you are now, when you first became the Contact?"

Contact looked inward. "I see. I see, no, I have grown much. I'm sure I was no more effective then... as someone new would be... someone like..."

"Lenth?" Messenger offered, fully expecting Contact's expression to sour a little a Lenth's name. "Or Gabe, perhaps?"

Contact's eyes brightened a little at an alternative to Lenth. "He does manage quite a lot, and the other Providers seem to agree with him a lo-"

Messenger bowed. "I, the new Actual, bow your wisdom, Contact. Gabe it is!" He took his leave before Contact could figure out if he needed to protest. The guard outside looked like he was on the edge of laughter.

"Be nice," Messenger said quietly to the guard with a smirk as he passed.

The little device that Tavish and Berryhill had given him made a strange series of sounds in his pocket. As the guard watched in bewilderment, Messenger dug it out and looked at it. The little screen had "Sergeant Berryhill" on it with a big green dot. He pressed it.

"Berryhill?"

Berryhill's voice came back, quietly, "Messenger? Knock knock!" Oh. Maybe it's supposed to be held to the ear. Messenger did so.

"Knock knock?" Messenger said.

"I'm here, and I brought guests." Berryhill said.

"Oh! Very well, I'll be there shortly. I have to get the Grand Elevator back, I'm a handful of levels down, and the chief Engineer is at the bottom. She has the Elevator."

"Ha, well, I guess I should have called ahead. Okay, we'll wait outside. We're good to wait, we have AC."

"Who's AC?"

"... Air conditioning. It.. it's a system to keep us cool when it's hot. And it's hot out."

So, Berryhill's people were not entirely immune to the attack of the Enem.... the sun. Sun. There was so much to learn. "I see. I'll try not to keep you waiting too long, I have to call Engineering first, and I need to get the Elevator back."

"See you soon!"

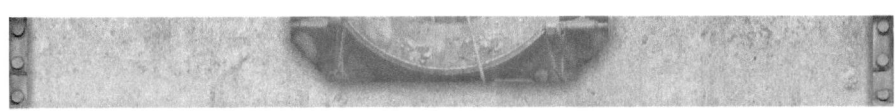

Chapter 15:

Snap

'*Pang*' went the lock inside the door from Citizenry loading bay to the Grand Elevator shaft.

'*Clangalang* boom' went the blade with no handle, and the hammer used to drive it.

'*Thump*' went Patricia as she dropped from the ceiling to the floor.

"Eeeheeheee," went Patricia as she planted her hands against the door, and began pushing it sideways. Bits of the broken lock crunched and rattled as the door came loose from the one side, and an opening began to widen.

A nearby Citizen noticed, and called out, "Patricia, you sniffer-head, you did it!"

People didn't notice when she had first started messing with the door. It had been dark, after all. When the lights came on, they asked. Even Leena had asked. *Why? Even if it were possible to break the lock, the lights were back, Actual and Messenger succeeded.*

Fine, yes, but it proved that Actual was not perfect. And if Actual wasn't flawless, he wouldn't be able to protect them from the monsters that came from the dark and the dust for long. And no one else believed in those monsters.

But she read it!

In a book!

So it has to be real!

So she had to help! No one else would!

She heard other Citizens coming, but she didn't have time for people who weren't going to help. She went through the door– *Oh no, there wasn't much floor here at all!* In fact, there's wasn't much ceiling! The walls stretched up, up, up, and down, down, down.

"This must be a hole for Actual to throw the monsters down into," Patricia thought. She'd never *seen* the monsters, other than in long-faded pictures in worn, torn, and flimsy books that she'd been allowed to take. A few people in the Citizenry had known how to read for a long time, and they usually preferred the thick, boring ones with no pictures.

Some of those people were dead now. Mostly deserved it, mostly. But they'd put up with her, and taught her to read. Well... not exactly taught. Answered questions, and never hurt her when they got annoyed. Never hurt her much. Finding the people who answered without hurting had been important, and there were more people like that now, and less of the hurty kind. And the non-hurty people brought in the papaya trees.

These tree things made food. Sounded crazy, but she'd seen it now. People were mad when Patricia had started sitting by the trees to read. "Don't hurt the other plants!" "Don't eat anything, it's for everyone!" "If you read your stupid books under the trees, everyone's going to think they can hang out in the garden, and the crops will get wrecked!"

'Stupid books' warned her about monsters. Even some of the non-stupid books told her where enough '*down*' ended up if you went far enough. And it was where monsters belonged. The books almost all agreed.

So now she saw it in front of her with her own eyes. This is were they were all cast down. She knew now that Iofus lived down there too, but probably above the monsters.

Lofus... or sorry, we know to call them Providers now, they make most of the food, and other things, with Actual's help! Or something.

Well, no monsters were visible now. But surely the Actual could use some help! Patricia would volunteer to help! Any way she can! There was no floor or ceiling, but there was a ladder nearby. *Up* it would be! Patricia grabbed on, and started climbing. She got up a little way, and heard Citizens below, discovering the floorless nature of their predicament. Yelps and hollers echoed in the Grand Elevator shaft.

Patricia swung one hand away from the ladder and looked down. No falling Citizens. The five people she could see were now looking up at her. They hollered confused things until Leena squeezed through to call up to Patricia.

"Patricia? What... uh... what's up, honey?" Leena asked. Kind people were understanding of Patricia, even when they didn't understand, and Leena had always been kind.

"Gonna go help Actual!" Patricia said, as she continued her climb.

Leena looked up, then down. "Patricia? This doesn't look so safe."

"I heard you've been in here!" Patricia called back.

"Yeah, but... but in the actual elevator. You know, that has a floor and stuff."

Patricia paused, looked up and then down. "It's not here. Maybe I'll get it later. Actual might be in danger!" She resumed climbing.

Leena sighed loudly. "Fine. If you're not coming back in, I'm coming along. Maybe I can... I don't know, make introductions." She moved over to the ladder, and her favourite, Cody, was right behind her. "Cody, you should..."

She was cut off by Cody's glare of 'as-if-I'm-letting-you-go-into-danger-alone.'

"Fine," Leena huffed. She turned to other Citizens behind Cody. "The rest of you stay here. You're safe, you have light, food, water pressure's improved, you're fine. Stay here."

Jen chirped up from somewhere in the pack, and called out, "Okay, okay, you all heard her, back up before you spill out and get killed."

Leena leaned off the side of the ladder to get a look at Jen popping her head out. "Jen? Keep em in line?"

"Yeah. Go make sure Patricia doesn't get herself hurt."

Patricia already had a considerable lead above Leena and Cody, and she didn't seem to be slowing down any time soon. Hollering up to Patricia to get her to stop was only met with insistences of the importance of Patricia's mission, and Leena decided to literally save her breath.

The climb went on, with Patricia officially saying (to no one in particular) things like "I'm coming to help, Actual, don't worry! I knew a guy who tried to build a tower to go meet you. What an idiot, this is waaaaay safer!"

Leena wondered for a moment why no one else had tried opening the door the way Patricia did – but remembering the door, she couldn't imagine what little feature Patricia would have noticed to accomplish what she did.

They eventually made it up to Actual level, and Patricia was already pushing the door open. "No lock on this one!" Patricia pointed up to a little latch near the ceiling. "Oh, there it is. It just isn't locked. Maybe Actual heard me coming, and opened it."

"Patricia, slow down," Leena said, pulling herself up onto the floor. Cody joined her, and they slumped against the wall. "Patricia, calm down. We're here. Can we just... relax? Don't go running around all bonkers. I've been here before. If you're insistent on meeting the Actual, let me take lead."

Patricia's eyes darted about. To Leena, to Cody, and around this new glossy, immaculate (compared to Citizenry) environment. The door was open to the cargo bay, and in front of it sat the new capacitor, hooked up to cabling. Patricia's gaze went further into the bay, and to all the supplies and equipment stored and arranged there. "Ooh."

"No, he's not *that* way. Let's not go that way, the Enemy is out that way." Leena said.

Patricia recoiled from that direction, and whispered to herself, "...monsters..."

"Come on," Leena said, "this way." She led Patricia down the hall towards the office where Leena had once met with Actual. Cody kept beside Patricia to keep an eye on her.

"Actual?" Leena called out, "Messenger?" They came to the office door, and found no one in there. Then they found Actual's personal room, and found no one there either. They went to other doors, finding uninhabited washrooms, janitorial closets, and so forth. They went to the room between the office hall, and the cargo bay. No one there. All the while, Patricia was getting jitterier and jitterier.

"*I'll save you, Actual!*" From under her clothing, Patricia pulled out a small but sharp-looking knife, and began running to the cargo bay. "*I'll help you! Those monsters won't get you!*"

With Leena and Cody giving chase, Patricia fumbled her way through the cargo to the wide rolling door to the Big Room... that is, outside. Not finding any way through this door, not knowing how it operated, she rammed the rolling door with her shoulder. "*I'm coming!!!*"

A voice came from the other side, muffled by the door. "Hang oon, ah'll halp, these kinds oof doors kin stick nae an then."

Patricia stepped back and looked excitedly to Leena and Cody, and whispered. "*Must be Actual! He's here! He sounds alright!*" Unsure, Leena and Cody only looked at each other and shrugged.

The big rolling door quivered, and began to rise. The light of the Enemy began to pour through.

"Why ye dun 'ave this thang ootoomat'd is beyoond me," said the voice outside, straining as he lifted.

"Actual!" With enough room, Patricia rolled under the gap, and popped up to stand next to not-actually-Actual Corporal Tavish. Startled, Tavish let go of the door, and it began to sink closed, but not before Cody and Leena stopped it enough to stick their faces through.

It was about this time that Patricia noticed the big box on wheels, this time not faced for unloading. It made noise, and had big white, rectangular glass eyes, and a handful of smaller red rectangular eyes.

"*Monster!*" Patricia lunged forward with her knife, jabbing at one of the large eyes. Her little knife slid off to the side, and her next strike was aimed at the series of horizontal slats of metal between the eyes. "*Die! Leave the Actual alone!*"

"I don't think that's a monster," Leena said, pushing the door back up a bit. By now, Corporal Muir had come out the side door of the 'monster', with the hairy thing named Caspar following behind.

"*That* might be a monster!" Leena said, now less enthusiastic about getting through the door.

Patricia jumped back, and took a combative stance, facing Caspar the German Shepherd, who stood awaiting orders next to Muir. As Patricia shifted her weight from side to side, preparing herself for combat, Muir casually pulled an item out of a pocket on her hip.

Muir pointed the device at Patricia, the device made a sharp 'clunk' sound, and Patricia collapsed on the ground, twitching.

Muir kept an eye on Patricia, petted Caspar, and said matter of factly, "Leave my bitch alone, bitch."

"Ye've been wantin' ta say tha' 'aven't ye?" asked Tavish.

"Been holding onto it for years, Tav."

By now, Leena and Cody had managed to get through the door, which now stayed hanging open by around a metre and a half.

"*You killed her!*" Leena cried, "She was just confused and scared! Granted, so am I, but I'm not an idiot."

"She's fine," Muir said. "Stun gun. She'll be tingly for a while, but she'll be fine."

"Who the heck is that?" asked Berryhill, who was coming out the door Muir had used. "For that matter, who are you? Do you work with Messenger?"

Leena stood straight, looking to Cody, then back to Berryhill. "We have. And I guess we still do what he says and stuff..."

Just then, a device on Berryhill chirped to life. He looked at it, poked it, and put it to his ear. "Messenger."

"Berryhill," came Messenger's voice from the device faintly, "I have to warn you, we've had a problem with some contained Citizens breaking cont-"

"Yeah, there's three of them right here. We had to taze one of them."

"... three? Three. Yes, that... that seems to be all of them. I'll be there as soon as I can. But I'm going to pick up some help first. I need to secure Citizenry. It should be quick. You're all right?"

Berryhill looked over to Cody and Leena, and called to them. "Are we all right?" Leena nodded, and Berryhill spoke into the device again. "Yeah, we seem fine. Don't dawdle." He poked the device and put it away before turning to Leena.

"I'm Sergeant Daniel Berryhill, commanding officer of Yute Central's Sixth Engineering team, under Colonel Mangual in the Agualian Army."

"That's a heck of a long name," Leena said. "I'm Leena."

Berryhill chuckled slightly. "Just call me Berryhill, that's what Messenger calls me."

"Um, yeah great. Can I check on Patricia over there?"

"Oh. Yeah," Berryhill said. "Technically, I suppose I should have restrained her by now. Is she going to get out of hand again?"

Leena went over to Patricia. She wasn't twitching or anything anymore, but she was breathing, seemingly asleep. Leena pulled Patricia onto her lap. She found the knife, and considered hanging onto it, but realized how that might look to these strangers who could point something at you and make you twitch yourself to sleep. Not to mention that hairy, four-legged monster that no one seemed to be concerned about. She tossed the knife into the cargo bay, then brushed some of Patricia's hair out of her face.

"She's not... not a bad person," Leena said, looking back to Berryhill, "she just... gets some odd ideas in her head. Most people in Citizenry understand her, and try to look out of her."

"I see. What's Citizenry, then?" Berryhill asked.

Cody answered. "It's an area inside there. There's a few hundred of us, and we're not allowed out."

"Are you... criminals?" Berryhill asked.

"What's that?"

"Well... dangerous people who broke laws, and had to be punished.. or contained."

"Ha!" Leena sighed, "Berryhill, there's been a lot of that in Citizenry. In the past it was way worse. But we seem to have things under control these days. Cody, when was the last attack, you think? A few hundred days?"

"Something like that," Cody said, "and they made up."

"What kind of attacks?" Berryhill asked.

"These days?" Leena mulled, "personal spats, fights. Arguments that get out of hand. But before... it was bad."

"Are things bad like that outside of Citizenry?" Berryhill asked, "Like, I know there's supposed to be a few thousand of you down there. Do they fight each other a lot?"

"I don't think so," Leena glanced to Cody to see if he agreed. "I've been to other areas in there. They're a bit afraid of Citizens. We... have a reputation. I guess I can't blame them for locking us in the way some Citizens were in the past."

"But they're not like that anymore?"

"Killed 'em." Leena said.

"*Excuse me?*"

"I personally killed one named Sledge? And at one point, we all got together and kinda hunted down all the rape-group people. Then Messenger and Actual helped us. We're farming now."

Berryhill, Tavish and Muir looked aghast.

"...Rape-group people?" Muir uttered.

"Yeah. A guy named Warren was the boss of them for a long time until he got into this white powder he found, and things got crazy."

"*Got* crazy?!?" Tavish blurted.

"Yeah, he tried to build a tower to meet Actual, but it fell, lots of people got hurt, he tried to fake his death, but my old favourite caved in his skull, but then Edgar started his own group, and they *seemed* okay, but before ya knew it-"

"Leena!" Messenger stood tall, pushing the door up the rest of the way. Behind him, Tara and Sasha followed along. Messenger shielded his eyes from the sun, but seeing Berryhill and the others here without a suit, he pressed against the impulse to avoid the 'Enemy' altogether.

"Oh, Hi, Messenger." Leena said.

"Uh, hi." Cody added.

"Messenger," Berryhill greeted, "Leena here has been giving me an abridged history of the Citizenry area."

"Well, I suppose she's pretty qualified," Messenger said. "Is *she* okay?" he said to Leena, pointing his chin to Patricia.

"She was worried about Actual," Leena said. "She broke out, got here, then sees this thing," she pointed at the big wheeled box, "and attacked it, and then saw *that* thing," she pointed at the hairy four-legged monster, "was going to attack it, but then got put to sleep by *her*," and pointed to Muir. "With a little thing that made her twitch."

"I... I see. Sounds like I missed quite a scene," Messenger said. "You were trying to stop her? And the three of you climbed up here?"

"And the door was unlocked, so she –"

Messenger frowned, and shook his head. "Door. Wasn't. Locked. No, I didn't figure on a grand Citizen uprising!"

"*Nobody* expects the grand Citizen uprising," Cody mumbled to himself.

Patricia mumbled quietly and incoherently, taking the first steps back to consciousness.

Berryhill sighed. "Well, I wonder what she would have done if she'd seen *that*." He pointed above the cargo bay door. Messenger, Cody, Sasha, and Leena all tried to see what he was pointing at, but it seemed they'd have to come further from the door. Sasha remained in the cargo bay, and without Tara at her side, she discretely moved further inside. Tara made sure to stay in sight of Sasha. Messenger stepped forward to be beside Berryhill, and looked up.

It was another big box, perhaps bigger, but not on wheels. It floated several dozen metres above the ground, and had four protrusions on its sides, each fitted with a large drum-like object that burned on their bottoms.

"What... is that?" Messenger uttered quietly. This caused Cody and Tara to come and look, while Leena remained with Patricia. Sasha remained safely a handful of metres in the loading bay, still not being pleased at all about the wideness and emptiness of the outside world.

"That is the Colonel's AirLimb," Berryhill said, "I'd guess it has at least two Stormfronts on it, which would figure out to eight troops. Colonel, you copy? Situation here seems contained. Just a mentally disturbed resident causing a problem. She's a non-threat. You're clear."

Tara looked up at the 'AirLimb' as it moved overhead. She pointed at the big box with wheels. "So, is that a FloorLimb?"

Muir looked at the big box with wheels, and then to Tara, as if she were an idiot. "No, it's a truck."

"Truck." Tara repeated.

"Ugh, combat utility engineering vehicle, whatever."

The AirLimb descended several dozen metres away, with the fiery machine parts kicking up dust the lower it got. The bottom of the AirLimb's body grew three metal feet, which met the ground and prevented the fiery parts from touching the ground – though it set down far enough away that the dust didn't reach the people around the truck.

Patricia woke up enough to speak, looking up to Leena. "Leena, did I do it?" she slurred, "Did I save the Actual?" She looked around and saw Tavish. "Aaaactual..."

"Leena," Messenger said, "If she's ready to move, it might be best if you take her and your fellow back to Citizenry. There's a handful of Providers inside near the Elevator. They'll help you."

"Yes, Messenger," Leena said humbly, "thank you."

"Thank you for caring for her," he replied.

As Leena and Cody helped Patricia to her feet, Berryhill and his three Corporals moved to stand side by side, facing the AirLimb. Even Caspar took position at one end of the line-up. Messenger and Tara shared a nod, and Tara went back to be with Sasha.

Feeling the need to follow a new custom, Messenger stood next to Berryhill. "And now?" Messenger's question was answered by the sound of the AirLimb opening on one side. A ramp slid out, and four soldiers began to emerge.

"Let's go talk to her," Berryhill said to Messenger. He turned to the others. "At ease, you three." Laird, Muir and Tavish shifted their stances in identical, specific ways that seemed trivial to Messenger. Berryhill started walking forward, and Messenger kept up beside him.

As they approached the AirLimb, the four soldiers formed two strictly ordered pairs to either side of the ramp. They had a similar array of pockets and gadgets all over their outfits, but where Berryhill and his people had designs of muted tan and yellow, the solders from the AirLimb wore a near-black shade of blue. They carried objects leaned on their shoulders that Messenger guessed to be weapons. It was only now that Messenger realized that one of the gadgets on Berryhill's hip was likely a weapon as well. Much smaller. Similar to one that Actual had, come to think of it. Where did he keep that thing stored? No matter right now.

One of the soldiers suddenly switched which hand supported his weapon, then whipped his now-free hand upward to beside his face, hand flat, palm facing Berryhill. "Sir." the soldier said sharply. He kept his hand in place.

Berryhill returned the gesture, albeit in a much more relaxed way. As he did so, he said, "Corporal." Before Berryhill got his hand back down, the soldier had already whipped his own hand down to take the weapon back from his other hand, returning to his original position to match the same as the other three AirLimb soldiers.

It was this time when a fifth soldier appeared at the top of the ramp. Her outfit had almost no devices attached to it. It was a deep blue, but nowhere as dark as the other soldiers. The most notable detail on her top was a cluster of colourful tiny squares and rectangles attached to the front, towards an upper corner. She wore glasses with slim, black frames.

Her short, tightly curly hair was a shade of purple so dark that Messenger thought it was black until she stepped further into the light. Atop was some kind of headgear that seemed to serve no purpose. It was just a wedge of stiff fabric, matching the colour of the rest of her outfit.

Before she got to the bottom of the ramp, Messenger took initiative.

He copied the thing with his hand, faster than he'd seen Berryhill do, but slower than the other soldier had. He guessed, "Colonel?" He lowered his hand, as keeping it up felt a little silly, especially if he was doing it wrong.

She smirked, with one eyebrow raised a little. When she got to the bottom of the ramp, she stopped. Berryhill snapped his hand sharply into position.

"As you were," The Colonel said, which seemed to be enough to release Berryhill's hand. "You would be Messenger?" she asked.

"That's correct."

"I am Colonel Veronika Mangual," she said in a formal yet kind tone. "I'm here for an exchange of information of sorts. We have very little idea what's going on in this 'Station Four', it seems, and I understand you have very little idea what's going on out here."

Messenger glanced back towards the others at the door into the cargo bay. "We don't generally call it Station Four. It's just home. We don't know about any other numbered stations, either."

Colonel Mangual sighed, and said, "I do."

Gabe and a few other Providers escorted the trio of escaped Citizens back to the Grand Elevator. The ride down to Citizenry was short, but Leena took the chance to ask, "So... Messenger was there. What about Actual? And just who are these other people?"

Patricia perked up at the mention of Actual, and paid stringent attention, hands clasped together. It was safe to say that she'd recovered from being stunned. "I saw Actual!" Patricia chirped, "He talked funny, had a beard, and no hair on top of–"

"That wasn't Actual," Gabe said. "That guy is with the outside people."

Patricia's enthusiasm melted along with her posture.

"Is Actual okay?" Cody asked. "I remember when Leena and me met him, he... well, is he okay?"

Gabe shook his head. "I'm told he collapsed during the blackout. There was no one with him when it happened, but it might not have mattered."

Patricia's eyes were now wide, and her mouth agape with disbelief. "What is that supposed to mean? He can't... he's The Actual, he..."

"Messenger's the Actual now," Gabe said morosely. "And not that it's directly related, but I guess I'm the Contact now."

"What's that?" Patricia whispered to Cody.

"Leader of the Providers, I think." he whispered back.

"Yeah, basically," Gabe said. "I just try to keep things organized.

That's not new. I just don't have to deal with the old Contact anymore. I don't even know what to call *him* now."

"Actual is Messenger..." Patricia mumbled to herself.

"He seemed kind," Leena said. "Actual that is... Hope he didn't suffer." Unlike the majority of the Citizens, (including Patricia,) Leena and Cody had previously learned the undeniable truth that the Great Actual was indeed just a man, and not some ambiguous force controlling everything. And Leena was ready for more truth.

"So who were those strangely dressed people up there with Patricia's 'monsters'? That small furry thing was pretty scary... behaved though. And one of the people had lots of colours in his hair..."

The Elevator had come to a stop at Citizenry. The Elevator's door was still closed, but presumably the bay's door itself was still open, or at least unlocked. There were two knocks at the door.

"I may as well tell a bunch of you," Gabe said before signalling one of the other Providers to pull the door open. As it slid to the side, a view of the Citizenry's loading bay was revealed.

Four Providers stood guard, two of them holding a stun-stick. Their clothing was similar to the Citizens in some ways. Both types wore a body suit. Providers in yellow, Citizens in blue. The Citizens tended to use old suits to make accessories such as scarves, belts and hair-ties, or rip and arrange things as they saw fit, in some cases, to show a little more leg or such. Citizens were also not quite as efficient with laundering.

The sum result was that the Providers were a stark contrast to the Citizens. And there were many more of the Citizens than the four Providers.

And yet there was peace. Because Jen said so. Under Leena's authority.

"*Leena!*" Jen called out as she was revealed, "you got Patricia back, I see! Everyone okay?" Jen didn't walk past the guards to approach Leena, but Leena wandered among the guards as if they were anyone else.

"Jen, yeah, it was a heck of a trip," Leena began, before Patricia interrupted.

"I saved Actual from monsters... maybe." Patricia said.

Jen looked past Leena, Cody and Patricia to see a handful of more Providers, including Gabe. "So... we all good here?" Jen asked nervously.

"Yes and no," Gabe responded in a light tone. "That lock's gotta get fixed, I guess, but Patricia apparently figured out how to crack em, so that complicates things. But at the same time, where Contact would assume that Citizens would be a violent murderous horde if you all got through this door... here we are. No horde."

"Nope," Leena said with affection for her fellow Citizens, "but it's worth mentioning... if this door had broken while certain nasty folks like Warren were in charge in here... things could have gone much differently."

"I wouldn't have opened it for Warren," Patricia said, "he was a bad person."

Leena chuckled. "You make it sound like you had this method of breaking out all along."

"Yeah, and?" Patricia said with a blank stare.

"How... how long did you know you could just.. open this door?" Gabe asked with a bemused smirk.

"Oh, I never *knew I could* until I did it," Patricia explained, "but I saw the lock on the inner door we could go by often, and I assumed a similar lock was on the outer door. From that, I knew where to strike it. The problem was crawling up close enough and hanging on while holding the hammer and the stick at the same time. I came up with the idea a *long* time ago, but would never have attempted it while Warren was around. So risky. Warren and monsters."

"And when Warren was gone?" Leena asked.

"Kinda forgot by then. If Edgar had asked me, I might have done it. Maybe. But it wasn't on my mind... and of course, monsters."

"Of course." Leena said.

"They could have been right on the other side of the door, you know," Patricia said with certainty. "but when the lights went out, well, that changed things. It was worth taking the risk. And then I found monsters, and saved... Actual?"

"That wasn't Actual you saw up there, remember," Leena said. "And those weren't monsters. Well... the hairy four-legged thing, maybe, but it was behaving."

"Citizens," Gabe interrupted, speaking to Leena, Patricia, and all of the Citizens further back in the loading bay, "what do you know about the Actual?"

Leena held her tongue, knowing that she knew more that most Citizens. Jen spoke up first. "He's the source of all things. Our food, water, light, and a couple of years ago, he visited us to help. He was totally covered by a black suit with scary eyes, and couldn't talk to us without Messenger. But after that, we started to learn that Actual has a lot of helpers, like the Providers and people even further down the Grand Elevator shaft than that."

"Okay, good, good, that's a great start," Gabe said. "There's people we call Subjects who do a lot of the work needed. They tend most of the farms, for example. Wash clothes, maintain certain parts that the Providers need to run the water and air. But until recently, most Subjects didn't know Providers existed, or that Messenger or Actual existed."

"Until recently?" Leena asked.

"Heh, you all know Lenth?" Gabe asked.

"Yeah... wait, he was... y*eah, he said he was a Subject!*" Leena remembered.

"That's right!" Gabe said. "He was in the lowest rung of authority, and he became my friend, and met Actual, even before I did. He's been working to educate the Subjects, and change a lot. He was making steady progress; he'd gotten hundreds of Subjects better educated – and then the blackout happened."

"Aw crap, chaos?" Leena guessed.

"Some!" Gabe admitted. "There's still so many more Subjects that Lenth and Karen hadn't talked to yet, and that's were a lot of trouble came from. And heck, the darkness was bad for everyone, but because there were so many better educated Subjects running around in the mix, it really helped. Better than a hundred Providers running into fifteen hundred uneducated Subjects."

"Were there killings?" Leena asked grimly.

"A couple of people got hurt a bit, but no, no killings."

"And none of the *other thing*, I assume," Leena said. "Well, they've got a cleaner history than the Citizenry then, by far."

Gabe held up a finger, and shook his head. "You can't compare Citizenry to the Subjects. Don't downplay what you've accomplished here. Citizenry today is a different place from a couple of years ago. We've established that. The door's been open for how long now?"

"And no murderous hordes," Leena said with a nod. "A lot of us *are* killers though."

"Like Warren's killers?" Gabe asked, knowing the answer. "I'm sorry Citizenry had been alone through so much of that."

Leena looked down. "*Are* you sorry?"

"We didn't know..." Gabe said. "We only knew that Citizenry was dangerous, and had been for a long time."

"...Which is why we were sealed off..." Leena said.

"Well... the seal is busted open," Gabe said, "and it's a different Citizenry now from what was sealed in back then."

Leena put her hands on her hips. "Well. You're welcome? I guess? I don't know what the hell I'm expected to say."

"Do you need anything?" Gabe asked.

"What?"

"Do you need anything," he repeated. "You, the Citizens... do you need anything?"

Leena scoffed lightly. "What, are you doing Messenger's job now?"

"I just got Contact's job," Gabe said, "but it's food for thought... If Messenger is Actual now –"

"*Messenger is Actual???*" Jen called out, "*Why isn't Actual Actual?!?*"

"Oh, right," Gabe said, "that's what I wanted to talk to you about when I started this. And about the world..."

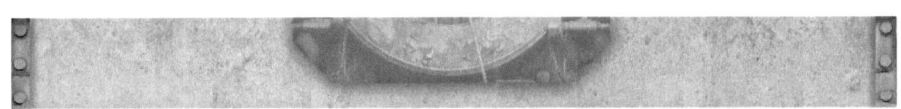

Chapter 16:

HDU

After some conversational pre-amble, Messenger was invited by Colonel Mangual to come aboard the AirLimb where they could be seated out of the sun to talk.

"This large box won't fly away with me in it, I trust?" Messenger asked.

"Not without your permission," the Colonel said with a polite smile.

Messenger didn't bother looking around him, but he was well aware that the four soldiers around him could have forced him inside if the Colonel was planning anything untoward. "Let me speak to one of my people for a moment. If they see me disappear into this, it may cause undue stress."

The Colonel glanced over to the bay door. "Sound decision," she said. "I'll be waiting inside when you come back."

"Thank you. I don't expect it to take long." Messenger went to the loading bay. Nearby, Laird was standing by the door to the 'truck'. Muir and Tavish had apparently gone inside.

In the loading bay itself were a few Providers, who looked overwhelmed enough by being on Actual's floor, much less the blinding expanse beyond the loading bay. Tara was there too, holding Sasha's hand, and watching Messenger come back.

"I'm going into that thing to talk," Messenger said. "I think it would be very useful to have our top two Engineers involved."

Tara had little time to absorb the idea before Sasha's grip on her hand tightened. "Us?" Sasha asked meekly, "going into *that*? And going out into *all that* to *get there*?" Her eyes were locked on the outside, wide, and darting around all that '*empty*' out there.

Messenger cast a sympathetic eye on Sasha. "I suppose just Tara would be– "

Sasha made a sharp whimpering noise. "N-no..." A mix of not having Tara with her, and worrying about Tara out there alone was terrible enough. But there was one final factor that she could address with less embarrassment. "I can do it. I'm going to do what needs to be done. I can do it."

Tara took Sasha's hands in hers. "Are you sure?"

Sasha blinked with a nod, and did her best to reset herself. "I can. It's just right over there. I can see it, I'll be back inside in no time."

"That's right," Tara said, looking closely into Sasha's eyes.

"If you're ready..." Messenger said quietly. He turned to one of the nearby Providers. "I don't know how long this will take. Maybe an hour? I'll call if it looks like it will go longer."

"We can do this together." Tara said, holding Sasha as if it were a dance. They began slowly towards the void, but Sasha's breathing wasn't calming down.

They got ever closer to that looming void, and Sasha's confidence crumbled. "I appreciate what you're trying to do hon, but it's not.. it's not..." Sasha's steps broke any rhythm of dance, becoming smaller and less frequent.

Tara leaned in with a kiss, and turned the dance more intimate. She held Sasha and did most of the work of moving into the light. "We can." she whispered into Sasha's ear, "We're together."

Tears came from Sasha with a gasp that turned into a gentle sob. "You're in just as much danger out here as I am. We have to go back." Sasha gently, but forcibly moved against Tara's body, trying to push them back inside.

Surprised at the strength Sasha was using, Tara couldn't bring herself to fight with enough force to correct their course. Instead, she simply stopped, and grabbed Sasha tight. "It... it's okay. I... you win." Holding her so close, Sasha's trembling breath seemed to overtake them both.

Messenger quietly stepped closer, and held out the comm device that Tavish had given him. "Hang onto this," he said softly to Tara, "I can probably get the Colonel to call you on it if we need to talk." After Tara took it, Messenger began walking back to the AirLimb.

"Neil," Tara called to him, with apologetic eyes.

"I understand." Messenger replied before continuing on, leaving Tara holding Sasha.

Sasha began to buckle, but caught herself. "I'm failing at my duty."

"Hush."

"And I'm causing you to fail because you need to take care of my weak ass."

"Hush."

"No *hush,* Tara," Sasha said, pulling away. Before Tara could react, Sasha bolted out into the void towards the AirLimb, head low, as fast as she could.

Tara ran in an attempt to keep up, but Sasha had managed a head start. They quickly passed Messenger. Tara only answered Messenger's puzzled look with a shrug.

Messenger broke into a jog.

By the AirLimb, the four soldiers watched with some alarm, but Berryhill was on the ramp between them, waving with his arms to encourage Sasha, "*You got this!*"

That caused a chain reaction. Sasha pushed harder, so Tara pushed harder to keep pace, and Messenger went from a jog to a full run. When Sasha arrived at the ramp, Berryhill ran in with her, followed by Tara and Messenger. The interior of the AirLimb was dark compared to the outside, but Sasha managed to lean against a two-metre tall container. Tara was quick to get an arm around her.

"Sash... Sash hon, you... you okay?"

"V...victory?" Sasha forced her words out with a mix of laughing, crying, and catching her breath. She took a moment to look at where she was as her eyes adjusted. This was a fairly big room, as far as rooms went, maybe thirty by thirty metres in area, but enough cargo was on board to make it feel smaller. And it had a ceiling. No Enemy. No sun.

The walls, floor and ceiling were near-black metal. The floor had a pattern of little bumps, and some of the walls had random looking additional conduits and panels. To either direction, she could see hallways leading away.

"That's some heavy agoraphobia there," Berryhill commented, "but that was a heck of a push! You want a coffee? After we get to the briefing room, I'm gonna get you some. Let's get seated, so you can chill out a bit."

"How's your gut?" Tara asked Sasha as they all got moving.

"I'll let you know when the shaking stops."

Messenger was the first following behind Berryhill along one of the narrow halls, and asked, "What's this agor..."

"Agoraphobia," Berryhill said as they reached the destination door. "Fear of wide-open spaces. Kind of rare." Inside the door was a long table, and seats bolted to the floor to accommodate ten people. One wall had a black shiny rectangle, and on the opposite wall was a picture of a grey and green mass, with blue on one edge, and points marked with text.

Tara presented Sasha with the nearest available seat, and Tara took the next one over. "How are ya?" She asked, taking Sasha's hand.

Sasha sat back, breathing deeply. She was smiling, but her eyes were glistening with tears. "Victory. Still gotta get back, though."

"I'll be back in a sec." Berryhill said before exiting.

"Blindfold?" Messenger suggested. "It just occurred to me, if you couldn't see the wide-open space..."

Sasha said nothing, but her raised eyebrow spoke more of scepticism than interest.

"We should have just told this Colonel to come to us," Tara mused.

As Colonel Mangual entered, she said, "Good thought. I have all the info I have for you *here*, but I could have carried it over." The two soldiers that came in *with* the Colonel implied other possible concerns.

"Colonel," Messenger said.

"Messenger. Have a seat," she said, walking over the chair furthest from the door. "And these two are..." The Colonel stopped when she got a look at Sasha. "Miss, are you all right?"

Sasha wiped her eyes and gave a large smirk. "I'm victorious, of course I'm all right."

Messenger spoke up. "She suffers from... what did Berryhill call it.. ago- fear of open spaces. He said it was rare, but I've seen it twice now, after having been out with only a few people. I suspect it might not be so rare for us."

The Colonel nodded. "That would make sense. Not that I'm an expert in agoraphobia... but you've all lived in there from birth?"

"For generations," Messenger replied, "and of the roughly two thousand of us, only a few of us in any generation are exposed to the ... the sun."

"I.. I've heard some of the details of your situation from Sergeant Berryhill," the Colonel said, "but I don't feel like I fully understand... but I've been doing research. You've... you've all slipped through the cracks."

"How so?"

"Well, do you know about Hiroshima, or Nagasaki?" The Colonel asked.

"No."

It was then that Berryhill returned with a tray holding five cups made of smooth metal. "Sorry, took a bit to get it all together. Sugars and cream, here, help yourselves." He put the tray in the middle of the table, and sat.

"Thank you, Sergeant," the Colonel said, taking one of the cups, a slender little one-centimetre white rod from one little dish, and a one centimetre white ball from another small dish. She looked to Sasha as she dropped the rod and ball into the cup. "Maybe you'd prefer a decaf green tea? Settles the nerves."

Unsure of what was in the cup, or what a *'green T'* was, she just smiled, and took one of the cups. It smelled interesting. Pleasant even, in similar way that new soil for the farms smelt. Sort of unappealing, but pleasant in its own way.

Looking down into it, the darkness was gracefully interrupted by reflections of light in the surface's ripples. Its warmth soaked into her hands, and radiated up to her face. It was a mildly pleasant experience, but she hoped she wasn't expected to *drink* it.

The entrancement was broken by the sound of Messenger sputtering, nearly coughing. Sasha looked over to him. His face was absurd, eyebrows twisted in anguish as if the liquid had kicked him somewhere sensitive.

"Oh, sorry, too hot?" Berryhill asked.

"You... *drink* this?" Messenger stared into his cup as if the liquid itself would provide answers. "And *intentionally*? And enjoy it?" He had heard that Citizens often ground bits of rust into their water to flavour it. That always sounded revolting, but in the light of this new liquid, rust-water suddenly didn't sound so bad.

Beside him, Tara had her cup tilted all the way back. Emptied, she set it back on the tray. "What? I was going to ask if we can find a way to make it, or get a supply from Division or something."

Berryhill peered at Tara. "Are you saying that was your first coffee ever? And you drank it as fast as water?"

Tara shrunk back a bit, smiling weakly. "Yes? Coffee, huh? Coffee."

Sasha had tried a small sip, and was unsurprised that the taste wasn't as pleasing as the smell. She quietly slid her cup towards Tara. Berryhill reached over, and put Sasha's cup back in the tray. "No wonder they made you head of energy. Maybe slamming back one cup on your first time might be a good place to stop for the moment. Can I get anyone anything else? We stock water, milk, apple and orange juice, Colonel said something about green .... you don't know any of these, do you?"

"Maybe it's best if we stay on topic for now," Messenger offered. "You were saying something about a hero-something?"

Not wanting to interrupt, Berryhill discreetly placed one of the little white rods in front of Messenger and Sasha before popping one into his own mouth.

"Hiroshima and Nagasaki were the only two cities in history to be attacked with atomic weapons." The Colonel produced a small device, and tapped it in a few places. The blackened frame on the wall came to life with "Atomic Bombings of Hiroshima and Nagasaki" in large letters at the top, followed by a copious amount of smaller text, and two black-and-white images. The images didn't look like anything recognizable.

"This gets taught to every student, fairly early on," the Colonel said, gesturing to the text. "129,000 people at Hiroshima, 226,000 at Nagasaki. Not huge cities by today's standards, but it horrified the world, and still is a ... a dark reminder of how ludicrous war can be. Humanity never did that again. There's been other wars, but not like that. The Erebus incidents got close, but even those weren't atomic."

"I don't even know what I'm looking at," Tara said, pointing at the images. "Are those plants of some kind?"

"Ah, no," the Colonel said. "The 'stem' in each of those images is the smoke and fire coming up from where the weapons were used. At the bottom, you can't see under the smoke, are cities that housed hundreds of thousands of people. Mostly civilians. The width of the blast at the ground was... if I remember right, about sixteen hundred metres across or so at Hiroshima. And all that crap in the sky came down all over, full of radiation. Anyone who survived the blast, w—"

"I... I get it." Tara said. The room remained quiet for a few moments.

Messenger sighed. "The great war... the one we thought took the world... was just two cities. Two cities, and our ancestors hid underground and lied to us."

Tara turned from the display about the atomic attacks, and stared at the tray of cups intensely. Sasha held Tara's hand, and looked back and forth between the photos and Tara.

"Well... essentially true," Colonel Mangual said, "but not exactly that simple. Those attacks marked the end of World War 2. The other major superpower on the winning side of that war, Russia, didn't feel comfortable with the Americans being the only ones to have this power, and suddenly people were either rushing to have their own atomic bomb, or being terrified of them, or both.

"It got to the point where it was accepted that any third World War would be the end. So, things were really stressful for quite a while. At this stage, it was Russia and the Americans staring at each other. If one launched bombs, the other would have launched back before the first set landed, and even countries not hit would have to deal with massive amounts of leftover radiation in the atmosphere and water, and potentially the sun being blocked off for everyone, for years, destroying farms and any source of food."

"That's when our ancestors hid?" Sasha said.

"No," the Colonel said, "but around then, the Aguolian government began digging facilities for if they were needed."

"Facilities like our own Station Four," Tara said. "So, where's Stations One, Two, and Three?"

"Station One was renamed Capitol Bunker in 1976," the Colonel said. "Its position isn't publicly known, same as all of them, but it's maintained, and close enough that the Prime Minister and a pile of other people can be brought there quickly if an attack is launched at us. Capitol Bunker gets updated regularly with the newest equipment."

"Lucky..." Sasha said, smoothly nabbing the comm device from Tara to admire it.

"No one... no one lives there," the Colonel said. "It has a crew to maintain it and keep it ready, but they come and go in months-long shifts. They're not cut-off for more than that."

"Why were we cut off?" Messenger asked calmly, looking mildly insulted.

The Colonel sighed. "Well, that's where Capitalism gets its fingers in."

"*Oh, who the bloody hell is Capitalism?!*" Tara cried, "I just found out Actual's mysterious buddy Division wasn't even an individual, and suddenly I'm dealing with Sergeants, Colonels, Corporals, some place called Yute, and did you say a *Prime Mini-store?*"

Berryhill blinked, and glanced at the coffee cup Tara had drunk so quickly. Her first caffeine was kicking in. Messenger put his hand on Tara's, and looked to Colonel Mangual. "I'm sorry, Colonel. Although, you have to realize how much all of this is for us. So... the... Government, whoever that is, made the stations, kept number one up to date, let them talk to people, then someone named Capitalism stepped in about Station Four?"

Colonel Mangual pushed her glasses up to pinch the bridge of her nose. "Oh, this is going to take a *while*." She looked over to one of the soldiers standing in the room. "Crewman, can you get us a carafe of coffee? And maybe one of the decaf green tea?"

The soldier saluted and left.

Colonel Mangual sighed, and continued. "Capitalism is the system where companies seek to acquire more assets. More money."

Sasha put her hands out meekly for a shrug. "Money?"

The Colonel rested her hand on her forehead, and looked for how to explain.

Berryhill broke the silence. "It's almost like they're like the Aguei people when Northers first came to colonize the continent."

The Colonel seemed to find the comparison useful, and decided to forego a lot of the specific words for now. "When the... the fear of an atomic war started to fade, the stations didn't seem to be needed so badly. So a corporation... ah... a group, got Station Four, and wanted to try different projects there."

She went back to her little device, and started tapping buttons. The display on the wall when through several clusters of text. Large headers passed by... '*records*'... '*archives*'...'*1960s*'

An image predominately of orange and black, with a band of green under the biggest text read "HDU INC. Harris Densfarn Utilities."

"*Eugh!*" Berryhill exclaimed. "That's one hideous logo!"

"I guess they thought it looked great back then," the Colonel smirked. "They had the money for the best." She tapped more buttons, and the monstrous logo scrolled up off the screen, replaced with mounds of text and dates. "I've read all this, so I'll paraphrase. Anyway, first, they thought they'd convert one of the lower levels into a prison."

"Prison?" Messenger asked.

"A place to put criminals for a duration. People who've broken the law. This prison was built to have three hundred units that could each house a handful of prisoners, they could eat there, sleep, do appointed work, and be supervised by prison staff from above–"

"–through a metal grate." Messenger interrupted with a near whisper, and wide eyes.

Colonel Mangual tilted her head slightly. "They're still intact, then?"

"And being used," Tara explained. "Most of those three hundred Units have four Subjects living in them, and a Rubberman to supervise, keep the Subjects' food and such stocked, that kind of thing."

"Rubberman?" Berryhill asked.

"Oh, sorry," Tara responded. "That's kind of a nickname we use for anyone using a rubber hazmat suit, but it especially means the Managers, since they use them a lot. Some more than others, and right now they... well, that's complicated."

"Why do the Managers have to use a hazmat suit?" Colonel Mangual asked, getting continually more puzzled.

Messenger gave a long, exasperated sigh. "Tell me, Colonel, is *'Big Farm'* something that exists? Or maybe it's something like Division, and we've been all backwards about it all this time."

"B.. big pharm?" Colonel Mangual asked, "As in the pharmaceutical industry?"

Messenger tossed his hands in the air. "Maybe?! We had been keeping Subjects separate, and handled with the Rubberman suits to maintain a sterile, neutral state to keep them ready for the day when Big Farm comes. That was part of the rules."

"*Good lord,*" Colonel Mangual exclaimed, "you're not running drug tests on them, are you?!?"

"No, no, no," Messenger said, shaking his head wearily. "We had to be ready to, in case Big Farm came. But now, I hope Big Farm won't be upset, because we've been tearing down those protocols gradually for the last couple of years. We're also educating them now, but with twelve hundred Subjects, it hasn't been–"

"Stop." Colonel Mangual said firmly. She Took a deep breath. "There's been generations of people you keep as 'subjects', at a state of readiness to..." She suddenly focused on her device, tapping, reading, tapping some more again. Reading, tapping, then – "Fuck, there it is. I found your big pharm."

Tara, feeling the brunt of caffeine, fidgeted her grip on the edge of the table. "What, bad news? Is Big Farm going to be a problem?"

"1958, HDU Inc. buys Station Four," Colonel Mangual read, "and starts generating electricity with the generator to sell back to the military. The next year, they're trying to make extra money with all the space they had, any way they could. Insane, as if the generator wasn't making enough for them? So they outfit the jails, and they try to set up a deal with several pharmaceutical companies, but the jail thing was blocked by the government, pharm had all pulled out, and HDU decided trying... tourism? A large hall with amenities for wealthy tourists who wanted to stay in a bomb shelter –"

"Citizenry," Messenger said. "I think you mean the area we call Citizenry. We know it used to be the most pleasant area in the facility. It... is not as fancy now. We have records stating that at one point, Citizenry was locked away, as the Citizens had become too violent, and were a risk to everyone else."

"Good lord, how violent?" the Colonel asked.

"At its lowest point," Messenger began, "it was lead by a man who used *my* deliveries of food as ransom to get the Citizens to do what he wanted. And he wanted bad things. He... had a number of followers who were of a similar mindset. They are dead now."

Colonel Mangual almost spit out her coffee. *"You executed them?!"*

Did you hold anything resembling proper trials?"

Messenger took a deep sigh. "No. The Citizens independently took it upon themselves to stand against their oppressors. It was a... battle of sorts, contained within Citizenry. My role was primarily to help them find stability afterwards."

Staring out the door in the general direction of the facility, the Colonel took a long moment to find words. "There's... how many people are there in that section? In Citizenry? How many died in this?"

"Close to a hundred died, leaving over three hundred Citizens in that section," Messenger said. "It was my job to take away the dead." He sighed, looking down into the table. "It was horrific. Honestly, it was horrific how long Citizenry suffered, but it seemed like an unbreachable situation. The rest of the facility feared them. They were locked away for generations, supplied their necessities. They came to a resolution, and in many ways, they're still healing. But I feel their current leaner, Leena, is their best–"

"So the surviving Citizens in there are killers," Colonel Mangual said flatly.

"Many," Messenger said with a nod. "But justifiably so, I'd say. They needed to purge the worst of them."

"And this is alright according to you? By your authority?" the Colonel asked flatly.

"My authority? I suppose. But I'm not alone in the opinion. The former Actual had the last say, and several Providers were in agreement."

"These Providers... they're a... a ruling class? Is there some kind of formal council of some sort? I'm trying to understand the... the society in there."

"Ruling class?" Messenger took a moment to digest the concept. "You might say that. They are the best educated group, and have the most access to areas of the facility, aside from the Engineers. The Providers deal with organizing the Managers and Subjects, do many repairs, and deal with basic infrastructure. Piping, extremely basic electrical, such as changing lightbulbs. Their leader is called the Contact. Traditionally, Contact was the only Provider expected to communicate to me, in my role as the Messenger, and I was their only connection to the Actual. But that's all changed bit by bit over the last few years. I've been in direct contact with several Providers, and I am now the current Actual."

"I need a graph or something," Colonel Mangual said, "Correct me if I mess this up, but as I understand it, on top is you, the Messenger, who is now also the Actual. You're the big boss. Then there's Citizenry, which are separate from the rest of the facility, but they're doing okay, now?"

"Quite okay, now," Messenger confirmed. "They're still a little chaotic, but they're peaceful. I'm actually rather proud of them."

"Yeah, okay. Then there's the Providers who do a fair amount of work, they know a lot, and are led by Contact, then there's the Managers, who run around in rubber suits, and control the Subjects, who do a ton of the manual labour, then there's the Engineers, who take care of electrical functions, and until very recently, an atomic generator, and they're led by..."

"That would be me," Tara said, "Chief Engineer, and Sasha here is second in Engineering."

"Right. Got it." Colonel Mangual said, clasping her hands. "Well, you folks have problems. I want to help, but I guess we need to address your power supply first. It seems like the most urgent."

"Thor..." Sasha said, remembering bits of an early conversation when they were first refused more uranium. "We should be using thor-something? Something about salt?"

Sergeant Berryhill spoke up. "Thorium salt generators. If you're thinking of installing one in place of your current uranium generator, I wouldn't get your hopes up. You don't build one of those into a facility, you build a facility around one. And it's not like they're cheap."

"The cost isn't a problem," the Colonel said with a minor scoff.

"Is the army just going to bankroll something like that for humanitarian reasons?" Berryhill chuckled. "Doesn't seem like something the powers that be would feel like funding!"

"Station Four *has* money," Colonel Mangual said.

"They do?" Berryhill responded.

"*What's money?*" Sasha asked.

Colonel Mangual began elaborating, "From 1958, to 2095, Station Four has been in an indefinite contract with the government, generating electricity, pumping it into the national infrastructure, and getting paid to an automated bank account that has been collecting funds for almost a hundred and forty years. Plus interest, minus a pittance for things like lightbulbs, which the army has been contractually obliged to supply. It's been such a long-running thing, and such low-maintenance for us, that it's slipped under the radar. When I heard of you just a while ago, my lieutenant told me he'd heard of Station Four, and assumed it was some top-secret weapons lab or something. You've been left alone because people assumed you were *supposed* to be left alone."

"The bulk discharge ground conduit..." Tara whispered, "it doesn't just go into the ground..."

"Ground?" Berryhill asked.

"All that time the generator was running," Tara explained, "we knew we were making way more than we needed. We didn't even have means to store extra, so we pumped the massive surplus into a conduit we thought was just going into he ground to be discharged..."

Colonel raised an eyebrow. "When you were outside, did you see the half-buried giant conduit leading away from Station Four?"

"I..." Messenger leaned back, and closed his eyes. "I've seen it. We assumed it was just wreckage from the war... that war that never happened."

"About two kilometres from here, it goes completely underground," Berryhill said, "and leads to the back door of a very big, very old power station hub."

"And it gets monitored," the Colonel continued, "and the value of the charge is paid to your account quarterly."

"What does *that* mean?" Sasha asked.

"You... Station Four... is rich." Colonel Mangual said.
"What does *that* mean?" Tara asked.

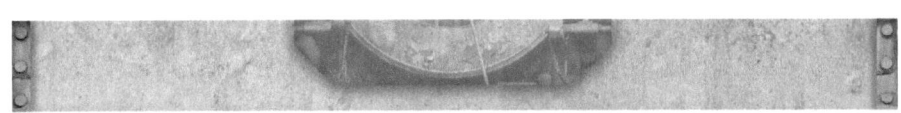

Chapter 17:

Leaky

Light had returned to the Units, but many, many Subjects were still roaming around the passages between the Units. The Managers did their best to maintain order, but the Subjects outnumbered them four-to-one, and during the darkness, many had gotten lost. Lost by accident, or on purpose.

Lenth came to an intersection in the metre-and-a-half wide passages where many Subjects were visible in all directions, and he tried yet again to apply order. "*Everyone?*" He raised his hands to attract attention. The yellow of his Providers' outfit made him stand out among the blue-suited Subjects. "*I know this is all a lot to take in, I know a lot of you are just finding out that there's a lot more people out there than you thought –*"

A few metres to Lenth's left, a Subject called out, "*Hey, you're Length, right? You came with my Rubberman to talk about a lot of things a bunch of days ago!*"

Lenth called back, "*Yeah*, and it's 'Lenth', not Length, w... *anyway, who here had had a visit from me or Karen? Raise a hand?*"

Of the thirty or so Subjects in view, about ten raised a hand.

"Good, good,"Lenth said, "So you know that I had planned to get all of you on a little exploration eventually, but not like this. Not all one giant mob, it's not safe! People need to get back to their own Units for now, and we–"

Somewhere down the corridor and around a corner, the rabble's meandering chatter was broken by sudden shouting by multiple voices.

Lenth squeezed past a couple of Subjects, and headed towards the ruckus. "Aw, crap, now what?"

Elise the wheat-farming Subject had managed to get herself good and lost during the blackout, and had no real urgent need to get back to her Unit. But she was close to the shouting when it started.

"You can't stop us!" hollered a Subject to one of the Providers guarding a hatch. "The guys at the ladder had those shock stick things, but you don't have em, we're going to see what's on the other side of that little door!" He was backed by three other Subjects, presumably his Brothers. The four of them advanced upon the two Providers, pushing them away from the hatch. The Providers did their best to stay in between the hatch and the four Brothers, but it wasn't long before one of the Brothers had gotten through, and managed to lift the hatch. He scrambled through, followed by another of the Brothers.

On the other side of the hatch, which had swung back down nearly into a closed position, the two Brothers were heard to yell in horror, and one of the screams grew quieter with increasing distance.

The two Providers struggled past the other two Brothers to get to the hatch. "Damn it, we told you not to..."

One of the Providers leaned out of the hatch, into the Grand Elevator shaft. The Subject Brother they found was trembling, eyes wide. He scrambled through the hatch to rejoin his other two Brothers. "It's some huge hallway!" he struggled to say, "but instead of going forward, it goes up and down! He fell down! I can't see him anymore!"

"Shit, I'm reporting to Gabe," one of the Providers said, before dashing down the hall.

The two Brothers who hadn't seen the Grand Elevator shaft pushed by the remaining Provider to *carefully* head out the hatch. "*We're coming!*"

"*No!*" the Provider said, "*It's too far, he's dead! Don't endanger yourselves!*" The two Brothers were already figuring out the ladder in the Grand Elevator shaft, and heading down. The Provider looked to the one of the Brothers who stayed behind traumatized, and to the two Brothers making haste down the ladder in the shaft. "Crap, crap, crap, idiots...!" He gave chase, getting on the ladder too. Before closing the hatch behind himself, the said to the other Subjects in the hall, including Elise, "*Now no one else go out this hatch! You could die!*"

Elise shrugged. "He said *could* die. Hey, anyone know what *die* is?"

Leena sat with as many other Citizens that could fit in the Citizenry's loading bay, listening to Gabe explain things. What news he'd heard about the world, and the lack of the big war, and about Actual. About how he'd died.

To most Citizens, Actual was an entity above being a mortal being. Hearing of his death was confusing, if not harrowing to many of them. But Leena had met Actual in Citizenry's darkest hour, as had Cody. Actual's being a normal person was not news to them.

Despite not knowing Actual that long, or that intimately, hearing of his death was ill news to Leena and Cody in a way that the other Citizens couldn't appreciate.

Much of what Gabe knew was second-hand news from other Providers. He himself hadn't been out in the outside, being busy juggling Subjects, Managers, Providers and Citizens. Some Providers that he'd talked to had met outsiders, seen the four-legged hairy thing, and the giant box that flew.

Also surprising, especially to the Citizens, was the idea of the room with a 'sky', not a ceiling, and the notion that the Enemy was an ordinary thing. Just an ordinary thing that was made of fire, and could fit over a million earths in it.

But it looked small because it was so far away. But don't look at it much, or it'll hurt you. But it's not an enemy. Because without it, everyone would die for some reason.

While Gabe had been answering questions, two other Providers were on-hand with shock-sticks. Just in case. In case the reputation of Citizens proved still true, and still dangerous. The door out to the Grand Elevator shaft had been ajar ever since Patricia broke it, and one of the Providers heard something.

He leaned out the door, and looked down towards the sound. He ducked back in, and caught Gabe's attention. "Uh, it's just Citizens and Subjects who wear the blue body suits, right?"

"Um, yeah?" Gabe responded, "You should know that, why?"

"I think Citizenry's not the only ones with the broken door!"

Gabe went to look, and sure enough, a number of blue-garbed people were coming up the ladder. From this angle, it was impossible to tell how many, but it was more than a few.

"What the hell?!" Gabe blurted, leaning over the gaping shaft. "Where are they coming out from?! What has Lenth been doing?"

The Subject closest, Elise, paused, looked up, and waved. "*Oh, hi! Another yellow-clothes person! Hi! I'm coming!*" She then resumed climbing.

"No!" Gabe called back, "Get back down where you came out of!"

Elise paused again, and looked at the stream of Subjects below her. "I don't think I can safely get around them," she said, just before one of the Subjects below her hollered something unintelligible. "Yeah, yeah!" She hollered back up at Gabe, "Sorry, yellow-clothes guy, it's okay, I'm coming your way."

Gabe shrieked, "*That's not okay!!!*"

Leena popped he head past Gabe and looked down. "Ooh, they wear blue like us Citizens."

Gabe jolted back, startled by Leena. "What are you –" He looked towards the other two Providers. "You two are supposed to be keeping Citizens from wandering out!"

One of the Providers shrugged, "Sorry, she's kinda the Citizen leader and she's been up and met Actual anyway, so–"

"That doesn't matter!" Gabe said, eyes wide, face turning red.

"It's fine, it's fine," Leena said, "I explained things to them."

"Explained *what?!*"

By now, Elise was pulling herself up into the Citizenry loading bay. "Ooh, neat place!"

"Ha!" Leena replied, "This is just the loading bay. You're from the levels run by Rubbermen, right? You should see the main Commons of Citizenry here, and our farms!"

"*Farms? I farm!*" Elise exclaimed.

"Can anyone actually even hear me right now? Am I talking to myself?!" Gabe cried, "*This isn't how things go!*"

Chapter 18:

Clamp

Aboard Colonel Mangual's AirLimb, Messenger, Tara, and Sasha had been given a rudimentary education about what money was. The Colonel had been very patient. She'd gone through a very simplified history of human bartering turning into currency, and how most people typically got it, and how it related to the way Station Four had amassed its fortune.

"So, what," Tara mulled, "with our generator dead, we use our money to buy those capacitors from the Aguola government? How long would *that* last?"

Colonel Mangual raised her eyebrows. "I mean, I don't have the numbers right in front of me, but I'm pretty sure you could run your operations like this for longer than any of us will survive."

"That's not long," Messenger said flatly. "I mean, compared to the life of our generator. It sustained us for generations, and −"

A soldier entered the room, and did that odd hand motion while facing the Colonel. "Sir, people are coming out of the station."

Elise wandered towards the biggest light she'd ever seen.

"That's the top level," Leena explained. Leena had followed along to be of help, understanding the desire to explore. Gabe wasn't far behind, trying to convince them all to go back.

It was about fifty Subjects who'd all decided that more *'up'* was interesting. A handful of bold Citizens were in the mix.

"Leena, they listen to you!" Gabe pleaded, "Can you get them to just go back?!" The handful of Providers in the area followed Gabe's lead, but the blue mass of meandering Citizens and Subjects was simply overpowering for the yellow-suited Provider resistance. Thankfully no one had become violent. So far.

The bulk of the blue mob was migrating towards the light. Cautiously. One Citizen found the Rubberman suits that had been kept near the door to protect from the Enemy's attacks.

"Actual?" the Citizen said to it – for this was the face most Citizens knew as the Actual.

"Nah, that's a Rubberman," corrected a nearby Subject. "They're people underneath those suits after all!"

Elise walked by them, giving the suit a glance for a moment, but she was much more interested in this huge, unending bright space – its cracked floor of dead dirt, and the ceiling of endless blue. Even the air had a different taste.

Nearby was the truck, but this truck was less interesting than the metre-high lump of brown and black hair sitting near it. The lump of hair was alive, and its mysterious eyes watched her. It smiled, releasing a huge lazy tongue, and displaying an array of teeth along the long opening that was its mouth.

".... Hello?" Elise ventured, "Are you smiling? Are you a friend?"

Elise had been fixated on the hairy lump so much that she didn't notice Laird standing right next to it.

"She's in a good mood," Laird said. She sighed, and looked at the enraptured Elise. "I gotta explain this again?" Laird's voice turned dispassionate to explain the seemingly obvious. "This is a dog. Her name is Caspar. *No*, she doesn't talk. She understands a handful of words, she does understand a tone of voice. *No*, she won't attack you unless really provoked, or ordered to. *Yes*, she would win. *Yes*, she is cuddly. *No*, you may not."

"May not what?" Elise asked.

"May not cuddle her."

Elise's eyes widened. "I wasn't thinking that until you said-"

"I said *may not*."

The door on the side of the truck opened. Tavish and Muir stepped out.

"Wut ar you lot up tae?" Tavish asked Elise, her being the closest of the meandering mob.

"You guys sure have complicated clothes," Elise said, looking across Tavish, Laird, and Muir, with their desert camouflage, straps and pouches.

Messenger bellowed from the AirLimb. He was standing on the ramp. "*What are you doing?! You all need to get back to where you came from!*"

"*That's what I've been saying!*" pleaded Gabe, who'd been running around fruitlessly trying to herd the Citizens and Subjects.

"Hey! That's Messenger!" hollered a Citizen. A few other Citizens took notice, but the majority of the Subjects were uninterested.

"He's the Actual, now, right?" another Citizen asked towards Gabe.

"Yes! Yes! Will you obey the Actual and go back inside?!"

Some did. Almost all of the Citizens did, and almost none of the Subjects did, as many Subjects had never heard of Messenger or Actual. Most that went inside only went so far as in the loading bay, out of the sun. On top of that, a trickle of Subjects was still coming out.

Colonel Mangual's voice came through the communication device Messenger had reclaimed from Tara. "Messenger, do you require assistance containing your people?"

Messenger held the device, and was about to answer "no," but then he saw the growing group of blue, with not enough yellow among them to control it. There was easily a hundred blue-suited people, and on the edges, some were getting farther away than was comfortable.

"Citizens," he called out, "can you h..." the Citizens didn't number many, and several seemed a lot less than motivated. Leena stepped forward however.

"Hey Mess, what a mess, right?"

"Yes, yes, Leena. Some of these people are going to end up lost if they go too far. Ack. Is your... confused friend out here?"

"Confu... Patricia? Crap no, there's monsters out here. Last I saw her, she was painting a picture of that hairy thing on a wall in Citizenry."

"Messenger?" came the Colonel's voice from the device again. The crowd was still slowly growing, and even if a quarter of the Subjects climbed the ladder, it would be three hundred... give or take those who just stayed at Citizenry, and those too afraid to come out into the open... it was too many hypotheticals. Too many unknown variables. It was indeed a mess.

"*Fine!*" Messenger said into the comm, "I mean, yes, thank you," he corrected himself with a calmer tone.

"Okay," the Colonel said, "is it fair to say that yellows are authority, and blues need to be contained?"

"A lot of them are scared, Colonel. Please handle with care."

"Kid gloves, Messenger, got it. The AirLimb will be lifting off shortly. Are you going to come aboard, or stay on the ground?"

"Lifting off? The ground?" A thrilling thought, but the internal debate of thrill versus fear was immediately made moot by responsibility. "I should stick around my people, it may help smooth things." He jogged the few steps off the ramp.

"All right, let's get to work," the Colonel said across the comm. "Berryhill's crew, assist at the doorway. Encourage blues in, assist yellows. Stormfront 1, come aboard. All Storms prepare for low-speed, minimum alt rolling drops, stun loadout."

The soldiers posted around the ramp ran into the AirLimb as its four turbines roared to life. The warm air from them blew around Messenger, and he realized that getting much closer to one of those turbines would likely be a bad idea.

The AirLimb lifted up, and flew about a hundred metres to the side, and began a slow path around the perimeter of the loading bay. As the AirLimb moved, it periodically dropped a soldier from about three metres up, who hit the ground and rolled, getting to their feet and surveying their immediate area. Instead of the arm-length weapons they had carried by the ramp, they held smaller weapons with both hands.

Once Messenger saw the third soldier land, he turned his focus to the Subjects. Terrain and the facility's structure was already blocking wanderers on one edge, but the other directions were open for Subjects to roam.

He yelled out, "*These people in the dark outfits are helping us organize, so no one gets lost! Please co-operate and get back in where it's safe!*"

Some seemed to be feeling obedient, many mulled around confusedly, but three ran for it. One of them was laughing his head off. He was running away from the soldiers that had already dropped into place, and a Provider was chasing behind him, yelling, "*Stop, where do you think you're going!?*"

One of the other runners stopped to watch the laughing one, and the third was planning on running between two of the freshly-dropped soldiers. One of the soldiers faced the runner. There was a '*thok*' sound and the runner fell, seemingly motionless.

Messenger talked into the comm. "Colonel! What are these soldiers using?!"

"Relax," came the reply. "Stun guns. Hits the target with a dull pellet carrying enough electricity to put most targets to sleep. One of your people was hit by a similar one after she stabbed the utility vehicle." Messenger figured electricity shouldn't work like that, but the results seemed to speak for themselves. The attack had to be more complex than the Colonel's quick assurances.

The Colonel might have recommended that Messenger relax, but the Subjects and Citizens certainly *did not* relax. Panicked screaming erupted all over. About three quarters of the mob fled indoors. The remainders fled away from the fallen Subject. Making a break for the portion of the perimeter that wasn't yet guarded. It was obvious that they wouldn't make it before that way was closed off. As it was, the laughing runner who'd gotten an early start quickly found himself on the ground, unconscious.

Now, all of the Subjects and Citizens were rushing to get inside. Some of the Providers, too. Those that *weren't* fleeing were only that confident because they caught sight of Messenger, who wasn't running.

Since the semicircle of dropped troops was finished deploying, the AirLimb itself moved to herd people inside, moving slowly towards the door of the loading bay. It was flying low enough that its turbines were kicking up a lot the dirt, ripping up several of the cracked chunks of ground, filling the air with dust.

It would have been a good day to wear a Rubberman suit after all.

Tara and Sasha were alone in the meeting room where they'd talked with the Colonel earlier. Berryhill had left. The two other solders had left. And at some point, someone locked the door.

They had been patient for the most part, but when they felt the AirLimb move, Tara found cause to give the door a few bangs, and holler "*Anyone coming back? What's going on?*" Sasha was slow to complain, as leaving this place would mean another dash through the open space back to the facility.

After a couple more bangs on the door, a voice came from the ceiling. "Sorry, ladies, the Colonel will be with you as soon as possible."

Tara waked towards the direction of the voice, and looked up at the speaker. "Great. How come *now* isn't possible?"

"There are operations in progress requiring her attention."

"*Operations?!*"

It was then that Berryhill came back in, looking frazzled. "Hey." He closed the door behind himself, but didn't bother to lock it.

"Okay, what the heck is going on?" Tara asked him.

Berryhill sat down at the table. "A pile of those 'Citizens' came out, with even more 'Subjects'. Then the Colonel asked Messenger if he needed help herding them back home, Messenger said yes, and it went mostly okay."

"Mostly?" Tara asked. Sasha had seated herself, but Tara remained standing.

"Two Subjects ran, and had to be stunned," Berryhill said, glancing behind his shoulder to the door. They should be waking up, any time now."

Sasha followed Berryhill's glance, and asked, "...So, are they back home now?"

Berryhill sighed. "The Colonel wants to talk to them. They're in other rooms here on the AirLimb. She wants to know if they're okay."

An awkward quiet followed. Tara finally broke it. "Why wouldn't they be okay? Is the stun sometimes damaging? I don't know much about how that works."

Berryhill sighed again. "They're physically fine. The Colonel is more... more worried about their living conditions."

"Subjects?" Tara asked.

"Yeah," Berryhill replied, "and why they'd be so interested to leave, where the Providers and Engineers don't feel the need so badly."

"Everyone likes to explore a bit," Tara said.

"Yeah – not everyone." Sasha mumbled.

"And most Subjects had no idea what they were getting into," Tara said. "They're not the best-informed sorts."

"Why are they so much worse informed than the Providers?" Berryhill asked.

Tara scrunched her eyebrows. "Well, they don't need a ton of knowledge to do what they do. It's not like they're keeping an atomic generator running or anything."

Berryhill folded his hands, and tapped his thumbs together a few times. "If they asked... are they told? Are they allowed to know things?"

"I guess?" Tara said. "I don't know who they'd ask, or why."

"If a Subject came up to you and asked about... about the generator, for example. What would you say?"

Tara shrugged. "I... I guess I'd explain that it makes the power to run the lights and Grand Elevator and stuff, but they wouldn't come to me. I don't go to the Units. They'd have to ask their Managers, and until recently, the Managers weren't allowed to talk to their Subjects."

"... they aren't?" Berryhill asked, "And Subjects can't come to *you*?"

Tara felt uncomfortable, but couldn't pinpoint why. "They... they have everything they need. Food, water, place to sleep, three siblings to socialize with..."

"And exorcize stuff," Sasha added.

Tara nodded. "Yeah, and that."

"Can they leave?" Berryhill asked, becoming a shade grimmer.

"They have a bunch of rooms," Tara said, "The sleeping room, exercise room, work room, washroom. They don't really need anything more. If it's a farming Unit, that's usually a lot more space."

"Can they *leave?*" Berryhill repeated.

"Well... well no, I guess. Why would they want to?" Tara answered, "Where would they go?"

Berryhill's eyes widened, he shrugged in an exaggerated way, and looked towards the door. "*Outside?* All around the place, wandering around the salt flats? And why?! You tell *me* why they wouldn't happily sit in these '*Units*'! Maybe I should bring you food, and lock you in here for a week or two, and then you tell me why Subjects might want to go out!"

"*It's not the same!*" Tara protested, "I wasn't *raised* in this room, it wouldn't be normal for me! I was raised as an Engineer, and that's my normal! If you put all the Engineers in Units, and all the Subjects in Engineering, it'd be chaos!"

Berryhill held out his hands, taking a moment to process. "Raised. Is everyone in there raised for a specific job, and are stuck in it?"

While Sasha nodded along in agreement, Tara explained. "Most of the time. There's some times when a person changes jobs, but it's rare. When a person is born, they get assigned to the group that will be needing someone next. Providers, Engineers, Subjects, Managers. You get brought up in that area, and learn the skills."

"I'm afraid to ask what your relationship with parents is like," Berryhill asked.

"They were both Subjects, so I never met them, since I was designated as an Engineer. I was raised by the nursery in Engineering," Tara said, while Sasha gave a humble smile, and nod. "Me too," Sasha added.

Berryhill looked horrified. "And if you had a child?"

Tara burst out laughing, and threw her arm around Sasha. "Berryhill, I don't know if anyone anyone told you where babies come from, but it's pretty darn unlikely for *us!*" Sasha giggled along with Tara's upswing of mood.

"*Okay! Fine!*" Berryhill cried in exasperation, "Say some other Engineer had a baby! Is the baby then just taken away to be a Subject if a Subject is needed?!"

"Probably," Sasha said matter-of-factly. "Subjects are the biggest group, so the odds are high that a baby will get assigned there. They get raised by Providers for a few years first, in a section set up like a Unit."

Berryhill shook his head slowly. "And you're all *okay* with this?"

Tara shrugged. "Duh. It's what's best for the facility, and so it's what's best for everyone's survival."

"But there was no war." Berryhill said almost in a whisper. "You're surviving a non-existent war."

"So?" Tara said, "We still need Engineers to handle the electricals, Providers to organize and repair, Subjects to farm, and all that. This 'no war' thing is big, but unless I'm missing something, we still need what we need."

Berryhill couldn't put together the words to explain the wrongness. He was pale with a sort of horror. A broader idea seemed to apply. "But there's... they have rights. You have rights. You're still all members of the same nation as me. There's rights that have been violated, *damn it*, for generations!"

"You need to calm down," Tara said, "I have no idea what you're talking about."

"I'm taking the first group down," Messenger said. The Grand Elevator had been loaded with Subjects (including Elise) and a handful of Citizens (including Leena). Three other Providers were on board, and between them, they had two of the stun-sticks. They had been guarding the controls, keeping Subjects and Citizens three or so metres back.

Leena was at the front, and she watched Messenger come onboard.

"Leena, what were you thinking?" Messenger asked, "I thought you to be more reasonable."

Leena scowled slightly, and said with a touch of spite, "I figured they were going up one way or another, and if I went along, I might be able to help keep them a little safer."

Messenger grimaced, turning to the controls. He huffed, softening his tone. "Next time... next time maybe it would be better to wait for Providers to help. One Citizen can't herd a hundred Subjects." He started the Grand Elevator, and the descent began.

"Messy, do you think of me as leader of the Citizens?" Leena asked.

"I suppose so."

"Maybe it should be official. Maybe if Citizens can pull themselves together – and we have been – maybe we should be more involved with the facility in general."

With a raised eyebrow, Messenger asked, "Is this your way of saying you don't want to be locked in Citizenry again?"

"That could be part of it," Leena said, "but maybe more than that. Maybe some people could be Citizens who officially organize Citizenry and stuff. I mean... it sounds a bit like the old groups who terrorized Citizenry in past years. They had guards and thugs and stuff..."

"You're no Edward," Messenger said, referring to the last would-be tyrant of Citizenry, "and you're no Warren," referring to the one before Edward.

"I sure as heck aren't!" Leena confirmed with a clenched jaw.

Messenger smiled softly. "Well, I guess we have a lot to talk about later."

"And them?" Leena pointed her chin at Elise and the other Subjects on board. The Subjects had little idea what Leena and Messenger were talking about.

"They're... a bit more complicated," Messenger said. "There's well over a thousand of them in total. Lenth's working on them with Karen, but it's a ... it's a big task."

"So they're not forgotten."

"I'm sorry," Messenger said, "Subjects and Citizens... they've been plugged into routine. If it kept the facility running, it was all that mattered."

The Grand Elevator came to a rest at Citizenry. Providers opened the door, revealing Cody and two Providers waiting inside the Citizenry loading bay.

"That was too long," Cody said to Leena with a forced smile, "You okay? You found everyone?"

"Ha," Messenger gave a mirthless laugh. "There's still dozens left up there. The trickle stopped some time ago." Messenger looked to one of the Providers who'd been guarding Citizenry. "News?"

The Provider nodded. "Word came up; we have the hatch re-sealed. Also, Engineering reports no Subjects made the long climb to down there. They have the one that fell, though. Died instantly."

Messenger bowed his head. Messenger had climbed up and down in the shaft so many times that he'd lost all fear of it, but a death stirred a bit of that old dread. "Hopefully they ... they don't mind holding onto them until I've gotten all of the Subjects back home. You fellows keep an eye on things here."

Leena and the other Citizens had unloaded from the elevator, back into Citizenry. Leena gave Messenger a pensive nod and a wave as the Providers remaining on the elevator closed the door. Messenger activated the controls, and got the elevator moving. He looked across the remaining passengers. Elise was still in the front of the Subjects.

"That big, bright area," she ventured, "I... there's so many people. Everywhere."

"Yes," Messenger quietly agreed. "More than I thought. I need to get more people working with Lenth to talk to Subjects about... about the world."

"Who's Lenth?" Elise asked, "What's a Subject?"

"You're a Subject," Messenger said. "Lenth used to be one. He's been going around talking to Subjects and filling them in on a lot of things that... things that some people long ago, decided you didn't need to know."

Elise frowned a little. "Like the big bright area."

Messenger glazed over a bit, nodding slightly. "Like the big bright area." It felt so recent that just seeing the outside was a horror. A burden of 'truth' that was carried only by a Messenger and an Actual. But the old Actual – the one he'd served under – Henry – he began breaking the old rules. He let Lenth quit being a Subject, showed him the outside, and let him teach Subjects. So many old rules broken.

Did the old man realize the generator's days were numbered? Impossible. No more than he could know about the outside world not having that dreaded war.

Unless... did his communications with 'Division' make him wonder? Did he notice that the voice wasn't always exactly the same? On some level, did he know?

No way to ask him now. Questions for the dead. Easy to dwell on, and fruitless to do so.

The Elevator stopped at the Provider-level loading bay, snapping Messenger out of his pondering. The door was opened, and Gabe was there with more Providers to accept and escort the Subjects back to Unit-level.

"I want to see it again," Elise said softly.

Messenger only replied with an ambiguous grimace. The other Subjects around her were hard to read. Some perked up at the thought, others ignored it. Soon enough, Messenger was alone on the Grand Elevator with his thoughts. It was time to go up and get the next batch, but he paused.

A moment to breathe.

The moment was shorter than he expected. That little comm sparked up. He dug it out. "Hello? Colonel?"

"Messenger. Please come meet me on the AirLimb." returned Colonel Mangual's voice.

"I'm in the middle of settling the Subjects back in. Can it wait?"

"I think you should come see me first." Not that Colonel Mangual had previously presented herself as particularly bubbly, but her tone now was notably firmer now.

"I suppose I can get my subordinates to handle things from here." Messenger said.

"Please discontinue that operation for the time being. Come see me, please."

Messenger attempted to weigh the meanings and intentions being implied. "I'm coming."

He started the Grand Elevator back up and began ascending. Past Citizenry, and reaching Actual-level. Opening the door, he found Gabe and a few other Providers ready to load on. As they loaded on, Messenger took Gabe aside.

"Gabe, that Colonel has asked me to go talk to her," he said quietly.

"Okay," Gabe responded in the same hushed tone, "that's fine, I can handle the rest of this. Looks like one more load after these folks."

"She told me to stop bringing them back down."

Gabe frowned. "Okay, why?"

"I don't know," Messenger replied, "but keep doing it. Nice and smooth. If anyone asks, you didn't see me, I *must* have been in *such* a hurry, that we didn't talk, and you assumed you needed to continue."

"Messenger?"

"When I'm gone, quietly look for a chance to close it all up. Both doors of the cargo bay, leave one person listening for me to come back, and leave Actual-level otherwise abandoned. Keep the Grand Elevator off Actual-level unless absolutely necessary. Lock things, and keep an ear out for me."

"Are... are the Colonel and those guys... Enemies?" Gabe asked, face now gaunt with concern. "Tara and Sasha haven't come back yet."

Messenger sighed. "Then keep an ear out for them, too. I don't know if we can call the Colonel an Enemy. I don't know. Be careful."

"Be... be careful."

Messenger left the loading bay behind, and went across the central hub room, to the cargo bay that led out. Just across the final threshold, on the cracked dirty floor that was now known to be 'ground', he awaited Berryhill. A handful of metres behind, waited four other soldiers.

"Berryhill," Messenger greeted flatly. "Come to fetch me?"

Berryhill tilted his head. "Well, yes, but do you have time for a story?"

Glancing back into the facility, and then at the AirLimb, Messenger replied, "I suppose I have time if *you* have time."

"Have you heard of the Aguei?" Berryhill asked.

Messenger shook his head and shrugged.

Berryhill sighed. "Long, long, long ago, the only people in this country were the Aguei people. Then, over three hundred years ago, people from Europe came, and more or less took over. They had better weapons."

"Europe? That's a country, yes?"

"Well, a group of countries, yes. And we're on Aguola. Anyone whose ancestors were from places other than here get nicknamed *Northers* –

Because the Europeans especially, came from far north of here."

Messenger paused to absorb. "So Europeans are Northers, and Aguei people come from Aguola."

"Yes. And for a long time, Northers treated the Aguei really badly. Really badly. But peace was eventually found, and through a few scuffles, and a lot of negotiation, the Aguei won rights, and respect, and lands."

Messenger frowned. "They were victorious in getting all of their land back?"

Berryhill sighed. "Well, not all. The Northers were pretty well-settled by that point, and multiple generations of Northers were born here."

"So they weren't Northers, they were Aguei," Messenger said, squinting.

"Well – the original Aguei look different, darker than most Northers."

Messenger had a laugh, and held out his arm, showing off his dark, dark skin. "So, I'm Aguei?"

Berryhill smirked. "The Aguei aren't nearly as dark as you! I'm half Aguei, on my mom's side. My Aguei heritage affords me a few rights others might not have." He reached back to flick his ponytail, and showed off the many colours it had been dyed in. "If I had to guess, you can probably thank a country in Africa for your skin tone. *That's* a whole other story!"

"Well, finish your first story first."

Berryhill's nodded, and his expression grew more serious. "The Aguei are a people who had their rights stripped away in the name of civilized culture. But a balance was found. They have a proud nation of Aguei, led by elders who are revered by the Aguei, and respected by ... most Northers. Their leader is the Grand Elder, Armil."

"Armil. The Aguei from Aguola." Messenger said.

"Grand Elder Armil. Okay, let's go."

"Sure. Mmm, hang on," Messenger said. "We've been taking on a lot of dirt with this door gaping open." He reached for the pull-strap to pull the door down. When it got close enough, Berryhill reached the edge and helped. When the door reached the bottom, it clanged soundly. Messenger stood and stared at the bottom edge.

"Must be kind of a bewildering time for you," Berryhill said softly.

Messenger put his hand on the door and sighed. "I just want them to be safe."

"Well... so say we all, Messenger." The word 'but' seemed to hang in the air, however, it was not spoken. They headed to the AirLimb, and the four soldiers allowed them to pass, then followed behind. When they arrived at the AirLimb, Berryhill stopped. "I'm headed back to my truck. My Corporals are waiting there."

"See you soon, I hope," Messenger said.

Berryhill paused. "I hope, too," he said gravely, before heading back to his squad's utility vehicle. Messenger watched him go for a few steps before the voice of a soldier came from the top of the ramp. "Sir? If you could come this way, please?"

The Colonel had been generous with the word *'please'* earlier, using the same pragmatic tone. It was not overly pleasing to Messenger, but he walked up the ramp. Glancing back, Messenger saw some manner of large flying box in the distance approaching. It had some similarities to the AirLimb, but at this distance, it was hard to see specifically what was making it different.

The soldier prompted Messenger to keep up, so he went inside, following along to a small room. It was pretty bare, with a bed and a toilet.

Before Messenger had time to turn and ask the soldier about it, the door was closed behind him.

He tried to open it.

Locked.

"Excuse me?" Messenger called clearly through the door, "Is this right?"

No answer.

"Hello?" he tried again with two knocks.

No answer.

Finally, a panel that Messenger hadn't noticed before across the room, lit up. It was about twenty by fifteen centimetres in size. Colonel Mangual's face appeared.

"Messenger."

"Colonel. What is going on?"

"I have some concerns," Colonel Mangual said, eyes down, seemingly looking at something else.

Messenger tried the door again to illustrate: "Evidently."

"I have a number of concerns about human rights violations occurring within Station Four. I've discussed this with General Westmore, and he shares my concerns."

"Who is General Westmore?"

"My boss," Colonel Mangual said. "Aguola has four Generals in the military, and Westmore is stationed in the Yute central base. That's a little over a half-hour flight in this AirLimb. It'd further into the desert."

"He's part of Division?" Messenger asked.

"Not, but the division you know is a fairly small group that is under the General's command."

"I see. So, he's important, and agrees with you about human something?"

"Rights. We believe the basic human rights of the Subjects are being violated." The Colonel said flatly, watching Messenger for a reaction.

"I haven't heard the term," Messenger responded, frowning slightly.

The Colonel sighed. "If what we're learning is correct, the Subjects are confined to a limited space, not generally allowed to interact with more than a few people, and are forced to work by a supervisor who isn't permitted to speak with the Subjects. Furthermore, they are woefully uneducated about the world in general, and are functionally illiterate."

Messenger nodded. "This is true, for the most part. There seemed no need to bother them with knowledge that didn't pertain to their role in keeping the facility running, and maintaining everyone's survival. This has been ch-"

"Yes," the Colonel interrupted. "Your senior engineers have told me there's one or two of you going about to the various cages, teaching the Subjects a little."

"Cages? There are no cages –"

"The enclosures. Whatever you call them."

"Units."

"Regardless!" the Colonel continued, "does it seem efficient for two or three people to educate … what was it, over a thousand people?"

"Roughly twelve hundred," Messenger corrected, "and no, it is not comprehensive. Lenth and Karen's endeavours are experimental. As I understand it, they've had multiple talks with roughly a third of the Units so far."

"And that other group," the Colonel inquired, "the ones who apparently kill each other."

"I believe you refer to the Citizens. Thankfully, the killing is a part of their society that has been weeded out."

"By killing," the Colonel said. "So you have a floor full of murderers."

"I believe all those who have killed and remain in Citizenry have killed only for self-defence, or for justice."

"*According to who?!*" the Colonel cried. "You? Them? Certainly no court Aguola recognizes! At the very, very least, those people need to be examined by a counsellor! This isn't the kind of thing one person can, or *should* do alone, or have the final say!"

"You have to understand, we were surviving the war! We needed to maint–"

"*There was no war!*" the Colonel interrupted. "It's time for you to rejoin the rest of the world! You're all victims!"

"The world…"

Chapter 19:

Yute

As closely as she listened, no useful sound was coming though that door. Had it been an hour? Two? She'd tried to stay positive for Sasha's sake, but the longer they stayed locked in the meeting room, the harder it was to keep a light spin on things.

Then they felt the world move, and heard the turbines firing.

"The AirLimb's moving," Tara said.

"Any chance they're just putting it closer to the cargo bay, so I don't have to run as far in the void to get back?" Sasha asked.

This was seemingly answered by a change in the motion they felt. If they'd been standing, it might have been a danger, but as it was, they were sitting together on the floor in one of the corners far from the door.

"Feels like it's ... it's going the wrong direction for that," Tara said.

Sasha inhaled deeply. "Ohhh, and we're not going slow, are we?"

Tara put her arms around Sasha and gave a squeeze. "We... we're okay. It'll be okay."

Despite this assurance, Sasha shrieked out in the direction of the door. *"When are you letting us out? Where are we going?!"*

She didn't honestly expect an answer beyond the extra squeeze from Tara, but the video screen lit up. Some soldier's face was there. "Do you need to go to the bathroom, food, or water?"

"I think she asked for answers," Tara replied.

"The Colonel will be addressing your concerns before long, I believe. If you don't need anything a this moment–"

"Out! We need out!" yelled Sasha.

"Ah... thank you for your patience," the soldier said before the screen went black again.

"I have work to do!" Sasha said to the blank rectangle. "Ugh. He's probably still listening."

"Probably," Tara agreed. She looked to the blank screen. "Any idea how much longer?" she asked with tempered resentment. No answer came.

"What is this all about?" Sasha mumbled.

"Subjects, I guess," Tara said, "Colonel didn't seem to like how the Subjects live or something."

Sasha grumbled. "Subjects have a lot more room than *we* have right now."

Eventually, they heard a change in the engines, and felt the motion change.

"We're... stopping?" Sasha said.

"Yeah, where?"

When the slowing became a stop, and the sounds of the engines subsided, they were still alone in the room. The next fifteen minutes, which might as well have been an hour, was filled with Tara pacing around, asking the occasional question to the blank screen.

Many of those answers were answered when the door opened. Two soldiers stood there.

"Ma'am," said the closer one, holding out a little metal thingamabob with two sets of curved metal,connected with a chain. "Hands, please?"

Tara looked at her hands, and figured out that the little sets of metal were made to go around her wrists. It seemed like an inconvenient thing to use.

"What are these? Why?" Tara asked, frowning.

"Detainees are to be restrained during transport to holding." the soldier stated.

"I've been stuck in this room for ... I don't *know* how long, *and now this? This is crap!"* Tara declared, "I'm going back."

The other soldier fired his stun-gun, and Tara fell to the floor with a shriek that quickly slid into a moan, and then silence.

Sasha screamed at a pitch and volume she didn't know she could. It echoed and resonated in the room, and the soldiers jumped in shock, a moment before Sasha went down in shock.

The one holding the handcuffs looked over to the other and the stun-gun. "Was all that necessary?"

"That wasn't going to get any smoother," he replied.

"Where's Tara and Sasha?" Messenger asked. Four soldiers were escorting him from the AirLimb, across a wide area of cement, toward a low, grey structure with a handful of grey doors on it. He was wearing the metal things on his wrists, which he regretted agreeing to immediately.

There were few walls here, and no ceiling. This field of grey also had two other AirLimbs sitting around, several crew and soldiers tending to various tasks. Yellow lines and white lines were painted across the floor for various purposes, few of which had clear purpose. Numbers and letters that meant nothing to Messenger were several metres wide across the floor. Here and there on the floor were little glossy panels that Messenger guessed were lights or something. This floor didn't go on endlessly, and edges could be seen. They were on top of some structure of an unknown height. Beyond that, vast, soft hills of light yellow could be seen in all directions.

"My two Engineers were on the AirLimb with us, correct? Where are they now?" Messenger asked.

The soldier directly behind him only answered, "Keep moving."

"I want to speak with them, and the Colonel," Messenger said sternly as he continued toward the door.

"You will."

The door led to a small series of halls that reminded Messenger of Provider levels in many ways, even leading to an elevator. It was about the size of the smaller utilitarian elevators in the Provider levels, but more refined. No structural supports could be seen as with some of the Provider elevators. It was certainly not as Grand as the Grand Elevator, however. The comfort of his familiar ride in the Grand Elevator would be welcome, even if the blasted lights were to go out again.

This elevator smelled different. It was cleaned more often, there was no hint of dust, just a sterile hint of metal and cleaning chemicals.

When he got onboard with his four escorts, one called out. "Holding."

The elevator beeped, and repeated in a soft voice, clear with precision. "Next:Holding."

The elevator moved with a barely audible hiss.

"I wonder if I can buy some of these," Messenger joked quietly, mirthlessly.

The elevator stopped, and as the doors slid open, that soft vice announced, "Arrived at holding," with another beep.

The five of them proceeded down another hall, taking a left, and past a few cells. Each was a fairly large space with a toilet, a few benches, and enclosed by black metal bars. One of them had a soldier in it, wearing only a white undershirt for a top, but dressed in uniform from the waist down. Waist sideways, anyway, as he was laying face-down on one of the benches, passed out.

Messenger was glad to be not stopping at these cells.

A little way down another hall, they came to a door on the right. One of the soldiers opened the door, then turned to Messenger and said, "Cuffs."

Messenger held out his hands, the small chain jingling between his wrists. The soldier touched a spot on either of the metal loop contraptions, and they came loose. He took the cuffs, and pointed Messenger into the room. "Dinner's in like half an hour, bang on the door if you need to hit the can. Make yourself comfortable."

And without a chance for another word, Messenger was alone in this room. His wrists felt odd after the cuffs. Not sore... a little sweaty, and a little itchy. He rubbed them as he took in the room. Three chairs, not all that different from chairs back in the facility, and a two-by-two metre table. Everything was grey, grey, grey. Except one wall. Most of the wall on the left was a mirror. Messenger had never seen a mirror that large, but a room on the Provider-levels had a similar setup.

"Anyone in there?" he called to the mirror.

No reply. With little option but to wait until someone came along to talk, Messenger moved a chair to where he could easily see the mirror and the door, and had a seat. Tedium set in quickly.

"Does the world still have magazines?" he asked out loud, in the general direction of the mirror, on the oft chance someone might be watching. "We have a few in the facility. Station Four, that is. They're relics. Damaged, frail." He got up, and wandered over to the mirror, examining himself. "Books, too. Some of them are in better shape, but I think I've read every one in the facility." He wandered back to his chair. "Might be some in Citizenry I haven't read, I heard one fellow had a number of books. He's gone now, so I'm not sure what happened to –"

It was then that the door opened, and Tara and Sasha were ushered in by soldiers before the door was closed again. They looked like hell.

"What happened to you two?!" Messenger asked, "Are you alright?"

Tara snorted. "Apparently, spending time unconscious from being stunned doesn't count as a good night's sleep." She put her arm around Sasha, who leaned into Tara.

"What's going on? We weren't allowed to leave the AirLimb from the moment you left that room," Sasha said.

"A bunch of Subjects got wandering on the surface," Messenger said. "Colonel Mangual offered to help contain them before anyone got hurt. It turned into a bit of a spectacle, and the Colonel's people took in at least two Subjects."

"She's got a problem with them," Tara said, "and how they live."

Messenger nodded. "I can see her point. She fails to see the situation from the perspective of our survival in the wake of the big war."

Sasha rubbed her jaw, still a bit sore from how she landed when she was stunned."Did you tell her about how the Subjects are getting–"

"She was unimpressed," Messenger said, looking towards the mirror, "and called us all victims."

"They watching?" Tara asked, looking at the mirror.

"Good chance," Messenger replied.

"Lovely," Tara said. "Did she happen to mean we were all victims of hers?"

As was promised, (yet forgotten by Messenger,) food was arriving. First, a knock on the door with a soldier's voice, "Step away from the door."

Before Sasha could say, "We're already away from the door," the door was already opening. Two soldiers were there, one holding a stack of three plastic trays with plastic lids, all a greyish-yellow. The soldier set the stack down on the floor and said, "There ya go. If any of you are vegetarians or anything, you're all good, it's not real meat." The soldier left, closing the door.

Tara, Sasha, and Messenger looked at each other, and back at the stack of sealed trays.

"Meat?" Tara asked, picking up the trays to bring them to the table. They all sat down in front of their trays, and lifted off the lids.

Each contained a ten-centimetre wide, off-white, smooth, soft-looking circular thing about a centimetre and a half thick, with a slightly darker circular thing under it, on top of another lighter circular thing. These circles all seemed to be presented as a single combined object on the tray.

Another section contained a quantity of rice. They knew what rice was, but had never seen it served in this way, as opposed to mashed beyond recognition as part of a food disk.

Another section was filled with what looked like red water. It had a few bubbles in it, but the bubbles did not rise, and the red water did not flow.

Another featured a dozen or so green, roughly cylindrical things. They were obviously plant matter of some kind.

One section had six or seven purple balls, each of which had a little hole on one side. They were at least twice as wide as the green cylinders, but still only about two centimetres wide.

Each tray had a sealed, two-hundred and fifty-millilitre container of liquid. Tara's was orange coloured, Sasha's was red, Messenger's was yellow.

Lastly, to the side was a long section containing a one centimetre wide black ball, a white ball, a small container with red goop, one with yellow goop, and a utensil that seemed undecided if it was a spoon or a fork.

"This is food," Sasha said, looking at the bounty. Whether it was a statement or a question was undecided.

Attached to each lid was an identical slip of paper.

YUTE CENTRAL KITCHEN
LUNCH A, TUESDAY

1 CHICKEN BURGER, (SIM)
1 GREEN BEANS

1 RICE, WHITE
1 GRAPES
1 JELATIN (CHERRY)

1 JUICE (ASSTD)

1 PEPPER
1 SALT
1 KETCHUP
1 MUSTARD

1 SPORK

"Well, rice is rice," Messenger said, "but the rest?"

"Ooh, this looks like the sweet little stick things the Colonel had with her cough-ee stuff!" Sasha grabbed her little while ball and popped it in her mouth.

Her eyes widened, and a moment later she was spitting it into the lid of her tray. "*Ueeeughhh!*" followed by more spitting, and more splitting. "That's not sweet!"

"Have something to drink," Messenger said, picking up a juice container. The yellow liquid swished inside. "Oh not this one, it looks like urine!" By now, Tara had opened Sasha's and handed it to her.

Sasha hastily took a mouthful and swished it around. Her alarmed expression changed to confusion. She swallowed, took another mouthful, and her expression only changed to a deeper confusion. She read the container. *Unsweetened Cranberry.* She swallowed and said, "The food out here is terrible! Think they'll let me go home just to pick up a papaya?"

"Try the purple balls." Messenger said.

Tara beat Sasha to it, and gave a thumbs up. "That's a little more papaya-like."

Choosing to mostly ignore the black and white little balls, the three of them went on experimenting with the various foods. The unmoving red liquid was floppy and ridiculous to eat, but it was also sweet. The rest was less interesting, but they still didn't know what was what.

When they had had enough, (Tara being evidently the hungriest, finishing everything except bits of the non-flowing red liquid, the white and black balls, and the two little containers of goop, which proved disgusting,) they closed and stacked the trays where they had been delivered, by the door.

"Is that what people always eat in the rest of the world?" Sasha asked, "I suppose it's more variety than the food disks, and sometimes nabbing a papaya before it gets processed. I wonder if they have papayas?"

"There's apparently billions of people," Messenger said, "I'm guessing they have more than what we've just been exposed to."

"Done?" came Colonel Mangual's voice from the direction of the mirror.

"Yeah," Tara said tersely, "We'll have to add some of those purple ball things to our shipment if we get another of those capacitors."

"Purple balls?" The Colonel's voice paused. "Grapes?"

"Sure, if you say so," Tara replied.

"Are we considered a threat?" Messenger asked sharply, turning to the mirror.

"That's not a simple question," the Colonel replied.

"This isn't a simple room," Tara responded, "or we'd be at that table on your AirLimb thing, not talking through a mirror."

"True." A moment later, the mirror faded to white before becoming clear glass. "But there are safely questions to be considered."

The newly revealed room wasn't much different than the one they were in. A table, a few chairs. The Colonel sat at the far edge of the table. A soldier was by the door, and and another soldier sat at the table. The one at the table was in a uniform that was a bit different from the ones they'd seen so far. It looked thinner, and included no helmet. Both this soldier and the Colonel had a hat sitting on the table, similarly pointless little things, flattened down.

The soldier at the table held a flat device that the soldier watched carefully, poking it on occasion.

"Safety questions?" Messenger asked, "Have I given you any reason to think I held any hostility?"

"As of this point, no," the Colonel said, "but I'm concerned with the welfare of the 'Subject' individuals."

"As am I," Messenger said. "You took two that your people stunned. I was assured they would be fine."

"What?" Sasha cried, turning to the Colonel, "how many people do you do that to?"

"It was for their safety," Colonel Mangual said, "if they'd been allowed to run off into the desert, or gotten into direct confrontation with my troops attempting to stop them, someone could have gotten hurt."

"And where are they now?" Messenger asked as cordially as he could through clenched teeth.

"After a cursory debriefing, they were screened for any contagion, bio or nano, and will be joining the rest as they are processed. That reminds me, the three of you haven't been screened yet either. Sergeant Berryhill tells me you were previously screened for nanite presence, but those portable scanners aren't as g–"

"What the ever-loving faeces are you talking about?!" Tara hollered.

"Wait, wait," Messenger stepped up, "they're with the rest? Who's 'the rest'?"

Chapter 20:

Maw

The Provider remaining at the door on Actual level heard knocking from outside. "Hello?" she yelled to the door.

"Hello? It's Sergeant Berryhill. Are you in charge while Messenger's away?"

"You probably want Gabe. I'll call him."

"Oh. Okay, please do. Shame he doesn't have a modern comm."

"Uh, okay, hang on." The Provider went to the nearby portable communication device, and called Provider levels. "Hey, an outside guy wants to talk to Gabe." With a bit of back and forth, promises were made to send Gabe as soon as he was found, and could make it up to Actual level.

It wasn't all that long before Gabe indeed arrived, gave a nod to the Provider, and went to talk to the door. "Hello? Gabe here."

"Oh, have we met? This is Sergeant Berryhill. I've been here before; my crew delivered the capacitor."

"I've seen you, I've been up here at the same time as you," Gabe said, "You're the guy with the colourful hair, right?"

"That's right. You're in charge?"

"I guess so," Gabe said, "I'm the best you're gonna get without Messenger here. What's *his* situation, do you know?"

"He's at Yute Central," Berryhill said, "That's a large base not too, too far from here. He's talking with the Colonel about a ... about a new home for everybody."

"What do you mean, a new home?"

"Well, the Station Four facility is old, right?" Berryhill said, "It hasn't been properly maintained. It's only a matter of time something like the generator breakdown happens again, and hurts someone. Actually, this place is so old, it's a miracle it hasn't happened already. Even the generator as it is right now might be a heck of a hazard."

This stood to reason. The Providers did what they could to keep things in shape, but even with parts from Division, some things just don't get fixed quite as nicely as they could be. Past wiring and plumbing issues have been nightmarish, but the potential for much worse happening was always there. In some ways, concerns like that had been ignored because there wasn't much option other than to do what little they could, and hope.

"Do you want to do a maintenance check or something?" Gabe asked.

"Well, yes," Berryhill said, "but I think in the meantime, until we can be sure everything's safe, it would be best to get everyone out."

"That's like two thousand people," Gabe said. "Some of them might not be too keen on going. Are they all supposed to stay at that Yute place?"

"Messenger will be there," Berryhill answered, "It's... safer. And not in Yute Base, it's not really suited for two thousand guests. There's another location, and Messenger will be joining you."

Gabe looked to the Provider who'd been minding the door. She shrugged. "I... kinda don't want to."

"Agreed, but if it makes us all safer in the long run... Gabe leaned down and unlocked the door. Rolling the door up, he was greeted with Berryhill and about fifty other soldiers. Behind them, sat five huge boxes, much like the AirLimb, but several times bigger. Instead of four turbines attached to their sides, each had two giant fan-like protrusions on their tops.

As soldiers made their way into the Actual level, a decidedly troubled-looking Berryhill went up to Gabe and the Provider. "Come with me to the first carrier. Please."

This was the first time Gabe had actually stepped out of the facility. Last time he saw it, it was still pretty light, but now, the sky was nearly black – except for the endless, tiny, shining specks.

The immediate area was lit well enough, as the huge boxes had lights on their fronts, coming from the windows on the upper front, and out of the door on the side with a ramp sticking out.

Up close, the box they approached loomed even bigger. The fan-like protrusions on top towered above them threateningly. Soldiers could be seen in the windows up on the front. Seeing inside, it was the biggest room Gabe had ever seen aside from the outdoors itself. Ten or more soldiers milled about.

This big flying room could probably hold a lot of people.

A lot more if they were uncomfortable.

"Find a seat," Berryhill said quietly to Gabe and the other Provider. Inside, the walls were lined with benches. The floor sported several two-metre high partitions, with seating attached to either side.

A mechanical 'cough' sounded overhead, joined by mechanical humming. After another cough, the mechanical sound gradually increased. Gabe looked up, and saw the large imposing protrusion begin to slowly move.

"I'm not sure I like this much." Gabe said.

Berryhill, eyes cast down, sighed. "I'm not so sure either."

Leena stood on the edge of the Grand Elevator shaft. One of the two Providers stationed at Citizenry stood with her and they looked up, seeing the bottom of the Grand Elevator, parked on the Actual level.

"Does that sound right?" Leena asked, without looking away.

Cody came up and listened, too. "I hear people," he said.

The Provider said nothing, still straining to hear. In time he said "Yeah, now I hear them. People."

"*Too many* people," Leena growled. "A lot of people getting on the Grand Elevator from up there? There's not supposed to be that many up there."

The Grand Elevator's sounds reached them as it started moving.

"Okay," she said, tuning to nearby Citizens. "Get as far away from here as you can. I don't trust this. Go to Cody's and my place, go to the other upper section, go to that passage. Or go to any crack in the wall and tell the sniffers they have company. Go, spread the word." She pushed Cody gently away from the Grand Elevator shaft, trying to get everyone moving, while she stood her ground.

"Well, come on then," Cody said to Leena.

"I have my knife, you don't." She stared up at the approaching Elevator. "Keep the others safe." She then raised her voice for anyone nearby to hear, hoping it wasn't loud enough for the passengers of the Grand Elevator to hear. "Go, hide!" She pulled Cody close, and kissed him. "Go," she whispered hastily. "Hide them."

She had to shove Cody to get him moving, then turned to the Elevator shaft. She got on the ladder, and began climbing as quietly as possible. She looked down, hearing someone else on the ladder. It was the the Provider she'd been hanging around with, and he was climbing down. He was probably heading to Provider-level.

As Leena climbed, the Grand Elevator came down. Leena held herself tight against the ladder, not sure how much room she had. She held her breath as the Grand Elevator passed her by, stopping at Citizenry.

She looked at the roof of the Grand Elevator, and then upwards. She had planned to get on top of the Elevator, but had no plan beyond that. Up was interesting too, but who knew what she'd find there?

Climbing is hard. Riding on top of an elevator was easy. She climbed on board as quietly as she could. There was a hatch on the top of the Grand Elevator that she could theoretically open to get in, but at this time, that would be foolish. This position did allow her to listen, however.

The people from outside sounded confident enough. They were assuring any Citizens they could convince, that they were headed to somewhere safer. And that if repairs to the facility went well, (which of course, why wouldn't they go well?) everyone would be back here as soon as all that was done.

She heard someone say, "This is going to take two or three more runs with this floor. Theses aren't even the Subjects."

Soon enough, the Grand Elevator began rising. Leena hadn't taken much note of the assembly attached to the top of the elevator that connected the huge cables supporting it. The cables quietly groaned as the Grand Elevator gradually accelerated. She was less focused on listening to the passengers, and more on the shaft's dim maintenance lights passing by, and the ceiling that grew ever closer.

The motor churned above, taking in the cables, and feeding them out sideways into the wall at the very top. The machine's metal gears were partly exposed, and the machinations of its innards were nearly hypnotic. She wasn't going to be squished, was she? Surely if that were possible, someone would have been squished in the past at some point. There were no warning signs here. Would they put any? There also wasn't any corpses, or old blood stains. So that fact was encouraging.

But damn, that ceiling was getting close. No, no, don't worry, the size of the engine itself would prohibit the elevator from going too high. And the door to Actual-level was right there, it was going to stop. Stop. Stop please. Slowing... and.. okay. Not squished.

She looked at the cables, and the big motor. Had they ever needed repairs? Was it just built so well that it just kept going, or was there a time when Providers and some past Messenger were forced to fix this thing?

Her wandering thoughts were refocused by the mumblings and movements of Citizens being unloaded. These people had grown up only able to get the slightest glimpse of the outside of the Grand Elevator, and today, they were riding it. What's more, they were about to see that big wall-free, ceiling-free room, and maybe see that Enemy.

Gabe had told her that all this time, they'd been wrong to call it an enemy. Where was Gabe now? Where was Messenger? And now strangers from outside were bringing her Citizens out to where the Enemy was.

She heard the outsiders boarding the Grand Elevator again. Soon it was moving, and the metal gears above her came to life. She saw the ladder slowly coming into view again, and she stepped onto it smoothly as the elevator began gaining speed, receding below her.

The door to the loading bay was left open, but the ladder was just around the corner in the shaft, leaving her out of sight. She peeked and saw a few of the strangers. They weren't the same strangers she saw when she was up before, chasing Patricia. These ones had helmets with eye-shields. It was difficult to tell which were men, and which were women, as their bulky clothing burdened with accessories made discerning their natural builds effectively impossible.

They did not look like friends. Nothing about them felt friendly. The fact that they managed to fill the Grand Elevator with peaceful Citizens was surprising. Future runs might grow more and more difficult.

Citizens could die. Cody might die. Patricia's was probably terrified beyond her wits. Trying to guess who might have been in the load that just came up was pointless. All the speculation wouldn't change the situation.

One of the strangers was still in the loading bay, facing away. Their hands weren't visible, they seemed to be holding something in front of themselves, likely a weapon.

She rested her hand on the handle of the knife hanging from her hip. She knew how to use it well enough. Most Citizens did. She could deal with the stranger in front of her. But she didn't know for a fact that the strangers were enemies. And she couldn't be sure that she could do it quietly enough. She heard other people not too far away.

Most of the chatter she heard was from Citizens who were facing the reality for the Big Room. It started to get noisier. One voice got noticeably louder.

"*No, no, no, no, no...!*"

A Citizen ran into view, clearly panicked. The stranger in the loading bay ran to meet the Citizen. The stranger's weapon was now visible; not a blade, but not much bigger than her knife. It might be like the thing that was used to make Patricia lie down. A few other strangers ran into view, surrounding the Citizen. They were all far enough from the loading bay now that Leena took a chance.

She walked swiftly, hoping it was quiet enough to not attract any of the strangers. The group of sixty or seventy Citizens were being ushered towards one of the big boxes outside, but Leena only paused for a split second to glance out that way, seeing three of the big boxes, and the night sky. From Leena's position, it may as well have been oblivion.

That direction had at least twenty of the strangers, with five or more on the way to the big boxes. Who knew how many more were not in view? That direction was no good.

The absolute right hand side away from them was the hallway to Actual's office, and other rooms. The running Citizen had been convinced to not fear the outside, and had been coerced to go along with the rest. All that Leena could tell was that no physical force had seemingly been used. Was it reason, or threat that maintained order?

Leena moved on, down the rightmost hall. It had been a while since she'd been down this way, towards Actual's rooms. And now that old man was gone. Would this be happening if he were here? As she started down the hall, it occurred to her that the rooms might not be free of outsiders. The first two rooms were washrooms, and presumably the outsiders pooped on occasion, so she passed them by to a smaller room, closing the door behind her.

The small room smelled of chemicals, and was filled with a variety of items. There were a few shelves with coloured bottles on them, and a large sink about a cubic metre in size. There was a cardboard box much like the ones that brought food to Citizenry. It had different markings, but it was about the same size.

In a smaller metal container, a couple of spears stuck out, and leaned against the wall. These spears had cloth of some kind on the end instead of a point. Perhaps for cleaning. Like for cleaning people who smelled bad, and you didn't want to get too close. In short, the room was more chaos than a crap-sniffer's den. But arguably smelled better.

A woman's voice was heard from in the hall. "What kind of savages are they that the women's bathroom has no TP? I mean, I get that they might not have installed a sprayer in the nineteen-goddam-fifties, but for fuck's sake!"

Was the voice coming closer? Leena panicked. *Hide, hide! Where?* The sink was big enough, but it's not like it had a lid. If there was a blanket to go on top, maybe, but even climbing into the thing would be a trial.

The cardboard box! Leena reached for it, and remembered the time a couple of years ago that a violent Subject hid in a food box that was delivered to Citizenry. Flashbacks of his deeds rushed to her, and of having found her love, Mike, torn apart. It added to her panic, and breathing became a bit more difficult. Her hands, a little less steady.

Focus. Focus. She flipped the box, and as quietly as she could, got under it, as close to the box's original position as she could tell. She listened carefully. It was only a handful of seconds before she heard the door open.

The woman's voice called out, "Holy crap, the janitor's closet's a mess. If they store TP in here, it'd take all day to find. Screw it, I'm just gonna try raiding the men's."

And the door was closed.

Listening closely, Leena raised the box enough to peek out. Yup, she was alone. She waited a bit just in case. The more Leena was exposed to these strangers, the less she liked them. After untold years of terrible events in Citizenry, they'd just found a peace, and now this. Her people were being taken away, and it sounded like the strangers weren't stopping there. If they were operating down the Grand Elevator shaft, once they figured they got all of the Citizens, Providers would be next. If they can be so easily herded.

The Strangers must be back at Citizenry by now. Would the second load of passengers come as easily? The third? Leena wagered that past experiences had made most of the Citizens wary. It was hard to imagine more than half of them coming on their own free will. It would get violent, but the strangers with their stun-weapons would likely overpower knife-wielding Citizens. Then instead of trips of nervous Citizens, it'd be cargo-loads of unconscious Citizens, laid out the same way bodies had been taken down to compost.

That brought up another idea; what if the strangers were taking people to be eaten? She'd heard stories about a Citizen who did that. Maybe the strangers didn't have farms like Citizens and Subjects do. Or maybe they just preferred eating people.

That was silly. Wouldn't they kill them first? Then again, a dead person would be heavy. Maybe they made them walk to somewhere more convenient to kill. This was too high of a risk to let rest. Either way, taking the Citizens away felt wrong.

But now what? She had her knife, and perhaps she could take down a couple before one of them stunned her. If she didn't think the entirety of Citizenry could manage a handful of them, how was she even considering taking on that many, or more, on her own?

All she could do at this point was to warn the Providers, in case they were next. She knew Actual had a communications device built into the table in one of his rooms. It had been quiet long enough out there. She stood, holding the box with one hand. She only now read the two-centimetre-high text on one of its sides. "BATH TISSUE x180 ROLLS". *Whatever that means.*

Thinking about her next move to the room with the communication device, she considered taking the box as a portable hiding spot, or one of the cloth-end spear things. She already had her knife, but this dumb spear thing had a little more range. Less range than those stun-weapons the strangers had, though. Not that the cloth end was terribly threatening. And besides, if she took one, she wouldn't be able to use the box to hide.

So she had a choice, and both seemed stupid. Maybe she'd leave both. And then later regret having neither? *Spin the knife.* She took out her knife, and spun it on the floor. If it pointed more to the spear, or box, she'd take that. And if it stopped pointing more to the door, she'd take nothing.

It stopped spinning almost *directly* at the box. She put her knife away and picked up the box. It was a little awkward and floppy.

She felt like an idiot.

She put down the box and picked up the spear. The cloth end was wet, made a squishy sound, and dripped.

This made her feel like even more of an idiot. Box it was. Holding it with one hand, she carefully opened the door with the other, and peeked out. She could hear talking, but it was fairly distant. Out she went.

The idiotic box bumped loudly on the door frame.

Leena paused, looking back... no one seemed to hear it.

Okay. Idiocy full speed ahead. She got to Actual's office, and went to the desk. The communication device was different, but the controls and display looked like they followed the same method. A dial was tuned to a frequency. She didn't need to wonder what to set it to, as writing on the panel pointed at spots for ELEV, PROV, and ENG. Simple enough. She turned it to PROV, and grabbed the handset, which was a bit different than what she was used to.

She held the talk button, and said as loudly as she dared, "Providers?"

It didn't take long before she heard something, but it wasn't loud enough to make out. When it stopped, she tried again.

"Providers? This is Leena from Citizenry. I'm in Actual's office. Can anyone hear me?"

The sound replied a little louder, but again indistinct and muted. The sound was coming from... oh. There was a thing on the desk. It was made of metal and other things, and had a wire leading to a plug in the desk. The thing had two padded cup-things, and the sound was coming from those. She picked the device up, and held the cups to her ear, hearing the end of what was being said.

"-from him."

"Sorry, Provider guy," Leena said, "I'm still figuring out Actual's communication device. It's a bit different. I think I got it now. What were you saying?"

The Provider on the other end sighed. "Okay, for one, what are you doing there, two, where's Gabe? He left to talk to Berryhill like an hour and a half ago. We heard the Grand Elevator moving, but he hasn't come back yet."

"Crap, the strangers from outside must have him."

"We know that, Berryhill is one of them, but we expected him back by now. We just want to get in contact with him. Or Messenger."

"I'm telling you," Leena replied, "the strangers are scooping up as many of the Citizens as they can, and loading them onto a huge box out there. They said something about taking people somewhere safer. I snuck around and listened to them talk, and it sounds like they also want to get the Subjects, too. Maybe everyone, I dunno. I don't like them! A lot of Citizens aren't going to put up with this, someone's going to get hurt. Is Messenger okay with this crap?"

There was a pause before the next reply, and he sounded a little panicked. "Messenger or Gabe would have told people if they were going for long," he said.

Leena grumbled back,"Ugh, well, they got gotten, I guess! What do we do now? Who's running things down there?! Don't tell me it's friggin Lenth."

"N-no, he's not qualified or anything... I guess the previous Contact, but he's... he's not available, so I guess.. I guess the head Engineer?"

"Yeah, okay, whatever," Leena said, "So where the heck is he?"

"She. She's a she. Named Tara. She's... in Engineering?"

Leena looked at the panel. The setting for ENG was likely Engineering. "Fine. Fine, Provider guy. I called mainly to warn you. I guess I'm going to call Engineering. *Bye.*"

"*Wait, I–*"

Leena cut him off and turned the knob to ENG.

"Hey Engineering people. You got a Tara there? I think I met her before the blackout. This is Leena the Citizen, and I'm calling from Actual's place."

It took a bit of time, but a reply came back. "Hi? Tara's not here. This is Kevin. We're waiting for her to get back, she's been gone a while, and we can't get a hold of Messenger."

"Oh for fuck's sake!" Leena cried, "I'm betting the strangers from outside have them, too. Messenger, a Provider named Gabe, a whole pile of Citizens, and they're just loading more and more people into huge boxes outside to take them to a 'safer place', but I don't trust any of this crap!"

"What? The people from ... the ones who gave us the power capacitor?"

"*Whatever! The surface outside people! They're taking people away! Maybe to eat them!*"

"And they're using the Grand Elevator?!" Kevin asked.

"Well, they're not carrying people up the ladder on their friggin backs, now, are they?!"

"I'm cutting power to the Grand Elevator!" Kevin said, then issuing the order to other Engineers.

"Whoo! Sounds good!"

It was then that Leena heard voices coming. Oops, she'd gotten too loud! The box! Hide in the box! She pulled the box labelled 'bath tissue' over herself, and tried to remain silent.

"Can you make it down here?" came Kevin's voice. Oh crap. She stood with the box on her head and turned off the communication device before quickly ducking back down into the box.

By now, three soldiers were already in the room, and had seen Leena pop out of the box momentarily.

"Wow," said one of the soldiers, "We uh... I guess we found where they keep the TP. Right in their boss's office. By the desk. The boss was hoarding TP. What kind of idiot hoards TP?"

Leena listened, and held her breath. No sound came for a long time, but she didn't hear them leave, either.

Finally, a Soldier said, "Ma'am, we know you're not TP."

Fuck.

Chapter 21:

Camping Trip

Tara, Sasha, Messenger, and two Citizens were all wearing those wrist things. 'Cuffs' the soldiers had been calling them. They had also been given new clothes – bright orange jumpsuits that covered slightly more than their old suits. They wore new shoes, which were a bit bulkier, but shoddier than their old ones.

They rode in a transport truck, on the way to a facility where they would be held. They were told others would be coming.

"How deep is this one?" Tara asked one of the soldiers guarding them.

The soldier frowned, unclear on the question.

"This facility we're going to," Tara clarified, "How deep is it?"

"It's not underground," the solder answered, "it's just surface level, fenced in. It's in the Meston outskirts." His voice got a little grimmer when he said the word 'Meston'.

"What is a Meston?" Messenger asked.

"A city. Well, it was." The Soldier frowned. "You seriously don't know Meston?"

"You know where we came from." Sasha said, "We haven't been getting much news from out here."

The soldier paused. "Then you don't know about the Erebus incident?" His question was met with blank stares. "A terrorist who called himself Erebus attacked a couple of cities. The second was Meston. It got wrecked bad. Tons of deaths. He's long gone now, and we were left with this burnt-out city. We're salvaging materials from it... using a little of the land... but people aren't exactly swarming to build here. Bad mojo, you know?"

"So there *was* a war," Tara said quietly.

"War's always out there," the soldier said. "Last I saw, there were nearly 20 active conflicts in the world that you could call wars."

"But no atomics?" Messenger said.

The soldier huffed. "Ha. 'Atomics'. No, no atomics, no nukes, no bio as far as I know, no neutron, no nano, I hope. Humanity's been smart enough to skip most of all that, so far."

"I have idea what half those are," Tara said.

The truck stopped, and the soldier opened the back door of the truck. The first thing to be seen was the colour green. They disembarked, stepping on a field of countless, tiny green plants. Sasha knelt, hands still bound, and ran a hand across the surface. One of the Subjects with them joined her, equally fascinated.

"I... what is this crop?" she asked.

"Very funny," another soldier said, "it's just grass. I mean, feel free to eat it if you really want, I'm not about to stop you. What are you, a goat?"

Without standing, Sasha turned to the soldier. "What's a goat? Are you making fun of me? You're talking like it, I think."

Tara looked around. The grass went for a couple dozen metres in most directions. On one edge was a two-story building. Around all of it was an imposingly high fence with a top edge encrusted with barbed wire. The fencing was thin enough that you could easily see through it. Beyond the fence, patches of this 'grass' could be seen, but not consistently, and most of it less green. Most of the terrain outside the fence was rocks and cement, much of it broken, much of it charred. Further out, buildings could be seen. Short ones nearby, getting taller farther off. Some reached higher than Station Four was deep. All of them damaged, most of them charred.

"War..." Tara whispered. "Did war happened *here*?"

The first soldier looked out across the ruinous cityscape. "Officially it wasn't a war. But yeah. Pretty much. Nano-based stuff. Bodies walking around attacking others? it was sick. Had to be burnt."

"Sasha," Messenger said softly.

Sasha was still kneeling. A handful of grass she'd been caressing was now ripped up in her trembling fist. The oddity of this thing called grass could only distract her from the wide-open space for so long.

Tara looked to the first soldier. "Can we get in that building? Like now? Sasha and open spaces..."

"That's where we're headed," the soldier replied.

"Sash, go for it!" Tara said.

Sasha stood, took a huge gasp, fighting tears, and with bound hands dashed towards the building. The second soldier raised his stun-weapon. "Runner!"

Messenger stood in front of him. "Are you kidding? There's a fence."

The soldier fired anyway, right into Messenger. The charged pellet bounced off Messenger's chest, but not before transmitting the charge. Messenger collapsed.

"*Neil!*" Tara cried. Sasha was watching, having already made it into the building, less than a yard past the door. "*What happened?!*" she screamed to them.

"He'll be fine," the first soldier said, "Idiot." Who that comment was intended for wasn't clear. He looked to the second soldier. "Okay, Mister *quick-shot*, you get the feet, we'll get him onto a cot."

The two soldiers who'd been in the front of the truck were now with them, and as a group, they all went to the building. Messenger, unconscious, was carried. Tara thought she was leading the procession, eager to get to Sasha, but one of the Soldiers made it his business to be in front. When they got there, and got in the door, Sasha grabbed onto Tara. "Why, why, why..."

Tara could only squeeze back and watch as Messenger was laid out on a cot.

The first cot of hundreds and hundreds, arranged in close quarters.

And there was a second floor.

All empty.

For the moment.

"Alright Colonel," Sergeant Berryhill told Colonel Mangual over the comm, "The elevator's got juice again. It was a simple bypass in theory, but the actual work on it was a pain."

"So, we've got full control of the facility?" the Colonel asked.

"Not even close. The elevator was possible because the power source and the elevator's motor are both at the top. Other systems are still controlled from the bottom. They can shut off any other system; lights, water and air pumps, and who knows what else," Berryhill explained. "Any other system we want to safeguard has to be bypassed one by one. We can spend some time securing the lights on the top floor, but to secure any other floors, I need to be able to sniff around on them each to see how, and where it's wired in."

"Well, that sucks," the Colonel said, "but no, that's fine. I doubt these people have any sort of night vision."

"Night vision was invented in 1939," Berryhill said, being the type to know such things, "plenty early enough before this facility was closed off. And given the climate at the time, they might have just been paranoid enough to get some."

The Colonel paused. "Is that so. I don't know, how likely is that?"

"Good point, I guess. I suppose I would have heard about it when I first got here, and they were in the dark."

"And anyway, even if they all had it," the Colonel said, "they don't have weapons to speak of."

"We... we are only stunning them at most, right?" Berryhill asked.

"We're certainly not here to kill them, we're trying to help."

"Of course, Colonel. ...Some of them don't seem too interested in help though."

The Colonel scoffed. "We're dealing with over a thousand uneducated... savages, in all honesty. And five hundred people or so who were content to keep them that way. We need to secure this zoo."

With the Grand Elevator alive once again, fifty well-armed soldiers piled on, and headed down.

At Citizenry, no Citizens were there waiting to board and leave. Instead, the Citizens near the loading bay witnessed ten soldiers disembark, carrying a larger weapon, about the size of an arm, as well as the smaller stun-weapons. They also wore a bulky addition on top of their already-bulky helmets. The new additions had eyes. These dormant, metal and glass eyes were only slightly colder than the human eyes below.

"What's this?" Cody asked. "The Grand Elevator looks pretty full of you people already." He wanted to ask where Leena was, but there was a chance that asking might but her in more danger. If she was still sneaking, Cody didn't need to let them know she was out there.

"Just doing a comprehensive patrol," the lead soldier of the ten said as the Grand Elevator continued down with the other forty soldiers, "We're asking that everyone in this section remain on it for the time being, to ensure everyone's safety."

"Riiiiiight..." said Cody, "got it."

At Provider-level, another ten of the heavily armed soldiers got off. They were greeted by a pair of Providers and Lenth. Lenth asked, "You fellas seen a Provider named Gabe, who went off with one of your people, Berryhill? Or do you know where Messenger is?"

"Sorry sir," said this soldier-group's leader, as the Grand Elevator left these ten troops behind, and continued down with the other thirty soldiers, "I'm afraid I don't have that information. We're asking that everyone in this section remain on it for the time being, to ensure everyone's safety."

"Riiiiiight..." said Lenth, "got it."

At Engineering level, the remaining thirty soldiers moved into the loading bay. A row of empty clothing hooks lined the left wall. Ahead, a barricade of slightly-damp, taupe steel barrels greeted them, as well as Kevin's face peeking out from a gap near the top.

"Nice outfits," Kevin said. "Are you fellas here to tell us when Tara and Sasha are getting back? It's been a lot longer than we were expecting. We were told you might be coming, though."

The lead soldier answered back, "We're here to ensure that the facility's operations are secure. In the interests of public safety. Please remove the barricade."

Kevin looked to the side, to someone unseen behind the barricade, and said quietly. "He's here for safety. Yup. Kinda how I saw it." Kevin turned back to the soldiers with a smile. "Yeah, no thank you. We've been maintaining this facility for a long time, and things are secure here. I'm guessing it was one of your friends that cut our connection to the Grand Elevator. That's not safe. Also, I don't feel like moving these barrels again; they're heavy cuz they're filled with water. Water from the cooling pool. The one where we keep the depleted uranium – so, you know, handle at your own risk. I'm a professional."

Kevin flipped down his Rubberman suit's mask, completing his hazard suit. "So, you can leave, see ya!" Kevin's now-masked face disappeared from the gap, immediately replaced with a box to seal the gap.

The soldiers didn't need to know that the vast majority of the water in the cooling pool was entirely harmless. The pool was now a bit lower than it technically should be, but the risk was low, especially for what was hoped to be a short duration.

"Yeah, okay, now what?" Kevin said to a nearby Engineer, suited up just as Kevin was, as were the nearest twenty Engineers.

At that moment, a 'foomp' sound came from the other side of the barricade, and a canister barged through the box in the gap. The canister rested on the middle of the room and started belching out purple smoke.

Kevin looked at the smoke canister, and said *"Son of a crap-sniffer!"* He tapped the filter on his mask, and pointed vigorously at the gap in the barricade, and yelled, *"Am I a joke to you?!"*

He picked up the canister, hands quite safe in his gloves, and shoved it back out the gap. *"Guys, I think this is yours!"* He turned to the other Engineers. "Okay, they asked for it. Let's do the thing, and then the other thing. Same time."

The solders were debating their next move, when the lights went out. Before they could get their night-vision goggles in place, they heard a half dozen near-simultaneous blunt impacts right in front of them, along with the sound of tremendous rush of water.

"Back! Into the lift! Radiation hazard!" yelled one soldier.

"Damned feral caveman!" Hollered another.

As they fumbled, lights went back on. Sure enough the six top barrels lay open at the foot of the barricade, their watery contents spilled toward the soldiers. This formed a barrel-high gap in the top of the barricade, which Engineers were already busy filling with more barrels using the 'picker' used for hauling moderate loads around. (And as of today, used to dip barrels into the cooling pool to fill them.)

Lacking proper protective gear for radiation, (or a Geiger counter,) the soldiers officially retreated, and headed up on the Grand Elevator.

For now, Engineering had won.

Tara sat by the window, looking out across the yard to the gate of the outer fence. Citizens were being herded in from the large aircraft that brought them. Sasha watched from behind Tara, where she felt a bit safer.

"Well, Colonel Mangual told us we'd be with *the others*." cried one of the Citizens that had initially come on the truck.

Tara, Sasha, and Messenger stood watching the Citizens being unloaded. "What do you think," Messenger asked no one in particular as the new crowd of Citizens were steered closer, "a hundred?"

The behemoth of an aircraft lifted away, presumably to get the next load.

"Less," Tara said. "Looks like. I don't know. It's hard to tell from here."

The crowd had eight soldiers surrounding them, but when they got closer, it could be seen that the front solder was carrying some kind of case. He stopped just inside the door, asking the everyone to back away. Other soldiers already in the building were nearby to enforce co-operation.

With the new batch of Citizens outside, the case was unfolded onto a table. The soldier managing it turned to the prisoners already here, and picked Tara, being closest. "Okay, may as well be you first."

"What is this?" Tara asked.

"The bunch of you in that hole have been out of contact with the world, and are out of sync with immunities. This is going to catch you up so you're not killed by the latest version of the flu or something."

Tara sighed, and put out her arm. The soldier placed a cylinder's smooth-looking square tip against her skin, and less than a second later, it beeped.

"Okay, when does it jab–"

The soldier smirked. "You people still use needles down there?" He then stamped her hand with ink. It was a black mark of a circle with a check-mark in it. "Alright, next."

Sasha stepped up next, and was processed without a word.

Messenger went next. "How much fluid is in that shot that it's so quick and painless?"

"Fluid? No fluid, just a tiny flake of carbon. Okay, move along, next."

"What do you mean, a tiny–"

"Next!"

With unfelt flecks of carbon and an inky stamp on their hands, Tara, Sasha, and Messenger stepped aside, finding a few cots to make their own in the far corner by one of the staircases to the second floor.

Tara looked at the spot she was 'not-jabbed'. There was a slight, tiny mark. Small enough she would never have noticed if she wasn't looking for it. Even now, she wondered if this tiny dent wasn't just a naturally-occurring flaw in the surface of her skin. "Sash, can I see yours?"

Sasha complied, and they both sat on one of the cots together. Tara held Sasha's hand, and gently brought it closer to the light from a nearby window. "Yeah, I think I see it. Same," Tara said, "Didn't hurt you either?"

"No," Sasha said, reclaiming her wrist to look at it herself.

"They certainly have developed many interesting technologies," Messenger said, "though they've had... over a century."

"I guess we have a lot of catching up to do. Not just our immunities," Sasha said quietly.

"The one soldier mentioned a lot of words I'd not heard before," Messenger said, "Neutron and nano stuck out the most to me."

As Citizens trickled in, several were heard to complain about the process of being processed, and just as many seemed to be still in shock over the outside world. Statements like, "Wow, I thought *Commons* had a high ceiling!" and such could be heard.

One Citizen was hyperventilating and crying. Sasha perked up. "He sounds like he has the same problem as me," she said. Looking over into the crowd, the panicking Citizen could be seen. A friend had their arm around him and was trying to comfort him. Whether he was agoraphobic, or just generally distressed was difficult to say for sure. Many of the Citizens could be described as looking 'generally distressed'.

One Citizen looked particularly pissed off. "I better get my knife back." It was Leena. Messenger walked over after Leena had been processed. "Leena, are you all right?"

"Ughf, Messy, they got you, too?" Leena had a bruise on her left cheek. "Yeah, when they found me, they didn't like my knife," she turned to the solders at the door. "*Which I want back! I earned that thing!*" The soldiers ignored her, continuing with intake processing.

"You fought them?" Messenger asked.

"Can't really call it a fight," Leena said. "Those friggin' stun-things... I would have taken the three of em if they had to get a little closer."

Gabe emerged from the crowd, freshly processed. "So you would have won in a knife-fight, three on one? Hi, Messenger."

"These outsiders aren't so hot," Leena grumbled.

Messenger led Gabe towards the corner that he, Tara, and Sasha had colonized, and Leena followed along, inviting herself.

"Gabe, what's going on back home?" Messenger asked.

Gabe looked at the stamp on his hand. "These fellas are taking in as many people as they can. That thing we flew in on? They have more, and they intend to fill em."

"They're saying home isn't safe," Leena added. "Most of these Citizens came willingly. I doubt they all will. I didn't."

"They're making it sound like it's your idea," Gabe said to Messenger.

Messenger scoffed, and held up his hand to show his stamp. "I'd say not!"

"*Those crap-sniffers!*" Tara snarled.

"*That's what I said!*" Leena agreed, pointing to Tara. "I don't know how fast they're going to be bringing any more of us in though. I called Engineering right before these crap-sniffers got me, and warned 'em. I overheard the Grand Elevator got shut down."

"Kevin's a good boy," Sasha said, giving Tara a squeeze.

"The heck?" Leena asked, pointing at Tara and Sasha, "Is he your two's son or something? How's *that* work?"

Tara chuckled. "Nah, he's... well, with Sasha and I *here*, he's in charge of Engineering right now, I guess."

"And with *me* here," Gabe said, "I have no idea who's calling the shots for the Providers right now. Lenth isn't really qualified, and Contact... who knows what's up with him right now?"

"I left the Citizens with Cody in charge," Leena said. "Aww, sounds like those boys are gonna need us back. What say we bust the hell outta here? These outsiders have their funny stunny things, but they're officially outnumbered here now! If we rally the Citizens here, we can rush em, get some of those stun things for ourselves–"

"–And then?" Tara interrupted, "go for a walk in this?" She gestured to the burnt husk of a city outside the camp on its rim. "And walk home? Which direction, how far, and with what water?"

Leena growled. "We... we force one of them to fly us back in one of those big things!"

"And then what?!" Messenger hollered, quickly composing himself. "Even if that worked, to which I have serious doubts, they know where we live, so it wouldn't be the last of it."

"And we'd still have to face our electrical issue," Tara added.

Growling mainly to herself, Leena said, "I wanna punch one of them. Repeatedly. I gotta do something for Cody, and Jen, and Patricia, and all the others. This is going to get worse."

"Sergeant Berryhill," came Colonel Mangual's voice and visage over the terminal in Berryhill's utility vehicle, "is there anything more you can do right now at Station Four?"

Berryhill sighed heavily. "The elevator's working safely, you can keep... extracting people. The Engineers haven't seen fit to shut down the lights to slow you down, probably figured too many people could get hurt."

"But it's still a possibility, and there's still that old generator that could be any manner of hazard," the Colonel stated.

"True. But until we gain access, it's a moot point. That is, I can't do anything about it."

"How would you feel about half your team going on a little milk-run? Some easy installation work."

"Splitting us up?"

"Just for one task. I still want some of your team on-hand at Station Four to move quickly if things change in regards to access to Engineering."

"... All right then, who needs a lightbulb changed?"

"The camp needs some media. A way for me to communicate to them as a group remotely, and while we're at it, a bit of entertainment to keep our guests busy, and perhaps mitigate undue restlessness."

Camp. Guests. Berryhill covered his mouth, and struggled to process. He finally came forth with something the Colonel would want to hear. "Yeah. Yup, I can swing by Yute Central, pick up some hardware, and... yeah. Yeah, no problem. Can I hitch a ride in the air? It would make things a lot faster. It'd slow down the evacuation, but given other factors jamming things up, I don't think giving me a ride would be that big of a hiccup."

"Very well, I'll authorize that, and let the pilots know. I leave it to you, Sergeant!"

The Colonel disconnected, leaving a black screen.

Berryhill went into the utility vehicle's cramped mess, where the other three members of his team were. "Okay, did any of you hear?"

"Aye," Tavish said, "oo's goin' whar, nae?"

"You and Muir are staying here, Laird, you're with me on this 'milk run'. So the two of you, get what you need, and get out. You're attached to Station Four operations without Laird and me until we get back."

"Ah thought ye were flyin'?" Tavish said.

"Yeah, but I might need the truck," replied Berryhill.

Laird snorted. "You're driving this thing onto one of those choppers?"

Berryhill nodded, "and taking up about two-thirds the chopper's cargo capacity while wasting its time, running around to base before getting to camp with a third of the 'guests' it was originally going to take. Anyone have a problem with that?"

"Sir, no sir, Sir the third, Sir!" laughed Muir.

"Good, now get outta my truck."

With Muir gathering her necessities, and Tavish fumbling along gathering his, Berryhill and Laird soon drove up to a half-loaded cargo helicopter, which had already put down the big ramp. Berryhill had called the ahead to the flight crew. They weren't expecting the utility vehicle, but

Berryhill explained that the Colonel *probably* neglected to mention it, because *obviously* everyone would know he'd need it. *Obviously.* No need to confirm with the Colonel, she'd just think you were an idiot for not realizing that *obviously* he'd need the truck.

"So," Laird asked, "why precisely are we being irritants? We could have just drove."

"Yeah... I don't know...maybe I just wanted to slow things down. Give the Colonel a little extra time to think. A forced evacuation seems a bit reactionary, don't you think?"

"Isn't Station Four a big hazard?" Laird asked.

Berryhill scrunched his mouth to the side, and tilted his head. "Sure, I'd like to get a closer look at the state of that generator. It's probably a mess, but it's that deep below everything else on purpose. The only people in much risk from it...even if it blows, is anyone on that bottom floor."

"And what about those.. 'Subject' people? Aren't they basically slaves?" she asked.

"And that Messenger guy seems to get that. I mean, they are slowly doing something about it, in their own way. I just don't think yanking them all out willy-nilly is necessarily the best move. Sounds familiar." Berryhill thumbed a strand of his coloured hair – colours only permitted with uniform due to his Aguei heritage.

Laird scrunched her mouth. "That bad?"

"I don't know," Berryhill said, "but a little extra time to ponder it might be good for everyone."

Once at Yute Central, Berryhill and Laird went shopping for gear. A screen befitting auditorium use, an independent net media server to hook it up to, a modest little filled capacitor to run it all from, and a personal tablet terminal.

While they were there, they restocked the truck's food and general supplies. Such a pity it meant delaying the chopper just that much longer.

"She's in the building somewhere, you know," Laird said.

"It's a big base," Berryhill answered. "She has better things to do than come harass two troops just doing their duty."

"Right. You're not being subversive at all or anything."

"Just doing my duty!"

Eventually, they were back to the chopper, back in the truck, and airborne. They soon made it to camp, and drove out of the helicopter. The visage of the camp was laid out before them. With the horror of the burnt, fallen city of Meston behind it all, the fenced-in compound housed a weathered two-story building, with lost souls, men, women, and children milling about with no direction or hope, each with a mark on their hand as a smattering of soldiers kept order.

"It *is* that bad," Berryhill whispered.

He and Laird parked by the front door of the building, and began unloading the equipment. They were waved in by the posted guards, and set up the screen between the two staircases.

"Hey! It's that coloured guy!" Leena declared. Loudly. A number of eyes in the room landed on Messenger, who was himself was looking at Berryhill's brightly coloured hair.

"You can't just *say* that," Laird hissed.

Messenger nodded. "Yes, he's clearly been coloured, but I believe his hair is part of his culture. You need to show more respect."

Laird squinted, looked at Berryhill's hair, looked at Leena, and looked at the very dark-skinned Messenger. "Sure, whatever." she mumbled softly, going back to securing the screen.

"Messenger," Berryhill said, looking over his shoulder as he walked over. He pulled the tablet terminal out, and showed it to Messenger. "This has access to the general web. There's all sorts of information, whatever you think you need to learn about darn near."

"Ooh, I definitely want a turn," Tara said.

Berryhill nodded. "I've saved some leads that might be of interest. Not that It's in my authority to recommend anything... in fact, oh, where did you get that terminal?" Berryhill handed the tablet terminal to Tara. "I didn't give it to you, I worked on that big screen the whole time I was here," Berryhill said, "I might not have even said anything to you while I was here. I might not have recommended anything saved on that thing."

The soldiers guarding the door were beginning to take notice. Tara read the look Berryhill gave her, and she discreetly kept the tablet terminal out of direct view of the guards.

"Sarge," Laird quietly said to Berryhill, "I've padded this job as much as I can. Are you done?"

"Yeah, I think so." Berryhill moved over closer to the newly installed screen. "All right, everyone," he said louder to no one in particular, "I was just discussing programming options with your Messenger fellow, here, and it seems like a lot of you might get a lot out of documentaries. A couple lovely ones I was suggesting were the rain forest nature thing, or ocean life. Any preferences from the group?"

Messenger played along, but none of the intended audience knew what a rainforest or an ocean was, so the group response was primarily blank stares.

"Maybe this group isn't ready for high-definition, big-screen shark attacks, Sarge." Laird said.

"Good point. Cute froggies and lemurs or whatever it is, then." Berryhill turned to the screen. "Media, find a rain forest documentary."

The screen popped to life, and an array of titles slid into place with thumbnail title cards. The Citizens were fascinated already.

"Attenborough? Really?" Berryhill murmured. "Okay, media, play the first one."

As the screen went black, and opening title credits began appearing, Laird made a disclaimer. "Just so you all know, Colonel Mangual, our boss, can interrupt this to talk to you all at any moment, but don't be shocked if this gets interrupted by some lady in –"

Music was beginning to swell, and a soothing narrator was speaking as a close-up of a frog blinked. The audience was a mix of awe, fascination, and quiet horror.

"I think you lost em, Laird," Berryhill said. He turned to the guard by the door. "You good to be DJ here? Keep it easy-end educational and stuff?"

The guard nodded.

Berryhill turned to the Citizens. "We all good?" He was mainly interested in the responses from Tara and Messenger, who gave subtle nods.

The Citizens gasped as a fly was struck by the frog's tongue in vivid, widescreen, slow motion.

Laird and Berryhill looked across this improvised class. Exposed to so many new things, it was easy to momentarily envy the experience, until they turned around and saw the guard. Saw the fence. Saw the huge helicopter landing with involuntary additions to the student body.

Berryhill made eye contact with Messenger and Tara, and tugged on a handful of his coloured hair.

It was time to go.

Chapter 22:

The Fall Of The Bottom

Once the troops were suited properly, and equipped properly, knocking over the barricade protecting Engineering was simple enough. Very mildly radioactive water spilled the other direction this time, flooding around Kevin's feet. A few other Engineers stood around with him.

No weapons had been prepared by the Engineers, for they knew that ultimately, they were soundly outnumbered; that even if thirty outsiders were defeated, there were many more willing to avenge them.

Instead, Kevin stood his ground, gloved hands up.

The first soldier through the line shot Kevin with a stun-gun. The pellet bounced off the rubber, radiation-proof suit.

Kevin looked up at the soldier through his mask, and said, "What? It's *obvious* what I'm wearing! I mean...! Not that I want to be shot with anything stronger, but it looks like we're *functionally* wearing the *same thing*. First you tried to gas me *seconds* after you see me put the mask on–"

The soldier heaved a heavy punch at Kevin, wrenching the mask off.

Kevin slipped, and fell to the wet floor with his mask landing beside him.
"Too much sass? That was too much sass, wasn't it?"

Meanwhile on Provider levels, the military had kept watch over the loading bay connecting it to the Grand Elevator shaft. Lenth had given up trying to talk to them. They provided no useful information, and nothing overly reassuring.

Gabe was missing, Messenger was missing, and the Grand Elevator had been busier than Lenth had ever known it to be. Lenth was known to be somewhat chummy with Messenger, and random Providers asked him questions for which he didn't have any answers for.

Sitting around wasn't getting anything done, so he headed down into the Manager level. It was still swimming with Subjects no longer confined to their Units, but the chaos had subsided.

Many Subjects had settled back to their own Units – or at least, *some* Unit. The Subjects that came back down from Elise's adventure returned with stories of the outsiders and their huge flying thing that wouldn't even fit in any room they'd ever known *except* that huge bright room that seemed to be endless.

The wonder this sparked among other Subjects was tempered by the threat of the big thing dropping outsiders that would chase them down. Debate and speculation was everywhere, and the outsiders were becoming as popular of a topic as the Subjects' new (if limited) freedoms. They talked about meeting other Subjects, and compared experiences of their Units.

They also talked about their Rubbermen or women – the Managers – who by now, had pretty much all unmasked themselves. A few Managers who had been less kind, and had been quick with electric discipline, avoided their Subjects or locked themselves away.

Down the corridor, a voice was heard above the quiet murmurings, "Okay! Fine! If that's so weird, what do *you* have between your legs?!" Lenth headed in that direction just in case something needed to be broken up, but by the time he got half way there, it was obvious that a Manager was among the eight or more Subjects, and things were proceeding in a fairly civil manner.

Lenth made eye contact with the familiar Manager, and cast them an inquisitive glance. The Manager returned a bemused, reassuring smile, and Lenth was satisfied that things were as orderly as could be expected.

Order. Some would have to be enforced at some point. Enforced? Encouraged maybe? Some order was needed, but the balance would be a task and a half. When did this become his job? It'd be handy to have Gabe around right around now. Things could get looking like the old Citizenry if things weren't handled well.

As Lenth approached the Unit managed by his love, Karen, he noticed a slightly higher density of Subjects wandering around, and almost all of them were munching on papayas.

He let himself into Karen's space, and found her reading her nursery rhyme book to seven or so random Subjects, all hanging around and chomping papayas.

"Okay, this is odd," Lenth said.

"Oh hi!" Karen greeted, pausing in the little book. "Odd is normal now," she chuckled. "You've read this book, right? Doesn't make a lick of sense, but they like it."

"Yeah," one of the Subjects said with his mouth full, "This Jack guy gets into a lot of trouble. My Unit grows beans, and it sounds like we need to be more careful. And this cow thing? She's got a picture of it, it looks terrifying!"

"Yeah, I'd trade *that thing* for beans any day!" another Subject said.

"Down with beans! Up with papayas!"

Karen chuckled. "I bet the Units that grow beets aren't dealing with this kind of situation."

"*Oh crap!*" another Subject said, "I had a bite of one of those beet things before I came here! They put those things in our food! Man, no more of *that* for me. Papaya from now on, thank you very much!"

Lenth had a laugh. "All the stuff we grow is needed by your body to stay healthy, that's why it all gets put into the food disks."

A Subject rolled her eyes,and took another bite of her papaya. "that sounds like the talk of a woman who's never had a papaya," she mumbled.

"I'm not a woman." Lenth said with a smirk.

"Pfft, 'man', whatever. Just a woman that's flat in the wrong areas."

"*Anyway,*" Lenth said to Karen, "I was going to see if you wanted to come with me to go snooping, but I can see you've got a busy day ahead of you."

"Snooping?" Karen said with a slight frown, "You've been pretty much everywhere. What needs snooping? You're not going to do anything stupid, are you?"

"Nah. Probably not. Just with the strangers blocking off the loadi–"

"I've heard all about them. Leave it alone," Karen said sternly.

"Yeah, well, they're not leaving us alone. I just... I just want to know what they're doing. It might be nothing worth worrying about. I might find Messenger and he explains everything. If I don't... then I'll find something worth knowing. No risky stuff, though, okay?"

Karen grunted. "Take a damned papaya. No, screw that, I'm coming with you!"

"Hon... what about the Subjects?" Lenth asked,

"Oh, we can come along!" a Subject said.

"I might have to be sneaky," Lenth said, "that's pretty hard if there's ten of us."

"Two is plenty," Karen added.

"And leave the farm unattended for everyone to eat all the papayas?" Lenth asked.

"So we have to make a run of food disks light on papaya," Karen argued. "Big deal, they're getting the nutrients anyway, apparently."

"And if the farm gets damaged, and we lose half the ability to grow these nutrients for thousands of people?"

"You used to be fun, Lenth," Karen joked.

"I was *never* fun!" Lenth replied.

"I *make* you fun," Karen answered, "I make fun of you all the time."

Lenth pulled Karen closer and kissed her head. "Be good."

"Be careful," Karen responded, "dork."

Making his way to the maintenance hatch on the Manager level, Lenth was relieved to find the guards there were a pair of Providers, and not surface strangers. They had two of the stun-sticks with them.

"What news?" One of them asked Lenth.

"No change at the loading bay," Lenth said. "No one in or out since the ten strangers came. Any news here?"

"Nothing special. Now and then a curious Subject comes by and starts asking questions. If any of them get pissy about being let through, it's generally not long before another Subject comes by to tell them about the incident up top, and that tends to calm things down pretty quick. Haven't needed the stun-sticks so far. I doubt many of the Subjects know what they are, anyway."

"No noise from outside?" Lenth asked.

"Not beyond the sound of the Grand Elevator going by now and then," the Provider replied. "I don't think the strangers have noticed these hatches exist."

"Understandable," Lenth said, looking upwards, as if he could see into the loading bay one floor up. "The hatches kind of blend in with all the other junk on the walls. Excuse me, I want to take a peek."

The Provider guards stepped out of the way. "Keep an eye out, never know when that elevator's coming back."

"Sure." Lenth pushed out and looked down the Grand Elevator's shaft. The next stop down was Engineering, but it was a great enough distance that it wasn't easy to discern between the roof of the elevator, or the floor of the shaft.

No, wait... part of it was darker than usual. Like a stain spreading from the direction of the door. He pushed through the hatch a little farther so he could look up. He could see the lip of the Provider-level loading bay, and farther up he could see the Grand Elevator itself, departing from Citizenry, heading up. He went back in, making sure the hatch door didn't slam shut.

"What did you see?" asked one of the Providers.

"Elevator going from Citizenry, headed to Actual-level, and something weird might be going in at Engineering."

"Weird?"

"Looks like some kind of spill? Not a ton, not enough to cover the entire floor. At least that how it looks from up here. I think I'm going to do have a look."

"What?" The Provider blurted, "on the ladder?"

"Yeah. I've done it before, down is a lot easier than up." Lenth looked their stun-sticks up and down. "Hey, you guys have two, and you said you weren't even using them..."

"What, going down the ladder all that way is too easy? Going to do it one-handed?"

"Huh." Lenth took one of the stun-sticks, and shoved it down his collar, pushing it down his back and along his side. He fumbled with his pocket, tuning it inside out, then put the bottom end of the stun-stuck in his inside out pocket from the inside. "There!"

"Wow," one of the Providers said sarcastically as the other end of the stick scraped the ceiling. "Looks like super easy for ladder time. Want me to tie your ankles together? Maybe blindfold you?"

"Yeah... I won't fit through the hatch with this." With some difficulty, Lenth yanked it back out. "You're going to have to feed it down my collar once I'm on the ladder."

"You're bonkers. Fine."

Before Lenth was half way out the hatch, Elise made herself known. "Can I come? I want to come."

"And you are?" Lenth whispered, mostly through the hatch now.

"I'm Elise, I farm wheat, and I saw the outside, and... I want to see it again."

"Shh, be quiet, they're right above me. I'm going the other direction, Elise. We can talk about outside after we deal with these ... well, outsiders."

"Fine, I'll help," Elise whispered, matter-of-factly.

"This might involve fighting."

"I've fought with my Sisters plenty enough!" Elise said, holding a fist forward defiantly.

"They might want to kill you." Lenth said.

In response, Elise held *both* fists out defiantly. "Or maybe I should go get a spade."

"No. You have no idea what's going on down there, and you're not even taking this seriously. Go bug Karen for a papaya or something."

Elise stood quietly until the shock-stick was back in Lenth's care, and he was about to start climbing down, then she stepped forward to crawl out after him.

"Go back!" Lenth whispered.

Elise shook her head. "Shh!" She smiled, pointed at Lenth, then herself, then down the Grand Elevator shaft.

Lenth pointed back into the hatch. Where were those Providers? How'd they let her through?

Elise smiled, and pointed down.

Lenth pointed to the hatch again.

Elise leaned back, one hand on the ladder, the other by her mouth, and inhaled deeply, ready to holler. Lenth made a '*Tch!*' sound, tapping her ankle. Elise looked down. Lenth didn't point at the hatch, only scowled, and started climbing down.

Elise's steps were jaunty and loud. After 2 of them, Lenth made the *tch* sound again, and mimed soft steps with his fingers, and mouthed the word 'soft'. He looked up and listened for any outsiders at the loading bay. The door must have been shut, or they had moved further in.

The span between the Subject level and Engineering was the longest span in the facility for safety reasons. It was difficult to be grateful for climbing down being easier than up, when every step down meant that he'd eventually have to take the step back up. The closer they got to the bottom, the clearer it became that Lenth had guessed right; it was some kind of spill. There was no particularly strong smell coming up to them, so *that* much was encouraging, not that radiation had a smell.

Each step down gave time to theorize, and grow concerned. At least when they got to the Engineering loading bay, they could grab a Rubberman suit if they found more reason to be worried about contaminants.

They arrived at the loading bay. The row of hooks, half of which were usually in use to hold a radiation-graded Rubberman suit, were all empty. The floor was wet enough that any hasty steps made quiet little splashes. Near the far end of the bay stood about half of Kevin's barricade. Some of the barrels that *used* to be part of the barricade were visible beyond. Voices could be heard in that direction, too.

Lenth looked back to make sure Elise wasn't about to do anything reckless. As they moved to take advantage of the remaining barricade to hide, Lenth pulled the stun-stick from his clothing.

The voices seemed to be coming from the direction of the main control room.

"What a mess," came one of those voices. "Half this crap is ancient, and the rest may as well have been stuck on with duct tape. It's a wonder this whole place didn't crater decades ago."

"So can we get the tech guys in here now?"

"Nah. For one thing, half of them are at the camp doing who knows what, and we should probably get the locals out of here before we bring in Berryhill's people to poke around."

That was a terrifying thought. Secured them how exactly? Engineering had about a hundred and fifty or so people. They must be locked in their quarters. Lenth knew that a central room was ahead, and branching left from that was the control room, ahead was the decontamination lock to the reactor areas, and to the right was residential.

Lenth leaned out from cover to peek. The door to the decontamination lock was wide open. The spilled water was pretty much everywhere, but the floor grate of decontamination would have stopped it from going any further in that direction. Who knows how much of the floor in the control room was flooded? Was there anything electrical that would be exposed that low? Lenth didn't think so. Water going to residential wasn't a huge concern.

"Now what?" Elise whispered urgently.

"I'm thinking! We don't know how many outsiders are here. They locked in a hundred and fifty Engineers, probably most in residential. If they moved fast enough and are keeping the right doors shut... some had to still be in the reactor area, but if these outsiders are good enough, they probably got all the Engineers out of there."

"Let's beat them up! Use your fancy stick!" Elise quietly giggled.

"They probably have fancy sticks. Probably have better. I'm also worried they might have stuff that does a lot worse than stun you."

Elise's face flashed from enthusiastic energy, through puzzlement, to moderate existential horror. "Do you think they brought a *rake*? Those can mess you up! My one Sister got mad once, and now another Sister has some nasty marks on her arm that never really went away."

Lenth slowly turned to Elise, with narrowed eyes. "No. I do not think we have to worry about rakes."

"Well, phew! You had me worried!"

"It could be a lot worse," Lenth said. "If you want to go back, that might be best."

"Nuh uh. This is too cool. What is this place, anyway?"

"This is Engineering. The people who are usually here are the Engineers. Their main job is to run the electricity that keeps all out lights on, the Grand Elevator running, and a load of other things we need. I'm an Engineer, though I'm in training."

"The lights?" Elise smiled, eyebrows raised. "Y'all messed up bad a bit ago, huh?"

"Wasn't me, I was doing my side thing talking to Subjects."

"Maybe if you were here, y'all wouldn't have messed up so bad."

"I doubt it."

"Oh, so *you're* not good at that either."

"Look, I don't come to your beet farm and tell you–"

"Wheat."

"Whatever. We have other problems right now!"

"Shh."

Lenth signed, and closed his eyes. Things were pretty quiet out there. "Okay. If we're lucky, and don't get spotted by anyone in the control room, we can get to residential, overpower outsiders guarding things, if we're lucky, then of we can get people loose before any outsiders from the control room get involved, then we'll have the other Engineers to help."

"That's counting on a lot of luck," Elise whispered, "but it sounds good!"

Lenth looked at Elise's smiling face. "Yeah, it sucks. We should go get more Providers."

"Huh? That's not what I said!"

"That's what I heard. Let's go." Lenth began putting the shock-stick back in his clothes.

"*Up* the ladder?"

"Up the ladder."

"Ugh, why didn't you tell me not to come along?"

"These gazelles suck!" Leena hollered at the screen, "The cheetahs have faces full of knives and stuff, but frig! Throw a rock at them or something, you're losing so bad! That must be why they call them cheetahs, 'cause they *cheat!* Ever think of that? Go drink water by the.... nice-ahs!"

"You have a point," Gabe said, "The gazelles look to be taller than the cheetahs, you'd think they could make use of that to counter-attack. What are they even fighting over, anyway? Is it just the water? There was a lot of it, and it didn't look clean at all."

"Rust-flakes," Leena said, nodding. "Pretty ambitions to flavour that much water at once."

"Oh, look, those two seem to be friends. The cheetah is snuggled pretty close to that resting cheetah. Another cheetah-friend is –"

At that moment, the two cheetahs pulled on the gazelle's body, practically ripping it in half.

Leena, and nearly half the people watching the documentary screamed.

The narrator, whom almost no one was paying attention to anyway, continued on in the same calm tone. Soon it was obvious that the cheetahs were feeding.

"What kind of...!" Leena turned to the guards, "*What kind of thing are you showing us?!*"

One of the guards fought his amusement to explain. "That's nature! Animals eat each other! It's been like that for thou... millions of years."

"Well, why hasn't anyone stopped them?" Leena said. "I don't eat people, do you eat people?" She looked out the window to the fence holding hundreds of them in. "Seriously. Do you people... eat people?" she asked with caution.

"People don't eat people," the guard said. "I've had mammal meat a few times though. Cow. People used to eat a lot of them not long ago. Some countries still do."

"*Who the hell is mammal?!*"

The guard sighed. A good deal of the people watching the documentary looked distressed, even afraid. "Look, if you people aren't into this anymore, how about I put on some cartoon movie or something?"

"I don't know that that is," Leena said, "but if it doesn't involve eating people, that sounds okay."

"I'll try to choose something tame." He got up to be closer to the screen so it could hear him better. As he passed Leena, she was talking to herself primarily, trying to grasp the idea of eating animals or people. Before coming here, she'd only ever had the Station Four facility's food disks.

"Geez, I mean, I've killed people," Leena said quietly, "you know, rapists an' junk, but I didn't look at the body and think *'yummy'!* What kind of sicko...?"

The guard, wide-eyed, took a hard look at the energetic young lady who he'd just learned was some kind of homicidal vigilante – and wondered at how that didn't seem to unsettle any of the other people he was guarding.

"How about some kindergarten stuff?" he said, looking across the media terminal's offerings. "Here's something with a cute fox."

The people were fascinated with seeing their first cartoon character. The guard took this as an opening to play a series, and retreated to his station.

Leena looked at the show beginning, then to the guard. "Thanks, *guy-I-don't-know-the-name-of-who's-keeping-me-here-against-my-will*, I'm Leena."

The guard rolled his eyes, "Hi Leena, Just call me Corporal VonWaffles." he said, stealing a name from the cartoon.

"Ok, VonWaffles. Shh, we're watching the colourful thing."

"Oh for crying out loud, my name's not actually VonWaffles, it's Brandon H–"m

"Shh, VonWaffles, we're watching this."

In the corner, Tara and Messenger were focused on the tablet-terminal. Gabe was looking at it now and then, and listening, but his primary focus was being a barricade between the tablet and the guards' gaze. They didn't know if the guards would take it away, but Berryhill treated it like a secret, so it seemed wise to follow that example.

Sasha was cozied-up to Tara's side. This room was big, which on its own wasn't *too* bad, but the surrounding windows shared a view of that horrifying, infinite outdoors. Being near it was troubling before. Even back in the facility, being near the open cargo door was unsettling, but it wasn't typically for all that long. Sasha had a way to retreat in that situation. Usually.

Here, there was literally no escape. The closest she could find was to hide her face against Tara.

"Solar looks like our best option as far as I can see," Tara quietly said. "The Enemy can give us what we need. The windmills look difficult. I don't want to be on some huge ladder all the time. Those solar pads... that looks workable. It'd mean building some stuff outside. We could salvage quite a bit from Engineering that we can't make use of anymore. I mean, I'd need to learn more than what we seem to be able to get on this thing, but... it's a lead."

"Great," Messenger responded. "I'll see if Colonel Mangual will let us out and hand us a few thousand of those solar pads."

"How many of these guards and soldiers do you think we're dealing with?" Gabe quietly said over his shoulder, not neglecting his watch on the guards. "I mean, we've got a ton of Citizens here. They've been through some heavy crap, they're tough."

"It's not just the soldiers here, though," Tara said. "You didn't see their base. It's huge. They have a pile of those AirLimb things, and other flying things, and the base is under control of a thing called a General, which is like, Colonel Mangual's boss, and there's ... what did she say? Three Generals in this country?"

"Four," Messenger corrected, "and for that matter, no one said that our nearest General is even limited to that one base. There's billions of people out here, who survived our *not-war*, and we have no idea how many are against us."

"Or *with* us," Tara said, giving the terminal a tap.

"If Berryhill could have done more, I suspect he would have already," Messenger said.

"I like his hair," Sasha mumbled, "I wouldn't mind hair like that. Must be rare, I've never seen anyone else like that."

"He wasn't *born* with it," Messenger said. "He changed the colour, and the military let him because..." Messenger frowned at the tablet, searching his memory.

"What?" Tara asked, "because he asked nice? Maybe we just need to use better manners on Mangual."

"No..." Messenger said, poking at the terminal. "He made a point of telling me he was half... half something. Some kind of people that were here before Colonel Mangual's people. There was a conflict, and they made peace agreements, and..."

After a few tries, Messenger found the word "Aguei". He tried to ask the little terminal about the past, about the conflicts between the Aguei and the 'Northers'. Finally, he came across a picture.

A picture with no colour, but it plainly showed many people with black hair – men, women and children – dressed in the same drab clothes, kept in a fenced-in yard, with guards at the gate.

He, Tara, Sasha, and Gabe stared at the image.

"Berryhill wanted us to find this. This is help."

"You want us to all crawl down to help Engineering, while we have our own outsiders in our loading bay?" a Provider named Dawn said to Lenth in Contact's office. Dawn had been managing things with Gabe gone, and no one wanted to get Contact involved again.

"Well, that's just it," Lenth replied. "The outsiders aren't just sitting in their loading bay, they've gone in, busting through a barricade that it seems the Engineers set up. I'm worried about them. Have you called them recently?"

"I'll call them right now," the Dawn offered.

"Maybe you shouldn't. If they can't answer, you'd just be letting the outsiders there know we're thinking of them."

"And if like fifty of us all sneak down there, and find nothing wrong?"

"Then great," Lenth said. "If we're wrong, then we all come back. If we're right, but do nothing about it, they have their fingers on our lights and pumps."

"They already have that," Dawn said. "The capacitor is on Actual-level. if they wanted to stick us in the dark, they could have done that at any time."

"Well. Fine. But I'm still worried about the Engineers," Lenth said.

Dawn sighed with a shrug. "Well, if you can convince a pile of people who aren't doing anything to go with you down the ladder, I … well, what the heck would you all be walking *into* down there?"

Lenth looked down, grumbling. "I can imagine if a bunch of us rush them... if we had the numbers... some of us would get stunned. We have access to two stun-sticks? That gets us something."

"And if it gets you worse than stunned?"

Lenth thought about it, and thought of the Citizens who might start whipping out knives if the outsiders got aggressive with them – if it hadn't happened already. "They're not lined up at our loading bay and controlling the Grand Elevator for fun."

"I want answers, too, but is getting in their face the best way?" Dawn asked sincerely.

"They're already in our face, I think some answers are the least they can do." Lenth said.

"Ha. Then save yourself a climb, and ask the outsiders in our own loading bay," Dawn said.

Lenth nodded slowly as he thought about it. "But the ones up here are... peaceful, more or less. They're staying in the loading bay. If I went in too hard questioning them, could it end up making things worse here? And the Engineers still wouldn't be helped."

"Well, we know the outsiders have been making runs between Citizenry and topside," Dawn said, "and we know they've been causing some kind of trouble in Engineering. How long until they bump up activity here?"

"There's about five hundred Providers," Lenth said, "and just ten strangers in the Provider-level loading bay. They're better equipped, but... ten against five hundred?"

"Well now we just look stupid. We need to do this." Dawn said.

"Let me take … thirty? Providers with me through the Manager level, and down to Engineering." Lenth said.

"Take fifty," Dawn said. "I'll deal with our guests while the pack of you are on the ladder."

Gathering fifty willing Providers wasn't quite as easy as just asking the first fifty people Lenth ran into. For one thing, many Providers only had a vague understanding of what Engineering even was. As well, not every Provider was suitable to go on a raid. The especially old and especially young would be a liability more than a help, but as word of Dawn and Lenth's dual plans got around, the willing found their way to whichever goal they wanted to help with.

Lenth's mob was lining the halls, and organizing them was nearly impossible, but it felt like there were more than fifty planning on coming along. With plans being passed by word-of-mouth relay, more distant recruits were getting second- or third-hand information, but it was time to move.

Making his way down to Manager level, a steady stream of Providers followed Lenth through the darker, tighter Manager corridors. Most meandering Subjects got quickly out of the way when they saw a chain of yellow suits pushing along.

"You got some people!" Elise popped up by Lenth's side. "Gonna go fight those guys?"

"Probably," Lenth said, making room for Elise to walk alongside him.

"Can I come?" Elise chirped, "I can bring some of the friends I told about it all, they want to see, too."

"They might get hurt," Lenth warned.

"I can go get a rake," Elise offered.

"Oh crap, not the rake thing again!"

"You're right, that's a bit extreme. Spade?"

"Elise, your enthusiasm is great, but I have about fifty people behind me, I think we'll be okay. We can go exploring after this outsider business is taken care of."

Elise stopped, and the chain of Providers continued on by. "Oh. Well, okay. After the outsiders are taken care of."

Lenth and his followers reached the hatch to the Grand Elevator shaft. The guards there stood aside, and one by one they got on the ladder. As quietly as fifty or so people could, they climbed down the ladder; a stream of yellow-suited Providers. Most had not been in the shaft before.

Hesitation led to little stalls, breaking the flow here and there, but many found that once a few Providers were above them, turning back was not a readily viable option. Courage would have to prevail.

Shouts were heard above in the elevator shaft, muted by the door to the Provider loading bay. Dawn's attack was underway. If she rallied enough people, it could be over very quickly. Looks of confidence were traded up and down along the ladder. Relative silence was maintained by Lenth's group, and they continued down.

The spill at the bottom of the shaft had more or less dried, but the mark was still there. Peeking into the loading bay, nothing had evidently changed. The barricade was still there, compromised.

Lenth had tried to get a plan passed around before they'd departed, but how much got around accurately, and was still remembered, didn't matter much. It wasn't a complicated plan. Moving forward to the breach in the barricade, Lenth kept watch for outsider activity while Providers gathered behind him. Some idle chatter could be heard from the control room.

He stood in front of the Providers, and pointed to the reactor door, and shook his head, mouthing 'no'. He held out his hand to divide the group into two halves. He pointed to one half, and then in the direction of residential. He pointed to the other half of the group, and then in the direction of the control room. Lenth himself stood with the group going to residential.

He then whispered, "Okay, point where you're going." Most of them pointed correctly, a few needing to correct themselves, with their peers as example. "Okay, fast and quiet."

Lenth ran through the barricade, and could hear the group following. Not even looking towards the control room, he dashed down the residential hall. Two outsiders were found immediately, and saw Lenth coming with about twenty-five Providers backing him up. They outsiders went for their stun-weapons, and Lenth made it to the first outsider with his stun-stick before they could fire.

The first outsider dropped like a sack of compost, but the second outsider fired at Lenth, who fell on top of the first outsider.

This was about how he expected things to go. Darkness found him.

Meanwhile, Elise was intent to help, and quite a few enthusiastic Subjects were happy to follow. Sure, the two Provider guards at the hatch didn't seem to keen to let them through, but some Subjects were decidedly not interested in their opinion any more.

One of the Providers was telling the other that the Subjects should have been locked in their Units again as soon as it had been an option; that he thought Subjects running around loose in the Manager corridors had been asking for trouble.

The two Providers had one stun-stick between them. A particularly vigorous handful of Subjects who passed by Elise, lucked out and overpowered them. The hatch was open to all who cared to pass.

Elise stopped to check on the two roughed-up Providers. One was bleeding from his head. He didn't seem to want her help, but as the scuffle toned down, the Providers settled on just going out the hatch to see what the couple dozen Subjects were doing in the Grand Elevator shaft.

Elise went with them. Or at least, not far behind. By the time she got to the hatch, she'd lost count of how many Subjects had gone through. Many had come back in, terrified.

When Elise looked down, she saw many Subjects heading down. When she looked up, she saw about as many heading up.

"Hey folks, y'all are going the wrong way! We're helping that Lenth guy save other Provider-ish people called Engineers."

Only one of the Subjects that were climbing up paused, and only long enough to look down to Elise and holler, "Who?"

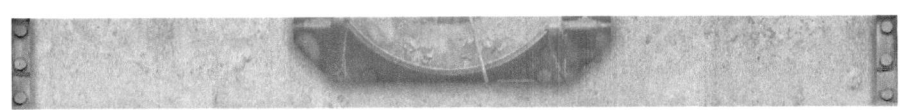

Chapter 23:

Hopeful

In the camp, Tara noticed a little '1' in the corner of the tablet's display. "That's new," she said. How long it had been there wasn't clear, but it had shown up at some point while she was reading about the operations and installation of solar pads. The information wasn't complete. She'd found a video but stopped it as soon as it started to make a sound. But at least she knew the information was out there.

And that '1' needed attention, apparently.

Tap.

The display changed to much like when Messenger typed a message to the Aguei.

'1' in the 'inbox'.

Office of Grand Elder Armil, RE: We are in a place like I saw in your past

Tara's eyes lit up, and she tapped on Messenger's lap. "They saw it! They sent something back?" she whispered.

Messenger nodded at the header expectantly, so Tara tapped it, still not sure if she was using the thing correctly.

Greetings, Mr. Neil.

Your message left us quite puzzled, but we investigated the existence of a camp operating in the region of the Meston ruins. Official channels were met with some resistance, but satellite imagery has shown us enough to put pressure on federal contacts to address your apparent situation.

We do not at this point fully understand your situation, but it is obviously worth understanding better. Prime Minister Leon has been advised that an Aguei envoy will be visiting the Meston camp. Expect us within twenty-four hours.

Regards,
Caitlin Aubrey,
Counsel to Grand Elder Armil.

"I don't understand half of that," Messenger said, "but it sounds decidedly hopeful!"

"Mr. Neil?" Tara asked.

"The thing wanted a 'last name'," Messenger explained, "and my last name before I was Messenger was Neil. I don't know where the '*Mr*' thing came from. Oh, I see. It must be short for *Messenger*."

Tara nodded. "Then we wait, I guess. I'm going to keep looking for solar stuff."

Meanwhile in the middle of the room, the bulk of the interned Citizens were still watching cartoons on the big media screen.

"That place looks great!" Leena blurted out, "Hey, Corporal VonWaffles! I wanna go there!"

The guard sighed. "For the last time, that's not really my name, and you can't go to places in cartoons, they're not real."

"Sure, sure, VonWaffles, so how come I can see it?! Ever think of that?"

Lenth opened his eyes, finding himself in his own bed in Engineering. His strength was slow to return, but a few brisk little exercises got the fog mostly cleared away. It was a great relief to find his door not locked, or barricaded, or anything. In the hall, he soon saw an Engineer, and asked, "Hey, what's go–"

"Hey! We like... just put you in there!" the Engineer answered, "You feeling okay? I'm told you were like the first person the outsiders stunned when you all ran in!"

"Their stun-thingies must be a lot different than our stun-sticks," Lenth said, "I've never heard of a stun-stick knocking someone out. But, yeah, I think I'm okay. Anyone else stunned? Anyone hurt? And where are the outsiders now?"

"Eight more Providers were stunned in this wing, and ten in the control room. A jaw got dislocated there, too. A bunch of scrapes and bruises all around, and that includes the thirty outsiders."

"It was thirty, then?" Lenth smirked. "Shucks, I brought like fifty guys; now it doesn't seem fair!"

A laugh came from Kevin as he came around the corner. "Just be glad they didn't use the knockout gas on you knuckleheads barging in here wearing no protection at all!"

"Kev! Well, looks like we're okay," Lenth said. "Knockout gas?! Is that how they took over here?"

"Ha! I was fully suited up when they tried that crap! It made it a bit harder to see though. They ended up crashing through the barrels, and tried their stun-crap on me, but the suit handled it, so I took em all on with my fists, and took em all out!"

"Kev, you lost."

"Okay, maybe I took one out. Maybe. Look, they're strong, okay?"

"Must be. So where is everyone?"

"About half your guys have already left, climbing back up," Kevin said. "Some are still coming out of the stun, some are just waiting for the others, etcetera, but the thirty outsiders are now our guests. By the way, do you want a can of sleepy gas, or one of their stun-weapons?"

"Oh! I ... well that makes total sense!" Lenth said. "In fact, if I could grab half of what you got, I'm sure Provider-level... frig! I just remembered! They started a fight with the ten outsiders there when I was coming down here! I need to–"

"Yeah, yeah, old news," Kevin said. "Dawn called. They captured three outsiders. The rest hit the ladder and bailed, which I'm told was difficult, since the ladder had a pile of Subjects on the ladder going up."

"Subjects?! Dammit, Elise!"

"Yeah, she's down here."

".... *Dammit, Elise!*"

"She said she was following to help."

Lenth pinched the bridge of his nose and winced. "I... I'm sure she was. Where is she now?"

"Last I saw her, she was in the cafeteria with some of the other Subjects who came with her,"

"Aw, frig. How many Subjects?"

Kevin leaned back, looking down the hall in the direction of the cafeteria. "Oh. Enough. Enough that there was no way any outsiders were going to be leaving by ladder. About thirty or forty."

"Ugh. I guess I'd better go talk to them." Lenth headed to the cafeteria, and found that it was a lively mix of Subjects, Engineers, and a handful of Providers.

"Sheesh, all we're missing is Citizens."

"Hey! Is *that* the guy?" Elise was pointing at Lenth, while facing to another Subject she was talking to.

"Yeah, yeah, that's the same Lenth," the other Subject said, as if Lenth were a common name, "He came to my unit and told us all that stuff. He's come like eight times so far."

Lenth kind of knew the face, but he'd been to so many Units talking to them about the rest of the facility, and why they were important, and about the war they were hiding from. "Oh, hey."

By now, almost all eyes were on Lenth. "Uh, raise your hand if you come from a Unit I've visited?"

About half the Subjects in the room raised their hand.

"Yeah, well, turns out I've found out a bit of what I told you was wrong." Lenth's statement was met with puzzled looks,but no direct questions. "Know that war I told you about? The billions of people that died?"

"Those outsiders are with the Enemy, right?" one Subject asked. "What should we do with them?"

Lenth gave a long, slow exhale. "Ohhh, boy. That war never actually happened. The billions of people are fine. Like, more or less, I guess. There were smaller wars, but nothing like we thought."

A surge of overlapping questions filled the room. "Then who are these outsiders?" "Can we just go out there?" "What about that bright Enemy?" and on, and on.

"The bright Enemy is just a thing," Lenth said. "It's called the sun. It doesn't have a mind any more than the lightbulbs do. It's just way bigger, way farther off, and doesn't need electricity from us."

"How does *that* work exactly?" Elise asked. "I heard sometimes it's off."

"It... it moves, sort of," Lenth said, "and its light gets hidden from us, then hours later, it comes back. I don't really understand it all. I heard something about it not moving, but... but *we* move, or something. But the point is, it's not trying to kill us. It's not *trying* anything, it just... *exists*. And it's existed before *this place* existed."

"You sure you've recovered from getting stunned, Lenth?" Elise chuckled.

"It's confusing!" Lenth admitted, "and we're all trying to figure it out, and these outsiders... they seem confused too. Some seem helpful, but then they try to take over. And they seem to be taking people away. Like right now, they've been taking away Citizens."

"Citizens?" a random Subject asked.

"They're like Subjects in a lot of ways, but there's like three hundred of them, compared to twelve hundred Subjects. They all live in basically one huge area, and don't have Rubberman Managers, and don't work."

"I wanna be a Citizen!" a Subject cried.

"But until recently, a ton of them were killing and hurting each other," Lenth said. "There used to be almost five hundred of them."

"So two hundred..."

"Killed. Violently," Lenth said. "Some bad ones were killing and hurting innocent ones; then some good ones killed the bad ones. They got rid of the worst of them, and then the ones that were left behind wanted to work, and now they run a small farm."

Many wide-eyed Subjects stared in disbelief. "Your 'sun' story was nicer."

One Subject leaned over to another Subject to whisper, "What's 'killed'?"

Lenth was suddenly taken back to when he was a Subject, and one of his Brothers died. Death was a concept he'd only heard his older Brother mention in passing, though he hadn't gone into detail about. His own understanding was minimal until then.

That was the life of a Subject. No knowledge beyond the controlled little Unit's function. This was why Lenth had been going to Units and bringing knowledge, but he'd only gotten to about half of them, and there never seemed to be enough time to help them understand so much.

He decided to take some time right now to explain the idea of death, how he missed his Brother, and how some people had decided to make death. To kill. Lenth explained that these people were a very small minority, and right now he didn't know of anyone running around making death.

This wasn't overly reassuring. So many of them had never considered the concept before.

To get their minds off of it, he told of the big open 'room' at the top, and that eventually, he wanted to show everyone. But for now, the outsiders were making that dangerous.

"And of course, everyone in the facility needs to do their jobs," Lenth reminded them. "We all need air, food, water, and all the other things we all have to get done. I think the *way* we all get everything done will be changing soon, but a lot has to be planned out to make sure we can make changes without anyone starving or anything."

"Are you saying you want me to keep farming rice?" a Subject asked tiredly.

"Please? And I'll keep explaining things to Subjects, and working with the Engineers to keep the lights on and stuff."

"A-ha!" Elise erupted, "Remember that time you all messed up the lights?"

"Yes, Elise, I think we all remember," Lenth conceded, "and remember how it was about running out of fuel?"

"You should have been making more."

"You can't *make* the fuel for it, that's the whole problem. I... I explained this."

"Sure, sure."

"Okay, anyway, I should go," Lenth said, "I'm going to go call up to the Providers. Between there and here, we have like thirty-three outsiders or something, and we have to decide what to do with them."

"Kill them?" a Subject suggested.

"No!" Lenth said, "I don't want to keep them around, but they're people! Besides, if we kill them, how would the other outsiders feel? They might want to kill us in return, or kill the Citizens they've taken!"

"What if they already killed those Citizens?"

Lenth grimaced. "I'm going to assume they haven't."

"And if they did? Do we kill the outsiders we have?" Elise asked.

Lenth looked into Elise's eyes for a moment, then at everyone paying attention. "Not if we can avoid it. That's something that can't be undone. Can't be fixed after. They're people. You're people. We don't kill people if it can be avoided."

"Kevin!" An alarmed shout came from the direction of the central room. Lenth went to see what was going on, running into Kevin on the way. They both found a frantic Engineer coming from the loading bay.

"I just saw a – he's dead!" As the Engineer pointed his thumb over his shoulder, Kevin and Lenth saw something drop past the opening to the Grand Elevator shaft. Then another, screaming. Both impacted with a thud.

"*No, no, no,*" Kevin cried as they all ran to the Grand Elevator shaft. At the bottom, two metres below the floor level of Engineering, three bodies lay in a growing pool of blood. One of them was an outsider, the other two were wearing Subject colours.

Kevin leaned into the shaft to look up. Muted shouts could be heard, but at this distance, nothing clear could be seen. "Dammit, we just hauled someone away from a fall like this! First in my lifetime! And now three more!? I'm gonna call Provider level."

"I'm going up," Lenth said.

"No, you idiot, you're just going to get into whatever crap just killed three people! Stay the hell here! Keep the Subjects here from going anywhere, too."

Lenth did as he was told, as Kevin went to the control room to make a call.

"Providers? Providers, come in, what the heck is going on up there?" Kevin released the talk button and waited.

Nothing.

"*Providers! Talk to me!*"

The population of the camp had grown and grown. As far as Leena could tell, all of the Citizens were here. Patricia was one of the last. She arrived unconscious, and had to be stunned again pretty quickly after waking.

The last of the Citizens to come were the most resistant, and many arrived with injuries to prove it. The screen which had entertained the interned was now mostly ignored. There was over six hundred people in the camp now, many of which were Subjects, with a few Providers mixed in.

Almost all had their original clothing – the most notable exceptions being Tara, Sasha, and Messenger, who'd been issued orange suits when they were at Yute Central.

Everyone here had that stamp on their hands, after being administered that tiny 'not-an-injection' injection, which they were assured was 'just a bit of carbon' that would keep them healthy.

An aircraft arrived, and while Messenger hoped it was the promised Aguei person, Caitlin Aubrey, it turned out to be just another load of prisoners. Seeing their yellow suits and the blue suits, it looked to be an almost even mix of Providers and Subjects.

Darkness soon came, and the lights in the building were turned down. Very few could sleep.

Messenger had been answering as many questions as he could. At first, Providers had questions, but they were easy to answer. At least, they were *quick* to answer as much as he knew, since he didn't know much about what was going to happen to them. He could only give the most generic of assurances that they'd be okay. There were no guarantees to offer.

There were more answers to give to Subjects. Half of them had only recently found out there were more than a handful of people in the world, and that the world was bigger than a few rooms.

The horror in their eyes was something Messenger didn't expect. Many were having a reaction like Sasha's. Even from inside the camp's fence, the world was just so unfathomably endless.

"Teach and comfort where you can," Messenger a handful of Providers. "We were all living a lie, but the Subjects most of all. We're all here. Teach and comfort where you can."

Some of the Subjects who'd been taught by Lenth overheard, and decided that they could pass on what they could to the other Subjects. Even if some teachings were remembered badly, or if some had been revealed to be incorrect recently, it was a step.

Many of the Subjects were seeing their Managers with no Rubberman suit for the first time, and hearing their voices. A few Managers found themselves welcomed, a few ostracised, but most landed awkwardly in between.

In any given direction, crying could be heard a lot. Whether the food here didn't agree with some people, or a mix of anxiety and agoraphobia, the smell of vomit was hanging in the air. Guards supplied materials to clean up with, but it only fixed so much.

Tara was sleeping on top of the tablet to keep it hidden, and partly on top of Sasha for similar reasons. Leena had been re-united with Cody, and they, like many Citizens, moved cots around to more defensible positions, turning them on their sides to create short walls, then laying on the hard floor. The padding wouldn't come off the cot frames. Not being able to fashion any sort of knife was a bit of a discomfort for the Citizens.

Someone had tried to break the media screen by kicking it, but the screen proved immune. The guard turned it off, leaving only the sounds of the prisoners. Chatter had all but ended as evening descended. Crying had calmed, but by no means ended.

Messenger settled into his cot beside the one Tara and Sasha were on. Gabe and Dawn were nearby as well. Dawn was just sitting in her cot, knees up, just staring forward, almost unblinking.

"Dawn. You may as well get some sleep," Messenger said quietly.

Trembling increased in her breathing a little, and her unblinking eyes released tears. Being out of useless words, Messenger went over and put a hand on Dawn's shoulder. She curled into herself tightly, and began sobbing.

With nothing else calling for him, he sat with her until she relaxed, and seemed to be on her way to sleep. Looking around, he saw that Tara was awake, and just staring a the ceiling. Messenger went over to her and quietly asked, "Done your research?"

Tara shifted to check that the tablet terminal was still under her. "About all I can do from here, I think. Whatever good it might do us later on."

"I think I might go for a walk," Messenger said. "It still stinks in here. Care to join me?"

"Nah." Tara looked over to the sleeping Sasha nestled up to her. "I'm not leaving her to wake up alone again. Especially not here, and I'm not keen to take her out there into the open."

"Fair enough." Messenger turned towards Gabe, to see if he wanted to come, but he was passed out quite ungraciously. Messenger passed by Gabe's cot, and put his dangling leg back on the cot. He headed for the door, where two guards were stationed. The guards weren't preventing anyone from going through, as the yard was still fenced in and locked. These two guards were just keeping an eye on things.

The yard had at least a hundred people wandering around. More than half were Subjects. Though the Subjects and Citizens were dressed in the same colour, though Citizens could be spotted for how much generally sloppier they tended to look. Hair not as tidy, clothes often ripped and altered.

The Citizens also looked less... less lost. They'd been here a little longer, but they've also been through some pretty intense things over the last few years... or more accurately, the last few dozen years. If they all lived in this camp for too long, would it risk turning into what Citizenry used to be? If they couldn't get out, maybe Messenger needed to organize things in the camp for a new way of life.

No. This could not be accepted. *This cannot be the new normal.*

Messenger knelt down, touching the grass.

It was cool to the touch, and soft. Looking around, he saw a few people walking around on it barefoot. Did any of the farming Subjects ever walk barefoot among their crops? If they had, it didn't seem to have done any harm.

Maybe he'd just sleep here. In the grass. Why not? Shoes off, bare feet, he got himself comfortable flat on the ground. A rock a few centimetres wide was hiding in the grass under his shoulder. He plucked it out, and rested, holding the rock up against the view of the night sky.

That other big thing was up there. It was entirely round tonight. Berryhill had called it what? The moon? Was it supposed to be closer or farther than the sun? Holding up the little rock, he positioned it to look about the same size as the moon appeared to be.

Fools.

He dropped the rock beside himself.

Such fools they'd been. So afraid of... of the wrong things. Did any of the past Actuals know the truth? Besides the first few of course. Did an Actual think about the strict rules, and how they had to address 'Division'... and about the... sun... and figure it out? Did any of the past Actuals at least suspect?

But such suspicions about the outside world couldn't have been verified without breaking too many rules, and then what? There was that threat of never getting anything from Division again. Why disturb a system that was working? That was keeping them all alive?

Messenger sat up, and watched four Subjects not too far away – Sisters, so it seemed – explore the yard together. They were more free now, locked in this yard, than they had been in their Unit. But Unit life was known for them, it was accepted, it was the rule. Subjects needed to be contained, or essential work wouldn't be done, and people would begin dying.

It was accepted.

It worked.

For generations.

What did Colonel Mangual say? A hundred and some odd years? How far in the past would one have to go to find a generation in the facility that knew about the world? Who was it that feared the war so much, they decided to lie and say it already happened? Decided it was okay to live in the facility, to lock out the world?

In the distance, Messenger spotted a few tiny lights in the sky. Red. Oh, and a blue one also. After watching for a bit, it seemed that that the lights were attached to one of the big flying boxes. The now familiar sound of the transport helicopters drew closer with the '*whupa-whupa-whupa*' sound. It landed outside the gate, with blades still running.

The side opened, and with soldiers guiding and prodding, a stream of Providers mixed with Subjects started coming out, all with wrists bound. Messenger stood and watched them. They saw him, but inclinations to go talk to Messenger were discouraged by armed soldiers.

Many of the Providers hung their heads. In shame? Messenger hoped they didn't feel too much shame; after all, he'd gotten brought here too. Maybe it was disheartening to see their Messenger so defeated.

"*How many are still safe?*" he yelled to the procession.

One Provider hollered back. "*About a quarter of Providers still in the ground? Probably similar with Subjects. I don't think they've gotten any Engineers–"* He was cut short when struck by a soldier.

"Shut up, keep moving! I don't want to have to drag your stunned arse."

Messenger signalled with his hand, and a lowered head in thanks. The question could have waited until after they were processed.

As the soldiers from the helicopter got out, other soldiers from the camp went in, in roughly equal numbers. The engines of the helicopter got louder, and it lifted away.

With little else to do for the moment, Messenger just sat in the grass, and watched the line get slowly processed. Interesting that Subjects were being brought here before all of the Providers. If things were moderately orderly, it seemed that getting to the Subjects would require most or all of the Providers to be out of the way.

But order could no longer be relied upon.

An unexpected, deep hiss could be heard in the distance. It was another flying box. Not a helicopter – the AirLimb. Maybe now he might get some answers from Colonel Mangual.

Where was she landing? A talk was long overdue.

It flew around the camp gently for a little while, and when the lights from the camp caught it right, Messenger was sure he saw a hue of blue. This was not the same AirLimb. Finally it seemed to settle on landing much where the helicopters had been.

Messenger jogged towards the gate, and this close, its shape looked identical to the Colonel's AirLimb, as far as Messenger could tell. It bore the letters "G.E.G." on its nose and side.

The side door opened with a ramp, and four soldiers came out, much like the Colonel's AirLimb had, but these soldiers moved in a relaxed way. On their arms, they wore a symbol of some kind of animal, and the letters G.E.G.. Three of them had darker skin than most of the soldiers Messenger had seen so far. Not nearly as dark as his own, though. Their weapons were slung on their backs, while the guards of the camp usually held their weapons in front of them at the ready.

One G.E.G. soldier walked to the gate guard closest to him. They did their little hand-thing at each other, then began talking. It didn't take long before they parted, and began talking on their comms. The G.E.G. soldier went and stood with the others by the ramp.

Momentarily, a woman came out of the AirLimb. She was dressed in a light jacket that hung almost to her knees, and was trimmed with a design of colours and patterns that meant nothing to Messenger, but looked quite unlike anything he'd seen on any soldier. The coat hung open, showing a white shirt that didn't cover the upper area of her neck. Her legs were covered by a cloth that went across both legs, instead of having separate tubes, but it only reached to just below her knees. Below that, a darker colour covered both of her legs quite tightly. Her shoes were higher on the back section than looked practical. Maybe she needed to be a few centimetres taller for some reason.

She came down the ramp, nodding to the G.E.G. soldier who'd talked to the guard earlier. Another G.E.G. soldier joined as they walked to the gate. By the time they got there, the guard had opened the gate enough for them to pass through before it was closed again.

She led as the two G.E.G. soldiers followed behind.

She stopped, and looked around at the wandering prisoners, and the building where the majority of the prisoners were.

Her shoulders slumped, and she lowered her head for a few moments before starting a walk toward the building.

"Excuse me," Messenger called to her, "would you be Caitlin Aubrey?"

She turned to face him, and her two escorts did as well. "I am," she said. "Does that make you Mister Neil?"

Messenger bowed his head. "I do not get called Neil very often. And I don't know this name 'Mister'. Most call me Messenger."

She tilted her head a little, and said quietly, "We thought that was a typo or something. I'm sorry. Messenger? That's an unusual name."

"It was given to me when I became my people's Messenger to the Great Actual."

Caitlin's eyes widened a little, her jaw slightly agape. "Great Actual? Is that a spirit of your people?"

"Spirit? He... he had spirit. But he has passed on recently. Technically, that makes me the Actual now, but it doesn't feel like the time to assume that title."

"You speak of him with great reverence," Caitlin said. "He was your leader, then?"

"Indeed. I am almost glad he's not here to see this."

Caitlin turned to look at the building again and sighed. "Satellite pictures don't... they didn't really prepare me. May I go inside?"

"I have no power here," Messenger said. "If you feel you need permission, ask Colonel Mangual."

"I don't *have* to ask her. I represent the Grand Elder. By Aguei treaty, I have permission to go almost anywhere I want on the land of Aguola."

"Because..." Messenger thought back to what Berryhill had told him, "because the Aguei were here long before the... Northers came."

Caitlin smiled a little. "Yes. But... you speak like this is all new information to you."

Messenger lowered his head, going onto his knees. "There is so much that is new to us." He began softly, silently sobbing. "I am so tired. And I am so afraid for my people."

Caitlin sat on her knees as well, facing Messenger. "Tell me about your people. I will tell you about mine, and maybe we will understand."

Chapter 24:

Armil and the Emptying

"I kind of miss the flat monsters, Leena," Patricia whispered loudly to a sleeping Leena. "Did you hear me? I think I miss the flat monsters."

Leena opened her eyes enough to frown and squint at Patricia. "What are you talking about?"

"The monsters in that flat box that run around and sometimes eat each other!"

"That screen thing? It got turned off because people were wanting to sleep. They're called animals, not monsters," Leena said.

"So, flat monsters are called animals. Whatever. Why don't they just walk off the edge to hide from each other?"

"Off the side of the screen?"

"Beats getting eaten!"

"Go to sleep, Patricia. They'll probably turn it on again tomorrow. Maybe we can find something we can use as a knife in the daylight. You can stab your flat monsters, like you stabbed that truck, and I can stab... I don't know yet."

"Maybe Messenger's new friend can give us knives."

"New friend?"

"Yeah!" Patricia said, "That lady who flew in on her blue box."

Leena sat up and saw Messenger walking into the building with Caitlin Aubrey and her two escorts. Messenger and Aubrey were talking, and heading over to Tara and Sasha, who were asleep.

"I'm gonna go ask her for a knife!" Patricia said, scrambling over towards Caitlin. "Hey lady! Got a knife?"

Leena was slow to get moving, but she caught up to calm Patricia down before soldiers took too keen of an interest. "Lady, I'm sorry," Leena said, "Never mind Patricia. She gets ideas and sometimes she gets a little over-excited about them."

By now, Tara and Sasha were awake, barely.

Caitlin was still being stared down by Patricia, who was still waiting on her knife request. "Ya see, if I had a knife, I'd be able to do something about the monsters. They aren't dust-monsters, but half of em eat the other half, and I'm thinking I could help the nice monsters. Guzils."

"Gazelles," Leena corrected, "and I'm pretty sure they're not actually in there, and you'd only end up wrecking the screen thing."

Patricia scrunched her face and peered over at the media terminal. "If one of those lion things pop out, and I don't have a knife..."

Caitlin followed Patricia's gaze, and began to piece it all together. "That won't happen," Caitlin assured Patricia. "The nearest lion is a long way away, probably in the nearest zoo, secure in a..." She lost the will to finish the sentence, and instead lowered her eyes.

Messenger stepped in to break the awkward quiet. "Caitlin Aubrey, this is Leena. She is effectively the leader of the Citizen group I mentioned."

With a bow of her head towards Leena, Caitlin gave a kind look, and said, "You've overcome much, I hear. It sounds like you're much loved by your people."

"Oh, only one, these days," Leena said. "He's passed out over there."

Caitlin chuckled politely, assuming it to be a joke. "And your friend, here. You... take care of her? Are you sisters?"

Patricia snorted, and wandered off.

"Patricia is just someone that a lot of Citizens keep an eye out for," Leena said. "She gets odd ideas sometimes, so it's best to make sure none of her ideas are... harmful. Not to say she's dangerous or anything. Not on purpose."

"Hide your truck, though," Tara said, rubbing sleep out of her eye. "Or anything else she might think is a monster. Hi. Caitlin-something was it? I'm Tara, Chief Engineer of... well, lots of nothing, right now." She gave Sasha a squeeze, "And here's my head assistant, Sasha."

Sasha nodded. "Assisting with that lots of nothing that she mentioned. But that nothing *was* the generator at the facility, and getting it to power everything."

"And then your uranium ran out," Caitlin said, glancing to Messenger to confirm what he'd told her earlier.

"That's the short version," Sasha said. She caught a look out the window, and was reminded of the endless emptiness around her. Her gaze remained on it as she commented, "I don't know what's worse, seeing it all with the light, or seeing it less with the sun off, but still knowing it's out there."

Caitlin was confused, so Messenger explained. "When she first came out of the facility, we found out that Sasha is quite agoraphobic. None of the people who have been brought here are used to it, many dislike it, but a few..."

Sasha hung her head in shame. "I'm sorry. I just can't de-"

"Shh," Tara said, administering a renewed squeeze. "You don't need to be sorry."

Unconvinced, Sasha just kept her gaze low, and leaned into the squeeze.

"Is there anything I can do?" Caitlin asked.

"You can get us home." Tara responded.

Caitlin looked across the room and the hundreds of prisoners interned on this floor, and knowing there was a second floor. And at the handful of guards at the door, staircases, and out in the yard. "I don't think I can." Her expression changed to one of sudden focus at the faint sound of a buzz. She reached into her hip pocket, and produced a comm. She answered it. "Hello?" She glanced out the window. "Really? Can it be used like that?"

Glancing between the window and Sasha, Caitlin listened to her comm for a few moments, answering, "Well, which is it then? You know there... okay. That might be difficult, she... really? That's going to really piss off... If you say so! I'll let the local guards... oh, sure, thank you."

She put away her comm, and moments later all of the camp guards held their hands to their ear, listening to their small comms.

"Okay, I was wrong," Caitlin said. "I very much *can* get you out of here."

"All of us?" Messenger asked.

"No. A few. For now," Caitlin said. "He hasn't decided if he's going to call it a humanitarian gesture or an investigative envoy, or whatever, but he feels he can justify bringing a few of you out."

"Who is this 'he', and who is he justifying to?" Tara asked.

"*He* is Grand Elder Armil," Caitlin said, "and by this time tomorrow, he will have had a talk about what we're about to do with Prime Minister Lachlan Leon."

By this time, the blue-tinted G.E.G. AirLimb was in motion, rising above the fencing, and moving over to the building.

"Okay, Sasha, you're invited," Caitlin said, "and Tara, and Messenger. We can go."

The AirLimb approached the building's doors, and the local guards moved out of the way of the turbines' expulsions. It landed gently, as close as possible to the building's doors. Close enough that the ramp could not be deployed. The local guards made their presence known. No one but those attached to Caitlin were about to get through.

"Best we can do," Caitlin said. "Shall we?"

"What we... we're just leaving?" Tara asked. "To where?"

"Aboard the G.E.G. AirLimb for now," Caitlin said, turning for a moment to gesture to the waiting loading bay of the AirLimb. "It's much more hospitable than here. Several staff happily stay onboard for months at a time. It will serve as a much preferred venue for meaningful discussion. After that, I can't say right now. But I won't throw you back *here*."

"Sounds good," Messenger said, "but I think I should stay here."

"Neil?" Tara asked quietly.

"You and Sasha should absolutely go, but I think I need to stay for everyone else."

"That doesn't seem right," Tara replied. "Gabe is here, let him handle things."

"Gabe is very busy upstairs last I heard, and we're just getting more and more people. Unless that flying blue box can fit us all, it's not right anyway. It sure doesn't look big enough for everyone, unless it's somehow bigger on the inside." Messenger said. "Just come back for me. For all of us."

Following behind Caitlin and her escorts, Tara and Sasha passed between the camp guards, out into the open for two metres before entering the AirLimb. Sasha made a point to keep her head held high, but her grip on Tara was quite secure, arm-in-arm.

What looked like darkness from the outside was revealed to be warmer than expected. Ruddy tones of pattered fabric lined the walls instead of sheer metal. Supporting vertical structures were painted to match, and were adorned with lights that looked less 'built' than 'crafted', in shapes that neither Tara or Sasha could identify. The floor was light brown tones with darker lines flowing through it. It was solid enough, but somehow didn't seem as hard as metal. It smelled nice – although whatever the smell was, it was alien to Tara.

"Welcome aboard!" Caitlin said as the door closed behind them. "Can I interest you in coffee, tea? We're pretty well stocked. Have you eaten? Were they... were they feeding you well in there?"

Sasha broke down quietly, holding tighter onto Tara's side. "I think we need to sit down," Tara said.

"Oh... of course!" This first room in the AirLimb was inviting, and on the opposite wall were a handful of plush looking seats, each wide enough to seat two or three people comfortably.

Tara helped Sasha to one of the seats, and joined her. Sasha had a hand over her eyes, and she was obviously crying, her breathing shallow and trembling. Tara held her close, kissed her forehead, and looked to Caitlin. "Thank you? Sorry? I... I have no idea what to say. We're just..."

An old man came from the hallway. He wore a robe made of blue and light-yellow fabrics that looked like they were held together by meticulous, precise folds that created a patchwork of centimetre-wide squares by his neck, turning into larger, looser folds down his form, until it formed loose, floating bands of cloth reaching the floor. He stood before Tara and Sasha, and began to kneel, refusing Caitlin's hand for help. It did look difficult for him. His skin was the tone that Tara was learning was common among the Aguei.

"Honoured guests," he said, head bowed, "I am Armil of Aguei. I would hear your words."

Tara frowned slightly, unsure how to respond. "I'm Tara. I... I have words."

"Caitlin has shared much of what your Messenger has told her," Armil said, "but I don't understand. You all came from one town? What is its name?"

"Your army calls it Station Four," Tara said, "and yeah, if you look closely, it does say that on the outside, but none of us call it that. We... don't really call it anything. Just the facility, I guess."

"I see. But you should know, those soldiers that brought you to that camp are not my army," Armil said. "I have been granted guards to assist me, who are given to me by the army, but they are no longer of that army, and have been chosen and taught to be... less military." This seemed to be evident in the way Caitlin's escorts moved, and the decreased amount of gear they had strapped to them. "Your home doesn't have a proper name?" Armil asked. "I find that a little disheartening. Do you love your home?"

"Engineering," Sasha meekly offered. "The section of the facility we come from is called Engineering. Tara and me, and the people we live and work with... we're the Engineers. But yeah, I'd love to be there. And for things to go back to normal."

"It's a lot further down from the next lowest level," Tara elaborated, "So that if the generator had an accident, supposedly no one outside Engineering would get hurt."

Armil nodded gravely. "That is a heavy burden you bear for your people."

"Well, that's nothing to bear now," Tara said. "Uranium ran out. We're running on a pretty hazard-free capacitor that the ..." Tara paused. "Were, we *were* running on it. They're taking our home. They're still pulling people out." She held up her hand, where she'd been stamped after her 'not-a-needle' was given. "And then they do this to us. Something about diseases and a little fleck of carbon."

Armil's brow contorted with pity and anger. "What do you know of my people, the Aguei?"

"Very little," Tara admitted. "Mostly just that you were here before anyone else."

"And what do you know of your people?" Armil asked, "The ones not from your facility?"

"Not much more. We only found out they survived. We thought they were dead for over a hundred years," Tara said. "I know they have an army, weapons better than ours, flying vehicles, better ways to make electricity, and they get called 'Northers'. I... don't feel like they're my people."

Armil lowered his head and was silent for a long moment. He sighed, and said, "Long ago. Before I was born by many, many generations back, and the Aguei were the only people on Aguola, the Northers came. They had weapons better than ours. Nothing like they have now, but still far better than the Aguei had. They took our land. Our homes. Often put us in camps."

"That's why Berryhill wanted us to learn about you...!" Sasha said, stunned.

"Have they killed any of you? Or ... defiled?" Armil asked.

"N... no."

"You look more like Northers than an Aguei," Armil said. "Maybe that is why it's not as bad for you. Or maybe they've just become a little kinder over the decades. Or they don't want your land as badly."

"They ... killed Aguei?" Tara asked.

"By the thousands," Armil nodded. "Of course, this was many generations ago, many agreements and treaties have been made. Many broken, most restored. Respect slowly fostered, for the most part."

"... but?" Tara asked.

Armil nodded slowly. "And yet, here we are, seeing Northers putting people they find inconvenient into a camp."

Tara and Sasha sat silently for a bit, before Sasha spoke up. "Maybe we're not much better."

Armil gave an inquisitive look, but said nothing.

"Subjects and Citizens?" Tara asked.

Sasha sighed. "But it's not so simple, is it?"

"It never is," Armil said. "Who are these citizen subjects?"

"Okay, the... the Citizens are easier to explain? Our history is pretty unclear in a lot of spots, but Colonel Mangual gave us some missing pieces. When the facility started, the Citizens were the lucky, who didn't have to work. The whole facility was meant to serve them, I guess. But they got violent and dangerous, so they got locked into their section to keep everyone else safe. And it just became the way of it. Stay away from Citizens, keep them locked away, or they'll kill you. And they also killed each other, and we just kind of... ignored it. For generations..."

"They had been thrown away," Armil said, "and their descendants continued to pay for the crimes of their ancestors?"

"Something like that." Tara said.

"But in the last couple of years, something new grew in Citizenry," Sasha said. "Innocents fought the cruel members of Citizenry. A lot of Citizens died. A couple managed to get to Messenger and Actual, and they managed a new peace."

"And this brings you shame?" Armil asked.

"They were ignored too long," Tara said. "Too many died or worse, when we could have been doing something to help. We didn't really know how bad it was in there... but we knew it was bad. And we did nothing for generations. Now, they're farming, and seem to be... I don't know. They're all in the camp right now. I'm sure a lot of people don't trust them much. Most of them are killers, even if they killed bad people."

Armil folded his hands and stared down into them, "Would you punish these Citizens who are killers?"

"I... I wasn't there. I don't know what they've been through," Tara said. "I can't judge."

"They seem nice," Sasha added. "Really weird, some of them, but... friendly enough."

"Have you wronged Citizens?" Armil asked.

"No, not personally," Sasha said, "and we're Engineers. We're as far from Citizenry as you can get."

"Wronged with inaction, maybe. I don't know," Tara said.

"Inaction is something that's wronged the Subjects, for sure," Sasha said. Armil said nothing, allowing Tara and Sasha to explore the notion.

"It could have been us, easily," Sasha said. "We were just lucky enough to be born when the facility needed Engineers, not Subjects."

"So your families raised you to be Engineers, knowing you could find work in it?" Armil asked.

He got blank stares from both ladies.

Armil tried again. "You showed more skill in it than those who became Subjects?"

"When we were born, the numbers showed we'd need an Engineer. The person born next was likely given to a Subject Manager to fill a role in a Unit. When you're born, most likely, you're a Subject. It's like... almost ten times more likely to be born to be a Subject than an Engineer. An okay chance at becoming a Provider. Still less likely than Subject by a lot. Engineers are kinda rare in comparison."

Armil frowned, not really understanding. "What... your career is decided at birth? And this is fine with you and your parents?"

"Why would parents be involved?" Tara asked. "We don't see our parents after we're born, they're not involved."

"Your... your parents aren't involved? Do you have a good relationship with them now?" Armil asked.

"Never met 'em." Sasha said, "at least I don't think so. I mean, it's possible, odds are they're Subjects, or Providers."

Armil's face widened with shock. "*Who raised you?*"

"Engineering nursery," Tara said, "obviously."

"You were taken from your parents at birth, and put in a nursery?"

Both ladies nodded. What was so hard to understand?

Armil searched for the question that would help him understand, and just maybe make it all seem okay. "And this is the same for Subjects and Providers, and Citizens?!"

"Well, not Citizens," Sasha said, "Citizens have always been separate. Citizen babies are Citizens. The rest of us are assigned by what the facility needs at the time for survival. We... were trying to stay alive after the world was burned by the war. But we just recently found out the war never happened... and we've been..."

Armil got up, and held out his arms. "I ... how does this happen?"

"Fear," Tara said. "Fear and stupidity of our ancestors. And we kept it going."

"And now you are learning," Armil said, maybe as a statement, or maybe as a question.

"And our people are in that camp," Tara said, "and we have a lot of learning to do. And teaching. To the Subjects especially."

"I fear the answer... but tell me why the Subjects especially need teaching?"

Purple fog choked the air in the facility's composting section. Trying to usher anyone he found to safety, Lenth could no longer see who was following him between the tall composting tanks, and he could no longer hear their footsteps.

But he heard other footsteps. Outsiders, yelling orders between each other. They had masks that operated much like a Rubberman mask. The one Lenth was wearing made him immune to the gas's effect. Obviously the outsiders were immune for similar reasons.

The random handful of Providers and Subjects that had been following him were not so lucky. Lost in the purple haze, Lenth stepped carefully to find anyone. He was not surprised when his foot bumped someone. He took off the glove of his suit, and checked for breath. This person was alive, but unable to see the colour of his clothing, there was no way of knowing if this was a Provider of a Subject.

Presumably, if they'd acted fast enough, plenty of Managers got into their Rubberman suits, and were doing alright. The first place Lenth had tried to get to was Karen's Unit, but he heard too many outsiders in the way. Either Karen was in her suit hiding somewhere, or they'd already taken her.

She would not have left her Subjects.

Lenth then tried to get to his old Unit; the one in which he had been a Subject in just a handful of years ago. The Rubberman of his Unit, Phil, was older and not terribly nimble, but his eldest Brother Joints was an even greater concern. He had a history of heart trouble.

The fog seemed even denser as he got closer. Blindly finding his way to an intersection, he heard some outsiders. "This crap wasn't meant for use under the damned ground," one complained, his voice muted by his mask, "and we're *still* finding these arseholes in hazmat suits."

"I heard the bottom floor has a ton of em," another soldier responded. Lenth knew this to not be entirely correct. Engineering had a few dozen Rubberman suits, but the Manager and Subject levels had three hundred Managers, each with their own suit. The Managers' suits weren't shielded for radiation, but they were probably enough to stop the outsiders' stun-weapons.

"There's no wind down here," complained a soldier. "This gas is going to take forever to settle."

Lenth also knew this to be not entirely true. The facility had an air filtration system designed to scrub carbon dioxide and such. Lenth used to help maintain the filters when he was a Subject. Surely it could manage this purple crap *eventually*.

How many Subjects and Managers were still free? Lenth had heard nothing but the outsiders for quite a while, but presumably Subjects and Managers would be keeping quiet as much as possible.

The outsiders were confident enough to run around shouting. Their heavy footwear didn't make them any quieter either. With sufficient caution, Lenth could get to his old Unit to check his Unit Brothers. Then, with any luck, maybe he could find another path to Karen.

With quiet steps, and well-worn memory of the Manager-level corridors, Lenth was able to quietly make his way around, despite not being able to see through the gas. There were moments he came across thinner patches, and could see a little, but it was never terribly useful, or much more than a tease. The thinner patches did seem to line up with the air vents, though, suggesting systems were working – if slowly.

Lenth found the door into Phil's space, and pushed it open as quietly as he could. It made a faint scraping sound, but he hadn't heard an outsider in a while. It was fine. He got in, and closed it.

The gas here was about as dense as anywhere else. It didn't bode well for his Brothers, but Phil might be running around in his Rubberman suit.

"Phil?" Lenth called out into dense haze. "You here?"

No response. Could he be in bed? It would be kind of a dumb thing to do at a time like this, but if his suit had a leak, he might have succumbed to the gas anyway. A lot of the suits the Managers had were damaged over time and wear. Broken seals, dead filters; a Manager didn't actually need their suits to perform all their functions. Usually.

It was simple enough to check Phil's bed, even if it was a long shot. Lenth shuffled blindly to Phil's bed, and reached out to feel if anyone was on it.

No. For better or worse, Phil wasn't here, and Lenth hadn't stumbled over anyone unconscious, either.

Lenth took a moment to decide whether to search blindly for anyone in rest of the Unit, or if he'd be better off to go back to Engineering... then he found out that the outsiders could be quiet when they wanted to be.

The weight of one of the outsiders tackled him from behind, and he fell across the edge of Phil's bed. He tried to get turned around, to get up and face his attacker, but his mask was soon yanked off of his face.

That purple gas didn't stink as bad as he had expected.

As sleep wrapped itself around Lenth, he heard one of the outsiders complain,

"I'm getting sick of this Marco Polo hide-and-seek crap!"

Kevin stood behind his re-constructed barricade in the Engineering loading bay. Only a handful of barrels were actually toppled, so it hadn't been too much of a task for the team to repair. The fact remained that it didn't stop the outsiders long at all when they finally had decided to breach it.

Ideas were tossed around about how else to slow or halt attacking outsiders. A lot of ideas involved electrical hazards, but makeshift traps and weapons would be equally hazardous to the Engineer using them without proper time to develop a concept. Anything they make along those lines would also be pointless if the outsiders came in insulated suits, which seemed very likely.

One plan was to attach weights to the corners of bedsheets. With a few sheets layered on top of each other, the plan was to toss these weighted sheets at outsiders to foul them up long enough to be tied up in a cable. Tests found that the sheets generally ended up bundling together on themselves, so they included a length of thick conduit cabling to play to that strength. Any part of the sheet that stayed open would be a bonus, maybe obscuring their vision.

It would likely take at least two Engineers to subdue one outsider, so it was a sketchy plan to begin with.

The Grand Elevator arrived, no doubt with a group of outsiders behind its door.

And then the lights went out.

"*The capacitor's been disconnected!*" That also meant that any plans for an electrical hazard would have failed. The Engineers in the loading bay area were suited up, though, so at least they'd still be immune to the gas and stun-weapons.

They heard the sound of the elevator door being dragged open. "Okay, okay, get a corner, go wide, we can catch em," Kevin called out to his team, but the outsiders' footsteps were coming. Fast.

People didn't generally run in the dark. It meant that they could see. Somehow, the outsiders could see in the dark.

The sound of the barrels being rammed came next, and Kevin got out of the way enough to only be glanced by a falling barrel. Yells of other Engineers sounded more like panic than injury, but it was impossible to tell in the dark.

The water in the barrels rushed across the floor, making things slippery. He felt an outsider grab at him, and he tried to resist, but he slipped on the wet floor. He managed to take the outsider down with him. This didn't prove to be much of a help.

He heard many other outsiders around him. His arm was grabbed before he could get to his knees, then the other, and before he knew it, his wrists were bound behind his back. Struggling to stand and not slip without use of his hands was a challenge. He could hear other Engineers having similar problems.

What now? With his hands bound, he couldn't exactly run to the Grand Elevator shaft and start climbing the ladder. No, he'd ram his way blindly into any outsiders he could find. Maybe Engineers further from the Elevator were having better luck.

Or he could get rammed against the wall by an outsider, and have his mask yanked off.

"Could you *not*?" Kevin called out to his assailant, "*I am so sick of you people!*"

"Feeling's mutual, Donkey Kong," the outsider replied.

"Who-ey what?"

Chapter 25:

Worrisome

"Sarge, your lil stunt's working," Muir called over to Berryhill as he boarded their utility vehicle parked outside the facility.

"What *stunt*?" Berryhill scowled, "I just *followed orders* and yanked their power."

"Nooooo no no," Muir said, turning the screen of the terminal his way, "this is *not* about following any order."

The monitor was viewing a news story with the headline, "Grand Elder Flies to Hidden Camp of Unidentified Prisoners."

Berryhill coughed in shock, eyes wide. "The *Grand Elder?!* Went *there?* I was thinking, *oh, Messenger might get a little buzz, draw a little attention –*"

"Well, it looks like he managed!" Muir said, "and with *your* tablet!"

"Oh, I am so fired. I can hope for a not-so-dishonourable discharge," Berryhill said. "Laird! I'm sorry I got you caught up in that! I'll tell them you didn't know what I was doing!"

"What?" came Laird's voice from the driver's end, "I'm innocent! What am I innocent of?"

A single deep laugh with a Scottish accent came from elsewhere in the vehicle.

"I went over the Colonel's head... or side-stepped it, or whatever," Berryhill answered, "when I gave Messenger that tablet and basically told him to email the Aguei. And I set up an email account for him. And saved relevant links..."

"Oh shit, you're guilty as fuck," Laird responded, "to the gallows with all of us!"

"Ahm completely innocent!" Tavish called out, "boot yer over-reactin'. Thar noot gunna link it to yer lil tablet."

"Tav, there's literally no other way Messenger could have contacted anyone," Berryhill said, "even if he found a way to hack the media screen or something, that *could* put doubt on the actual device used, *but his emails!"*

"Yah," Muir said, "That crap's traceable."

"Ah, right," Tavish said, "yer fooked."

Not far from the truck, the carrier helicopter landed, ready for another load of prisoners. The other helicopters had been dismissed when it became obvious that the elevator's capacity and speed made additional helicopters pointless to have around.

Berryhill watched for a moment before closing the door behind himself and heading to the truck's little mess. "I guess I wait now. I'll either get orders to hook the capacitor up again, or I'll get arrested for my gift to Messenger. Just depends on what happens first; the troops secure the engineering floor, or Colonel Mangual sees the news."

"Arrested? Are you serious?" Laird asked.

"Well, it probably counts as treason or something," Berryhill responded. "Going against the spirit of prevailing orders? Giving aid to an enemy? I don't know. My career's done. I wouldn't be surprised if I'm a civilian by sundown, and not shocked if I'm in cuffs."

"They're not enemies," Muir said. "Isn't Colonel Mangual trying to help them?"

Berryhill stuck a ration in the microwave, and raised his eyebrows before mumbling, "Drag em out, give em civilization. A fine Norther tradition. And I tried to foul it up."

"Good," Tavish said, "Ees people – ey've go' a life, thar own tradition. Give em the new toys, sure, boot all this?"

"Mangual has a point," Berryhill admitted. "They basically have.. *had* slaves. But this is a bad way to do this. I suppose I should have made some noise about this through regulation channels, but..."

"Ahm old," Tavish said. "I got yer back. If ah git fired, ah have me nest egg."

"And your retirement?" Berryhill scoffed. "They can take that."

"As if ah opted to roon mah r'tiremen' through th' military. It's all squirrelled in anoother pile."

Muir perked up. "You can do that? I want to do that! How do I do that?"

"Proobably harder fer ye now, since ah suppose ye signed ool th' usual papers when ye joined. Ah'll send me banker at ye tho," Tavish said.

"Ha, probably a bit late for me," Berryhill said, "but if this all –" he stopped,to answer his comm. After listening for a moment, he responded. "Berryhill here. Yup. Okay." He put it back in his pocket.

"Arrested or capacitor?" Laird asked.

"Capacitor. For now. They have everyone secured, and are ready to start shipping them on the elevator. I'll be back in a sec, I have to go assist forced relocation a bit more."

"Nice toy," Colonel Mangual said over a video chat. Her image came through nice and clear on Messenger's tablet-terminal. "I see you've been making good use of it."

Messenger tilted his head at the Colonel's image. She seemed to be addressing him directly. This was different than the people in the documentaries on the large screen. "You can hear me? See me?" Messenger asked.

"Yes, that's correct. I intended on calling you on the large screen I had set up in there when everyone from the facility was there, but that's been taking longer than anticipated. And now you have that little tablet, and have been busy. Tell me, did the same person who gave you the tablet tell you to contact the Aguei?"

"Truthfully," (and Messenger very much wanted to adhere to the truth,) "he never told me to do that," and Berryhill hadn't... directly... "but we had the tablet to do a little research, and someone mentioned that the camp looked a lot like other camps from your history."

"Yes. I can see your search history," Colonel Mangual said. "That tablet is a military unit operating through military servers, just in case you were any impression you were hiding anything."

"We have had many questions," Messenger said, "and this device is very helpful. The Aguei and solar power were especially interesting."

"I see that," the Colonel said, eyeing another screen. "Your camp isn't like the old Aguei camps," the Colonel explained. "It's not a fitting comparison. Your camp is temporary, with plans to get you all to better places as quickly as is safe."

"I wonder; were the Aguei people told similar?" Messenger asked. "Things got much worse for them before they began to get better. When are we able to go home, then?"

"It's not that simple! I'll be honest – I'm wondering if charges should be laid on you specifically, and other members of you staff for abuse and confinement of your workforce! Not to mention that group with that allegedly violent past!"

"Charges? You want to electrocute me?"

"Elect... oh, charges. No, no, it's a legal thing... which... you really don't know about..."

On the other end of the room, a shriek was heard. "*Leave it alone! It's a nice monster, not like you!*" It was Patricia's voice. She'd gotten hold of a knife somehow, and lunged at the large media screen.

"Colonel, one of the Citizens needs some help now, I need to go," Messenger said, before dropping the tablet-terminal on his cot, and running off towards Patricia. In the few seconds it took to get there, weaving between people as he went, soldiers who traversed less gently had arrived first.

One fired a stun-weapon, and Patricia was quickly on the floor. The knife sat lazily in her hand, and the screen was a malfunctioning display of wrong colours, black, and cracks that spread out from the two points where Patricia had stabbed it. Two solders were keeping people away from her while another collected the knife, then began dragging her away.

Gabe was nearby and spoke up before Messenger could. "Where are you taking her?"

One of the soldiers answered, "She can sleep it off in another room. We'll see where her head's at when she comes to." As the surrounding people began to lose interest, one of the soldiers who was assuming crowd control began helping to carry Patricia.

"Did you see what happened?" Messenger quietly asked Gabe.

Gabe sighed. "She started getting agitated. On the screen there was this animal made mostly of arms that moved like a... slow rope? Lots of arms, and it was attacking a smaller orange animal that flew somehow. I think they may have been in water, which is confusing all on its own. Anyway, Patricia wanted to save the orange thing. I have no idea when she got a knife away from one of the soldiers."

Messenger and Gabe followed along behind the soldiers carrying Patricia. They soon came to a smaller room that needed to be unlocked. It was big enough for two cots, a toilet, and not much else.

"She's not so stable," said Leena who now showed up to check on Patricia.

"I noticed somehow!" one of the soldiers replied as they locked Patricia in.

"Do you need to lock her in?" Messenger said. He realized the irony. Patricia and the other Citizens had been locked away. The Subjects had been locked away. And now he was complaining about being locked away in a section of a place where they were all locked away.

Messenger looked towards Gabe, and Gabe was looking around at everyone else.

Leena was quietly seething. Others here and there looked similarly agitated. The ones watching most keenly seemed to be largely Citizens, although their energy was infectious.

The Solders gave no sign of reading the room, but Providers and

Managers exchanged knowing, worried looks.

Picking up the tablet-terminal again, Messenger found that Colonel Mangual had disconnected at some point.

Aboard the G.E.G. AirLimb, Grand Elder Armil considered the things he'd been learning. His brow tightened in concentration for a moment before looking to Tara and Sasha. "Can you accept your wrongdoing?" he asked them.

"We thought it was for survival," Tara replied, "If we'd known the world was fine, the Subjects wouldn't have been forced into their jobs. I didn't choose my job either. I was put on the Engineer path, and that was it."

Armil sighed. "Would you agree that your Subjects were wronged?"

"They were slightly unlucky to be chosen as Subjects."

"Only slightly?" Armil asked with eyebrows raised.

"They're fed the same as everyone, they were unaware the world out there was fine, like everyone.

Sasha cleared he throat, and said under her breath, "Most of them didn't know there were more people than their siblings and their Rubberman. And they got shocked when they didn't do what was expected of them."

"That could have as easily been us," Tara said to Sasha, taking her hand. "It's not any..."

Armil once more decided not to speak, and just listened to Tara and Sasha hash it out.

"If it had been you," Sasha said, "wouldn't you want to know other people are out there? Wouldn't you want the chance to learn to read? And what if it was me, bossed around by a silent Rubberman? And getting shocked?"

Tara frowned "I... that would be unfortunate, but... it'd be fair?"

"Save me, then," Sasha said.

"What?"

"If I were a Subject, come save me," Sasha said. "Let me meet other Units' Subjects, meet my Rubberman, meet Engineers and Providers. Let me ride the Grand Elevator and meet the Actual."

Tara looked to the floor and spoke quietly. "The work needs to be done. Or we starve, or whatever..."

"Engineers do their work," Sasha said, "and we're not locked in Units."

Tara sat quietly for a moment, thinking. She finally came out with, "You're saying they should all be loose, and get told everything."

"Including *why* everyone needs to do their jobs," Sasha said, "and that they're appreciated, and others are doing their own jobs for them as well."

Tara smiled faintly. "That simple? And if a Unit of beet farmers decide they're all going to go hang out with the Citizens for a month?"

Sasha shrugged. "Maybe an Engineer could plant a beet or two. We could adapt."

"The system's been working for so long by not changing," Tara said with a grimace.

"Working just fine for me and you," Sasha said, "but not as fine for everyone. We're not just a couple thousand people huddled in a hole in a dead world. I think we could manage a bit of change."

"Change. Scary." Tara said, mocking herself.

"Change is already here anyway, hon," Sasha took Tara's hand and gave it a squeeze. "If I can run from the facility loading bay to Mangual's AirLimb across the war field, through the wide open-void under the radioactive glare of the big bad Enemy, you can deal with beet farmers going for a walk."

"Change scary. World scary. Sasha good." Tara said, tiredly staring into Sasha's eyes.

"Tara good."

Just then, Armil's assistant Caitlin stepped back into the room. She held a terminal in her hand. "Grand Elder? A Colonel Veronika Mangual is on hold, wanting to speak to you. Do you want to take it? I can put the call on this tablet, you could take it in your study, or I can tell her you'll call her back."

With a soft huff and groan, Armil took his time standing, getting a hand from Tara. "I don't think I've met a Veronika. Oh, I may as well take it in the study. We've been lingering around in the front room for long enough."

As he took a step towards a hall, he turned to Tara and Sasha with an understated smile and beckoned that they follow. It wasn't long down the AirLimb's hall before they reached a room slightly larger than the one they came from.

At the middle of the room sat a wooden desk that looked like it might have grown here. Most of it was still covered in dark, lumpy bark, and its base spread out as if roots should be showing out the bottom of the AirLimb. At first glance, the only part that looked looked like a desk was most of the top surface,which was flat, smooth, and free of bark.

Behind the desk waited a wide, soft-looking seat. It rose at an angle to accept Armil gently before it, and he, settled into a typical seated position.

The walls were laden with fabric weaves that seemed the share the feel of Armil's robe; small, tight meticulous folds, flowing back and forth to wide, gentle stretches, all in soft tones of earth and sky.

An image on one wall was of some kind of hairy animal, with dark-blue flowing hair, and curved protrusions from either side of its head. Behind the animal in the image were countless tiny stars in a sky of black, and deep blues. The animal seemed to be looking down at the viewer, watching silently with blackened eyes.

On the opposite wall was another image of an animal. The one was less grand, looking up at the viewer. It had no hair, but a skin covered in little light-yellow panels that overlapped each other. Only its little black, shining eyes seemed to be not covered by these panels. It stood on dirt that looked a lot like the ground outside the facility. Perhaps finer. The ground was a similar colour to the animal's many little skin-panels. Where the blue hairy animal seemed powerful, perhaps even judgemental, this other one (as bizarre as it seemed to Tara and Sasha,) seemed meek. Friendly.

Armil touched something on the desk, obscured around the edge nearest to him.

A rectangle of light appeared floating over the desk, and from Tara and Sasha's side, it seemed to quickly darken. Armil reached to its edge, and pulled it smoothly to the side so that Tara and Sasha could see the other side a bit. This side was still fairly bight, and a handful of indicators and text labels were visible at its edges.

"It's... a screen?" Sasha asked.

Armil nodded. "A bit much, I know, but the fellow who made me this desk put it in. All right, then. Vee-ron-i-ka... All right, answer line 1."

The screen flickered for a moment, and the image of Colonel Mangual appeared. She looked like she'd been doing something else while waiting for Armil to pick up the line.

"Veronika, I presume?" Armil said.

Mangual's eyes opened wide, and she sat up straight, before stammering in an apologetic tone, "Gra... Grand Elder?! I didn't know you were... I was trying to get in contact with two detainees from the camp, your assistant must have forwarded me to your own line. I was just–"

Tara stepped more in front of the screen. "Hi, Colonel. You found us. I'm here with Sasha."

"Uh.. hi?" Sasha added.

Colonel Mangual frowned with quiet panic. "Grand Elder! I had no idea you were on board that AirLimb, I thought that your Caitlin Aubrey person was leading this... whatever it is. I'm sorry, I'll send troops to fetch those detainees immediately."

"No, no," Armil said, "there's no need, they're welcome guests. I had Caitlin invite them and that Messenger Neil fellow."

"I was just talking to Messenger!" the Colonel said, fumbling hurriedly with her words a little, "I knew he had a terminal, and I called him assuming he was on your AirLimb, and he wasn't there, and I was talking to him but he had to go be because some kind of fight started. As soon as I heard the camp was secure, I wanted to ask an Aguei contact what your AirLimb was doing, and–"

"A fight?" Tara interrupted, "in the camp?"

"One of your people stabbed the media terminal," Colonel Mangual said tersely.

"Bloody Citizens," Tara mumbled, covering her eyes with her hand. "Bet you anything it was a Citizen. They seem to have a thing for knives." Tara moaned, "Is anyone hurt?"

"No one was hurt. The knife-user was stunned, and she's resting it off in a solitary room."

Tara turned to Sasha. "Remember that Citizen who stabbed Berryhill's truck, and got stunned for it?"

"Berryhill?!" Colonel Mangual barked, "One of your people stabbed his truck? I didn't hear about it."

"Not one of *my* my people," Tara explained, "a Citizen. Different section of the facility. Different... different way of doing things."

"Citizens, Engineers, Subjects, Managers, Providers," Colonel Mangual said, frowning. She shook her head, letting a curl of her dark purple hair pop loose, to dangle on her forehead. "I'm still figuring all your messed-up little sub-cultures out, but they all need to remain orderly while we figure out what to do with them, and figure out who needs to be held accountable. They're *all* your people, and-"

A voice would be heard on the Colonel's end, and she turned to the side to pay attention to them, then replied, "What? How many? Well is it secure now? No, no, how did *that* happen?! No, you can't. Focus on the camp, get anyone in the yard into the building. I'll send another unit. Damn it."

"What's going on?!" Sasha pleaded.

Colonel Mangual turned her attention back to Sasha and Tara. "I need to go. Things got stupid. Stay out of trouble and don't make things any worse. Two of my men are hurt. One, badly. Just stay out of trouble."

The Colonel disappeared from the screen, and it went back to the black, with indicators on the edges.

A moment of quiet left in her wake, Armil finally offered, "If you want to stay out of trouble, you're welcome to do so *here*. I had meant to offer something to eat."

"Thank you, Armil, I'll have to take you up on that another time, but the Colonel said it." Tara shared a nod with Sasha.

"They're all my people."

Chapter 26:

Visiting Ghosts

"How many left?" Messenger asked Gabe. "I heard a commotion by the room they put that Patricia Citizen in, and next thing I know, the guards are talking about runners."

The camp was immersed in more commotion than usual. Some guards ran around yelling for people to stay at their cots under threat of being stunned for non-compliance, while other guards were in the yard, attempting to herd detainees back into the building.

A Citizen they didn't know came up to Messenger and Gabe. "There was a lot of talk of going to those tall, wrecked things," she said. "Seemed to think surviving in there would be simple, because Citizens had survived in Citizenry for so long."

Messenger looked out the window. Even in the dark of night, the towering wreckage of that dead city stabbed upwards into the moonlight. "In there? The guards told us it was–"

"Whatever. I don't know what they plan to eat," the Citizen said, "without our farm, and without *you* bringing supplies, Messenger."

"Was this Leena's idea?" Messenger grumbled.

"Nah, she was trying to stop them. She didn't argue too much when the plan was just to bust down the door to get Patricia out, but Leena wasn't into going into that huge wreck."

"Where is she?" Messenger asked.

"She went into that huge wreck."

"*What?*" Messenger scowled.

"She chased after Patricia. Patricia was saying something about monsters, and –"

"I see. So just the two of them?" Messenger hoped.

"Yeah. And like... forty or fifty others. Mostly Citizens? Some of those Subject people? I don't know how they can stand to be out there with no ceiling. Freaks me out."

The guards at the door were standing instead of sitting. Usually one was sitting. They had their weapons at the ready, instead of slung over a shoulder. Messenger turned to Gabe. "Try to help get this mess calmed down here. I... I guess I'm chasing after our strays."

Gabe gave a sceptical sneer. "Not alone, you aren't."

"I need you here," Messenger responded.

"Yeah, you do. But hang on." Gabe waded into the chaos and stated yelling for Providers. Less than a minute later, Gabe returned with ten Providers.

"Take these. It's dangerous to go alone."

Messenger looked to his newly appointed squad, and gave them a nod. "Be safe, Gabe." He approached the door, and the two guards looked about ready to start stunning Messenger and his people.

"I have to go after them," Messenger said.

"Back to your cots," the one guard said. "We'll handle it. We have reinforcements coming."

"Reinforcements?!" Messenger responded, "You mean there's no one pursuing them already?"

"Back to your cots!" The guard made a show of readying his stun-weapon.

"*Soldier!*" came a voice from the field, as Caitlin Aubrey called to the guards. By her side, Tara and Sasha walked with her, looking fatigued and worried. Sasha looked worse off, with the wide-open space pressing down on her. She was trying very hard to only look at the ground, unsure if it was helping at all.

The guard ignored Caitlin, and addressed Tara and Sasha. "You're suppose to be in here, get to your cots."

"Ladies, I was going to take these Providers into those ruins," Messenger said, ignoring the guard. "We have about fifty of our people wandering around in there. Sounds like mostly Citizens and Subjects."

"We heard a little about it," Tara said, "that's why we're here."

"*Cots! Now!*" the guard barked. He then faced Caitlin. "And please keep out of the way, and get back on your pretty AirLimb!"

Caitlin narrowed her glare at the guard, and put on her most official tone. "Soldier! The Aguei nation is responding to assist in ensuring the safety of people the Norther Aguolian army have just lost track of. I would do so with the assistance of Neil Messenger, if he would agree."

Messenger nodded.

The guard stood his ground. "I'm not letting another pack of these nuts wander out of here!"

"You most certainly *are*, unless you want to discuss it with *him*." Caitlin forcefully pointed at the Grand Elder's 'pretty' G.E.G. AirLimb. "And he would no doubt bring it up with your Colonel. Meanwhile the detainees you were entrusted to guard are facing more and more danger."

The guard looked over to the AirLimb. His stern expression faultered, and began to go pale. "He's... he's here? He's right there?"

Messenger, ten Providers, Tara, Sasha, and Caitlin were soon underway. The gate of the fence hadn't been used, and a cluster of guards stood around a section of the fence in the other direction. The direction to the heart of the ruins.

As they walked towards the fence, Messenger commented, "Are you sure the great war never happened? That looks like about what I'd expect."

"What happened to the city of Meston was horrible," Caitlin admitted, "but it wasn't the war. I... I know you've only seen the rougher edges of the world so far, but this –" she held her hand out to the ruins, "this is not the world. This is such a small part."

"My favourite part so far is these tiny green plants we're walking on," Messenger responded. "We have plants in the facility back home."

They arrived at the soldiers by the fence. It could now be seen that the fencing had been ripped out of the ground, and hastily bent back into shape. "Stand aside," Caitlin called to the soldiers. "We're going through."

The soldiers protested a bit, but not as much. The confidence of Catlin's authority, and the thirteen people following her went a long way. Caitlin stopped Messenger before he ducked under the fence. "I'm going back to the AirLimb, I can help more from there. You have that terminal?"

Messenger raised it up to reply silently.

"Good," Caitlin continued, "There's a good chance you're going to see some ... bad stuff in there."

"*Dangerous* bad?" Messenger asked.

Caitlin looked towards the burnt husks of skyscrapers, and stared for a moment. "Well... it's rough terrain. The wreckage might be dangerous... but by 'bad'... there was a reason it got bombed."

The thirteen of them walked swiftly into the wreckage of Meston.

They were giving chase, yet they knew that too much haste could mean a clue missed, or a careless injury.

The ground was black and worn with an old but deep burn. Footsteps could perhaps be seen here or there, but the disorder and filth of the terrain made it impossible to be sure. They spent two minutes scaling an incline before anyone realized it was a collapsed wall. It looked like it had once been part of one of the nearby fractured, towering structures.

"War..." Sasha whispered to herself. The fear of the wide open was magnified by the shock of this place. They'd said the war never happened, but then – what was this?

Carefully passing through a hollowed window that was now diagonal, they passed through a massive piece of wall. They continued along the barely-identifiable passage, with the wall itself looming overhead for a while before coming back out into relative open. Charred and warped metal objects littered the passage. Some looked large enough for a few people to fit in. A few of the big metal objects might have been able to contain dozen or more people.

They seemed to have doors to access them, and broken windows. Inside, most had four or more objects that looked like they may have been chairs or seating, and one almost always had a wheel of some sort in front of it.

Other debris was found, smaller than the metal things. This other debris was more burnt than the metal, and even less identifiable.

Sudden realization made Messenger's eyes go wide, but he didn't speak of it.

His terminal beeped in his hand, and a hiss could be heard in the sky. He answered the terminal, and saw Caitlin's face.

"Messenger, I'm above you," Caitlin said. "The AirLimb can see the heat of everyone down there. I'm feeding you a live map of it." With a few taps, Caitlin's face disappeared, and a blue graphic of lines and stripes dominated the screen. A few patches of red littered the graphic. Messenger immediately noticed how the graphic adjusted its angle so that it was always facing the same way relative to the ground.

"These red blobs..." Messenger began.

"The ones in the middle are your group," Caitlin explained. "The group to the north and the group to the north-east are who you're out here looking for."

Messenger held out his hand to divide the ten Providers with them into two groups.

"You five, come with me. You other five, go with Tara and Sasha, and head that way," he said, pointing north.

Tara nodded, and then checked that Sasha was doing okay. Sasha was hauntingly silent. She was avoiding eye contact, staring intently at a nearby rock. But she stayed by Tara, holding her hand. They took their five Providers and headed north, while Messenger and his Providers took the map in the less simple-looking north-east direction.

The way north remained just as cluttered and burnt as things had been previously, and taller buildings loomed ahead. With a smaller group, they made less noise, and it was easier to listen for any Citizens or Subjects nearby.

They had only been apart from Messenger's group for about five minutes when Tara felt Sasha's hand slip from hers. Tara stopped and looked at Sasha.

Sasha was looking down another passage. Frozen, staring.

One of those non-metal lumps of debris was slouched against a wall, not entirely collapsed.

The partly-charred bone of an arm could be seen. It protruded from burnt lumps. Bones of a shattered hand lay nearby. A ribcage. Vertebrae. A skull, still clinging to some of its charred flesh. After noticing the nature of a few features, the rest seemed obvious.

Sasha's eyes widened slowly. Her jaw loosened, and her lips parted.

The other lumps they'd been seeing. Others in view right now. She knew what they were now, and she imagined how they died.

The endless void of a world that took her from her home pressed on her harder than even before. The charred dead stared at her with emptied eye sockets.

And a scream came from her. The world ripped it out of her, and the air from her lungs was not enough. It ripped her tears out. It pulled and ripped her courage and will from every fibre of her body, and wrung her out like a rag. Everything she had within her pushed out through her throat into the sound that came from her.

As she crumbled to her knees and inhaled, she didn't hear the words of concern from Tara, or notice Tara's arms around her.

And a scream came from her again.

Almost as forcefully.

And a scream came from her again.

Weaker.

Weakness broke her focus into incomprehensible speech, buried in uncontrollable sobs.

The scream reached Messenger's group. The group stopped. The screaming didn't.

Messenger looked at the map. All the little red marks had stopped moving. And then they began moving towards the scream. Messenger rallied his Providers and broke into a run.

The screams stopped, but it had been enough to get a reliable route. It wasn't that far. When they came to Tara and Sasha's group, the Providers were standing around.

In the middle sat Tara, wrapped around Sasha.

"*Is she alright?!*" Messenger asked.

Sasha was quiet, curled into a ball, staring into nowhere. Tara saw crying. "No. No she isn't. It's my fault, it's my fault, I should have *never* taken her out here, I should have never pushed her. We should be in Engineering. *I should have never taken her out here.* Never."

Messenger looked at the map. The other red marks were much closer now. People could be seen running towards them. All of the Citizens and Subjects in the ruins. They all came.

"What's going on here?" Leena was the first Citizen to get to them.

"No one's hurt," Messenger said. "It just... it got to her. Why did you all come back?"

"Mike's rule," Leena said, referring to her late partner. "When someone's in trouble, don't hide. Strength in numbers. Citizens strong together."

Several of the other Citizens repeated solemnly, "Citizens strong together."

"Sasha's not a Citizen," Messenger said.

"Close enough," Leena said. "Ever since those outsiders came and started scooping us up... everyone from the facility? They're all my people."

Tara kept holding Sasha, and nodded. "All my people."

"All my people," Messenger said.

A hiss was heard approaching in the sky.

From multiple directions.

Messenger expected the military AirLimbs soldiers to drop soldiers, like he'd seen back at the facility. He expected to be facing shots from stun-weapons. Everyone instinctively formed a circle around Tara and Sasha, who were still on the ground. Everyone was prepared for defeat, each person deciding whether to surrender, or go down swinging.

No such choice was needed.

Nearby, a new hissing was heard. Higher pitch, softer than the AirLimbs overhead.

In the darkness, a few people caught a glimpse of the purple gas.

At least the crying would stop for a time. At least the darkness of sleep would do them that favour.

For a time.

Chapter 27:

Divided

When Tara began to wake, she found herself coiled up in a coarse, dull-blue blanket, facing a wall. She was laying on a padding that was similarly coloured as the blanket. There was more dirt under her fingernails than usual.

As the little details of her surroundings made it through to her re-assembling consciousness, the memory of the moments before she fell asleep came crashing back at such a velocity that it knocked her out of bed, and onto her feet before another thought could form.

"*Sasha!*"

Sasha was not in this room. Four by six metres large with white walls, two cots, a stainless steel toilet, a door, and a little panel next to it.

It dawned on Tara that the last place she'd seen Sasha was in those ruins, with all those charred bodies lying around. And she didn't know what killed them. Or when. But Tara, having survived being put to sleep by the army's gas, had to assume that Sasha survived as well. Maybe Sasha woke up first, and let Tara sleep. She might have stepped out to... to what, find food?

Lacking any better plan, Tara tried the door, only to find it locked. The panel by the door had a button, and a speaker.

She held down the button, and spoke. "Hello? Is anyone out there?" She remembered the way the old Actual used to talk to Division, and added, "Over," before releasing the button.

A response didn't come soon enough for her, so she tried once more, holding the button again. "Hello, this is Tara. Chief Engineer of the facility... oh what do you call it... Station Four. Is anyone out there?.... Over?"

She let go of the button, and paced a few steps in a circle, and upon facing the button again, she hit it with the force of building frustration. "Look, I'm not even trying to get someone to complain about being locked in here or anything. Right now, I just want to know where Sasha is, and if she's okay. She wasn't really doi–"

A voice came back out of the little speaker. "It's not a radio, you don't have to hold the button. Please leave it alone. A single press is enough to let us know you want to talk."

Tara released the button, and took half a step back. "Mangual? All right. All right then. So, Sasha. What's going on?"

"She's in another room. She's not awake yet. Care to tell me what happened out there?"

"We were on Armil's AirLimb, we heard there was a problem at the camp, so we, Messenger, and some Providers went to go keep them safe. The Citizens might be tough enough to handle that place, maybe, but the Subjects? Not as much. Most of them, anyway."

"And, you weren't just looking for a chance to escape," Colonel Mangual inquired dryly.

"The only place I want to escape to is Station Four," Tara said, "and I'm pretty sure a walk through those ruins isn't getting me there."

There was a few seconds of silence before Colonel Mangual gave her response. "Fair. It's become clear that different groups from Station Four are... operating with different levels of education and experience. Can you tell me what happened with Sasha in the city?"

"You know about her agoraphobia, yes?"

"Yes."

"She was doing really well. I pushed her a little more than I should have, but she was doing really well. All things considered. Until we noticed... recognized the... the bodies."

There was another silent pause before Mangual replied. "Unfortunate she noticed," Mangual said, clearing her throat. "That city had to be burnt five years ago or so now."

"And all those people? Were they your enemy?"

"No. They were innocent, but an enemy... more of a criminal really, 'killed' them before we burnt the city. Nano-bio terrorism."

Tara stared at the panel in confused disgust. "What is that supposed to mean?"

"We had to burn two cities that year," Mangual said in a solemn tone, "it was the most violent event in our nation's history. Over ten million people died. We're still picking through the wreckage. We're having to be very careful about making sure there isn't a contamination as we go along. Just last year, another city was attacked, but we managed to contain the situation before – "

"The big war!" Tara cried, *"It's not that it never happened, it just hasn't even ended yet!"*

"No, no, no!" Mangual pleaded, "The nuclear war thing never happened, and it's not happening now. The attacks we've been talking about weren't nuclear, they weren't even a war, and it's over now!"

"It sure as hell sounds like war! Ten million?! And that's not a war?!"

"But it wasn't like–" Mangual stopped talking abruptly.

"Colonel?" Tara asked.

A moment passed, and Colonel Mangual's voice returned, brisker than before. "She's awake. You should go see her. Now."

The lock on the door clicked open.

Tara went through the door, and looked in either direction. Both directions looked identical until a man dressed in a light version of the splotchy-uniform came out of a room thirty metres or so away, and called out, *"Engineer Tara?! This way!"*

Tara ran as fast as possible. Getting closer, she could hear Sasha's cries, and another women trying to calm her down. Tara narrowly avoided bowling over the man before getting to the room.

Inside, Sasha sat in the corner, knees up, trying to stay back from the uniformed woman trying to comfort her.

"Back off," Tara said as she dashed in to kneel by Sasha and hold her.

"Tara! Tara! I woke up, and I had no idea where you were, and this place... and – "

"Shh, I know." Tara held Sasha closer, resting her lips on Sasha's ear. "I know, my love. I know. I came as soon as they'd let me."

Sasha's jagged, panicked breathing began to calm, little by little. In Tara's arms, Sasha's fearful, rigid body shook gradually less and less. Sasha was in Tara's arms, and the room around them become less and less important.

"Do you need anything?" the woman in uniform asked.

The answer came in the form of an unimpressed glare from Tara.

"I... I'll come back later and take some vitals," the uniformed woman said before exiting, and locking the door behind her.

Tara relaxed a little. They were imprisoned, but together at least. *"My* room had two cots, *this* room has two cots, why'd they bother to separate us?" Tara growled softly.

Sasha didn't bother theorizing. The tears were cooling on her face, and her Tara was here. She kissed Tara's neck, and just left her lips there to breathe. "I want to go home," Sasha whispered.

"Yeah. Me too, hon." Tara answered softly, "I think we're not done hiding from the war."

Messenger awoke alone in a room much like the ones Tara and Sasha had woken up in. As he woke, he heard shouting on the other side of his door, but it ended quickly. Now he heard voices, barely. Either from the other side of the door, or through the walls.

He tried the door, finding it locked. For that matter, the tablet Berryhill had given him was gone.

Seeing the intercom button, he held it down and called out, "All right, where's this? And where are my people?" He released the button and waited. He was about to try again, when Colonel Mangual's voice beat him to it.

"Messenger. I hear you're awake? I was dealing with something else," she said.

"Hello. As I had asked, where am I, and where are my people?"

"You're in Yute Central. You've been here before, but not this section. The cells you were in last time currently have most of the others you were gassed with in the Meston ruins."

"So, why am I in this room, and not with the others?" Messenger asked.

"I thought it would be easier to talk if you weren't in a crowd," Mangual said, "I also had your two main Engineers separated from everyone. The one with agoraphobia was examined as well as we could, and the two of them are now together."

"They... they're alright?"

There was a long pause before Colonel Mangual replied. "Physically, they're fine. The Sasha one is significantly distressed."

Messenger snapped back immediately. "I want to see her."

"Tara is with her," Mangual replied, "and they're fine now."

Messenger scoffed lightly. *"Fine?* I guess that's relative, isn't it? I'm guessing they don't want to be *here*. And what of the others that were with us?"

"They're fine," Mangual said. "Some are still asleep, but they'll be up any minute. You're among the late risers as well."

"You laid them all out unconscious in the cell?!"

"We provided matting where needed, but yes. After checking their vitals. There was enough of them that a few cells had to be used. Since they wouldn't all fit in one cell anyway, we attempted to sort by Providers, Subjects, and Citizens. Once everyone's awake, we'll issue a … brunch, I guess, a new set of clothes as needed, then back to the camp."

"I think they'd rather go home!" Messenger said firmly. "As would I!"

"That home is an underground slave camp!" Colonel Mangual

sharply replied.

"*They were just helping us to survive! We were all working together to survive the war!*"

"Your war never happened! Your facility is done. It was a disaster of human rights crimes from the first inhabitant who wasn't told the truth! The Subjects and the Citizens are victims, and we're going to find a way to re-educate them, and integrate them back into society! It's not going to be fast, and it's not going to be easy."

"Is that so?" Messenger sat on the corner of his cot. "I suppose Providers and Engineers don't need the education."

"Oh you do! But I'm not sure what's going to happen to you. You're all complicit with maintaining a society of slave labour. And I've heard how you manage your children!"

Messenger stood, muscles rigid. "*We were surviving! This is how we managed it! The Enemy stalked us daily! We survived! This is how we did it!*"

"You certainly need re-education," Mangual said flatly. "How you can repay the Subjects and Citizens for your crimes... I don't even know what your punishment will be yet."

After a meal, new clothes, and a ride in one of the cargo helicopters, Leena arrived back at the camp, along with the other Citizens, the Subjects, and about half of the Managers.

The Providers and some of the Managers didn't come along. She thought they might come on the next flight, but there were no Providers at camp, either. No Engineers.

Just Subjects, Citizens, and a handful of Managers.

The front room was different. Many of the cots were replaced with little tables connected to little chairs, all arranged in a wide grid, all facing a new media screen. The one that Patricia had stabbed was gone.

"Welcome to school," the guard at the door said.

"Corporal VonWaffles!" Leena said, looking at the changes. "What happened here?"

Having found that trying to correct Leena was fruitless now, Corporal 'VonWaffles' spoke to any of the incoming people who were listening. "Well, now that everyone's back, class will be starting in the morning. Gonna do a lot of learning."

"Where's the Providers?" Leena asked.

"You don't have to worry about them anymore," VonWaffles said, "They're going to learn other things, it sounds like."

Leena held her hands in front of herself as if expecting to be given something. "Yeah, but... Messy!"

"Messy?"

"Messenger!"

"Do you give goofy names to everyone?" VonWaffles asked.

"Whatever. Where is he? And these two lovey-love-girls, and Gabe, and..."

"They're fine," VonWaffles said. "The Colonel just thought it'd be better to split you all into groups."

Leena frowned slightly, looking around. "So... did they all go willingly, or did you use the sleepy smell on them and cart them off?"

VonWaffles grimaced. "There were some objections. But it went okay."

Hands on her hips, Leena fidgeted, and sucked her teeth. "*Some objections but it went okay.* Yeah. Yeah, fine. Okay, so what are we learning?"

"From what I hear, kinda a lot," VonWaffles began, "about the world, reading-"

"Ha, I can read!" Leena pointedly said proudly. "And I know plenty about the world now."

"Enough that if we flew you to the nearest city, you could find a job and an apartment?"

"Yeah! Yeah, what's an apartment?"

A new camp, a new fence. A different kind of building.

"This place smells," Tara said as she entered the building, along with a hundred and fifty other Engineers, five hundred Providers, and the Managers who had once been Providers. It was smaller than the building at the first camp, but that first camp was more than big enough for two thousand to sleep.

The ground here was grassy, like the first camp, but a bit more overgrown, and it didn't stop at the fence. Where the first camp had grass only to the edge of the fence, because it was planted and maintained there, the grass here grew of its own volition, with several other plants here and there of unknown kinds.

"This was some old food processing factory," a soldier replied. I hope you like bugs, there's bound to be a few still hanging around."

Sasha was leaning on Tara, and murmured, "Oh Tara, look behind the helicopter."

Looking back, beyond the fence the grass kept going until it met with drier land, with rocks and gravel, leaning into fine, grey dirt that reached a churning field of endless liquid, which seemed to try to advance towards them, only to break apart into white on the edges, and retreat. Over and over again.

Tara could now hear it a little, beyond the helicopter and the sounds of the people.

The liquid field was hypnotic, and she was not the only one watching. Sasha was less entranced. "Let... let's go inside now?"

Messenger stepped up. "Let's. I saw that liquid on Berryhill's little tablet thing. From the air. I believe that is the ocean."

By now, the guards were getting less interested in letting people gawk, and increasingly more concerned with getting people secured. Much like the other camp was now, the first room was an array of little desks, facing a screen. When everyone was inside, one of the guards at the door said, "Okay. For now, I'd appreciate if you all stayed indoors. Colonel Mangual will be addressing you shortly."

"What's that smell?" Gabe asked.

"A mix of fish, bug guts, and bleach," the guard said. Getting only a puzzled look from Gabe, he explained further. "Bleach is a chemical they used to clean this place out, but apparently not well enough. Bugs are tiny living things, probably crickets in this case, and fish are living things that live in that ocean." He pointed outside to the giant mass of liquid.

"We saw fish on the screen at the other camp," Kevin said. "They don't look great to eat."

The guard laughed. "You haven't seen a cricket then! Eh, they get processed,and they don't end up looking like they were when they were alive. 'Cept my kid... dunno how she got into whole baked crickets, but whatever. We're lucky whenever kiddo gets into anything that's actually nutritious."

"Kid..." Tara said, "that's a child, right?"

"Yeah. She's five. Great age. Lots of energy, not a ton of logic."

"And she... you're her biological father, and she lives with you, yes?"

The guard seemed a little surprised by the question. "Y...yeah?"

"When she was born, was she assigned to your section? Your job? Will she be a soldier also?"

"Ha. Right now she wants to be a cookie-maker, she says. Who knows?"

Tara was mildly alarmed, and many around who heard this were visibly concerned. "You... have no idea what she'll do?!" Tara asked, "no assigned duty?"

"At five?!" the guard laughed. "She just plays and learns! I won't be shocked if she's twenty before she knows what she wants to do, but figuring...." he looked at the mystified expressions on the faces around him. "You people don't have any idea..." he said, his own face becoming as mystified and concerned as the people listening to him. "You people have a lot of earning to do."

It was then that the media screen popped to life. After a quick flash of technical information and a military logo, Colonel Mangual appeared.

"Good day, everyone. Engineers, Providers. Messenger."

Messenger stepped forward, making himself closest to the screen. "Colonel. I ask that we be returned to our facility, Station Four."

"You're aware that I can't responsibly do that. You are to learn here, about the world as it is now. You're over a century out of date, and have been living in such a ... regressed society. But you are still citizens of this nation, and as such, the nation has a responsibility to aid you in recovering from that."

"Whether we like it or not."

"Education can only benefit you, Messenger."

"And the Subjects and Citizens? They're not getting education?"

"They are. They, especially the Subjects, have a good deal more to learn. When they're able, we'll help them make lives in general society."

"Even the Citizens who've killed?" Messenger asked, "they're not a concern?"

Colonel Mangual nodded with a raised eyebrow. "They most certainly are. Counsellors will be examining their mental status and conditions of their past violence on an individual basis."

Messenger leaned back. Would these counsellors be fair? Would they be accurate? "I trust Leena's judgement of the Citizens in general. Maybe that's too naïve, though given the resources in the facility, I had to trust the situation. Whereas you –"

"I have the resources to make sure their needs are met, and hazardous behaviours can be mitigated," Mangual said.

"That easy..." Messenger stated.

"Nothing easy about it. I don't envy the counsellors their jobs."

"Jobs. Yes, so once the Citizens and Subjects are all... educated to your liking, what kind of jobs do you plan to set them to?"

"That will vary based on aptitude and their interests. It's going to be freedom."

Messenger nodded. "And me?" He turned to gesture to the Providers and Engineers. "What jobs, what freedoms?"

Colonel Mangual's expression went from mild pride, to a much more dour look. "The... children among you won't be held accountable for the slavery of the Subjects, though they will need to be educated away from that system. The adults..."

"Will be punished." Messenger said, causing a ripple of quiet but discordant noises from the people behind him.

"Punished is a strong word," Colonel Mangual said. "There will be consequences. Accountability. But It's not like we're going to toss you all in a room and lock you away for generations like was done to your Citizens section," she said with a notably growing hint of spite.

"You realize why that was done," Messenger said.

"Yes. And now you're going to blame a lack of resources for leaving them there instead of trying to fix them decades ago."

"That's a factor," Messenger admitted. "Fear of them? And then it became just the way things were done."

"It seems like a lot of terrible things happened down in that hole just because that's the way it was always done." She glowered at Messenger, who had no reply. "You have ten hours," she said, addressing the entire room. "Then the guards will wake anyone asleep, and your first lesson will begin an hour after that, on this screen. Welcome to your future, people."

With that, the screen went blank, and six hundred and fifty prisoners were left in shock, breathing the lingering bleach, slaughtered fish and crickets.

"You can go into the yard now," said the guard by the door. "As far as the fence, obviously."

Some people interested by the sea went to watch it. Some people went out for fresh air. Others wandered the building, exploring where they could, finding the rooms with arrays of cots.

Messenger stepped up to the media terminal. Finding the small array of buttons on the bottom edge, he was soon in a menu that offered what looked to be the same selection of documentaries and approved entertainment. He looked for a way to access the mailing programme he had on the tablet that Berryhill had given him.

"Guard, does this thing have access to mail?"

"Nope."

"Can I call the Colonel, or anyone else using this thing?"

"Nope."

"I had a little tablet terminal when I was at the other camp – "

"And now you don't."

"Ah."

"How ya doin'?" Tara said, putting an arm around Sasha's shoulders for a squeeze.

"Oh. You know. Spectacularly." She grabbed Tara's hand and gave it a squeeze back. "Same as the rest of us. Grateful to our kind hostess, and looking forward to trying to sleep in a room with a couple hundred other people again. With this stink. Oh, and there's that little wet spot outside looking at me."

"Wet spot?" Tara glanced out towards the direction of the ocean. "Uh, yeah. That's... that's something all right. Hey. We gonna talk about what we saw in those ruins?"

Sasha's gaze shifted to a distant nowhere. "Can... can we not?"

"Okay."

Sasha nuzzled herself into Tara, burying her face into her shoulder, and squeezing as tight as she could. "Tell me that's not the world," she mumbled into Tara weakly.

"Well... yes, we're told that place is like one of two places like that, and the vast majority of the world isn't... that."

"No good," Sasha said, squeezing desperately, even tighter. "Tell me that didn't exist."

Tara nuzzled into the hair near Sasha's ear. "I don't know what you're talking about, Sash. We're home. We're in our room on our own bed. The generator's doing fine, and we even have the day off. I'm going to keep you in bed all day, and not let go."

"Never let go," Sasha whispered.

"Of course not. You're my Sash." Tara gave an extra bit of squeeze, unsure if it could even be felt against how hard Sasha was squeezing.

"You won't let go because I'm weak?"

"You're my Sash."

A few moments passed as they held each other, doing their best to ignore their surroundings.

"I hate being weak. I hate that it makes you have to … to deal with me."

Tara moved back enough to look Sasha in the eye with a stern expression. "*You. Are. My. Sash.* I know how big it is out there. I know how that's making you feel. I have trouble logically understanding that hugeness out there. You can't help how much it affects you, but you push through. I've never been prouder of how you handled that run to the AirLimb back at home, or how you followed me into those ruins. I've never been so ashamed of myself for bringing you there."

"Tara, no…"

Tara grabbed Sasha close again, almost forcefully. Hints of sobs struggled to push their way through Tara's voice. "Y-you are my Sash. You're *so* strong, hon. You're my…"

And they held each other. And others held each other. Some needed comforting, others chose to explore cautiously. Others stared at the sea. And night eventually came.

And they held each other.

Chapter 28:

Settle

"They weren't killed by monsters," Leena explained to Patricia again. "Stop telling people the ruins are full of monsters."

When their little group had been held in Yute central, the attacks on Meston were explained to them in terms that the under-educated Citizens and Subjects could understand. That the government didn't have a choice, and that the innocents were already either taken somewhere safe, or already dead.

This information was coming from a soldier in the army holding them captive, which cast a little doubt on it all, but in the interests of keeping Patricia calm, Leena accepted what they were told.

When they got back to camp, Patricia made it her mission to warn anyone who'd listen.

"Yeah, okay, maybe *full* of monsters is going a bit far," Patricia conceded. "We didn't *see* any of the monsters, but those ruins are huge. There could be like a *hundred* hiding in there!"

A guard nearby scoffed with a smirk. "A hundred, eh? Lass, if I thought you could handle it, I'd say you should read up on the recent history of that city. But no, I'm pretty sure all the monsters have been burnt clean."

"War..." Patricia whispered, wide-eyed.

The guard grimaced, and stared at the floor. "Something like that. Not all conflicts are wars."

Patricia tilted her head and ventured, "Questing...?"

Leena stepped in, "Okay, thaaaaat's more than enough. Patricia. There's no monsters, and it's not your job to kill em if there were." She gave the guard a pointed glare. "Don't encourage her."

The guard finally clued in about Patricia, and gave a small nod. "Right. Sorry. Class is starting any minute now, anyway."

Guards instructed people to sit in the little seats attached to the little tables. These were the first to volunteer, and most inclined to go along with the lesson, but of course many of the younger ones were more difficult to settle down.

Everyone who got a seat was told to touch a little device that beeped, and asked their name. When the seats were all full, it only accounted for a small part of the Subjects and Citizens. People who wanted to stay were also asked to touch the device and introduce themselves.

"You're class A," a guard announced. "In an hour, we'll get a class B set up, and so on." He pressed a button on a device, and put it in his pocket.

The screen popped to life. On it was a slender man in clothing like they'd never seen before; a pretty dull blue shirt, and some black bit of cloth hanging from his neck. He had some sort of decoration on his face; some slim bit of black that had big holes for his eyes to see through.

He introduced himself by some forgettable name, and as 'your teacher'.

"This is a course specifically arranged for the refugees from Station Four. Let's start with geography. We'll start at Station Four, and by the time we're done in an hour, we'll have gone around the world, popped by the moon, across our solar system, and beyond."

Leena leaned out of her desk, over to the guard. "We're not actually going around-"

"No, no one is leaving the camp," the guard said with a huff. "It was a poor choice of words. Now pay attention."

The screen showed the outside of Station Four, which most of the people in the room had only seen once, while they were getting herded to a helicopter. The scene zoomed back and up to get a look at the surrounding dried flatlands in a soaring view that few of the audience could have imagined was possible.

A young Citizen fell out of his chair, apparently the most stunned in the audience. Most were transfixed. Some were holding onto their chairs tightly. One Subject in the back row chose to sit on the floor behind his chair.

Cody was seated beside Leena, holding her hand, and trading the occasional glance with her.

The view rose further and further. They passed through some white smoke of some kind. Eventually they saw the greater shape of the land, tan in spots, more white in a patch off-centre, and greens, especially around the edges. It was all surrounded by dark blue.

"This is your country," the voice of the teacher said. "Aguola. Our home."

"My home's in the Citizenry Commons!" Patricia hollered out.

More than a few people in the class made their agreement known.

"He can't hear you," the guard said. "This is just a recording."

Patricia stood and screamed louder at the screen. "*My home is in Citizenry!*"

Leena squeezed Cody's hand and lowered her head.

Another voice came from the class, who were now all but ignoring the lesson. "My home is in a wheat Unit." Elise said, with her three Sisters seated nearby, agreeing. Others chimed in.

"My home's in a rice Unit."

"My home's beets."

"Citizen."

"Papayas."

"Lablab."

"Citizens strong together."

"Beans."

"Citizens."

The lesson had progressed automatically all the while, hearing nothing.

At the second camp, the lessons were going smoother. Providers and Engineers knew more about technology, and while they didn't understand everything about the workings of the screen, they were quicker to adapt to expected levels of interaction.

Even if the expected level of interaction was to sit down and shut up.

That's not to say that every student was happily, intently absorbing every nugget of knowledge. Some politely ignored it, some found it to be going too slowly, and many were frustrated with being taught about things millions of kilometres away, when they were not permitted to travel *one* kilometre.

Messenger found himself interested in the nature of the cosmos, despite himself. He had been quite determined to resent the lesson, and maintain a bitter disposition throughout until the promised break, when he'd planned to press the issue with the guard about getting communications out.

The guards kept a hand on their stun-weapons while overseeing the class. This seemed to send a clear enough message, but it gave Messenger time to consider exactly what he'd say to the guard during the break.

When the recording of the teacher came on to declare a half-hour break, it switched quickly to a connection with Colonel Mangual.

Some of the students were wandering off, but more than half stayed.

"Colonel," Messenger said curtly, not entirely sure this wasn't just another recording.

"Messenger, everyone," Colonel Mangual replied, "how did your first lesson go?"

"Very interesting," Messenger admitted, "though I've had other things on my mind."

With a hint of a smile that may have meant "Oh, what now?", Colonel Mangual instead simply said, "Oh?"

"We have money, don't we?" Messenger said, "I recall you saying that Station Four was making a great deal of money in our name ever since the generator went online."

Colonel Mangual's slight smile turned into a slight smirk, and a slight cock of he head. "If I recall... HDU incorporated. That money is being held. The generator's dead, so there's no payments coming in from that anymore, but it still is gaining interest, I think."

"I want to use our money," Messenger said, holding his arms out to indicate the other classmates.

Colonel Mangual's slight smile turned to a slight squint. "And what do you want to spend it on? You're learning exactly what you need."

"It's our money, I think we'd like one of those huge helicopters."

Colonel Mangual scoffed a mirthless laugh. "It takes a lot of training to fly one of those things, and then there's airspace regulations and a lot of things that go well beyond the curriculum of your classes here."

Undaunted, Messenger countered. "Then we'll use some of the money to get someone to fly it. And all those things not... not in our current curriculum."

Colonel Mangual returned to he meek smile, and shook her head. "I think that money will be locked away for a good while. I don't even think it's yours. And you're not going anywhere."

Tara stood abruptly. "*Why can't we just go? What danger are we to you?*"

"*None.*" Colonel Mangual snapped back. "You're a hazard to yourselves. I don't know when you'll be ready to be out in the world! You're regressed for over a century! If I had to guess, I'd say maybe *half* of the children there have any chance at having something resembling a normal life. What we're trying to fix now is generations of systemic ignorance your facility ran on! And that's not even addressing the issue of the Subject slavery! *Get comfortable folks.* You're here for the long haul."

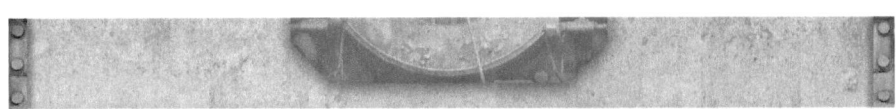

Chapter 29:

Deploy

Eight months passed.

The residents of Station Four learned of snow, and rain, and that the Enemy can indeed be dangerous, but not as severely as they once thought.

Those who'd never read, now could, a little. Those who used to a bit, now could read better. Those who read well, could now ready very well. Math improved, understanding of the world was better.

They learned of jobs, money, guaranteed incomes, higher learning, trade schools and apartments, and what life would be like in a 'transition home'.

Many wanted to visit the many places they'd been told about, and shown video of.

Most still spoke of Station Four as home. And wanted to return.

In the second camp, ideas floated around between Providers and

Engineers. Ideas that relied on a lot of 'maybe'. They wished to discuss their ideas with the Citizens and Subjects, but communication had not been allowed.

In the first camp, a day of lessons ended with a new woman appearing on the screen, with turquoise, curly hair. She smiled benevolently.

"Hello, people, My name is Becca Moorehead. Just call me Becca. How's everyone doing?"

The class in session responded as any group responds to a non-question, with a wave of half-hearted mumbles.

"Blue hair!" Elise commented, "Colonel what's-er-face has dark purple hair, is that kind of thing common with people out here?"

Becca took a second to remember. "Colonel... Mangual? Oh yes, she does have coloured hair, doesn't she? Huh. Never thought about it, I didn't think non-Aguei could have coloured hair in the military. I don't know exactly how common it is. A lot of people colour their hair a natural colour, like blonde or brown or red, or wherever, so they don't generally stand out like blue or pink."

"*Sky colour!*" Patricia hollered. "I want sky colour!"

Becca chuckled, "Well, that's an option you can look into some other time. I'm not here to talk about hair."

"You're not here." Leena said flatly. "And you're not military? Does that mean you're not a soldier?"

"That's right. I'm a civilian."

"We've been taught about those."

"Good, good stuff," Becca said. "At any rate, I'm coming to you as a *Social Councillor.* I've got some pretty exciting news. Due to how well your studies have gone, the higher-ups including the Colonel, think it's time that a test-group of thirty people get moved to a civilian home in the city."

Horrified gasps and shocked expressions erupted along the Citizens and Subjects.

"Why?!"

"What have we done?!"

"... I"m pretty sure it's still got monsters."

"What kind of test is *this*? Survival???"

Becca was stunned by the reaction, and tried to listen to as many people as were calling out objections. "You haven't even *seen* Densfarn! Have you? It's nice!"

"What, not *that* city?" Elise pointed in the direction of the adjacent ruins of Meston city.

"*That* ci... *Meston?! No,* no," Becca assured them, "No one's moving into there for... a long, long time, if ever. Sorry, I should have been more clear from the start. Densfarn's beautiful. Coastal city, easy access to the beach."

"No monsters?" Patricia asked with grim scrutiny.

"Ha... no, like a year or two ago there was an incident that... was stressful," Becca said, "but that's long taken care of."

"Did you burn it like Meston?" Leena asked. "That crap's horrific."

Becca took a deep breath. "I have to be honest with you. No, no it wasn't burned, but it was headed that way. The person responsible for that, and Meston, and one other city is gone. As much as I'd like to tell you that there's nothing dangerous out here, the fact is that danger exists. It will always exist. As much as I and anyone else wants you all to be safe and happy... as unlikely as anything unexpected and horrible happening... the world has dangers. If it makes you feel better, I live in Densfarn, and I'm in it right now. It's a really nice day out, sun's shining, birds are singing, all the rest."

The class didn't respond with cheers, but they didn't respond with jeers, either, so Becca continued.

"Now what I want to do, is bring thirty volunteers to a 'transition house'. You'll live there. You'll have your own money, you'll have freedom to explore the city, but for five hours every weekday, you'll be in class, learning skills that can help you find a job, and eventually your own home."

"I have a home in Citizenry," Leena said. Several others seemed to agree.

"That facility can't be your home anymore, sadly," Becca said, "it's not sustainable anymore, and the means that food was made there was under working conditions that really can't... just can't go on like that. Station Four is no more."

"Leena, you go to Densfarn!" Patricia said, "you go, make sure there's no monsters, and come back."

"Leena is...?" Becca asked, looking across the class.

"No way," Leena said, "if I go, who's gonna keep an eye on the rest of you dorks?"

"I can," Jen said meekly, giving her partner a squeeze, "I have help."

"Leena," Becca said, "Are you a leader of some kind?"

Amid positive responses from around the class, and a shrug from her partner Cody, Leena had to admit, "Yeah, I guess so. For some of the Citizens, anyway. I've never been a leader of Subjects, though."

"I'll vote for you, I'm a Subject," Elise said. This garnered other positive comments from the crowd.

"You vote on it?" Becca said with mild surprise.

"Nah, but we learned about voting a while ago," Leena said, "I kinda became leader-ey when Mike was killed, and the guy who wanted to take over offed himself after the Actual made him... feel bad or something."

With mild panic, Becca looked to the side, reviewing data. Making sure this didn't happen in the camp. "Wh.. when was that?"

Leena sighed. "Wow... Mike's been gone almost... almost three years."

Cody put his arm around Leena, then told Becca, "We named Citizenry's first papaya tree after him. He was a hero. He taught us a lot about... looking after each other, I guess."

Becca nodded. "Yeah. I read that Citizenry's had some rough times."

A gloom had been settling over Leena, thinking about the loss of Mike, but she broke out of it with a single harsh laugh. *Rough times? Ooh, a* moment or two were a teeny bit inconvenient."

Cody smiled warmly at Leena. "And now *you're* our hero."

A number of the class members voiced their agreement, and someone got off a 'Citizens strong together'.

Leena turned to everyone, and waved them off with a laugh. "Aww, quit sucking up."

"Well, it seems you're very *much* their leader," Becca said.

"Okay, for Citizens, maybe," Leena said, "but most of the folks here are Subjects, I was never their leader."

"Uhm?" Elise spoke up, "I didn't know you in the facility, but ... since we've been here? You... you've been looking out for everyone."

Elise's Unit Sister nodded and added, "Yeah, she's settled a lot of things. Our Manager got taken away with the Providers, a lot of Managers were, but Leena more than picked up that slack."

"You're blowing things out of proportion," Leena said.

"Nope!" Called out another Subject in the other end of the class. "If anyone's got an issue, they wanna go to you before they bother a guard."

"See, then?" Leena said to Becca, "If I'm so darn valuable as a leader here, what's going to happen to them all if I go to thems-farm city, or whatever?"

"It's entirely up to you," Becca said, "and it's *Densfarn* city."

"You should go," Jen said firmly. "Sure you're needed here, but thirty of us in a whole new place, trying out the ... the outside world? Gonna need a leader there."

A resounding outpouring of supportive cheers flooded across the group. Leena shook her head, and turned to Becca's image on the screen. "Frig. That sounds a lot like a vote," Leena bemoaned. She turned to Cody and asked, "So, feel like going to thems-farm, hon?"

At the second camp, Tara and Sasha watched along with everyone else as the guards carried out a body bag on a stretcher.

"Do you know who it was?" Messenger asked.

"I heard someone say it was a 'Joanne'," Sasha said, "A Provider. I... didn't know her."

Messenger shook his head and said, "Me neither. Our third suicide... it makes me wonder how the other camp is doing."

"I wonder how they manage to kill themselves," Sasha said. "No one heard it happening? They must have used some kind of–"

Tara squeezed Sasha. "Shh. Don't... don't talk about it. Don't give anyone ideas."

"It's not the *how* that's really at issue, it's the *why*," Messenger said.

"All my life I've heard of one Engineer suicide," Tara said. "We've been here less than a year, and that's three.

"I knew of a few in Citizenry," Messenger said, "though given their history, it's probably a lot more. I... like I said, I wonder how the other camp's doing."

"The Citizens are different than they used to be," Sasha said, "but being in the camp... ugh..."

One of the guards spoke up, hollering to anyone in earshot, "*Class is cancelled for the morning. Afternoon's optional.*"

The prisoners dissipated from watching the body being taken away, some going to their cots, some loitering around the class area, some headed into the yard for a walk.

Sasha and Tara headed to their cot.

"I'm going to go stare at the ocean," Messenger said.

Dawn and Gabe came along. "Weather's good. We're in."

"Either of you know this Joanna person?" Messenger asked.

"She worked in composting," Dawn said, eyes cast down. "The people out here... I don't think they compost the bodies of the dead. Or they do sometimes, but not always? It's unclear."

"I'm ready to stop talking about it," Gabe said. "Ocean staring?"

"Ocean staring," Messenger replied.

Escorted by a single soldier, and Becca the social councillor, Leena, Cody, and twenty-eight others from the first camp flew via helicopter to the Densfarn airport. In camp, they'd had a lesson about what to expect, but walking into the airport was staggering.

A bold sign overhead greeted them, "Welcome to Densfarn."

So many people. All very busy people dressed in so many different ways. After a life of blue standard issue body suits, seeing yellow suits, and later, the uniforms of the military, this array of random colours and forms was dizzying.

Lights overhead spewed data that meant nothing to Leena, but there was so much of it, it had to mean something important to someone. Other lights showed strange foods, and colourful drink containers, and there was a rack containing a vast array of items, from books, (new, real, undamaged books!) small foods in paper wrappers, and small hairy animals that didn't move, were often strange colours, and looked like they'd be quite unsuited to survive in any of the animal documentaries they'd seen.

"Don't buy anything here," Becca said, "everything's way overpriced for travellers and tourists."

"But we don't have money," Cody said, holding up the little hand-sized personal terminal he, and the entire group had been issued.

"Pay attention," Leena said, showing Cody on her own terminal. "Our first allowance. Press there.. and there..." She poked Cody's terminal, but his screen brought up Leena's name. "What..." She poked her own terminal and saw her own name there, too. "What. *Hey Becca, Cody's terminal thinks it's mine!*"

"Leena, remember, the terminals can read you, and accesses your own information for you, "Becca explained, "you can use anyone's terminal to get to your own information."

"Pay better attention," Cody smugly joked, earning an elbow in the ribs from Leena.

As they got a little further in, the interior opened up into a large hall that put the Citizenry's Commons to shame, a few times over. Filled with more busy people, going every which way, the dull roar of talk all but drowned out music playing from nowhere, yet everywhere.

"Come along, we have our bus waiting for us," Becca beckoned. The group managed somehow not to lose each other in the flowing crowds. Mostly. At one point, a Subject called out, "Where's Elise?" Becca checked her terminal, and saw on the map that one of her charge had broken off, so she changed the group's direction to intercept the lost wandering Elise, who was quite relieved to be back with her Sisters and the rest of the group.

Eventually, they were out of the building on the other side. A beautiful blue sky with a blessing of a few puffy clouds greeted them. A few bands of concrete stretched out nearby, servicing the comings and goings of ground vehicles while multiple behemoths streaked across the sky.

A minute more of walking along the building's outer edge, seeing a seemingly endless concrete field of parked vehicles, they came to their bus, dark blue, and imposing. "Huh. Reminds me of that truck Patricia stabbed. Kinda... longer but narrower. Kinda." Leena remarked.

"I've seen more people in the last ten minutes than I knew existed," Elise said as she stepped up into the bus.

"And we're not even in the city yet," Becca said.

Cody pointed back at the gargantuan airport building. "*That's not a city?*"

Becca looked at the airport, and at Cody's shock. "Nope. But you have a point. There are cities out there that are about that size. People work at the airport, you can eat there, there might even be a few people who live there, but no, it's not a city. This place is just about air travel. It's not even part of Densfarn city, officially, I think."

Cody tinkered with the map of his terminal. "Oh... oh I see... hon, I'm getting the impression the world might be kinda big."

Leena chuckled nervously. "Yeah... having it explained on a screen is one thing, but... even at the camp, there wasn't all these people. And this place? This place makes the camp look like a crap-sniffer's den."

The group all boarded, including Becca and their soldier escort. The seats were unlike any they'd seen before, and each had a screen of its own. The windows that provided a somewhat tinted view of the outside ran the length of the bus, but they weren't noticeable from the outside.

"Oof, I could live in *here*." Leena said, discovering the ability to recline her seat.

Once everyone had found a seat, Becca called out, "Saved Destination two, go."

A gentle voice came from the ceiling. "Confirming: Becca Moorehead request transit to saved destination two."

"Yup, go already."

A soft electric whine could be heard from somewhere under the floor, and the bus began moving.

Half of the passengers held on to their arm-rests despite the bus's motion being a slow, gradual acceleration as it manoeuvred the parking lot, and the rest of the passengers were glued to the windows, watching the world move around them.

"This thing... controls itself?" Leena asked nervously.

"Yeah," Becca said with a mild smile.

"Do you trust it?!"

"I wouldn't trust *me* controlling it!" Becca laughed. "It's huge, and there's a lot of cars and stuff I'd hit!"

"Can't *it* hit things?"

"There's well over a billion and a half cars out there driving like this, I think we'll be fine."

"A bill... Leena gazed out the window as they joined other vehicles turning onto a larger, straight road. "So many..." Hearing the numbers and having them explained and shown on a screen did little to prepare her for being among the masses. "Do these people know about us?" Leena asked.

Becca took a moment to decide how to answer. "It did make the news when the government told the world that... a 'large community of cold war survivalists' had been discovered. It kind of started fading from the news in a week or two."

"We... we're a curiosity. We were. We're just..." Leena trailed off into her own thoughts.

"Do they know about that dead city?" Cody asked.

"Oh yes," Becca said gravely. "Between Meston and Autar, and the smaller attack on Densfarn, people are still talking about it, and how to keep it from happening."

"*The thing that did that to Meston could happen to the city we're going to?!*" Leena cried.

"No! No, no. It almost happened, but we figured out how to stop it. That threat is gone. Even this bus has sensors onboard to look out for the weapons used in those attacks."

"So it's still a possibility." Leena said.

"So is lighting and earthquakes." Becca replied.

"*That shit's real?!*" Elise yelped.

As they travelled, they saw cricket farms, wheat farms, (which stunned Elise especially,) and a number of indeterminate facilities. "Storage or factories", Becca would often explain, often guessing. These sorts of buildings became fewer, and the metropolis of Densfarn's core could be seen in the distance.

"Are we going to live *there?*" Elise asked.

"Well, what we're seeing from here is the tallest buildings in the middle. Very few people actually live there. It's more for businesses and stuff. A lot of people come from the edges and the middle to meet close to the core for work, then return home later. Some people spend nearly an hour in their cars going back and forth every day. We won't really have a practical need to go into the core, since your school and the apartments are fairly close to each other ... in the middle between the edge and the core. I do assume most of you will want to go check it all out, and I've picked some popular places we can go see, like the view from one of the middle towers, a museum, a fun park... we'll go over our options when we're settled."

"View from the..." Cody stared out the bus window, into the sky. "Why didn't the helicopter have windows like these? It should have had windows like these!"

"The helicopter was a military vehicle," Becca explained, "military vehicles are boring."

Their soldier escort snorted with a smirk, but otherwise kept to himself.

"Hey wait, did the helicopter control itself, too?" Leena asked.

"Yes, but aircraft require a human pilot supervisor to keep track of things. I don't know how much they actually do."

"Not a fuck of a lot," the soldier said, "Nice gig if you can get it. Half a year of training over basic. Heard it's not so hard, but supply is bigger than demand."

The view of passing buildings turned to smaller houses, small businesses, wide arrays of matching homes, two stories high. Then three, then four. The sizes and types of buildings varied considerably when the bus left the long road and turned down a smaller side road.

People were a common sight walking along the sides of the street.

"They don't have cars?"

"For short distances, cars become less convenient than just walking," Becca explained. "Our apartments are about four blocks from school, so we'll be walking *that* daily.

"I kinda want a car..." Cody said, mainly to himself.

"Well, that can be a future goal," Becca responded, "and later on, I'm sure you can get one, but that's a bit of a ways down the road."

"Can I walk to it?"

"Walk to... no, ah... down the road means 'in the future.'"

"... how long?"

"I'm not sure. A year or two?" Becca guessed.

"Long road."

"A lot shorter than if you still lived in that Citizenry place."

That earned Becca a less than warm glance from Leena, and Cody was suddenly stoically lost in thought.

Elise broke the sudden silence. "Does a wheat farm like the ones we saw need workers, or do those farms drive themselves?"

"I'm sure they're not *totally* automated," Becca said, "We can certainly look it up later. Buuut, here we are!"

The bus drew closer to a four story building with windows and balconies all about. "Four apartments to a floor, two people to an apartment. That accounts for everyone on the bus."

Cody did the math quickly in his head. "Uhh, are you and our soldier buddy staying with us?"

"I will be, for a month or so," Becca said, "and I'll be sharing one of the ground level apartments with the apartment manager. A guy named Juho. He's like... Swedish or from Denmark or something? Anyway, our military escort's gonna get back to the chopper."

"What's a chopper?" Cody asked.

"I have one back home," Elise and Leena said at the same time.

"Neat," Elise said, "It's what I call the tool we use when we harvest the wheat."

Leena scrunched her mouth for a moment, eyebrows raised. "Yeah! Wheat! Citizenry has farms now, I use mine for wheat! And just wheat! Wasn't ever used for anything else!"

"Eek. *Actually*," Becca said, "It's another name for a helicopter. You guys know those. Anyway, let's get moving."

The bus had parked itself, and everyone but the soldier got off. As they got closer, a man in a striped shirt and blue pants came out the main door to greet them. "Ah, you must be Ms. Moorehead?"

"Yup, call me Becca, if we're going to be flatmates for a month."

"Good, good. Then I'm Juho."

"Swedish?"

"Danish."

"I knew that. The... accent threw me off?"

"...accent?"

"Anyway, you got your clearance to be responsible with these tenants?"

"Of course."

"Because while they *are* adults, they're very not accustomed to our ways, and are in some ways naive and vulnerable."

"Yeah, it's been explained to me," Juho said.

"And if the documentation is correct, about half of these people have fought in a literally underground gang-war of some kind and have slain a lot of very bad people with knives and things."

Leena smiled and waved.

Juho's eyes widened. "That's..."

"Don't say that's hot," Becca warned. "You looked like you were going to say *that's hot.*"

"What? What no! That's... harrowing! I'm glad they were bad? I mean the bad people who were... slain? Congratulations? I honestly don't know what do do with that."

Once everyone had apartments assigned to them, the idea of just settling in interested no one but Becca. "Fine, let's... just go check out the convenience store I saw on our way in. It's less than a block away."

Of course, very quickly it had to be explained that a *block* didn't mean an individual tile of pavement.

"That's dumb, they should have a different name for it," Leena said.

"Ooh, look! Tiny crops! Different than that 'grass' stuff at camp. Can we eat *these*?" Elise asked.

"What? Where? Don't eat things until I tell you it's okay!" Becca said in a bit of a panic.

"Tiny walkway crops," Elise said, pointing at the ground.

"Those aren't crops!" Becca said, "those are just weeds coming up between the blocks of the side-walk!"

"Oh, *now* they're blocks," Leena said.

Becca held her hand to the ground, and then down the street. "*Both* are *blocks.*" She pointed at the weed. "*That's* not food, it's yucky, it's called a weed, they grow wherever they feel like, and you don't want them in with your crops, because they'll try to take over."

"Too bad I don't have my knife," Leena said, eyeing the malevolent little growth.

"That's not..." Becca sighed. "That's not necessary. It's not doing anyone any harm, okay? Can we just get to the store?

With a thirty-member entourage, Becca led the way less than a block to the store. People touched things. Ground, buildings, a tree trunk, the pole to a light fixture. More than once, people had to be reminded to keep off of the actual street. More than one vehicle had to employ caution around the barely-cohesive group, while the passengers of those vehicles looked on in curiosity.

The storefront itself was fifteen or so metres across, with the street-facing walls being glowing, slowly shifting displays of the kinds of things available inside. Images of fast food items floated upward, along with various beverages, interrupted by the occasional electronic gizmo, each with a glossy name and slightly less glossy price.

As the group approached the doors, they slid open, silent, other than a pleasant little tone.

"Okay people, you all have money in your accounts," Becca said, "and I guess it'd be mean to come here and tell you not to buy anything, but try not to get more than ten dollars worth. That's more than enough to get an assortment of little junk foods, a drink... the half-frozen things in the dispenser in the back are all probably going to be interesting, but do not touch things you don't plan to buy! Let's not make this the worst day of the month for the attendant. No messes!"

"Uh... welcome, everyone?" the store attendant said with a meek wave. "Let me uh.. let me know if I can help you find anything, or if you have any... ah... questions."

"Oh, you'll regret that," Becca said. "They have questions."

Before the attendant could ask details, Cody approached. "Half-frozen things? I've seen frozen things in our lessons, but I've never actually touched ice. Do you have ice?"

"Yes, in the back corner we h-"

"I'm a beet farmer," a Subject asked, "do you have beets?"

"We can go look in the canned sec-"

"Holy crap! This is so good!" proclaimed a Citizen who had already gotten into a bag of chips.

"*Don't eat anything you didn't buy!*" Becca pleaded to the little mob she'd inflicted upon the store.

"How to I buy something I ate already?!" came the earnest reply.

"*People!*" the attendant called out, having come to some level realization of the people's level of understanding. "It's really best if you don't eat anything while in the store, but if it's too late, just hang onto the packaging, and you'll be charged automatically as you leave."

"Yeah," Becca added, to explain further, "*any product you take past the doors gets detected, and you auto-buy it. But like I said, try to keep your totals under ten dollars!*"

She turned to the attendant as the group continued to explore every nook and cranny. "I'm so sorry, I should have taught them more about how this kind of place works before we came. Let me toss you my ID," she said, poking a button on her terminal. "If there's damages or anything after we go, I'll make sure it gets taken care of."

From the back, an elated cry was heard, "You can just suck the frozen stuff out of the machine! You don't need a cup!"

Eyes wide with terror, Becca turned her attention towards the back. "*Whoever that is, stop it! That's not sanit-*"

A mewling, anguished scream came out of Elise. "*My head! Oh why the pain?! My head! It's killing me!*"

Becca huffed. "Calm down, that's brain freeze. Too much cold, too fast, and that's what ya get!"

"How long till I die?" She wailed, nearly slurring as she struggled against the sensation.

"It goes away on its own, just give it a minute. You're fine."

"I'm dying...! No... I guess it's getting a little better. But *ow?!*"

After some marginally effective clean-up, Becca reinforced requests to everyone about what to touch, and what not to. With great deliberations the group eventually got their candy, or drinks, or hot dogs, which needed additional explaining as to how they're not dogs. And how they're made of other meats. In this case, cricket meat and various seasoning and processing, like the majority of meats one can find.

On the way out, Elise spotted a modest little rack of seed packets in the corner, almost hidden by a display of earbuds, whatever those were. The pictures on the packets told her what each looked like, but only a few were of foods she knew. They were all really cheap. Potato? Watermelon? The seed packet with a picture of a 'rose' was interesting to Elise. This rose thing looked kind of like the 'ketchup chips' she'd seen Leena gobbling. Worth the meagre price to try to grow. The bag of chips cost way more than the seeds, so it seemed like a prudent purchase. A growable alternative to the bagged chips sounded great, and they're probably better fresh.

She could surprise Leena when the roses are ready to harvest. Assuming she could find a spot to plant them. It didn't look like there was soil available here. She thought about asking the attendant, but between mopping spilled frozen stuff, and answering an endless barrage of questions from everyone, Elise didn't feel like pushing her luck.

When the group finally left, most with more than ten dollars worth of junk food, Becca embarrassedly thanked the attendant, sandwiched between apologies. This would require an impromptu lesson or three, but that was why she was here, after all. It was fine. Things went fine. Not smoothly, but fine. They learned, they experienced.

On the way back, Leena glanced down the street with a critical eye...

Chapter 30:

Sprout

Camp two's lessons progressed, day after day. What had started out on the fantastical side, about the world, the universe, and micro-science basics, had gradually shifted to what a lab assistant does, or even less enthralling, proper methods for the cleaning of public spaces.

After one of the more depressing lessons, Kevin went to commiserate with his Engineer bosses, Tara and Sasha.

"Banal," he said. "That's about all I can call it."

"I've asked the guard about getting more info about solar power," Tara said. "The one lesson was good, but it was introductory at best. I get the concept, I want to know more about actually getting the components, not to mention installing and deploying an array."

"They don't think we need that," Sasha mumbled. "They never

planned on taking us back home. It must be totally abandoned right now. Or with *them* crawling all over messing stuff up."

"Well, at least there's hope they want something more than keeping us here," Kevin offered. "I mean, the lessons lately seem to be teaching us skills we can use *some*where."

"They have 'robots' for more than half the stuff we just learned about," Tara said, "I'm not a robot. I could fix a robot with a little training, we *have* the basic skills for that kind of thing. We have mops here right in this camp. We don't have a robot. They're really only teaching us to take care of camp."

Kevin nodded, and gave it some thought. "There was that video about the weather patterns thing... *that's* not training us for anything in camp. Or the mid-Atlantic ridge... and... useless. They're just keeping us busy."

"And the garden," Sasha added, referring to the micro-farm that the Providers requested to start last month. "Busywork. We know real farms are way more automated, way more efficient. It's not like tending our garden teaches us anything we can use out there to contribute to the world. It's not even big enough to reliably feed *us*. They won't let us expand it, they won't give us *real* gear. They don't have a future planned for us. Messenger knows it, he's figured it out. That's why he's almost always just at the fence, watching the ocean."

Shortly after a helicopter arrived for re-supply, Messenger was approached by Corporal Kay Laird. "At least you have a view here of something other than Meston," Laird said, pointing her chin at the ocean.

Messenger turned away from the fence to look her over. "You're... I know you, you're one of Berryhill's people."

"Corporal Laird, yeah. Berry says hi. I wormed my way onto the resupply chopper, and I wanted to check in."

Messenger gave a nod, and sighed. "Good to know we're not totally forgotten. I don't suppose you have another one of those terminal tablet things for me."

"Afraid not. I'm probably going to catch hell for coming over to chat as it is. I'd bet the guards are watching, so acting casual will probably lead to the least hassle about this later."

"The Subjects and Citizens," Messenger asked, "are they all right?"

"From what I hear, slightly better than here," Laird replied. "Some of them have been moved into Densfarn city, learning skills to just be regular residents."

"How long has it been now?" Messenger asked.

"A month, I think. They don't report to me or anything, I hear it from Berryhill, so he hears it though the grapevine, I guess."

"Grapevine?"

"Uh... kinda means rumours. A bit more reliable than that."

"I see. How's their morale? Have there been suicides?"

"Oh crap!" Laird said, "I have no idea! I don't get that level of information."

"There's been a handful here," Messenger said,."Not a ton of hope. No communication to anyone, even the Colonel. It's like we've been thrown out. Kind of like we once did with Citizenry."

He turned back towards the ocean. "If this is supposed to teach us a lesson, it would have been better delivered five or more years ago. We were in the middle of opening up Citizenry when the power ran out. We were in the middle of teaching the Subjects. All the things Colonel Mangual are accusing the Providers... accusing *me* of... were true. But we were fixing them. We were making progress."

"And then the power outage, and then us," Laird said.

"And then you. You and Berryhill's other followers weren't the problem, you just brought the attention of the Colonel."

"That capacitor we brought you wasn't just a box of lightbulbs..."

"I know. I know," Messenger said, "I guess we're just lucky that the occasional uranium reloads were … were routine. Established in the original agreements."

Laird scoffed softly."Ha. to think that *uranium* was something that *didn't* rock the boat."

Messenger furrowed his brow towards Laird, taking a moment to disassemble the boat axiom. "On the other hand, maybe it was *un*lucky. If people asked questions the first time the facility asked for more uranium... It could have all been different. I could have been born *out here*."

"I can *kinda* get why the Colonel doesn't know what to do with you," Laird said, "but it's awful."

"Oh, I'm pretty sure she's decided." Messenger spread his arms wide to present the camp. "Here we are. Right where she's content to leave us."

Becca had left the transition home a week or so ago. She checked in now and then, less and less. Leena made sure that they had been going to 'class' regularly, and Juho didn't have any significant complaints as building manager. Nothing that raised any alarms.

This was the plan. Becca had let slip that their spending was tracked. Fine. Fine, they had soil, and a garden had been started along the side of the building. Those roses tasted like shit, but it seemed to impress Becca and Juho.

No one paid to much attention to how *much* soil had been purchased, and how much was needed for those roses. No one tracked what other types of seeds were purchased.

Also, it was discovered that duct tape was awesome.

So was a nearby construction site that had its construction put on hold for reasons that Leena didn't care about.

Leena knew ever since their airport experience, that their positions could be tracked, but she didn't know how much that was being watched on a regular basis. Paranoia had become the watch word, but some chances had to be taken.

Leena had assigned field trips. Distractions that if they were being tracked, enough time was seen in a wide enough area that the construction site didn't stand out too much. It was not hard to get people to spend time at a nearby park, or theatre, or museum, or mall. Things like this were indeed noticed, and they merrily reported visiting such places.

And yes, they were indeed beneficial and educational, and such outings were even praised by Becca. Becca and those who read her reports felt this was a sign that the integration into society was going well.

Swimmingly, even.

Oh, yes – Also, it was understandable that everyone would desire some kind of personal defence device, being strangers in the big city. It was a hiccup to explain these purchases, but Leena explained how people were eager to do things, to explore, but they had never had to deal with so many strangers. In a worst case scenario, the "PDD"s were non-lethal deterrent spays.

As well, vocational exploration classes went well enough.

Allowances were saved, purchases were made that fit well into projects relating to chosen courses. Many of them were even paid for by Becca's federal funding.

And quietly, the construction yard gained a water condenser. Gained a compost accelerator and waste management system. Things that would have been a miracle in Citizenry, and a notable upgrade for the Station Four facility in general.

And one day, Juho realized the apartments were especially quiet.

"Uh, Ms. Moorehead?" Juho said into his terminal. "Becca?"

"Hey Juho. How's it going over there?"

"Did I miss a message? When exactly did you pull them out?"

"Pull them out?" Becca pulled up screens of data, and began locating them with increasing irritation. "Why are *none* of them home?!"

Tracking the location of her charges, Becca arrived in front of the construction site. From the outside, it looked like 10 stories of metal framework. The entire property was enclosed by a ten-foot-tall temporary security wall. The signage on the front promised a ten-story office building.

The entrance to the property was a gate with a little damage where a lock surely once held it shut.

Currently, it was closed. Becca tried to press it open, but it wouldn't budge. She could hear some talking inside, and her portable terminal showed all thirty of them inside.

So she knocked. "People?"

"Hi, who's out there?" came the reply.

"It's Becca. What's... what's going on?!"

"Oh, you may as well come in."

The sound of sliding metal preceded the gate swinging open. Inside, two-thirds of the ground was covered in soil, marked into sections by string held five centimetres off the ground by little wooden posts. Various crops grew in every available spot. The other third of the available space featured a makeshift shack made of sheet metal and plywood, partly leaning on the pre-existing construction. A dozen or so people poked around the garden, most obviously working in it.

The person who'd opened the door stood proudly with a spear fashioned out of construction materials, and his PDD on his hip. "Welcome to Citizenry II!" he declared.

Leena popped up from the fields. "Becca! Yeah, kind figured you'd show up pretty soon."

"What is going on here!?"

Leena looked down at the crops surrounding her. "Lablab here, peanuts there, beets, beans, wheat, sweet potatoes, rice goin' on over there, what a pain that stuff is. Papaya's slow to grow, but I'm lookin' fo-"

"Why?!"

"Food," Leena said. "All ya need. We'll expand into bonus yummies later."

"W...why?!

"To eat!"

"There's food in stores!" Becca wailed.

"Yeah, but it costs money. And you need a job doing something stupid to get money, when you can just make food your job. What the heck. When we start getting a surplus, we're going to sell it, and pay you back these allowances."

"You can't do that! There's rules on agricultural... industry or safety regulations, or... *it's not this simple!*"

Leena smiled and scoffed softly, waving away the criticism with her hand. "It's food. Simple."

"You can have the roses at the apartments if you want," Elise said, popping up from her familiar wheat. It was still extremely young, not much more than a hand-span tall.

"People will buy those rose things," Leena commented.

"Why?! They taste horrid." Elise said.

"This isn't simple!" Becca cried.

"Yeah, we're going to have to set up some greenhouse tents for some of these," Leena said, "and did I mention the rice is a pain in the arse? But the people are the garden shop are super helpful."

"This isn't even *your* land!" Becca cried out, "You can't just start a farm on it!"

"No one was using it," Leena said. "Also, we might live here now."

"What's wrong with the apartments?"

"Lack of farming space."

"This is ridiculous! A company owns this space! They were in the middle of making a big building!"

Leena leaned back and looked at the metal framework overhead. "They gave up, I think. If they want the building, they can have all those huge heavy pieces, they're useless to us, but we're keeping the sheet metal, the pipes and junk."

"You can't do that!"

"Ugh. Fine. We'll buy the junk from them, or go buy our own. Might take a little time though. Crops can't be rushed."

"Are you going to buy the *land*, too?!" Becca asked.

Leena looked down. "Buy land... whoever owns it didn't seem to care for it too much, I don't think it'll be an issue. They probably forgot it, and are making their thing somewhere else."

Becca scoffed. "I can guarantee that's not the case. Land... realty... is a big thing! Especially in the city!"

"Seems like it isn't."

"It is! They're going to find out about this, and have you forcibly removed!"

"Doubt it. We have spears and those PDD spray things if they try anything."

"That wouldn't end well," Becca said. "You have to leave this place and come back to the apartments. Finish your training, and get real jobs! You'll be lucky if the owners don't press charges!"

"What's that?"

"Have you arrested! Fined! Maybe taken to jail!"

"Well. I guess we need to build up defences."

"I don't have any grounds to operate in the city," Colonel Mangual said. "I can notify the local police."

"I... I guess?" Becca responded. "I mean, they're in the middle of fortifying their... their base. I'm not welcome back in, they have spears and PDD sprays."

"Spears?! Where did they get those?"

"Made them out of construction scrap. They're calling the site their 'stack' for some reason, and named it Citizenry II."

"... Well, it's going to be a problem for *the police*. They can call me, I can advise, but I can't act. I'm not even allowed to take military gear into city limits."

And so, the police were contacted. District chief Weaver came himself, with one other officer, and met Becca across the street from 'Citizenry II'.

"You say no one's been hurt?" Chief Weaver asked.

"Not as far as I know, but they're... they should have some degree of supervision, and the property is owned by someone else."

"Who exactly are they? Is this a protest of some kind? Or have they made demands?"

Becca sighed. "They... just want to live there, it seems like. I brought them here on behest of the army, and I thought things were going well, you know... integrating them to our society... and then this happens."

"Ah. Immigrants, hm? How's their English? Where are they from?"

With a chuckle hatched from misery, Becca shook her head. "Oh, they're from here, their English is fine. Uh.. do you remember last year when it hit the news that two thousand people were found living underground?"

Chief Weaver squinted towards Citizenry II. "There's two thousand people in there?!"

"No, no, thirty. At least there should be. They're a test group. I guess they're failing."

"Where are they supposed to be?" Chief Weaver asked.

Becca sighed. "Not here. They have an apartment building paid for them, but they have the freedom to go wherever, as long at they show up to class. Which today, they haven't. After this ... stunt? Ugggh... Can't you lob a bunch of crazy purple knockout gas in there or something?"

"Hah, if you want something like that, you should have called the army."

"I did. They sent you."

Chief Weaver sighed. "Well, no gas, no guns, sorry. I guess I should address them." He went to his car and grabbed a bullhorn. He walked over to the gate, and knocked. "Hello?" he called out, leaving the bullhorn off, and at his side, "This is police Chief Weaver, Densfarn PD."

Cody's head popped up from the other side of the wall, handmade spear at his side. "Hello police Chief Weaver, Densfarn DP,"

"PD. I'm from the police department."

"Right, whatever. You already said you were police, I didn't think you were from the pudding department. Do you start all conversations like that? Seems awkward. I don't mean to be picky, I'm honestly curious."

"Protocol. I need to be clear. How should I address you?"

"Me? Oh. Uh... Beet farmer Cody, Citizenry II... FD? Farming department? Am I doing it right?"

"FD would be the fire department."

"Oh, we certainly don't have one of those. Weather's nice enough and we have an electric heater if things turn cooler."

"... Right. Would you be the leader of your group?"

"Nah, I guess that's Leena." Cody turned towards the inside of the site, and called out, "Hey Leena! There's a police guy here who wants to talk to you!"

"What? Hang on."

"She's coming," Cody said with a smile.

"I get that, thanks," Chief Weaver said.

Soon, Leena appeared over the edge next to Cody, holding a hoe. "Hey there, we weren't planning on selling anything until we have our own supply sorted out and stuff. I guess I could make on exception. I'm betting papayas will be our most popular, but that tree is far from ready. Want a potato? They're doing fine, I could sell ya a sweet potato. They're still tiny though. Like... another month at least before they're fully grown."

"H... how long have you been here?" Chief Weaver asked.

"Well, it's been a step-by-step thing, but stuff was planted about a month ago."

"And you're doing this to make money?"

"Nah, we're doing this to eat, but we're going to have to make *some* money. We gotta pay Becca back for the money she's been giving us, and there's been some talk about having to buy this land."

"So right now you're all squatting."

"Nah, I'm standing." Leena looked behind her. "A few people working the crops are squatting, tho."

"Squatting means living somewhere you don't own. It's illegal."

Leena looked out to nowhere and sneered. "Pff. We're gonna fix that. If the people who own the land are so worried, they can come talk. I can hook em up with some crops or something. We can work it out."

"That's not how things work. I doubt you'll be making enough in crops on a plot this size to make enough to buy this land any time soon. I'm going to have to ask you to return to the apartments you've been assigned. What was wrong with them?"

"Not enough space for crops."

"Regardless, I'm going to have to ask you to leave these premises."

"Yeah, okay."

"Yes?"

"Yeah, ask away, I'm getting back to work. Feel free to go away! Bye!"

"Grand Elder?"

Armil opened his eyes. Caitlin was not typically prone to interrupt meditation. "Yes?" he asked her.

"Remember when we talked with a few of those people who'd lived underground?"

Armil took a moment to search him memory, and then scowled slightly. "Yes. The ones the army told us they were honestly caring for? The ones they were going to 'give civilization' to?"

"Yeah, those are the ones. Some of them have... come to attention." Caitlin replied.

"Is that blasted camp still running?" Armil said.

"Yes. Turns out they split it into two camps for some reason, and then sent a handful to live in Densfarn."

Armil grumbled, and rubbed his jaw. "Well, that last part sounds positive. Better than a camp, anyway. What's gone wrong?"

"They ran off, took over a construction site, moved in, and turned it into a farm. It's all over the news."

Coughing out a couple sudden laughs, Armil reclaimed his composure, and gave it some thought. "This is still going on? The army's gotten involved, I assume?"

"The army's not permitted to act against civilians. Local police are handling it."

"The army sure acted when they pulled them out of their little hole and threw them in a camp!"

"True," Catlin said, "though I don't suppose there was any police department overseeing the area of that facility... and there was an atomic generator involved, so..."

"What a mess...." Armil held out his hand to get help getting up off the floor. "So the group in their city-farm –"

"They're calling it Citizenry II" Caitlin said.

"And the military isn't moving on them... because they count as ... as *more civilian* than the ones in the camp? Sorry, camps?"

"They're in the public eye in the middle of a major city, Elder."

"Hrmhrm. Surprise... when you drag people out of a hole, you end up in the light of day. What's going on at... Citizenry II? Is that Messenger fellow, or those nice ladies in there?"

"Police have currently have ten or so cars surrounding it," Caitlin said, "but as far as I can tell, none have tried to break their way in. No one's been hurt, and I haven't been able to tell if anyone we've met is in there."

"Are the people in the camp armed?"

"Spears and PDD pepper spray is all anyone's been able to tell."

"And the police?"

"The usual stun-guns, I think. So far they've just been talking."

"You don't need ten cars to talk. Do we have their contacts?" Armil asked.

"I can connect to the police, easily enough. Any time."

"No, no, the farmers. Citizenry II."

"N..No, we don't have any way to talk to them."

Armil sighed. "How big is the farm? How big is the street it's on?"

Before long, Armil's blue AirLimb had entered Densfarn airspace, cruising politely over buildings, careful not to affect anything below with jet wash.

"G.E.G. AirLimb, come in," said the communication panel in the control room, "this is the Aguola Transport Authority, Please advise your purpose in Densfarn."

The designated operations pilot looked to Caitlin. "Do you want to take this?"

"Not really," Caitlin said, sitting to answer the call. "Hello, A.T.A, this is G.E.G. AirLimb actual. The Grand Elder wants to visit Citizenry II."

"You're aware military hardware isn't permitted in civil airspace?"

"Yes, I assume you know we're not military, and Aguei treaty–"

"Yes, yes, G.E.G., are you intending to land?"

"The Grand Elder isn't a certified skydiver, A.T.A."

"Well, that would be interesting. A street landing, then?"

"Yes, we'll assess when we get there."

"Hooboy. Note that a fair number of civilians have gathered outside the police line. Be careful in there. "

"Will do, A.T.A.."

All eyes were on Armil's AirLimb when it took position over Citizenry II.

"Aww, these guys again?" Elise bemoaned, "Becca wasn't happy with the police yellin' at us, she had to call in the army?"

"Doesn't quite look quite the same," Cody observed, neck craned up to see.

"Hello," came the booming voice of Armil, amplified from an unseen speaker somewhere on the front end of the AirLimb. It had to overcome the sounds of the engines. "This isn't the most ideal way to speak with you. We've asked the police to move their cars so we can land in the street. I wouldn't want to damage your ... fields, and there isn't a good space to land in there, so if you'll wait, I'll be with you momentarily at your front gate."

The AirLimb floated back, to take position over the street.

"Who's this arse?" Leena said, keeping an eye on the AirLimb while slowly walking to the gate.

"He didn't say," Cody answered.

"Yeah. I heard. Half the city heard."

Leena nodded to the two guards she'd posted at the gate. They tossed Leena a face mask. They'd bought a box of fifty disposable masks, using them while working with dirt, but the main reason for getting them was in hopes of defending against sleeping gas. Behind her, everyone was going for their masks.

When the police pushed civilian onlookers back and moved their own cars, the AirLimb sank gently down to land. Leena and her people could still see the top third of the AirLimb, as it was taller than the construction site's wall. Tensions rose.

"He sounded friendly, but don't relax too much," Leena said to her guards.

Shortly, the engines silenced, and a little while later, three knocks were heard on the gate.

"Hi, flying person," Leena called out.

"Hello," the reply was the same voice that had boomed down at them, but the voice was not assisted by technology now. The old man's voice was barely loud enough to be understood. "Oh, of course. Call me Armil. I am the Grand Elder of the Aguei. I think you have some people nervous out here."

Armil paused, giving Leena a chance to speak, but not getting a further reply, he continued. "Who among you is the strongest? Bravest in battle?"

Leena looked behind herself at a number of people. "Battle?" The people only looked towards Leena. Cody smirked, and shook his head.

"Well crap," Leena said, "I'm a little tough. I've killed like... two, maybe three people if you count that one guy..." Leena searched her memory and trailed off. "It's been like a couple years. Like before the blackout at the facility... ah, Station Four. Before the old Citizenry farms."

Armil's asked, "Are you feared?"

Leena shrugged. "Not especially. I mean, I know how to take care of myself, but you know..."

"These people you killed," Armil asked, "you admit it freely?"

"Oh sure, they deserved it. They were the type that hurt other people, you know? If they went on living, they'd have hurt or killed other people who *don't* deserve it." Nods and affirmations came from behind Leena.

"Are you proud to be a killer?" Armil asked.

Leena's expression soured, and she looked about with her eyes, formulating her response. "Well yes but no, you know?"

"No."

"Well, I mean... I hated doing it." Leena looked at her hands, and remembered the feel of her knife. "I hated the moment. I hated the need to do it. But I'm proud that it protected others."

"Would you do it again?"

"I fucking hope not!"

"But?"

"If it meant saving someone? And there was no other way?" Leena took a deep breath. "I'd really rather not have to."

"Would you kill for this land?"

Leena hesitated. "If... if we're attacked, we'll fight back. I wanted those fancy electric stun things, but we could only afford pepper spray. We... we've made spears. I don't want to use them."

This hung in the air for a little while. Leena could hear other people on Armil's side of the wall, outside Citizenry II. Police? Curiosity seekers? There was nothing to be heard that helped a lot.

"You've told me so much," Armil said, "and I don't even know your name."

"Ah... Leena. I'm pretty much leader in here, which basically means people in come at me with their issues. You said you were a ...Grand Elder... sounds big. Are you like... an Actual? Nah, you people have Colonels and Generals and Prime Ministers and junk."

"No, I am Grand Elder of the Aguei. We are separate from the Aguola government."

"Aguei, Aguola? That's confusing, they sound a lot alike."

"Aguei means people of Aguola. The first people to live on this land, before the Northers came, and took the land. Aguola's actually a slight mis-translation from an Aguei word if you want to get picky."

"Wow. If they're gonna be such– waaaaaait, I learned about this," Leena said, "it was in our lessons back in that camp we'd been held at for months."

"They taught you..." Armil said, almost inaudibly.

"A ton. Then they sent thirty of us to an apartment building, and started teaching us things to help us get jobs, to get money, to get food, which seemed dumb. We can farm. If you just let us be."

"This isn't your land, though, child."

"Oh. Well, can we have it? I mean, I can give you some crops when they start coming up proper."

"... It isn't my land either," Armil said.

"But you're the head guy with the people who were here first, is it..."

"Northers own this land now."

"What, why?"

"A long time ago, a Norther either bought it, or took it. I'd have to look up exactly which, in this region."

"What do you mean, '*took it*'?"

There was a bit of a pause. "Assuming they didn't buy it, Northers who wanted the land either started building when no one else was here, or drove off any Aguei who got in the way."

"You mean killed them."

"Often."

"Northers suck!"

"That was a long time ago. We negotiated treaties that helped us share the land."

"Sounds like a crap deal," Leena said. "How much would they have paid for this land? I'm willing to pay, once the farm starts making money."

"I fear they'll want more than your farm can make," Armil said.

"Well then, they'll just have to ... what did you say? Negotiate? If they come looking for a fight, I've been there. I'm not marching back to that apartment and leaving the farm."

"They've been very patient with you, but I don't know how long their patience will last. The police will bring more more than spears and PDD pepper spray."

Leena clenched her fist, and stared sternly at the gate. "Let em come!" Leena hollered, walking away, "Citizenry II isn't going anywhere!"

Armil made his way back between his guards and up the ramp into his AirLimb. Caitlin was waiting for him. "The PM is on the line."

"What? You should have come told me!" Armil said, pausing for a moment after making it up the ramp.

"He knew what you were doing. He was watching on satellite."

Armil snorted, and knocked on the door-frame of the AirLimb. "Huh! I wonder how he found me?"

"He's a clever fellow, Elder," Caitlin said with a smirk. "I have him on the big screen in the den."

Armil smiled softly and nodded, heading towards the den. "Thank you, Caitlin. Could you or someone bring me a cranberry juice in a bit?"

"Unsweetened?"

"More bitter the better!"

"Want me to put in some lemon?"

Armil paused his progress for a moment to think. "No, that's been causing indigestion lately,and I think I'm already headed for that today." He made it to his den to see Prime Minister Lachlan Leon waiting patiently on his large screen. Armil smiled and greeted the Prime Minister. "Ah, hello, LL. Checking up on me?"

The Prime Minister smiled politely, and nodded. "Taking your AirLimb into municipal airspace... I assume you've done this for a good reason?"

"Yes," Armil answered, "I heard you're having problems with some of those poor underground people. I thought I might come try to help. See that no one gets hurt."

"How did it go?"

Armil huffed. "Well, no one got hurt. But they have no idea who I am; they aren't ones I've met before. I was hoping it would be that Messenger fellow, or those two electrical engineer ones."

The Prime Minister looked to another screen. "Sasha and Tara? No last names?"

Armil nodded. "They were quite sweet. Some flawed reasoning they grew up with, but... quite open to new ideas."

"They are... still in the second camp," the Prime Minister said.

Armil's expression soured. "Second camp. A lot like the first, I assume. You must be aware how familiar those camps look..."

The Prime Minister paused, eyes cast down, and was about to speak, but Armil spoke before he could. "I don't have to tell you exactly what they look like," Armil said, "or do I need to review some terrible events in history with you, Lachlan?"

Prime Minister Lachlan Leon shook his head slowly. "It's a lot of people to deal with at once, it's the best way we have, and we're starting to integrate them into soci–"

"*And how is that working for you?!*" Armil snapped.

The Prime Minster sighed. "And what else could I do?" he asked.

"I'll go get some people they'll talk to," Armil said, "just send me the location of this... second camp."

The Prime Minister shook hie head, holding his hand out. "I have people close to it. I'll bring them."

"The world is watching, Lachlan," Armil said sternly. Do all our peoples proud."

An army AirLimb touched down in the yard of camp two, as everyone watched. A Stormfront of soldiers poured out of the ramp, and took formation. Their commander called out, "*We're here for Messenger and the the head engineers.*"

"*What does Mangual want with us?*" Tara asked, from the door of the camp building, with Sasha right behind her.

"Some of your people have illegally occupied property inside Densfarn city," the commander replied. "Grand Elder Armil wants you to talk them out before anyone gets hurt."

"Armil?" Tara was a little surprised.

"Which of 'our people' are doing this?" Messenger asked, having a hunch already.

"I don't have that information, Sir, please come along."

Messenger grimaced. Rides on these AirLimb things hadn't been great experiences so far, but it couldn't get much worse than one of these camps, could it? "Fine. I'll come," he said, pretending he had much a of choice.

"Armil also mentioned engineers," the commender said, "Tara and Sasha. You people need last names."

Tara turned to Sasha. Sasha was trembling. Her agoraphobia was hitting hard just at the thought of making the walk to the AirLimb. "Honey, I... maybe you can stay here," Tara suggested.

Sasha's breathing was bringing her to the edge of sobbing. "Without you? In this place?! You don't even know how long you'll be gone, or if you'll come back!"

"I'll come back, I prom–"

"*I'm fucking going with you!*" Sasha screamed at the top of her lungs, sobbing.

Tara pulled Sasha close. "Oh honey, I'm so sorry..." and they began their way out in the open, clinging to each other.

Messenger walked with them, and as they got to the ramp, passing the commander, the commander asked, "Is... is she going to be alright?"

Tara turned to glare at the commander and growled, "She was perfectly fine before you people ripped her from her home."

The three of them found themselves in close quarters with well over a dozen soldiers. One of them handed Tara a tablet-terminal. A large green "answer" button blinked in the middle of the screen. With Sasha clinging to her other arm and trembling, Tara pressed the button with her chin.

Colonel Veronika Mangual appeared on the screen.

"Tara," she said, "I was expecting to be talking to Messenger."

"You got me, instead," Tara answered. "Neil can hear you. What's going on?"

"Thirty Citizens and Subjects were moved to a property inside Densfarn city to begin assimilating them into general public life. They soon decided to take over a nearby construction site, and set up a farm there. They're calling it Citizenry II. I believe a Citizen named Leena has been chosen as their leader."

"Yeah... that fits," Messenger scoffed.

"You know her, Messenger?" Colonel Mangual asked. "Think you can talk some sense into her?"

Messenger rubbed his jaw, thinking back to all of Leena's past exploits. "I've kind of gotten to know her. She's remarkably intelligent despite her lack of real education. Her sense of... sense... is unique."

"You're going in to defuse this," Colonel Mangual said. "They need to willingly leave the site they've invaded, before something more extreme has to happen. That Aguei Elder Armil thinks you're capable."

"*Grand* Elder," Messenger corrected.

"Yeah, whatever."

Colonel Mangual disconnected, and Messenger borrowed the tablet terminal to try to contact Armil, but the soldier who had originally given Tara the device took it back without a word.

After a hurried flight, and seeing that Armil's G.E.G AirLimb was out of the area, they landed outside Citizenry II, and prepared to disembark from the AirLimb, with the ramp feeding close to the door.

Messenger stepped out first, looking around as well as his position would allow between the AirLimb and the Citizenry II wall. Around them was a city. A living city. It took a bit of effort to compare this to the ruinous Meston they'd stepped into before being taken to camp 2.

Nothing here was destroyed or burnt. The building under construction visibly sticking out of Citizenry 2 was incomplete, but clearly not due to damage.

The city was built up significantly more than the camps in almost every regard. It was constructed so much differently than Station Four, but presumably much of Densfarn City's structures were younger than a hundred years. Maybe?

Messenger looked back to Tara and Sasha. They were all surrounded by soldiers who stood on guard. Sasha had her eyes clenched shut, breathing roughly, hanging onto Tara. Tara nodded to Messenger.

He turned to Citizenry II's door, and knocked three times. The answer did not come quickly, so he knocked again before a voice responded from the other side.

"We're not ready to sell crops yet! If you want anything else, tough!"

"Am I speaking to a Citizen, a Subject, or maybe a Manager?" Messenger asked.

"It's Citizenry II, we're all Citizens now!"

"You've gotten the surfacers upset," Messenger began, but was quickly interrupted by another voice from inside.

"*Messy? I know that voice! Messy! What are you doing here?*"

"Leena?"

"Messy! You're okay! Where the heck have you been?"

"Providers and Engineers and some of the Managers are all in another camp. Basically the same, but a much nicer view. I think the Colonel might be planning to keep us there forever, but you seem to have a better deal – they brought you here. Or to this city, anyway."

"... are they treating you okay?" Leena asked tentatively.

"We're... unharmed." Messenger slowly said.

"Are there soldiers all around you right now? We saw that AirLimb come down."

Messenger turned back, seeing four soldiers in formation at the end of the ramp, and a few inside the AirLimb, along with Tara and Sasha. He turned back the Citizenry II door. "The nearest soldier is about four metres away."

The door to Citizenry II opened a little, and Leena peered out. "Messy. Good to see you." She pointed her chin towards the AirLimb. "That chick... they're Engineers, right? That one doesn't look like she's having a good time."

"This is extremely difficult for her," Messenger said. "How is Patricia?"

"Not here, thankfully. She's back in the camp. The people here are the only ones that they tried to... 'assimilate' into the city so far."

"Do you have shelter in there?" Messenger asked.

Leena's eyes widened a bit. "It's cramped, but we have a thing we threw together that will even block rain if that happens. We sleep there in shifts."

"Excellent. Leena, do you trust me?"

"You helped save the first Citizenry from a really bad situation, when you had no reason to help us at all. Of course I trust you."

Messenger turned to face Tara, and nodded slightly.

Tara nuzzled her lips by Sasha's ear. "Hon, we're going. Keep your eyes closed, I'll guide you."

Sasha eyes shot wide open, pleading to Tara. "We're what?!"

Tara squeezed Sasha's hand, and whispered, "Strong girl..."

With a shuddering exhale, Sasha closed her eyes tight, and squeezed Tara's hand back. They began down the ramp.

Between blindly managing the ramp, and her nerves, Sasha stumbled. Tara caught her. Half-way on her back, Sasha opened her eyes, and a wounded cry seeped out of her as the city's vastness pressed down on her from every angle.

Two of the ramp-guards moved to assist, but Tara held them back with an outstretched hand. "I have this."

Sasha was outright sobbing now, and Tara pulled her closer, burying Sasha's face in her shoulder. Tara scooped Sasha up, held her as tight as possible, and began carrying her towards Citizenry II.

Leena, shaken by this, stepped back and opened the door wide. "Come on, ladies."

Tara, Sasha, and Messenger entered Citizenry II, and the door closed to the world.

Chapter 31:

Descend and Rise

"They've been in there quite a while," Colonel Veronika Mangual said to the AirLimb's commanding officer, through the display in the AirLimb control deck, "They should have gone with some kind of terminal. Go ask for them."

The commander's second in command went to Citizenry II's door and knocked.

"Still no crops for you people!" the Citizenry guard inside replied through the closed door.

"I'd like to speak with Messenger," the soldier said.

"... Yeah, lemmie see what I can do."

After a bit, Messenger replied, through the still-closed door. "You wanted to speak with me?"

"The Colonel wants to know when you plan to come out with the prisoners. We saw from the satellite that you entered their inner structure. You've had a long while to talk to them?"

"Prisoners? I thought they were being … assimilated into the city. They're free, I thought."

"Just get them out here so we can wrap this up," the soldier replied.

Messenger inhaled deeply, and replied for all to hear, "*Citizens strong together!*"

Cheers and repetitions of the Citizen mantra erupted behind Messenger.

"*Just get out of there!*" the soldier yelled back, barely heard over the Citizens.

"I'm home now." Messenger replied.

From a command room in a section of Yute Central, Colonel Veronika Mangual watched the satellite feed of the Citizenry II residents crowded around Messenger, celebrating. The two Engineers had disappeared into the ramshackle inner shelter near the far edge of the site almost immediately after they entered. Colonel Mangual was only now hearing about the mental state one of them had been in. She should never have been cleared to go into that situation.

Maybe that had been the tipping point of instability that led to the current situation. Someone on the scene should have identified the risk. But speculation was fruitless now. The Grand Elder's way had been tried, and had failed miserably.

An order was sent.

The military AirLimb rose over Citizenry II, crossing the wall, and dropping soldiers armed with stun-guns.

Inside the shelter, Sasha and Tara heard the movements of the AirLimb, and the commotion outside. Screams. Yelling. A few people in the shelter ran out to find out what was going on, and another ran in. "*Soldiers attacking!*" Sasha gripped onto Tara. Tara wanted to go look, but decided that staying put might be the best option, both for Sasha and her own safety.

"*Forget the masks, they're not gassing us! They've got guns!*" a panicked voice was heard to yell.

"*It's just those stun things!*" a reply came back, "*Don't let em scare you!*"

Out the doorway, Tara saw a Citizen retreating, then suddenly jolting stiff, only to fall limp.

"*Use corners!*" Leena's voice called out, "*make em get closer, then let em have it!*"

"Right! Got your back," Cody replied.

"I knew I kept ya around for something! *Messy! Where are you?*"

"Being distracting!" Messenger's voice called back.

The soldiers moved to immobilize anyone they saw moving, cautious of the spears and other tools most of the Citizens had armed themselves with. It had been only seconds, but about half of the Citizenry II residents were already stunned to the ground.

"Okay! Got ya!" Cody was heard to yell. The commotion quickly died down.

Tara peeked out to see most of the soldiers facing Cody. Cody was holding one of the soldiers from behind, while holding the handle of a rake firmly against the soldier's neck. Leena was picking up the soldier's dropped weapon, and waved it at the other soldiers around them.

"*Get back!*" Leena yelled at them, "*Just go away, leave us alone, and-*"

One of the soldiers tackled Leena from behind, pinning her.

"*Leena!*" Cody yelled, jerking his hostage. Another soldier shot the hostage, which fell limp out of Cody's gasp, a split second before Cody was also shot.

Tara ducked back into the shelter as soldiers drew closer. "*Neil! Where are you?*" Tara, Sasha, and a few other Citizens remained in the shelter as soldiers closed in towards the entrance.

The sound of the overhead AirLimb grew notably louder.

The soldiers stopped their advance, looked at each other, and began backing away,keeping an eye on any Citizen still standing.

The soldiers paused for a few moments, looking at each other, before backing off. Methodically withdrawing.

Tara stepped safely but carefully out of the shelter as the soldiers exited Citizenry II in an orderly manner, carrying the stunned soldier. Tara saw why the AirLimb was so much louder. There were two now.

Armil had returned.

"Hey!" Leena pointed at Armil's blue AirLimb overhead. "He was here before. Old guy, talked a lot about his people, and stuff... and thought we'd be better to leave here, before..." She pointed to the grey military AirLimb, which now was rising further into the sky with Arimil's blue AirLimb.

"He's a friend," Messenger said, "I've talked to him several times."

As some of the stunned Citizens began to stir, an uneasy quiet settled around Citizenry II, marred only by the hiss of two overhead AirLimbs, and the crowd of onlookers murmuring from the street. Were there soldiers left behind to control them? Police? No one was banging on the door.

Sasha joined Tara at the doorway of the inner shelter. "Tara? What are they doing?"

"Talking to each other?" Tara guessed. "I wouldn't mind having a communication device to listen in. We should have at least hung onto that tablet-terminal thing."

"Yeah, tell me about it," Messenger moaned.

Sasha yelled up at the looming aircraft. "*Just gonna stare, or are we going to talk?*"

As if on cue, the grey military AirLimb drifted up and away, headed out of Densfarn city airspace.

"Damn," Leena said, "why didn't you just yell them away in the first place?"

"Heh," Sasha chuckled meekly as she stroked a bit of hair out of her face. "Didn't know I had it in me."

"I did." Tara said, giving Sasha a squeeze.

A voice boomed from the Elder's AirLimb. Grand Elder Armil's voice. "Who among you is the most wise?"

At that, a little personal terminal fell from the AirLimb and bounced on the ground, coming to a rest, blinking.

Despite a gentle nudging by Cody, Leena backed away from the device, wide-eyed, hands up.

Tara looked towards Messenger. He shrugged.

"I wish Actual were here," Messenger muttered. "I carry the most information of everyone from the facility, and I am called upon to make many decisions. If that makes me wise, maybe I'm stuck with that..."

Tara picked up the little terminal. "You're not alone. Let's be wise together." She pressed the button to answer. "Grand Elder Armil? We can be wise together." She looked up to the blue G.E.G. AirLimb, wondering if they were watching.

A few moments passed before the reply came from Armil through the terminal.

"Very well. Wisest of your people, tell me the one thing that is the most wise."

Messenger shifted his weight uncomfortably. "I... I don't know such wisdom..." he said quietly, "I just don't know." His hopeless wide eyes sharpened with realization. "I don't know!" He smiled fiercely. Proudly. "The wisest thing to say is *'I don't know!'*"

"Oh yes?" Armil responded, holding back a chuckle, "go on!"

"We are *so lost!*" Messenger cried, his brief joy splintering into a focused misery. "My people are *so lost*. Our wisdom is not enough! I don't know what to do next! *I just don't know!*"

"And?" Armil asked forcefully.

Tara responded. "And what wisdom we have is... is asking for more wisdom! We need... we need help!"

The world became still and quiet. The hiss of the AirLimb and the sounds of the surrounding city paled against the empty anticipation of a reply. Many Citizens were still recovering from being stunned, trying to figure out what was going on.

"We're coming down." finally came Armil's reply as the AirLimb moved to land in the street outside the walls of Citizenry II.

Before long, there was a knock at the door. Leena went to answer, rake in hand. She tossed it aside before opening it. When the door swung open, Grand Elder Armil was flanked by his assistant Caitlin. Also with them was a man in a dark suit, with Colonel Mangual standing behind him, frowning. Around them was a formation of soldiers and attendants in suits. Half a dozen matching black ground vehicles littered the street behind the AirLimb.

About half a dozen small flying objects buzzed thirty or so metres overhead, drifting slowly about.

Armil opened his arms wide in greeting, his robe dangling braided strands from his arms. He nodded to Tara and Sasha, and to Messenger. "So wonderful to see you all again. Is the young lady I spoke to before here? The leader?"

"I guess you mean me," Leena said, stepping forward. "Who's all your buddies?"

"I am Counsellor Caitlin Aubrey, assistant to the Grand Elder," Caitlin introduced herself to everyone with a slight bow. "We have the honour of being joined by Prime Minister Lachlan Leon, and Colonel Mangual, who I believe some of you know."

Colonel Mangual grinned tersely, more of a grimace, but Prime Minister Leon smiled genuinely enough. "Greetings," he began, "I'm hoping we can come to some resolution that lets us all walk away from this happy."

"What's a Prime Minister again?" Leena asked, "I think I heard that in a class at some point..."

"I am the elected leader of our nation, Aguola."

"....Elected?" Leena had been taught this, but the lessons felt so long ago now.

"Every half decade or so, all the adults of the nation vote to decide who the Prime Minister should be. I've won twice now, and I'll likely run for another term when the time comes."

"So everyone can just decide to get rid of you?" Leena smirked, "and you'd go without a fight?"

Prime Minister Lachlan Leon chuckled. "Yes, so far, they like my work enough to keep me, but if I lose an election, I'm out."

"With no stabbings or anything," Leena said to confirm.

"That's the idea."

"You'll have to excuse her," Messenger added, "Leena grew up in a section of the facility where leadership... was a difficult and... violent process."

"Yeah, we ended that." Leena explained.

Colonel Mangual scoffed quietly, earning a quick little glare from the

Prime Minister.

"We need help," Tara said flatly, looking to the Prime Minster, trying hard not to look at the Colonel. "Some *better* help. Not camps."

Prime Minister Leon grimaced and cast his eyes down. "I don't know what I can do. There's a lot of you. You need modern education, and the camp system... it's terrible. It can be refined, improved, but I don't see a much of a better way."

Messenger looked down as well, voice nearly trembling. "I don't wish to be a burden. I don't think any of us want to be. I don't know if I have any right to ask, but will you help my people... Armil?" Messenger looked to Grand Elder Armil, eyes beginning to well up.

Colonel Mangual stared with an incredulous gaze, Prime Minister Leon resisted a smile. Tara and Sasha felt the weight of the situation, and held hands tightly to the edge of pain.

Grand Elder Armil took a moment to stand as straight as his bones would allow, and asked clearly, yet warmly, "Are you... Neil Messenger, rightful heir and Actual of Station Four, leader, and among the wisest of your people, asking the Aguei Nation for aide?"

Messenger's smile broke through his tears. "Yes, Grand Elder Armil, I suppose I am."

Armil smiled. "As Grand Elder, I invite you and your people to be as Aguei. We are the same people. Our home, our land, our lives, we are the same."

Leena gasped, fighting tears. "Are... you giving us this land?" she asked.

"It is not mine to give," Armil conceded. "I told you that before, but you don't need it."

Messenger chuckled softly, rising into a laugh. "I *have* land!" Messenger said, pointing to Colonel Mangual. Enough for every Citizen, every Subject, every Provider, every Manager and Engineer All of us! I *have* land!"

Sasha's eyes welled up, and she stuttered. "H-home? Home-home?"

"That facility is under the military control and authority," Colonel Mangual snapped.

"Why?" Tara asked. "You said it was still legally held by the company that originally built it."

"*Over a century ago!*" Mangual countered.

"So?"

"That company... Harris Densfarn whatever... HDU, they're gone!" Colonel Mangual snapped.

"But they have a healthy bank account," Messenger reminded Mangual.

"And now that we know it exists, and the company is dead, they're lost funds! It'll be absorbed by federal systems, right?" Colonel Mangual said turning to Prime Minister Lachlan Leon.

"The company belonged to the people who ran it," Caitlin Audrey said, "and they moved into Station Four before they sealed it."

"Next of kin," Grand Elder Armil said, looking across Messenger, Tara, Sasha, Leena and the other Citizens behind them.

"That's ridiculous!" Colonel Mangual said.

"Seems... logical," Prime Minister Lachlan Leon said.

"And now all that money's just going to end up in Aguei pockets!" Colonel Manual complained.

Armil shook his head slightly in disapproval.

"Colonel," the Prime Minster said, "You are dismissed. Take the rest of the day off. I will be contacting you. Or a lawyer representing you."

Colonel Mangual stared back with a shocked glare. "Sir?!"

"Dismissed."

They stared at each other for a moment, and Colonel Mangual turned and left, leaving her soldiers behind.

"What... what just happened here?" Tara asked.

"I ... I have no good excuse for not acting sooner about those camps," Prime Minister Lachlan Leon said. "It looked good enough as statistics in a report. I saw photos. They were.. carefully chosen and framed photos. When I actually looked at them in person..." he glanced to Grand Elder Armil, "those camps looked familiar. There's going to be an investigation into their operation."

"Fire that Mangual chick!" Leena said.

"Something like that is likely. Some kind of charges are also likely."

"Jail?" Armil asked.

"It's too early to say. But it's on the table," the Prime Minister said, "But the Colonel's concerns about the slave-class Subjects... that's very valid."

Elise chirped up from the crowd of Citizens. "Hi, I'm okay with farming, mostly. We'll still need that, right?"

"Indeed. But there will be changes," Messenger said. "Changes I hope you'll like. If the Grand Elder will help us make them..."

"And if some farmers and stuff want to stay out of home? To stay out of Station Four?" Leena asked.

"They are welcome to go," Messenger said, "I think we can help. And if they want to come back, it's still home."

"If it's all decided, I have some arrangements to make," Prime Minister Lachlan Leon said. "See you all soon enough!" He shared a nod with the Grand Elder, before vanishing into thin air. The Prime Minister's guards filed out of Citizenry II.

The Grand Elder saw the astonishment on people's faces, then looked to where the Prime Minister had been standing. "It was just a projection. He does that a lot. He's probably actually on the other end of the country. *Security.*" He chuckled a bit of a scoff. "A very norther way to get things done."

Leena laughed, standing where the Prime Minister had been. "Cool!" She then poked the Grand Elder lightly. "Are you able to touch one of th–"

"I'm actually here," the Grand Elder said, "but let's, perhaps... *not* be here. Does anyone want a ride?"

"Home..." Sasha squeezed Tara's arm. "We...we're going home..."

Chapter 32:

Nothing. Everything.

By federal order, the residents in both camps were brought back to Station Four. Plans were made for the Aguei council, with some federal supervision, to redesign how things were done in the facility. Work was to be shared more evenly, voluntary classes were available, and supply lines and agreements were made with Division, and private suppliers.

The assigned designated military contacts and engineering consultants were Sergeant Daniel Berryhill, and his Corporals, Alison Muir, Kay Laird, and Tavish. And their dog Caspar, who enjoyed celebrity status as every Station Four resident eventually had to meet her.

Renovations began in Citizenry. The ramps would be repaired, scrap metal shacks replaced with proper housing sections. One by one, the Subject Units were being outfitted to be more like dorms and workplaces, and less like prisons. Farmers like Elise soon had modern tools that made the old tasks considerably easier. Nearly every job done by Subjects was suddenly much easier. The farms were able to expand. The menu changed vastly, no longer just 'food disks'.

The Rubberman suits were retired, except the shielded ones for Engineering, and even those had less use now. New communications systems were installed, as to rely less on radio and batteries. A panel could soon be found at every Elevator port, and all significant rooms. Portable terminals such as the surface people liked became more and more common.

The Grand Elevator was tuned up, refitted in what ways could be done, and new passages were opened. Old forgotten side lifts were retooled and reopened, and stairs were installed here and there, all for the new freedoms spreading through the facility.

The atomic generator was gutted, ripped apart and hauled away chunk by chunk, to be sold for scrap once remnants of dangerous materials were cleaned out. Kevin took charge of turning the newly-claimed space in Engineering into housing. He was also charged with figuring out how to turn the fuel rod cooling pool into a swimming pool, but that plan had some very obvious safely concerns, specifically for the bottom few metres. In time, They would be overcome.

On the surface, a vast field of solar collection panelling began being installed. At first, just enough to run facility operations, but set to slowly expand into a minor industry to assure future finance flow. The HDU savings were vast, but not infinite.

The former residents of Citizenry II were keen to point out that income could also come from the updated farming practices, and although Station Four would never be nearly as big as established farms in the country, it was hard to argue with a bit of income diversification.

And this was to be home. Indefinitely. For generations more to come.

Almost everyone chose to continue to call Station Four their home. Some Subjects who had been under especially harsh Managers were among the handful to leave, as they had no great love of Station Four.

Others who left were simply curious and brave enough to step out into the world, to forge a new path in this new world. All who left were given some support, and an open invitation to return.

"So what the heck has the old Contact been up to?" Lenth asked Gabe.

"Is he like... bitter with you?" Karen asked.

Gabe stood from the desk that was now his. "I don't think so. He's more stunned by the changes than anyone. Every time I heard of a suicide back at the camp, I thought I'd hear it was him. I think he's just trying to adjust. Being the Contact isn't what it used to be," Gabe said "It used to be that the Contact was the only one supposedly allowed to talk to the Messenger, but the old ways..."

Karen chuckled, "Anyone can talk to him now. You're just stuck with organizing the Providers."

Gabe nodded. "And the Managers, and Subjects, but those titles are all kind of tossed in the blender, too. Want to know what an Aguei advisor suggested I call myself?"

Karen and Lenth smiled, inviting the answer.

With a chuckle and raised eyebrows, Gabe said, "Chief Administrative Provider."

"Rolls *right* off the tongue, doesn't it?" Lenth commented.

"I think I'll stick with being 'Gabe'. And 'Contact' can just be the job. Not my name. And now I have to pick a 'last name'. The surface Northers are so big on last names. Whatever! I have no idea what to pick."

"Have you seen that book being passed around with suggestions?" Karen asked. She hugged Lenth's arm. "We're going to pick the same one. There's something about marriage or something..."

Gabe laughed a single, loud, mirthless laugh. "*And* I'm supposed to keep track of *marriages!* There's so many things now! And who wants which jobs, and how it affects what we need, and–"

"Going bonkers, Gabe? Can I help?" Lenth asked.

With a somewhat tired-sounding chuckle, Gabe waved the notion away. "I have help. Between Messenger, some good Providers, and Aguei help... consultants they like to call themselves... It's good. It's all good. It just takes time. What are you officially now, Lenth? I know Karen's an *agricultural manager* still..."

"So far," Karen interjected, "The farms are changing, lots of Managers are becoming redundant."

"I'm a... an Assistant Subject Educational something, something..." Lenth replied.

"Eventually Subjects are going to get all.... educated up," Gabe said. "Then what... you two going to raise a kid or something? The way it's done *now?*"

"Ooh, easy there, not so fast." Karen chuckled.

"Yeah, I think I'll be busy for quite a while," Lenth said, "There's still tons and tons that the Subjects don't know about. Me too. You too. We have a lot of *stupid* around here still. Then the *kids* will need to be less stupid, then there's going to be *new* kids that are going to be *born* stupid. Arg. I'm going to be dealing with stupid people for the rest of my life!"

A new plaque adorned the wall on the Actual-level. It would be the first plaque of a new tradition for Station Four; to mark the lives of those who'd passed on. Taking his earned title as a surname, the man once known as Messenger was now named *Neil Actual*.

He ran his fingers across the top edge of the plaque. It read:

Henry Actual

2010-2095

He led us against the Darkness
and is missed by all those lucky enough to have known him

Neil rested beside the plaque, and stared at it with glassy eyes. "So. I got them home safe. Most of them. It's just as well that you missed a lot of that, Actu... Henry." He swallowed hard, and began to quietly cry. He suddenly remembered the last time he saw Henry's face, down at composting. He forced that image out by remembering him at his desk, minding the minutia of the facility, and pecking at a meal.

He sniffed, and breathed deeply. "At the same time... it would have ... it would have been great to have you with me. I... I only..."

He looked to the door to the outside, and wiped a tear from his face. "They know a lot about DNA now, Henry. They've going to let anyone who wants to know who they're related to... who's whose parents. How we handle babies is going to change a lot, too."

Neil chuckled through his tears, looking at his dark skin. "I have a feeling DNA's going to try to tell me I'm not your son." He chuckled softly again, wiping fresh tears. "Oh, I'll find out who my birth parents are... if they're still alive, I guess they deserve to know I'm around. And there's medical reasons to know all this for everyone, but..."

He raised his eyebrows towards the plaque. "I'm talking to a hunk of metal on the wall. And you'd know how I feel anyway. You know. I'll do my best for them, Henry. And I won't be alone. I'll do my best. I had a great teacher."

As the old 'Enemy' faded into the horizon, Sasha sat alone among the solar fields, gazing out across the vast nothing.

The vast everything.

Tara returned to sit with her, bringing a couple of drinks they'd learnt about in the city. She put her arm around Sasha, and saw her that eyes were close to tears.

"Hon. You okay?"

Sasha took a deep breath. "Terrified," she calmly said. "It's still terrifying."

"You want to go inside?"

Sasha nodded, but didn't get up. "In a bit." She bit her lip, and looked at Tara, then back to the sunset. "The world is big. It's terrifying. But here I am. I'm in it."

"And with me."

"Always."

"Always."

Thank you for reading Rubberman's Exodus. I hope you enjoyed it!

Please consider giving it a quick little review on Amazon, or anywhere you see fit. It helps a lot!

If you haven't already, the first two books of the Rubberman series are available, as well as my Lifehack series, and a few other smaller works.

Of course, I love to hear from readers, and feedback is more than welcome. Knowing what does, and doesn't resonate with people just helps the next book become better.

Find me at www.ozero.ca, or Amazon:

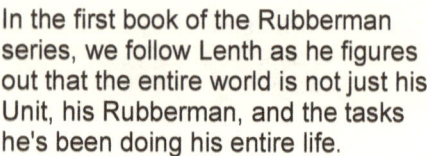

http://www.amazon.com/Joseph-Picard/e/B002LPT7VA

In the first book of the Rubberman series, we follow Lenth as he figures out that the entire world is not just his Unit, his Rubberman, and the tasks he's been doing his entire life.

As he explores the facility, and learns about the the existence of different groups, elevators, papayas, women, and the BIG ROOM, another wandering Subject roams the innards of the facility with malice and revenge on his mind.

The second Rubberman book focuses on Leena and the Citizens, as they struggle, exiled from the rest of the facility for generations.

Under the cruel Citizenry leadership, and a culture of systematic abuse and control, Leena finds a chance to rebel, and challenge the cycle of one dictator after another, with herself and her loved ones at grave risk.

The Lifehack Series books all take place in the same world as each other, and in the same continuity. While nanotechnology is the basis of each, the characters and tone of each are significantly different in each.

As Regan flounders out of a relationship to crash on her brother's couch, a bored, evil genius repurposes nanotechnology to create a plague of zombies.

Soon assumed dead in a quarantined city of undead, Regan seeks her dead brother fruitlessly until she's found by Alicia, a soldier who's surprised to find Regan, and more surprised that she's the new subject of Regan's desire– all while fighting back against the rise of Erebus.

Cassidy faces death. Her love's, her enemy's, and her own.

An ancient temple guarded by modern soldiers becomes the scene of misguided violence, and a tragic death that shatters Cassidy's world.

While covering up banned nanotech, a scientist studying Erebus' work tries desperately to avoid blame, and manipulates a fringe faction into acts of terror in the name of freedom.

Born of forbidden science, Sarah is the secret creation of the most feared and hated entity in the world.
(Also, she's made primarily out of fish that died of natural causes. Because.)

And that hated entity lives in her skull.

Horrors emerge not long after she does, and her deathly heritage stands between claiming a peaceful life, and a new massacre fuelled by her father's other creations.

Joseph Picard

Year of hatching: 1976
Last seen: Lower Mainland,
              B.C., Canada
Current level: 46
Blood type: Red and tangy

Identifying features: Drives a manual
wheelchair fuelled by taurine.

Do not approach. Suspect won't shut
up, especially if his books come up.

Known to be easily distracted by
polyhedral dice. And crows. And dogs.
And kids. And the colour 47.

A generally creative type, a lifelong interest in writing became a greater focus when a short story spawned a sequel... and another sequel... and a prequel. Fleshing them out and cleaning them up eventually became his first novel, Lifehack.

While cycling to a computer repair job in 2001, Joseph was struck by a car, resulting in T5/6 paraplegia. Since then, he has married, and had two children, Caitlin and Lachlan.

Later dealing with significant paraplegia-related pressure wounds that resulted in another six months of hospitalization, Joseph gradually recovered to a 'healthy' paraplegic condition.

Joseph began volunteering at the local seniors centre, leading to a job. This position ended less than a year later due to Covid-19. A few months later, Joseph began working online for another non-profit organization dealing with community projects and seniors, and a company facilitating supervised access, for which he edited reports and co-ordinated supervisors.

These were cut short by the emergence of multiple sclerosis, which was diagnosed after a significant attack of the condition. Thankfully, Rubberman's Exodus was well into editing when MS appeared.

Due to the cognitive and other effects of MS, added to his paraplegia, Rubberman's Exodus will most likely be Joseph's last novel.

www.ingramcontent.com/pod-product-compliance
Lightning Source LLC
Chambersburg PA
CBHW020349120726
47904CB00002B/519